THE WORLD RAPERS
by
Jonathan Black

A lusty novel spread across three continents and climaxing in the seething cauldron of the oil-drenched Middle East, where cosmopolitan princes of profit, bejeweled sheikhs, and commercial cutthroats of every hue gather to batten on the golden riches of the world . . . where power is an aphrodisiac and a whore, passed from hand to hand among her insatiable lovers . . . and where sleek, cold, beautiful predators vie for the most dazzling stakes in the deadly gambit of Mid-East petro-politics . . .

THE WORLD RAPERS

"A powerful and compelling novel of international intrigue."

—Irving Wallace

THE WORLD
RAPERS

Jonathan Black

BANTAM BOOKS · TORONTO · NEW YORK · LONDON

This low-priced Bantam Book
has been completely reset in a type face
designed for easy reading, and was printed
from new plates. It contains the complete
text of the original hard-cover edition.
NOT ONE WORD HAS BEEN OMITTED.

THE WORLD RAPERS

*A Bantam Book | published by arrangement with
the author*

PRINTING HISTORY
Published in Great Britain in 1974 by Hart-Davis,
MacGibbon Ltd.

Bantam edition | September 1977

*Bantam Books are published by Bantam Books, Inc. Its trade-
mark, consisting of the words "Bantam Books" and the por-
trayal of a bantam, is registered in the United States Patent
Office and in other countries. Marca Registrada. Bantam
Books, Inc., 666 Fifth Avenue, New York, New York 10019.*

PRINTED IN THE UNITED STATES OF AMERICA

TO SYLVIA

To be a Levantine is to live in two worlds or more at once without belonging to either, to be able to go through the external forms which indicate the possession of a certain nationality, religion or culture without actually possessing it.

—ALBERT HOURANI

Money is the greatest coward in the world.
—YOUSSEF BEIDAS
Founder and Board Chairman Intra Bank

THE WORLD
RAPERS

BOOK ONE

One Week
April 23rd—29th

1

New York City. Tuesday, April 23rd.

The girl looked up at him. Moments before, she had been docile. Now her desire reawakened.

"Jimmy."

Jemel Karami stood beside the bed, not yet sated but conscious of time, shrugging his tall lithe-muscled frame into a white bathrobe.

"Jimmy, come back."

"I will. Later."

She groped in the folds of the robe, found what her fingers sought, and held him. His response was quick, but he moved away and freed himself from her grasp.

"Later."

It had to be later. In half an hour Miles Langford Palmer, financier, senior statesman of American banking and economic adviser to presidents, would arrive.

Jemel Karami's aquiline features were meditative, and there was a taut, expectant set to his broad shoulders as he went into the bathroom. The meeting with Miles Palmer, significantly being held in Jimmy's duplex penthouse apartment rather than in either of their offices, was important. It would be decisive, setting in motion an awesomely intricate and ambitious apparatus.

Money in sums that few could even comprehend was at stake. Money and much else, Karami reflected. He was gambling all that he owned, far more than he did not. No, he corrected himself, gambling wasn't the right word. Although the game was vast in scale and lethal, he'd eliminated most of the risks. Those remaining were known, meticulously calculated—and they included Miles Langford Palmer. The weeks ahead would require strong nerves and stomachs. Palmer might weaken.

Jemel knew how to handle Miles Palmer, and he could manage—or manipulate—the other calculated risks. Still, he dared not become overconfident, complacent—or careless. There were always inponderables. To say nothing of hyena packs . . .

Having showered and shaved, Jimmy returned to the bedroom. The girl—he'd met her at a dinner party the night before—slept, curled small in the great round bed. A loose mesh of fine ash-blonde hair was filmy gauze fallen over her face, blurring her exquisite profile. The nipple of a bare breast gleamed pink in the cradle formed by her arm.

Karami pensively surveyed the familiar surroundings: his "million-dollar bedroom," a recent newsmagazine cover story called it, only slightly overestimating the value of the furnishings and of the superb French Impressionists that hung on the walls. Jimmy's teeth flashed white as he smiled, recalling the paean orchestrated by the magazine's Business Section editor —in return for an inside-price option on 500 shares of a Karami company stock.

"Jemel 'Jimmy' Karami was hardly an anonymous tyro when he first set out to conquer the occult world of international banking. Then in his mid-twenties and already hailed as an entrepreneurial prodigy . . ."

It had been good publicity, Jimmy mused. Good for five- to ten-point spurts in the stock prices of the American corporations the article touted as being "among the solid-gold building-blocks forming today's $1.5 billion Karami financial pyramid."

But the most difficult and delicate stages of the pyramid-building job lay ahead, Jemel reminded himself, no longer smiling. If he blundered, the results would be fatal. Everything would go.

He dressed quickly now—in slacks, open-throated sports shirt and loafers—and quietly left the bedroom.

Outside, in the corridor, he encountered Dowling, his butler.

"I was coming to tell you Mr. Palmer has arrived, sir. He's downstairs in the library."

The spacious library overlooked Central Park. The day was clear and light from the late April sun streaming through large plate-glass windows. Subdued modern furnishings mirrored expensive, impeccable taste. Floor-to-ceiling shelves along one wall were solid with books in tooled-leather bindings. Miles Palmer stood at one of the windows staring down at Fifth Avenue, thirty-eight floors below.

"Hello, Miles."

Recognizing Karami's robust baritone, Palmer turned. He moved a bit ponderously, a short, fleshy man nearing sixty with thin gray hair, a type to whom ultraconservative clothing and an awareness of his own importance were equally mandatory parts of a self-prescribed uniform.

"Good morning, Jemel." Karami was almost twenty years his junior, and they knew each other long and well, but Palmer disdained nicknames.

They shook hands. "Care for coffee or anything else, Miles?"

Dowling had entered silently, depositing a tray with cups, sugar bowl, creamer, and Thermos carafe on a low table. Then he vanished just as silently, closing the library doors behind him.

"No, thank you," Palmer replied.

"Mind if I have some?"

Miles Palmer said he didn't mind at all. The men seated themselves in comfortable armchairs set at complementary angles next to the table.

"Well, Miles?" Karami asked.

Muddy eyes gazed back at him through rimless glasses. "My associates and I met yesterday, Jemel."

"And?"

"We agree to your proposals—in principle." He paused. "But, to be perfectly frank, there is still some hesitation—even reluctance—about committing ourselves on the terms you demand."

"Really?" Jemel's bronze-hued face was bland. "Any particular reason?"

"Actually, there are several. First, the financial statements . . ."

"Are airtight." Jemel completed the sentence without losing a beat. "The SEC or anyone else can examine them under a microscope."

Palmer grimaced. "But my associates and I know . . ."

"Who cares what you know? You break the fifty up into chunks small enough for your various boards to swallow. Nobody will choke." Karami placed his empty cup on the tray. "When you people came to me, I told you I was willing to carry the ball. I also made it clear I needed the money fast. Right away. For lubricating oil, to coin a phrase."

"I've said we agree in principle," Palmer declared. "However, the other members of the syndicate have left the final decision up to me."

Jimmy pretended surprise. "Oh? And on what does that decision depend, Miles?"

"It depends on what develops from our conversation this morning—on our candid exchange of information, on your giving me assurance . . ."

"Not again!" Jemel groaned protest.

"Our caution is not unreasonable. I have been working on—ah—the overall project for several years without seeing much return, as you are aware. There is no guarantee that you'll be able to accomplish more —or even that the project is feasible."

Jimmy swung a long leg over an arm of his chair. "It was feasible as far back as '58, when you made your first try," he declared coolly. "But you flubbed, Miles. You listened to the Washington oracles who predicted the tin soldier wouldn't make a move. Only he did—and the next thing you knew, the Marines were landing and your situation was completely out of hand."

"I miscalculated. Foster assured me . . ."

"Secretaries of State feed everyone bullshit. That's their job. In any case, forget '58. It's ancient history. Your work on the 'overall project,' as you put it, has been a series of bungles, Miles. Bad bungles. Remember Enrico Mattei in 1962 and Emile Bustani in '63?"

"Coincidences. They died in aircraft accidents." Palmer was unruffled.

"Of course," Jemel nodded. "Accidents due to faulty maintenance. Very common in Mediterranean countries. Unfortunately, while tragic coincidences may remove troublesome people who erect obstacles, the obstacles often remain. You've learned that, haven't you, Miles?"

There was no response.

"We could discuss even more recent events," Jimmy said. "There was the June 1966 fiasco, for example. I warned you that the Egyptians would be smeared by the Israelis. But you preferred to listen to the CIA pratboy you carry on your Cairo bribe-roll. I 'lacked the requisite training and experience to assess military potentials,' he told you."

Palmer blinked, blurted: "How did you. . . ?"

"Miles, you're typically American. You don't have a clue as to how things really operate on the other side of the ocean. Any ocean. I've been prereading the supposedly secret reports sent to you from the Med area for years!"

Palmer's facial muscles pulsed. Karami chuckled, jabbed deeper.

"You've been trying to steal oil concessions for more than ten years, Miles. But you infallibly backed the wrong side or chose the wrong time to make your plays." The older man remained silent, glowering, and Jemel snorted. "You and your crowd pissed away fortunes. Then, as a last resort, you asked me for help. I agreed—because I have the machinery and can make it roll. Now, all of a sudden, you're hedging, back-pedaling!"

"Reasonably so," the financier argued defensively. "Those fortunes we spent laid some of the groundwork. You'd need far more than fifty million if you were starting alone, from scratch."

Karami leaned forward. "Granted. But then I wouldn't have to share any of the concessions—or profits—with you or anyone else. Which doesn't alter the fact that I need the fifty to spread around, pay for brewing up the storm."

"I've bought storms before, as you've seen fit to remind me," Palmer grated. "What did they produce?"

"Mainly wind," Jimmy replied amiably. "They were engineered by solid, clean-cut white Anglo-Saxon types. Oh, they're good—in their own environment. In the Middle East, they're ham-handed infants at the mercy of the shrewdest, sharpest dealers on earth." He laughed and waited while Palmer lit a cigar.

"You're familiar with the old wheeze about setting a thief," Jemel continued with a grin. "In the Middle East, substitute 'Arab' for 'thief' and you begin —just barely begin—to make progress."

"My associates and I have bought our share of Arabs, too, Jemel."

"Precisely your mistake. Only an Arab can buy another Arab and have any hopes the deal will stick. Even then, the buyer has to keep both eyes on his investment—day and night."

Palmer exhaled cigar smoke. "Who's to keep an eye on you, Jemel?"

"You people aren't buying," he countered. "You're simply underwriting a new stock issue for Karamcorp, an American company in which I hold the controlling interest. Period. If anyone gets hurt, it'll be the little old lady in tennis shoes—and I find it difficult to visualize your losing sleep over her welfare, Miles."

"The basic premise is a half-truth at best. You want the money immediately, months before we can begin unloading your paper. If you fumble the ball in the meantime, we're out fifty million—and every federal and state regulatory agency is on our necks."

"There's an element of risk in any form of investment," Jemel conceded blithely. "Or haven't you read the management training manuals?"

Palmer glared at the end of his cigar.

"Guns are expensive, as if you didn't know, Miles —and dissident sheikhs cost even more. I have to bid against oil-company money."

"You purchase the arms from your own companies."

"*Through,* Miles, not *from.* The preposition makes all the difference."

The portly financier cleared his throat. "I suggest we try for a compromise." He was testing, seeking signs that Karami's position was weaker than it appeared.

"Go ahead and suggest."

"I propose our syndicate puts fifteen million up front now and advances the balance later, when the picture has begun to clarify."

Jemel suppressed a disdainful laugh. The offer was preposterous, a transparent snare tactic. Palmer's investment syndicate could shove him into a corner, grab the new Karamcorp issue at thirty cents on the dollar, and acquire a massive minority interest in the company. Palmer could then pack the Karamcorp board with his own directors or even jockey the company into receivership and wrest away actual control. And, while Karamcorp—like Jimmy's bank and other enterprises—was currently tight on cash, the company did have some $200 million in eventually realizable assets.

Jimmy studied Palmer and thought, "The old bastard must be getting senile if he can't set a better trap than that." He said, "The answer is no, Miles."

"Be realistic, man!" Palmer exclaimed—a shade too quickly and too forcefully. "With your holdings, you can always obtain short-term interim financing to remain fluid. You'll have the assurance that we're behind you, ready with the other thirty-five million when . . ."

"You mean as, if, and when—and provided you and your bunch aren't sneaking through the back door to hijack Karamcorp."

"Now you're being . . ."

"Stop the shit, Miles! You say your associates left the final decision up to you. So make it. One way or another."

No indication of weakness here, Palmer realized

—but his nature and training demanded he make a last attempt. "Meet us part of the way, Jemel, so we have room to maneuver until the paper is off our hands."

"Balls! We're not discussing the takeover of a corner grocery. We're after three-quarters of the oil in the Middle East. I can think of a dozen concessions, each worth at least fifty million *a year*—in clear, tax-free, and eminently siphonable profits. Rand Oil, Shelby, Whitehead MidEast . . ."

Miles Palmer stopped listening. His eyes narrowed. He might have been contemplating some sensually pleasurable vision—and in fact, he was.

". . . make up your mind. Do we have a deal, or don't we?"

The question jolted Miles Palmer out of his daydreams. He focused his attention on Jemel. He sensed that further bargaining would be futile. But then, he and his associates had already agreed that Jemel Karami offered them their sole remaining chance for success. Karami knew the Middle East and was a part and product of it. Through his ownership of the Lebanese-based Incombank, Karami controlled an imposing array of facilities for accomplishing desired ends.

"You don't give me much choice, do you, Jemel?"

"Au contraire," he replied. "I'm offering you the widest possible latitude of choice between diametrically opposed alternatives. Yes—or no."

The simple French phrase *"au contraire"* chafed on Palmer even more than did Jemel Karami's casual, almost contemptuous arrogance. It reminded him that Karami was the cosmopolite, the sophisticate fluent in half a dozen languages, at home in any of half a hundred countries. On the other hand, despite ancestry, Old Money wealth, Social Register and *Who's Who* listings, he—Miles Langford Palmer—remained what Karami had said. Typically American, parochial, provincial, a stranger anywhere but in his own land. He forced himself to counterfeit an affable smile.

"All right, Jemel. The money will be transferred to your bank in Beirut this week." He stood up. Jimmy followed suit, his lean, six-foot figure making Palmer look even shorter and flabbier. "When do you plan on leaving New York?"

"In a few days, Miles. There are reasons for me to stay on this side a little longer."

"Business or pleasure?"

"Officially, business. As you know, we're opening the second New York branch of Incombank day after tomorrow—and that's my excuse. Off the record, now that we've reached agreement, my people on the other side can take certain steps—and it's advisable that I be here when they're taken."

Miles Palmer wisely decided to make no further inquiries.

Jemel accompanied his guest from the library to the elevator that served only his penthouse. When the elevator doors snicked shut, Jemel hurried to his bedroom.

The subtle frictions of his hour with Palmer had honed all his senses razor-fine, intensifying the need that had not been fully satisfied earlier. Jemel abandoned conscious effort to restrain the millrace of blood surging into his loins. When he entered the bedroom, his sex was already tumescent, swelling heavily against the cloth of his trousers.

The girl was still asleep. He removed his clothing swiftly, noiselessly. Naked, he went to the bed. eased himself gently down on its edge. He touched the girl, stroking her throat, caressing her breasts, feeling her nipples come alive and erect. She stirred, opened her eyes, blinked slowly to focus them and smiled.

"Jimmy."

The craving was there, heightening his own.

His hand moved over her, pressed between her open thighs. His fingers found moist warmth, lost themselves in it, and the muscles of her supple young body contracted. She locked her thighs and, arching her back, moaned softly. Then, abruptly, she raised herself up on one arm, twisted her torso towards him. She bent her head down, her hair loose silk brushing lightly against his thighs.

"God, Jimmy—let me feed . . ."

The greedy sheath of her mouth closed over him.

2

Beirut, Lebanon. Wednesday, April 24th.

The strident contrasts that assail the senses everywhere in the Lebanese capital become bedlam in the Bab Edriss sector.

There, faded miscegenations of Third Republic bourgeois and quasi-Moorish architecture line bogus Parisian boulevards. Behind these pathetic monuments to the abortive zeal of the French empire-builders who held a mandate over the country from 1920 to 1944 lie rancid soukhs—market-alleys teeming with haggling, polyglot humanity.

Garish new office-blocks—bizarre hybrids of bastardized Le Corbusier and depraved Saarinen mass-produced by fast-money contractors—amplify the discord.

Trough-narrow streets, malodorous in the humid heat, are a tumult of blaring automobile horns, cursing pedestrians and the whinny and bray of draft animals.

Soaring high above this anarchy, a tower of latticed white stone and tinted glass arrogantly dominated the Beirut skyline. Massive, opulent, it symbolized the prestige and stature of the giant international banking organization best known by the evocative acronym, Incombank, and served as its global headquarters and nerve center.

Incombank—the Industrial and Commercial Bank of the Levant, Societé Anonyme Libanaise—was freely chartered to perform all banking functions: savings, commercial and investment. It had branches in a score of countries and owned or controlled a wide range of business enterprises in five continents.

Incombank had been founded in 1953 by Jemel Karami, who was its board chairman—and who retained clear-cut numerical control of the bank's voting stock. Thus, the parent organization and all its world-wide subsidiaries and affiliates were his property.

Karami's first deputy and closest confidant, the ex-patriate Englishman Brian Lockhart, served as president of Incombank.

The two men formed an ideally balanced team. The extroverted, peripatetic Jemel Karami was a flashy virtuoso possessing uncanny intuition and observing few conventions. Brian Lockhart—aloof, aristocratic and tightly self-disciplined—relied on intellect rather than instinct, and during Jemel's frequent and pro-tracted absences from Lebanon, directed the bank's home-office operations with icy efficiency.

Seated behind a predictably antiseptic-neat desk in his sumptuous-for-show fifteenth-floor office, Brian Lockhart prepared to deal with an irrelevancy that would consume time and require mental effort on a day when he could ill afford to spare either. Jimmy Karami's telephone call from New York the previous day had wound all the springs tight, activated a com-plex train of gears and levers that demanded intense concentration and close supervision. But now he would have to attend to this damned nuisance, Lockhart cursed to himself—and glanced at his wristwatch.

It was 2:57.

In precisely three minutes United States Senator Frederick Hayworth and his wife would leave the American embassy on the Avenue de Paris and would be driven to the Incombank Building for what some bloody fool of an embassy clerk had described as an "informal goodwill visit."

Lockhart scowled, rose from his chair. Although of only medium height, his Guards Brigade bearing made him appear taller behind his fifty-two years. He went to the outer office of his executive suite, pausing there to speak with one of his assistants.

"Everything laid on for the reception?"

"Yes, sir. I've just made a final check."

Brian Lockhart took an elevator down to the main floor.

The Cadillac limousine with the Corps Diplomatique plates was making only slow, fitful progress through the chaotic traffic.

Senator and Mrs. Frederick Hayworth were alone in the rear seat. Insisting that his visit to Lebanon was unofficial and impromptu, Hayworth had rejected offers from embassy officials and attachés to accompany them. Only a single security man rode up front with the driver—but even so, Fred Hayworth was grateful that a soundproof window separated passenger compartment from front seat.

He'd rolled the window up. Tight. He didn't want anyone to overhear the abrasive-to-vituperative conversation he was certain would ensue between his wife and himself.

The limousine was forced to halt at a vehicle-jammed intersection.

"Look, Fred! There's a man wearing a burnoose waving at us!" Michele jeered. "If he's a camel-driver, you can take him home. That's what Hopalong Cassidy did. It helped him get where you want to go so badly."

"For Christ's sake, Mickey, shut up!" Hayworth snarled.

"Oh, the senator isn't enjoying his trip to glamorous Beirut!" she taunted. "What'd you call it yesterday? A 'half-assed Miami full of greasy big-nosed Arabs instead of greasy big-nosed Yids'?"

Frederick Hayworth cringed, his matinee-idol features reflecting something akin to fear. He'd hit the bottle a little too hard himself the previous day and sounded off after seeing the flamboyant beachfront hotels along the Corniche Chouran. If anyone except his wife had heard him, each booze-inspired word could mean ten thousand votes. Lost votes.

"Straighten up!" he rasped. "We'll be there soon."

"Go fuck yourself, Freddie! You've fucked just about everything else."

"What are you today, the Virgin Michele?"

"Hardly. I've done pretty well keeping up with you." She knew his rawer nerve ends, went for them.

"Wouldn't it be a laugh riot if your adoring constituents knew?" She giggled. "Senator Fred Hayworth, America's charismatic perfect-husband symbol—the call girls' best friend, and his lovely wife—with the roundest heels on either side of the Mississippi. You'd never get within a mile of that Oval Room, Freddie-boy. You couldn't even stay in the Senate—or get yourself elected to anything again."

Hayworth wanted to hit her, but didn't dare. "Easy," he warned himself. "Don't let the temper-control slip. No public scenes." The image of "Freddie and Mickey" Hayworth, eternally honeymooning couple, was one of his biggest political assets.

The Cadillac crept forward, was forced to stop again as a large red-painted truck and a horse-drawn wagon loaded with watermelons reached an impasse at the next intersection.

Michele's mood changed. "Why this junket to Jimmy's bank?" she demanded, turning to her husband. "He's not even here. He's in New York."

Hayworth's shrug was exaggerated. "Jimmy is an American citizen—thanks to your father, the people's cash-in-advance tribune—and . . ."

"Leave Dad out of it!" Mickey flared. "If it hadn't been for him, you'd still be a two-bit state assemblyman!"

What she said was true, infuriating. He'd married Michele to obtain the political backing and patronage of her father, Michael "Iron Mike" Ferrenbaugh, his state's party-boss. Hayworth despised them both for what he owed them.

"I'm waiting for an answer, Freddie-boy."

He droned an improvised reply. "Karami is important, influential—makes big contributions to party campaign funds. A visit to the home office of his bank is a gesture."

"You're lying, Fred. As usual." Mickey tucked a stray lock of auburn hair back into place. "What's your real reason? Jimmy told me you'd got him a bundle of Uncle Sam's butter-and-eggs money and that he'd paid you off—but that was months ago."

"I'm aware you sleep with Karami," Hayworth said, his voice brittle. "But I thought he could keep his mouth shut."

"Why should he with me?" Mickey responded, her hazel eyes softening. "I've known him most of my life."

At last, the limousine drew up before the Incombank Tower's rue Raid Solh entrance. Mickey instantly transformed herself into Mrs. Frederick Hayworth, lovely, warmly smiling, and devoted wife. It was a conditioned response. Her father had spent his life in politics, served several terms in the U.S. Senate. She'd been trained from childhood to maintain appearances in public.

The motorcycle policemen dismounted, cleared the sidewalk in front of the bank entrance. The embassy-assigned security man leaped out, opened the limousine door for the Hayworths. Brian Lockhart, several Incombank officials and numerous Lebanese newspaper photographers clustered around the senator and his wife. Greetings were exchanged, photographs taken.

"Mrs. Hayworth." Brian Lockhart offered his arm. The police waited until the entire party was inside the building before allowing the pedestrian flow to resume.

A reception was held in the luxurious Incombank boardroom. Members of the Lebanese press and Beirut-based foreign correspondents were among the invited guests. White-jacketed waiters served drinks—soft to the handful of devout Moslems present, hard liquor to the others.

Michele Hayworth drank sparingly. She watched and listened, alert for clues that might indicate why her husband had abruptly scrapped their planned itinerary, flying from Zurich to Beirut the day before. Above all, she was interested to learn why he'd insisted on making the visit to Incombank less than twenty-four hours after their arrival in Lebanon.

Senator Hayworth was at his charismatic boyish best, she observed. His remarks to the journalists and his responses to their questions were friendly, apparently spontaneous—and, Mickey recognized, artfully ambiguous. "Back home," a gullible electorate would interpret them as confirmation of hurriedly planted hints that "Young Senator Fred's" spur-of-the-moment detour to Lebanon was yet another of his famed altruistic private "missions." Beguiled Hayworth supporters would be convinced he was employing personal diplomacy in an effort to help ease the tensions that remained at flashpoint peak in the Middle East.

". . . I look upon Lebanon as a strong stabilizing factor in a troubled world," Fred Hayworth was saying to a journalist. "It is the financial and banking center, the Switzerland of the Middle East. Much—if not most —of the enormous wealth the other Arab countries derive from oil revenues finds its way into Lebanese banks. I feel that it is to America's best interests that we establish closer ties with Lebanon and the Lebanese. . . ."

"Oh, hell, I suppose I'll find out what it's all about sooner or later," Mickey told herself—and, bored now, asked a bank official to bring her another highball.

The hour allotted for the reception ended. Hayworth told Brian Lockhart he would like to speak to him—alone. They left Michele and the security man with a group of bank executives and went to Lockhart's office. There they seated themselves—the senator on a long, low couch, the bank president on a matching, equally low-slung chair facing him—and lit cigarettes.

"And now, Senator Hayworth, how may I be of service to you?" Lockhart inquired in his clipped old-school-tie accents.

The American cleared his throat. "I think you know that Mrs. Hayworth and I came here from Zurich?"

The opening wasn't at all what Brian Lockhart expected. It served to make him even more wary. He'd never met Hayworth before personally, but had heard much about him from Jimmy Karami. "Yes, I understood that you flew in from Switzerland. Was your stay there enjoyable?"

"Yes and no, Mr. Lockhart." Hayworth's smile was bland. "I picked up some rather disturbing rumors in Zurich." He tapped cigarette ash into a silver tray. "I suppose I should pass them on to Jimmy directly. However, I'd rather not do it over a transoceanic telephone line. Too many ears. And he may be gone from the States before I return there. Hence my trip to Beirut—and here, to Incombank."

Brian Lockhart registered polite interest. "I take it you wish to give me a message for Jimmy?"

"Yes." Hayworth busied himself extinguishing his cigarette. "The word in Zurich is that Incombank's liquidity ratio has—well, nosedived—and that your most important depositors among the oil sheikhs are growing worried and uneasy. Supposedly, they've sent a representative here to close out their accounts."

If Hayworth anticipated a strong reaction, he was disappointed. Lockhart placidly snuffed out his own cigarette, smiled. "There are grains of fact in most rumors, senator. This no exception."

"Then you . . ."

"I beg your pardon, senator. Abdul el Muein, a representative of the ruling Kuwaiti Sabah family and of other important Kuwaiti sheikhs, is actually in Beirut. He won't be leaving here until tomorrow, as a matter of fact. The business he has been transacting with us is, of course, confidential. Nonetheless, I can assure you that the people he represents are not 'worried' or 'nervous.' No accounts have been closed out." He cocked his head to one side. "If you'd care to speak with el Muein, I can probably arrange a meeting for you this evening."

Lockhart felt himself on safe ground. Senator Frederick Hayworth could hardly afford a face-to-face meeting with Abdul el Muein, emissary-at-large and hatchet- and bag-man for archreactionary oil sheikhs. The Englishman's pewter-pale eyes betrayed no amusement when Hayworth rejected the suggestion by ignoring it.

"Regarding our liquidity ratio," Lockhart continued. "As of this moment, it *is* down—to something less than twenty percent. The dip is technical, however, due to accounting complexities arising from the merger of three of Incombank's wholly-owned subsidiary companies and the consolidation of their assets."

Lockhart leaned back, assured and at ease. "By week's end, our ratio will be close to thirty percent. That's about as good as you'll find in any banking operation anywhere. For example, British clearing banks are among the world's most closely regulated. They're required to have very high liquid asset ratios —of only twenty-eight percent." He knew Hayworth would not ask how Jimmy Karami was going to boost the ratio. It was all going to be quite simple. The fifty million being advanced by Miles Palmer's investment syndicate was part of the answer. The rest? Adroit accounting permutations would shuttle funds and figures among subsidiaries and affiliates, inflating them at each step, and finally reflect ballooned totals on the parent company's books. The patches would hold for as long as they were needed. And afterwards there would be no problems about liquid cash, Lockhart grinned inwardly. None at all.

"I shall be pleased to send you a consolidated balance sheet on—mm, let's see—on Friday, senator," he said. By then the patch job would be completed and the on-paper liquidity ratio up to the 30 percent level.

"Your word is all I need, Mr. Lockhart," Fred Hayworth smiled broadly. "Jimmy is my friend, and I'm naturally glad to hear that there was no real basis to the Zurich rumors and everything is okay for him. I'd hate like hell to see Jimmy in a tight spot." He lit another cigarette and then looked at Brian Lockhart, his smile benign. "Being on various Senate subcommittees that deal with questions of international relations and finance, I'm happy to be in a position to reassure any of my colleagues who might hear the same rumors."

"I understand, Senator Hayworth," Lockhart nodded. He didn't understand really—not yet—but the first dim outlines were emerging.

"Oh, a last item, Mr. Lockhart. A personal favor."

"Certainly. A pleasure."

"My own account with Incombank . . ."

"Ah, yes. The one opened for you when the Commodity Credit Corporation transaction went through?"

"That's it. I'd like to have the money transferred to the Heinewald Brothers bank in Zurich."

"In your name?" the outlines were less dim now.

"No. I opened a numbered account with Heinewald. To make certain I didn't forget it, I simply doubled the number of my account here."

All sharp and clear at last, Brian Lockhart thought and said, "I believe you have $150,000 plus accrued interest in your account, senator. Suppose I transfer an equivalent amount to Heinewald's in Zurich, but maintain your Incombank account intact as proof of our trust and confidence. I'm certain Jimmy will approve my action."

It was Senator Frederick Hayworth's turn to read between the spoken lines. If he cooperated, muddied no waters, kept his information and his educated guesses to himself and did his bit for Incombank in Washington, he'd be another $150,000 richer. Karami would double the money he'd paid to Hayworth for steering $11 million in U.S. Government money—Commodity Credit Corporation credits—into Incombank's vaults.

Of course, the extra $150,000 would be held by Incombank, blocked until Karami was satisfied he'd lived up to his end of the newly implied bargain, Hayworth realized. But that was fair, a reasonable precaution.

"Then there's no need for me to take up any more of your time, Mr. Lockhart," he said. "I'll leave everything to you."

"Excellent. And please call me Brian, senator." Lockhart congratulated himself. The $150,000 price was cheap, for it could avoid catastrophe.

"Thank you, Brian, and by the same token, it's Fred, not senator." After escorting the Hayworths to their waiting limousine, Brian Lockhart returned to his office. Jaw set in a hard, determined line, he sat down at his desk and jabbed a button to summon his secretary.

He had crucial orders to give, vital work to do.

3

*Aboard Pan-Arab Airways Flight 106, bound from
Beirut to Kuwait City. Thursday, April 25th.*

Abdul el Muein had sprawled wearily in his first-
class compartment seat ever since the Caravelle took
off from Beirut's Khaldeh airport.

He now shifted his position, sighed, tried without
avail to blink away the burning sensation that pained
his bloodshot eyes. His lips were parchment; his
mouth tasted foul. Every fiber of his scraggy body
ached with fatigue.

Yet Abdul el Muein was content, immersed in
euphoric reverie.

For once—*min kan bisadik!*—a Zeitouni Quarter
pimp had told the truth. The boy the *'akrut* had
procured for him the night before had been young
and, if not exactly a virgin, still fresh, still so little
used that it required much effort to effect entry into
the passage. The boy had whimpered and bled—
which intensified Abdul's enjoyment—while quantities
of hashish enabled him to prolong his pleasure through
the night until dawn. But Abdul el Muein was savoring
memories and thoughts of much more than his de-
bauch with the submissive catamite.

He had enjoyed rare success in Beirut. He had
concluded extremely delicate business affairs for his
employers, accomplishing all he was sent to do—and
more—in less than a week.

Abdul ruefully admitted to himself it would have
been much more difficult if he'd had to deal with Jemel
Karami personally. El Muein had encountered Karami
frequently in the past and respected—and even feared
—him. Americanized or not, the falcon-faced Karami
was a Levantine. An Arab. His ruthless cunning was

21

almost legendary, and it had enabled him to create the largest, most powerful banking institution in the entire Middle East.

Largest and most powerful to outward appearances, el Muein laughed silently. He could afford to laugh, for he'd been the one to see what lay behind the façade. Luckily, Karami had been away from Beirut, and the ultimatums were delivered to—and the ensuing negotiations conducted with—the *inglizi*, Brian Lockhart.

Abdul el Muein indulged himself in a derisive grimace. Lockhart had proved no match. He was weak as a woman, offering only halfhearted resistance, merely dithering and delaying until Wednesday morning—when suddenly he'd capitulated, conceding everything, agreeing to all of Abdul's demands.

El Muein gloated, glancing at the locked dispatch case that lay on the empty seat beside him. The case contained the signed documents that were at once proofs and trophies of his triumph. He grunted happily, contemplating the praise and rewards he could expect to receive after his arrival in Kuwait City.

While it was entirely possible that he'd crippled —even destroyed—Incombank and Jemel Karami, he had saved Kuwait's ruling Sabah family and other influential shiekhs immense sums and much *sharaf,* much honor. They would be grateful. Grateful and generous.

Abdul reflected that he had been very wise in not sending reports of his progress to Kuwait. In the first place, such reports could have been intercepted, compromising the secrecy so necessary for the negotiations. Beyond that, the Sabahs and the others would be all the more pleasantly surprised when he delivered the fruits of his labors in a final, complete-to-the-last-detail package . . .

". . . *mnusal ba'd nuss sa'a.* Ladies and gentlemen, we will land in half an hour. *Mesdames et messieurs . . .*"

The trilingual announcement broadcast from the flight deck brought a halt to Abdul el Muein's meditations. He stretched, sought to rub life into the exhaustion-numbed flesh of his gaunt face, found the effort futile, and cursed.

Perhaps it might help if he went to the lavatory and bathed his face in cold water, Abdul thought. He levered his seatback into vertical position, stretched again and stood up. He eased himself out into the aisle, started walking forward.

He took three, possibly four, steps.

The explosion was sudden, awful in force. The Caravelle blew apart like an artillery shell detonated in midair. Fragments of wreckage and wispy shards of human flesh and bone erupted from the roaring ball of flame—and began falling, to scatter themselves over several square miles of arid wasteland 27,000 feet below.

4

Jeddah, Saudi Arabia. Friday, April 26th.

Russell Stanton had arrived in Jeddah on Monday. As a key—and ascendant—Whitehead MidEast Oil Co. vice-president, he made such visits periodically to inspect the company's Saudi Arabian and Kuwaiti operations. Normally, Russ Stanton spent a few days at the Whitehead MidEast administrative center in Jeddah, a week or so in the field, two or three days in Kuwait City and then returned to the New York home office.

But, on this trip his schedule was already a shambles. On Tuesday Stanton had been confronted with two major problems he could not in good conscience leave for Lloyd Emmerick, the resident superintendent, to face alone.

First, the Saudi labor delegate, representing the company's two thousand or so indigenous employees, had raised myriad baseless complaints and irresponsible demands. Then a typical Arab bureaucratic snarl blocked customs clearance of an entire shipment of urgently needed drilling equipment.

Russ Stanton glumly resigned himself to a protracted stay. Endless dickerings and liberal doses of what American oilmen in the Middle East call the "B-and-B—the baksheesh and bullshit treatment"—would be needed to avert labor trouble on the one hand and slash through red tape on the other.

Not much progress had been made by Thursday night. The Saudi officials were dragging out the suspense, insisting that all the maddening, time-consuming rituals of negotiation be observed. That evening, Russ Stanton had dinner with Lloyd Emmerick and his wife in the miniaturized American suburban community Whitehead MidEast maintained outside Jeddah for its administrative employees and their families. Afterwards, he went to his own temporary quarters, the VIP guest bungalow also situated in the company housing compound and spent a few hours sorting and reviewing his notes and papers.

Deferring to orthodox Moslem customs of the Saudis, Whitehead MidEast closed its downtown Jeddah offices on Fridays. American administrative personnel did what work that had to be done in their homes or at the comfortable clubhouse in the housing area.

Russ Stanton rose early on Friday. He had asked Lloyd Emmerick to come over to the guest bungalow so that they could catch up on routine matters they'd found necessary to postpone.

Stanton ate the breakfast made for him by one of the servants assigned to the bungalow and went into the living room to wait for Emmerick. It was not quite 8 A.M., but outside the sun was already superheating the whitewashed, flat-roofed and concrete-walled house. Stanton kicked up the air-conditioning control and decided he'd listen to the eight o'clock VOA English-language news broadcast.

He switched on the Braun T-1000 receiver in the living room, tuned it in and settled his athletic, six-foot-two body into an easy chair. The VOA newscaster's nasal voice droned from the loudspeaker.

A high-level Washington spokesman was quoted as warning of new, menacing developments in Southeast Asia. A Detroit sniper had gunned down three pedestrians in broad daylight. Britain's Chancellor of the Exchequer announced an improvment in the country's balance-of-payments situation.

Then:

"In Beirut, Lebanon, Pan-Arab Airways officials have revealed that one of their Caravelle jet transports vanished yesterday while on a flight to Kuwait City. Air and ground searches are continuing in an effort to find the craft, which carried forty-three passengers and six crew members . . ."

The ruggedly handsome features that Russell Stanton had inherited from his clipper-ship-captain forebears became alert and serious. He made a mental note to inquire if there were any company personnel aboard the plane, for Whitehead MidEast employees frequently traveled between Beirut and Kuwait City.

The newscast ended and Stanton switched off the set. Moments later, he heard a car stop in front of the bungalow. He guessed it was Lloyd Emmerick's Chrysler.

The door buzzer sounded. Russ made no move to answer it. The door-opening task was for the barefoot *khaddam* already hurrying along the hallway; in the Middle East, a master who did his servants' work made himself an object of contempt.

Lloyd Emmerick, a spare man grizzled by decades in the oil fields, was ushered into the room. Russ stood and they shook hands warmly.

"Heard the news about the Pan-Arab plane?" the resident superintendent asked, taking a black cigarillo from his pocket and lighting it.

"Only what came over the VOA," Russ said. "Could any of our people. . . ?"

"I'm not sure. I'm always behind on what happens out of Kuwait."

"Then maybe you'd better use your pull with Pan-Arab and have them give us a passenger manifest.

Use the phone in the corner while I go get my papers and other stuff."

Emmerick went to the telephone, called the local Pan-Arab Airways office and spoke to the manager. Returning to the living room, Stanton found a somber-faced Lloyd Emmerick chewing hard on his cigarillo.

"Ungood?"

"Ungood, Russ. They spotted the plane—or what's left of it—a little over an hour ago. No signs of survivors. The jet must've come apart in the air about two hundred and fifty miles due west of Kuwait. That's all the manager has so far. He's promised to squeeze a passenger list out of Beirut and call me back when he has it."

Stanton folded his husky frame back into the easy chair, spread documents on the table that stood before it.

"I always smell a stink whenever there's a plane crash in these parts," Emmerick mused aloud.

"The only stink I smell is from that cheap rope you're smoking," Russ grinned. "Sit down, Lloyd, and let's take care of the trivia."

"Sure, Russ." Lloyd Emmerick approved of Stanton, liked him. Russ was an exception in the newer generation of petroleum-industry executives. Most were dudes, overpolished deskbound types lacking the balls that the business demanded. Stanton, despite his comparative youth, was like the old-timers. Balls, he had —plus horse sense and a genuine feel for the oil business.

The work went smoothly. Both men knew their jobs thoroughly. They covered the items on Russell Stanton's agenda with swift efficiency. They were almost finished an hour later, when the telephone rang.

"Take it, Lloyd. It's probably Pan-Arab."

The older man went to the telephone and answered it. He nodded to Stanton. The call was from Pan-Arab.

"Yes, just read off the names," Emmerick said. "No, any order will do fine." He placed a gnarled hand over the transmitter. "He's apologizing because the

tourist-class passengers are listed first," he said to Russ
sourly. "When it comes to being snobs, the airlines . . ."

He didn't complete the sentence, turning his attention back to the telephone, listening intently. Occasionally, he spoke a few words.

"Could you spell that name? Thanks. No, it's not
one of our people."

"No. You're not going too fast."

"First class now? Okay . . ."

Russ noted with apprehension that Emmerick's
back stiffened when one name on the first-class roster
was read to him.

"You're sure?" the superintendent rasped. "Yes,
I suppose you would be. What? No, not a friend. A
business acquaintance."

The last names were read off.

"None of our personnel, thank God." Emmerick
said into the telephone. "Many thanks for all your
trouble." He replaced the instrument, swung around to
face Stanton. "You have a surprise coming, lad," he
growled. "Guess who was among the first-class passengers."

"Who?"

"The one and only Abdul el Muein."

Russell Stanton's eyes widened, then narrowed.
"Are they certain?"

"Absolutely." Emmerick returned to his chair, lit
a fresh cigarillo, and frowned. "Can't say that I'll
mourn Abdul the Anointed," he muttered, "but all of a
sudden we have a flock of new headaches, Russ."

"You're so right," the younger man nodded
gloomily. Abdul el Muein had long played an important—albeit equivocal—role *vis-à-vis* foreign oil companies operating in Saudi Arabia and Kuwait.

He acted as intermediary for numerous oil sheikhs,
presenting their requests (or demands) whenever they
wanted something not stipulated in their contracts—or
outside the law. He also collected—and paid out—the
clandestine extra baksheesh that bought the oil companies, Whitehead MidEast among them, protection from
dissident sheikhs and have-not Bedouin tribes. The

bribes purchased immunity from raids by "bandits" or "unidentified marauders" who would otherwise shoot up or dynamite drilling rigs and other installations or steal or destroy valuable supplies and equipment.

"Abdul's passing won't affect our relationships with the Kuwaiti or Saudi governments because we deal with them formally and directly," Russ Stanton mused aloud. "It's the smaller-fry sheikhs and tribal chieftains we have to worry about. Abdul handled all the transactions with them. We don't even know how he doled out the graft, how much he gave to each." He drew a deep breath. "And if all those bastards don't get their monthly baksheesh on the dot, they'll start to raise hell without even asking why their payoffs are late!"

Asking any dissident sheikh or nomad chieftain how much he had been receiving from Abdul el Muein would be sheer folly. Any reply would be a square of the actual amount—and once stated, the price would have to be paid thereafter, or else. Attempts at guess estimating would be equally fatal. To give a chieftain a penny less than he's previously received would invite instant and violent retaliation. Pay a cent more than usual to one—and all would demand increases.

Emmerick cracked his scarred knuckles. "Should we ask around to find out what the other oil outfits intend doing?"

Russ shook his head. "Not unless someone topside orders it. We take care of Whitehead MidEast—and on our own. Period."

"I reckoned you'd say that."

"Maybe you were right about that stink." Russ said. "Airplane accidents happen all the time—but when they happen with somebody like Abdul el Muein aboard . . ."

"They're suspicious until proved otherwise."

"It could have been a curtain-raiser—only for what?"

"You name it, lad," Emmerick shrugged. "The pot's constantly boiling out here. Lots of people would love to see the lid blow."

Russell Stanton lapsed into deep thought. It was essential to learn who would replace Abdul el Muein as go-between and bag-man. However, inquiries would have to be made circumspectly, circuitously. Beirut was the logical starting-point—for several reasons.

Beirut was the Middle East's money capital—and el Muein spent much of his time there. The Caravelle had taken off from Beirut, and it belonged to Pan-Arab Airways, a Lebanese airline owned by Incombank...

Incombank!

Of course! What better source of information was there anywhere in the Middle East than Jimmy Karami?

Russ smiled. Jimmy practically owned Beirut outright—and held a first mortgage on the rest of Lebanon. Sure, he was a banker—but his Incombank was the biggest and most influential in the Middle East. Its depositors included the leading Arab oil princes. If anyone could tell him what had happened—or was going to happen—it was Jimmy Karami. Jimmy would have the inside dope at his fingertips—or he'd be able to obtain it faster than anyone else.

"Oh, hell!" Russ blurted. "That's no good!"

"What's no good?" Lloyd Emmerick inquired with evident curiosity.

"I was hunting for ideas about where we might find out something fast," Stanton explained. "I thought of Jemel Karami—and then I remembered he's in the States."

"The Incombank Karami?"

"The same."

"Oh, yeah. You went to school together, didn't you?"

"That's exaggerating it a little. We were roommates during our single year in college. We've stayed friends, though we don't see each other often."

Stanton's voice trailed off as he recalled when he had last seen Jimmy Karami. It had been a little more than two years before. When Pat—died. When he'd heard the news, Jimmy had dropped everything, flown to New York immediately. Damned few friends would do as much as Jimmy had done for him—and for Pat.

Now all the bitter, agonizing memories and the unanswered questions boiled up again.

Pat, Patricia, his wife. Mrs. Russell Stanton. Who was gone, dead, but could still be alive if only—if only what?

Why? Why wasn't Pat still alive? Even if she hadn't wanted the baby, why in the name of God had she—of all people—acted like some hysterical, panic-stricken, and totally ignorant adolescent?

Why, for Christ's sake?

Russ passed a hand over his eyes, blocked off the memories and forced himself to concentrate on the present. On the right now—and his work.

Jimmy Karami couldn't help because he wasn't in Beirut, and if Stanton and Emmerick were to accomplish anything, they would have to act quickly. Immediately.

Russ rearranged the pieces into another pattern.

"When did you and your missus have your last vacation, Lloyd?" he asked.

"Four months ago."

"Then you're due for another—deluxe and all expenses paid by Whitehead MidEast. I'm authorizing it —and I recommend Beirut and a suite at the Phoenicia. Can you make the MEA flight this evening?"

"Which means you want me to bird-dog?"

"Yes. Aside from Jimmy Karami—who isn't there right now—I don't know many people in Beirut. You do. What's more, if Mr. and Mrs. Lloyd Emmerick show up in Beirut on vacation, it's normal and natural —which it wouldn't be in my case. So, while you're vacationing, you ask some questions, pass out company money whenever you feel it'll do any good—and listen and look. Okay?"

"Sure, Russ."

"I don't want the Saudis to know why you're in Beirut," Stanton told Emmerick. "So, if you learn anything, call Quentin Yeager in New York—day or night, at the office or his home."

"Yeager himself, eh?" Quentin Yeager was the president of Whitehead MidEast Oil, second only to R. Daniel Whitehead, the petroleum-industry magnate who owned the company.

"Yep. This thing is touchy. Yeager should be kept posted." Stanton grinned. "You can tell me everything when you get back."

Emmerick got to his feet and went across the room to the telephone. "I'll call MEA and make flight reservations," he said. "Then I'll tell the wife to start packing."

5

Oceanside, California. Monday, April 29th.

R. Daniel Whitehead belonged to the same breed and generation of oil tycoons as H. L. Hunt and J. Paul Getty, but he differed greatly from both men in many respects.

Whitehead shunned publicity, scrupulously avoided expressing his opinions publicly on any topic. He had been married only once, in his youth. The marriage ended in amicable divorce, and he was childless. His numerous affairs with women thereafter were consistently brief in duration and discreet in nature. Well—if largely self-educated, he could be suave and gracious or bluff and irascible as occasion and his best interests demanded.

Daniel Whitehead began his career as a wildcatter in the Texas oil fields. Over the decades, he parlayed his first gusher into a dozen or more operating companies, including at least three rated as petroleum-industry majors.

He lived in unobtrusive but regal luxury on a hilltop estate overlooking the town of Oceanside and the limitless sweep of the Pacific that lay beyond. From there, he ruled his far-flung domains in the manner of an absolute—if relatively benevolent—despot.

Despite his seventy-three years, Whitehead remained a gritty, vigorous autocrat—"the boss sits wherever I happen to plant my butt"—and actively directed the operations of his companies. Senior executives of Whitehead corporations went to the Oceanside estate by summons or sufferance, as though before an imperial presence. While "R. D." solicited their opinions and suggestions, he was the final arbiter and authority whose last word—whether calmly murmured or impatiently thundered—terminated discussion and constituted decision.

On warm and sunny days, R. D. Whitehead made his office in the patio of the large rose garden that was separated from his Spanish hacienda-style mansion by a vast expanse of green lawn. Comfortably dressed in short-sleeved sports shirt and slacks, he would sprawl on a foam-rubber-padded outdoor chaise longue. Flanked by secretaries, extension telephone close at hand, he dictated letters and memoranda, issued orders and instructions, and conferred or conversed with those to whom he had granted audience.

It was near noon on Monday, and the weather was warm and clear. R. Daniel Whitehead was in the rose-garden patio, but the secretaries were absent, and instead of lolling on the chaise, he sat ramrod straight at its foot.

A rough-hewn figure with a leathery face and gun-metal eyes now aglow with rising anger, Whitehead listened to the neatly dressed, fiftyish man sitting opposite him in a wrought-iron garden chair.

Quentin Yeager, president of Whitehead Mid-East Oil Co. had flown in from New York that morning. He'd brought news that added ominous dimensions to a picture Daniel Whitehead first glimpsed taking shape on the preceding Friday.

". . . and Lloyd Emmerick phoned my house at five this morning, New York time—eleven at his end," Quentin Yeager was summing up. "He says there's all kinds of wild talk about dissident sheikhs coming to

Beirut for a sort of renegades' summit meeting. He also claims his sources suspect the Pan-Arab crash was caused by deliberate sabotage . . ."

"They 'suspect,' do they?" Daniel Whitehead snorted.

"So far, there's absolutely no proof," Yeager said.

"Proof? There's no proof, Quent. Remember the Trident that 'disintegrated' over the Red Sea a few months ago? And the Comet that dived into the Persian Gulf? Think back a few years. When Enrico Mattei beat the competition out of too many oil concessions, his private jet crashed. A year later, Emile Bustani started to make life difficult for the poachers—and what happened? He climbed aboard his Aero-Commander at Khaldeh. His pilot took off—and fifteen minutes later, that plane 'disintegrated,' too." Whitehead scowled. "Let a plot start hatching anywhere in the Middle East, and right away you have 'unexplained aircraft accidents' happening to people who might somehow gum up the machinery."

Yeager looked unconvinced. "This could be an exception, R. D.," he said quietly. "We've done everything with that Caravelle passenger list but fluoroscope it. The only person who could conceivably tie in was Abdul el Muein. Wrecking an airliner, killing forty-nine people, strikes me as too much of a risk merely to eliminate one man—especially one like el Muein. He was nothing but a glorified errand boy."

Whitehead made no immediate comment. He reached for a tall glass of bourbon and water on a round metal table at his elbow. He sipped, replaced the glass, spoke. "Errand boys sometimes learn too much from the messages they carry—or they carry messages some people would rather not have delivered."

Yeager nodded, willing to concede the point, and admitted to himself that he was out of his depth. He had almost no direct Middle East experience. He wasn't even an oilman in the commonly accepted sense of the word, for he'd come up through the sales and marketing side of the business.

"Quent," Dan Whitehead said after a moment's

silence. "Suppose I told you that Miles Langford Palmer has formed a new syndicate and advanced Jemel Karami fifty million?"

"What?" Quentin Yeager's head snapped up as though he'd been struck in the jaw. "You're joking!"

"Wish I was," the oil magnate rasped. "I got a confidential and fully verified report last Friday."

"Jesus Christ!"

"And then some. The pirates have picked a new captain—Jemel Karami—and they're off and raiding."

Whitehead lapsed into oil-field idioms when he spoke again. "It's plainer than a baboon's ass to me, Quent. The sons of bitches are going to make another try—all out and straight for everybody's balls. How Abdul el Muein fits in—or didn't fit in and had to be given the permanent flush—is a side issue, but you can bet there's a connection somewhere."

Yeager stared at his employer. "Palmer, I understand," he said. "He's been trying to steal Middle Eastern oil concessions for years—and he's always operated by proxy, keeping himself covered. But Karami? He's got the biggest bank in the Middle East. The Saudis and Kuwaitis have poured tens of millions they've received from oil royalties into his bank. Why in the name of God should he get mixed up with Palmer and his crew and run the risk of losing. . . ?"

"Desperation," Whitehead cut in. "Karami is overextended. Incombank, and his main American holding company, Karamcorp, is spread thin. Oh, he can juggle, stave off the day of reckoning for eighteen months, two years at most. His sole long-range hope is to score a major coup. A Middle East oil grab is an obvious answer—especially with the game room being right next door to Incombank."

Yeager's brow seamed. "Palmer made other attempts. He was always stopped before."

"Now isn't before, Quent. The whole Middle East is primed for a giant-sized blowup. Ba'athists, Nasserites, Reds, and God only knows who else are all stirring and stoking. Rulers of Arab countries that have oil are terrified they'll be deposed by outsiders or the don't-haves and dissidents in their own countries.

"I accept what you tell me, R. D.," he said. He did—and as gospel. Daniel Whitehead hadn't amassed an almost billion-dollar fortune by misjudging the situations that confronted him. "My only question is what should we—what can we—do?"

The old oilman grimaced. "We—meaning Whitehead MidEast as a company and yours truly as an individual—gird our loins and sally forth to do battle with the motherfuckers."

"Alone?"

"Alone."

"But there's a real threat to the entire Middle Eastern structure," Yeager protested. "Why don't we pass on what we know—and suspect—to the Arab governments concerned? They would . . ."

"They would nail us to the nearest wall. Not a year or two ago, maybe. Today, yes. The governments of the oil-producing Arab countries are infested with informers, power-players, traitors. We pass along a tip—and within hours, wild-eyed fanatics will be screaming that Whitehead MidEast is playing imperialist tricks, meddling in the country's internal affairs. Finish. The government concerned would be forced to cancel our concessions in order to save face."

"How about Washington?"

"Useless. Miles Palmer is a public-spirited, economic-advising fixture in Washington with friends in high places. Jemel Karami owns a stable of senators and congressmen. Teamed up, they're two pimps with more whores than we can handle."

Yeager looked grim. "Let me run down my mental checklist, R. D. We're not the only foreign company producing oil in the Arab countries. The others stand to lose as much as we do."

"Sure," Whitehead agreed calmly. "And we all worked together when similar situations arose in the past. Once again, it's different now. Because of the conditions over there, each outfit is running scared, looking out for itself. How many would you estimate we can trust?"

"When you put it that way, not many."

Daniel Whitehead turned his head. "Say for argument's sake we did cooperate with the few companies we can trust. We'd be hamstringing ourselves. This mess isn't going to develop slowly and gradually. Karami will have to act fast—very fast. There won't be time for us to form committees, hold intercompany conferences, obtain majority approvals."

The old man is right, Quentin Yeager admitted. Most other oil companies were cumbersome superorganizations run by plodding directors and nervous hired-hand executives. R. D. Whitehead exercised one-man control over his enterprises, could make instant decisions and obtain lightning-swift action simply by rapping out an order.

"Anyway, I've always come out ahead when I was the bull of the woods," Whitehead said, turning back to Yeager. "I can afford to be an altruist and try to save the other guys' hides along with my own. Jemel Karami is our problem. He's smarter and deadlier than Miles Palmer—and he's got guts."

Whitehead stood up, walked to the far end of the patio, toyed absently with the leaves of a rosebush, returned and sat down. He leaned forward, resting sinewy forearms on his knees.

"We have to get to Karami," he declared.

"Can we buy him off?"

"Hardly. I'm convinced he and Palmer are playing for more than all the oil companies in the Middle East put together could afford to offer."

"You say he's spread thin. What if we grabbed the edges and tugged hard?"

Whitehead shook his head. "He's not that thin on the surface, especially not with the fifty million transfusion. Incombank and his other holdings show considerably more than a billion in assets. While they aren't net and they aren't fluid—and some aren't even assets —his balance sheets convince a lot of people. I could bust him open, given enough time. But there isn't time."

He waited for Quentin Yeager to exhaust his modern-business-executive idea resources.

"Women?" Yeager offered tentatively.

Whitehead laughed. "Guess you don't read the gossip columns. Jemel Karami is a bigger cocksman than Flynn, Rubirosa, or Aly Khan ever were. Women stand in line, panting to be laid by him."

Yeager spread his hands.

Good, Whitehead thought. *The instant-suggestion store is empty.* He said, "Quent, I'll be seventy-three years old next month. Just being around that long has made a cynical old fart out of me. I've learned there are two last-resort approaches for getting to—or at —people. Through their past or their friends—and for overkill, through both."

Yeager's upper lip curled slightly. "I don't doubt for a moment that there's plenty in Karami's past. What I can't understand is how he manages to make the friends. With him, everything's one-way. His."

"You underestimate the man. He's loaded with what's called 'charm,' and he's got the rare talent for making one-way look two-way. He can make it appear that he does most of the giving and takes nothing in return. He has more than just talent for it. Almost genius." Whitehead grimaced. "He's got friends who swear by him. Male and female. Believe me. I know. I've been keeping tabs on Karami ever since he opened up shop as an international banker in our Middle East backyard. I've got quite a file on the Boy Croesus."

"Oh." Quentin Yeager knew the extent and efficiency of his chief's awesome private intelligence apparatus. It had few equals in an industry where almost every major company maintained large industrial and political espionage systems. "Oh, I see."

"No, you don't see, Quent," Whitehead disagreed in an amiable tone. "Not really. You and I come from different generations. You read about Teapot Dome. I lived it."

He continued. "You didn't grow up in this business during the days when the local banker and the county clerk would get together and forge courthouse records to swindle you out of a lease. You never had your drilling crews worked over and your rigs wrecked by hired goons to make you abandon a property after you'd brought in a producing well or opened up a new field."

He put his empty glass on the table.

"What I'm driving at, Quent, is that Jemel Karami can't be stopped with writs and injunctions. It's going to be a vicious brawl. People are likely to be hurt. Physically hurt. Maybe killed. And even if we win, the dust we kick up in the process may attract the wrong kind of attention and get us run out of the Middle East anyway."

Quentin Yeager read the message. This was the last opportunity to climb off. Stay, and he'd have to ride to the very end of the line. Wherever that was. He made his decision.

"Whitehead MidEast is your company, R. D.," he said evenly. "I'm paid to run it the way you want."

"Thanks, Quent."

"None needed. Just tell me what you think of our chances."

"I calculate the odds at around five-to-one. Against us," Whitehead replied. His mouth slanted into a diagonal grin. "That's before we turn over our hole cards."

"Which, I presume, are the banking wizard's past and his friends."

"Right." Whitehead got to his feet. "Let's go up to the house. After lunch, you can plow through my Karami, Jemel *et al.* files. You'll find they're packed with surprises that might be used to lower the odds."

The two men walked along the flagstoned path leading from patio through rose garden and across the lawn to Daniel Whitehead's huge, gleaming red-tile-roofed mansion.

"So," Yeager murmured, half to himself. "We fight dirty."

Whitehead heard him. "We haven't much choice," he said. "We're up against a man who's originally Lebanese. A Levantine. The end product of a mongrel culture that threw away all the rulebooks before the dawn of civilization." He gave a short, harsh laugh. "Men like Karami have been raping the world for three thousand years and more, Quent. They pass the fine art down from father to son, with each generation improving on the techniques."

They paused outside an entrance to the great house.

"People in Texas believe that if a centipede crawls over fresh beef, there's some poison in its feet that rots the meat," Whitehead said, the remark tossed off, seemingly irrelevant. "Karami's like that, Quent. He's famous for having a magic touch. The Midas touch. Everything he puts his hands on seems to turn to pure gold. But what he touches, he corrodes. That's his weakness. That's liable to be our strength."

They went into the house.

Protasis I

A millennium before the Christian era, what is now known as Lebanon was inhabited by the Phoenicians. Precocious, unburdened by scruples, they were traders and usurers, princes and profiteers of commerce in the ancient world. After their decline as a race, Egyptians, Persians, Greeks, Romans, Byzantine Christians, Saracens, Crusaders, and Turks in turn swept over the land. Each left marks and influences, traces of customs and cults, swarms of bastards and handfuls of colonizers.

In mid-nineteenth century, Lebanon was part of the Ottoman Turkish empire—and an ethnological absurdity. Less than two million people were splintered into countless inimical ethnic strains, tribes, factions and twenty-nine identifiable religions. Roughly half were Moslem: Shiite, Sunnite, Metwali, Malikite, or Druse. The remainder were Christians, ranging through a spectrum of Eastern Rite sects from a Maronite majority down to a few thousand Syrian Jacobites.

The "Lebanese" had in common only a vague concept that, since Arabic was the language spoken and understood by all, all were somehow Arabs. Despite nominal Turkish rule, any real and effective power over this motley populace was exercised—as ever—by the spiritual heirs of the Phoenicians: the merchants and moneylenders of Beirut.

In 1860 the Druses began a systematic massacre of Lebanese Christian Arabs. Turkish bureaucrats were indifferent, Turkish garrisons impotent. France had long enjoyed special trading privileges with Lebanon and intervened, sent an army corps to save Christian lives. America sent another army—of zealous Protestant missionaries bent on saving Eastern Rite Christian and Moslem souls.

The French troops crushed the Druses within a year—and departed. The missionaries remained, competed fiercely for converts and superimposed a layer of "American Protestant" Lebanese on the existing social and religious structure.

Of all the American missions, the one maintained by the Presbyterian Church was the largest and most liberally endowed with funds. Not surprisingly, it won the greatest number of converts. Among the first of these was Ibrahim Karami, the patriarchal head of a prosperous Maronite Christian merchant family in Beirut, a man of considerable imagination who recognized the potential advantages of apostasy.

1

For generations, Karami men had been traders, arbitrators, moneychangers and lenders, financiers of ventures sometimes illicit but seldom unprofitable throughout the Levant.

The conversion of Ibrahim Karami and his immediate family to the Presbyterian faith brought them immediate benefits. Ibrahim and his sons became stewards of mission and missionaries' funds, acted as brokers and buying agents for the mission when it began building a "Protestant College" in Beirut. The evangelists, satisfied that their commercial affairs were in competent hands, pretended not to notice that the Karamis were indifferent toward all religions, and that their conversion had been one of convenience.

Born in 1871, Ibrahim Karami's grandson, Bakr,

attended the American Presbyterian schools and college in Beirut. He received a one-year mission scholarship for further study in the United States.

Returning to Lebanon, Bakr Karami went into business as a general trader and importer-exporter.

Bakr's son, Hassan Karami, attended the same schools as his father and also spent a year studying in America. Hassan arrived back in Lebanon in July 1914, just before World War I erupted in Europe.

The Turkish empire's entry into the war as an ally of Germany caused Bakr and Hassan Karami no hardship. Christian Arabs were exempt from service in the Turkish army, and the Karamis were left free to deal nimbly in fluctuating currencies and trade in scarce and contraband goods. By paying baksheesh and providing women or boys to Turkish officials, they obtained lucrative contracts for food and supplies needed by Turkish military forces in Lebanon, Syria, and Mesopotamia.

During the last year of the war, a typhus epidemic raged across the Levant, wiping out almost a third of the Lebanese population. Hassan Karami's parents and most of his relatives were among the victims. He was left alone to take over the family business in October 1918, the same month that victorious British and Australian forces entered and occupied Lebanon.

Hassan Karami's fluent English and Western manners won him the confidence of British and Australian officers. Gifts of liquor, women, or money—or all three —gained him new supply contracts and purchase orders. But the "Anglo" occupation ended swiftly. Lebanon and Syria passed under French mandate, in effect became French colonies.

This development was a source of deep concern to Hassan. He spoke French with an atrocious accent and was known as "American Protestant Arab." His worries were short-lived. He discovered that in French idiom, a bribe or baksheesh is called *"pot-de-vin."*

Otherwise, nothing had changed.

2

Hassan Karami wanted to marry a European woman. He disdained the bovine daughters of merchant families in Lebanon's hidebound, inbred Christian Arab community. Besides, such a marriage would give him added prestige and advantage in his steadily increasing dealings with Westerners.

In 1924, Major François Tallier was transferred to Lebanon from France. A widower with no income aside from his army pay, Major Tallier was accompanied by his daughter, Annette, who, at twenty-four, remained a spinster due to the squalid petit-bourgeois customs prevailing in the French army. Annette could offer a suitor no *dot,* no dowry.

Major Tallier was assigned to the Beirut military headquarters and appointed local contracting and purchasing officer. He could hardly believe his good fortune. At last, he would be able to augment his pay, accumulate a respectable *dot* for his daughter.

Hassan Karami soon contrived to meet the new contracting and purchasing officer, and they reached an agreement. Tallier would receive a 5 percent commission as *pot-de-vin* on all contracts and purchase orders he awarded to Karami *et Cie.*

After they had done business together for a month or two, Major Tallier invited Hassan Karami to dinner at his quarters. It was Hassan's first visit to the drab, army-standard house allotted to Tallier—and his first meeting with the major's daughter.

Although no ravishing beauty. Annette was attractive and shapely. Tawny hair framed a good face and clear blue eyes. Hassan's speculative interest was quickly aroused.

Annette seldom met men who were not in the army. Hassan Karami was a sharp and exciting contrast. Hawk-faced, his skin a shade darker than western Mediterranean olive, he wore his expensive double-breasted suit with the easy air of the rich cosmopolite, and he was more the elemental male than any booted, bemedaled chasseur. To her dismay, the young woman found that his dark-eyed gaze made her blush, caused her thighs to flex involuntarily as the juices of the female hunger welled between them.

Conversation at dinner and in the dreary, cramped parlor afterward was polite, banal. Hassan took his leave at eleven. When he held Annette's hand to bid her good night, he pressed it and felt response.

"Pas une mauvais pomme, pour une pomme— not a bad apple as apples go," Major Tallier commented when Karami had gone. It was the highest praise he could bring himself to give any civilian.

"He seemed nice, papa," Annette said, feigning indifference. Alone in her bed, she found sleep impossible until her trembling fingers finally provided sterile release for the tensions within her.

A week later, Hassan Karami invited François Tallier and his daughter to dinner at his own home. It was a spacious two-story villa with Moorish-arched windows and much decorative tiling located in the Ras Beirut quarter. Major Tallier ruefully noted that the wines were vintage, and the excellent dinner was served by a squad of servants. At least he pays me promptly, Tallier consoled his envy pangs. The evidences of wealth were not lost on Annette, either. She saw their equal only on the rare occasions when she and her father attended functions in the homes of commanding generals or ambassadors.

Hassan inquired if Mademoiselle Tallier had done much sightseeing since her arrival in Beirut. No, she had not. He offered to place a car, driver, and guide at her disposal. "With your permission, of course, m'sieu," he smiled at François Tallier.

The major nodded and expressed his appreciation.

There were other dinners and Karami made other generous gestures during the next several weeks, but he and Annette were never alone. It was painfully clear that Major Tallier would tolerate no kind of relationship between his daughter and a civilian—least of all a civilian who was a dark-skinned colonial. Christian Arab or not, in Tallier's eyes Hassan was a native, no different than an Annamese yellow, a Moroccan Jew, or a Senegalese black.

In early September, Major Tallier was ordered to Damascus for a fortnight's temporary duty with the headquarters there.

He left Beirut with a motorized supply convoy on a hellishly hot and humid day. Shortly after arriving in Damascus, he suffered an attack of nausea and diarrhea and reported to the garrison hospital. An army doctor, puzzled but not alarmed, ordered him to bed and gave him a mild sedative. Tallier slept six hours, awoke and vomited blood.

His temperature soared to 105 degrees. By midnight he was delirious. Shortly after dawn, he lapsed into coma. An hour later, he died. Medical officers, unable to make a diagnosis and fearing epidemic, ordered immediate burial.

The Beirut headquarters was notified by telephone. A staffcar and armed escort were provided to take Annette to Damascus, where she was shown her father's freshly filled grave in the garrison cemetery.

When Annette returned to Beirut, Hassan sent his chauffeur to her quarters with a note expressing condolences. He was not surprised when the *ujak'ji* brought him a sealed envelope that contained a message asking him to call that evening. After ten o'clock.

Annette was alone and wore a plain black dress. A single weak light burned in the foyer. When Hassan entered, she closed and locked the door, switched off the light. She seized his hand in the darkness, digging her fingernails deep into his palm and wordlessly led him through the house to her bedroom.

"Hassan." She had never called him by his first name before. She fumbled at the fastenings of her dress, undid them, let the dress fall to the floor. "Hassan!" She flung herself into his arms, ground her mouth against his, and he felt the ripeness of her body.

He led her to the bed and undressed. She grasped his wrist, pulled him down on top of her.

Annette Tallier's ardor was unpracticed, instinctive. She was a virgin, as Hassan had guessed she would be, and there was savage ecstasy in her cry of pain as he probed into her, felt the membrane resist, then yield, and her hips flail in frantic, spasmodic movement.

Hassan's sure, insistent promptings subdued her, established rhythm, subtly varying and amplifying it, increasing and protracting pleasure. Only when he sensed that her sensual demand was total did he carry her—and himself—to completion.

He felt the violent constriction of her vaginal muscles, heard her expectant yet disbelieving gasps burst into a long, frenzied moan as she climaxed, straining against him, then falling back, trembling, still holding him inside her.

Hassan waited long minutes, turned and lay on his side.

"Annette."

There was an interval before she replied. "Qui, Hassan."

"You have been told you must return to France?" The daughters of deceased officers were not permitted to remain alone in military cantonments.

"Oui, Hassan." That was all, but her tone was like the dry scratch of crumpled paper blown along a sidewalk by the wind.

Yes, Annette thought bleakly. She must return to France. To do what? Work as a governess? Marry some man who'd never let her forget she brought him no *dot?* Live in shabby-genteel poverty with relatives?

At least she'd done this, Annette told herself. For once, she'd experienced sheer animal pleasure—and retaliated against the obscene restrictions with which her father and the *systeme* he worshipped had so long stifled her.

Hassan spoke again: "Annette, listen to what I say . . ."

Money circumvented secular and religious rules, and they were married the following week.

For Hassan, it was the attainment of an objective; for Annette, deliverance.

3

Hassan Karami gained much *sharaf*—honor—by his marriage. Annette proved to be an excellent manager of his household and a charming hostess to his guests. Annette's gain was no less in degree—security and affluence.

It was a time of prosperity and change in Lebanon. The French poured enormous sums into the mandated area in an effort to make it productive and self-sustaining.

Adroit maneuvering by the city's merchant elite caused most of the money to be diverted to Beirut. Acres of scabrous stone and mud hovels were demolished (and their occupants sent packing) to make way for preposterously wide streets that aped Parisian boulevards. Scores of four- and five-story commercial buildings were constructed. Something of a start was made toward saving the ramshackle port from total disintegration.

Profiting handsomely, the businessmen of Beirut and their families imitated the customs of the French upper-middle class.

Hassan and Annette Karami fitted themselves to the pattern and were content. Idealized romantic love was not an element in their marriage, and neither had expected it. Hassan satisfied Annette sexually, and he was reasonably discreet about his extramarital adventures.

Hassan's clothes were made for him by a London tailor. Annette's came from Paris, as did any new furniture, linens and similar items needed in their house. Marvelously silent American electric fans cooled their rooms in the summer (when they did not take refuge from the searing heat in the mountain resorts), and remarkably efficient and clean German oil heaters eliminated any chill or damp in winter.

By any standards, the Karamis lived well; by those of the Levant, none lived better.

Two years after their marriage, Annette had her first child—a son.

The boy was christened Jemel.

Jemel Karami.

Among Arabs—Moslem or Christian—a father's feelings toward his firstborn son transcend any familiar to Westerners. They are at once mystical and crudely possessive. The father sees his son as a projection of himself, to be cast and trained—at whatever cost and by whatever means—into a duplicate of his own image.

Hassan Karami was determined that he, and he alone, would guide Jemel's development, mold his mind and personality.

Hassan monopolized Jemel. Annette, having learned much about Arab mentality and comprehending the father-firstborn son mystique, accepted the inevitable. She stood aside, played a less-than-subsidiary role in Jemel's upbringing.

Four years passed and Annette gave birth to another child—again a son. Hassan was pleased, named the boy Nuri—but he was by then too deeply absorbed in Jemel to show Nuri equal attention.

Annette Karami's suppressed maternal instincts now found their outlet. Hassan had usurped Jemel. Nuri would be hers—her son. She engulfed the boy in protective, permissive love, denied him nothing, forgave him everything.

Each parent was making grave errors. Neither was aware of them.

In 1938, the year of the Munich Pact and the *Anschluss,* Annette Karami became pregnant for the third time. She hoped for a girl, chose Felicite, her own mother's name for the unborn child.

Annette had borne her sons in the Hospital de la Maternité Française, Lebanon's best maternity clinic, and went there again. She was attended by Beirut's foremost obstetrician, and routine medical examinations indicated she was in good health.

But Annette was a European woman who had lived fourteen years in Lebanon. Climate, frequently dubious water, primitive public sanitation—all had eroded her physiology, carried her past childbearing prime.

Organic adynamia made her labor long and agonizing, and she was delivered only with great difficulty. The baby was a girl—normal and healthy. However, Annette had been exhausted by the ordeal of giving birth. Complications set in. Her condition grew progressively worse over the ensuing days, and the doctors were unable to save her life.

Hassan remembered his wife's wish, and his daughter was christened Felicite. He employed Mademoiselle Claire Viete, a plump matronly French nurse to care for the baby and further augmented his domestic staff with a housekeeper and a governess to look after Nuri. He did not need or want anyone to assist him in raising his oldest son, Jemel. Less than a year later, Germany invaded Poland and World War II began.

The Nazis paused for several months, then conquered Norway, the Low Countries, France.

In Lebanon and Syria, the French defeat caused dismay and turmoil. Order was restored by the pro-Nazi Vichy-appointed military governor, General Dentz. Deploying Foreign Legionnaires and Senegalese levies, Dentz established an iron regime administered by subordinates who were ruthless, brutal—and corrupt. Wealthy Lebanese had but one thought: to flee, preferably to the United States, which was neutral, far removed from the war, safe—and rich.

It was against this background that Jemel Karami entered his fifteenth year.

4

Automobile headlights swept the dockside wall of the metal-roofed warehouse, briefly illuminating a signboard: "Karami *et Cie*."

The car stopped before the building entrance. A night watchman peered out through a window, recognized the Renault sedan, unlocked and opened the door. Hassan and Jemel Karami entered, accompanied by a thickset man wearing the khaki uniform of a full colonel in the Vichy French Army.

"*Alaiyi shral mhimmi*—I have important business," Hassan told the watchman, who promptly scuttled off, to wait until summoned in a dingy seamen's café on the rue Hajj Douad.

Hassan switched on the yellowish lights in the cavernous warehouse storage area. Jemel went to a tool rack and took down a steel crowbar shaped like a truncated cane. Watching them, Colonel Henri Perrot was again struck by the similarities—and subtle differences—between father and son. Both were tall, Hassan the taller by only an inch or so, and alike in build —save that the man was lean and angular, the boy slender and supple. Their facial resemblance was startling, except that where Hassan's features were hawklike, Jemel's seemed to have been refined into those of a highly bred prize falcon.

"Please follow me, *mon cher colonel*," Hassan said. They went along an aisleway flanked on both sides by heaped bales, crates, sacks, objects difficult to identify in the gloom.

Turning off at a pile of bulging jute sacks, Hassan stopped beside two triple-tiered stacks of identical wooden crates. Colonel Perrot stared at them greedily.

"Open that box!" Hassan ordered, jabbing a thick forefinger.

Jemel wrestled the crate down to the packed-earth floor. Using the crowbar, he loosened the lid, then pulled it free, exposing a layer of small, flat tins with colorful labels that indicated they contained stuffed Portuguese anchovy filets. Perrot bent, dug among the tins, removed one. He pulled off the slotted key soldered to the tin, fitted the slot to an overhanging metal tab, and rolled back the top.

"*Bien,*" he grunted, standing up. "And now?"

"The *capres* must be tested with the fingers," Hassan said.

Perrot grimaced at the prospect of crushing the oily, smelly anchovies between his fingers, but placed the tin atop the two-crate-high stack and began. "*Voilà!*" he exclaimed triumphantly seconds later, extracting something very small. "You say there are four in each tin?"

"*Oui, monsieur le colonel.*" It was Jemel who replied. "Each weighing two-and-a-half grams. Ten grams per tin, twelve dozen tins per case. Six cases, a total of eight kilos, six hundred and forty grams. All twenty-four carats fine."

In 1941 neutral Portugal was already doing a brisk trade in selling and smuggling gold. Sold at high premiums, gold was cast into two-and-one-half-gram "*boutons,*" which were lacquered *capre* green and stuffed into anchovy filets. In belligerent countries and their colonies, gold was worth astronomical prices in terms of currencies it could buy on the black market.

Importers of the gold-stuffed anchovies took grave risks. Germany, Italy, and Vichy France had decreed summary death sentences for private individuals possessing gold bullion. No one knew this better than Colonel Henri Perrot. Assistant chief of staff to the military governor in Lebanon, he had countersigned death warrants for more than ninety "gold hoarders" in Beirut alone. However, Perrot had no fears. His rank and position placed him above the laws he administered.

"Ah! Another—and another!" Perrot chortled, finding more pellets. He calculated the worth of the gold in the six cases. *Mon Dieu!* At black-market rates, equal to three years' pay in Reichsmarks, much more in the Vichy francs! "The last!" Perspiration oozed from his pores. "Open the next crate." He wanted to continue his random inspection and assure himself the Arabs weren't cheating.

"Soir, messieurs!"

Jemel's head snapped up. His father and Perrot whirled around.

First they saw the nine-millimeter Belgian Browning that was pointed at them, then the man who held it—a short, hard-eyed Frenchman in a rumpled white cotton suit. Felt-soled Arab slippers on his feet explained how he'd approached without being heard.

Colonel Perrot's eyes bugged recognition. He flushed, made an attempt at bluster. "Capitaine Andrieux! As your superior officer. . . !"

"Your mouth is a cunt!" The Browning muzzle yawned its menace. "All of you move close together. There. *Bien.*"

"Andrieux." Perrot's bluster had vanished. "We can make an arrangement. There is enough for both of us." He was pleading now.

"Merde! Shut your face!"

Hassan and Jemel were afraid, but they could not suspect what Perrot knew. Capitaine Raoul Andrieux was a Gestapo-trained agent only nominally subordinated to Beirut army headquarters. He reported directly to Vichy and, worse, to the Gestapo kommandatura in Occupied Paris. It was a standing joke in the Beirut staff-officers' mess that if Capitaine Andrieux pissed at all, he pissed ice water. Henri Perrot realized with growing horror that if Andrieux was determined to make an arrest, nothing could save him from drumhead trial and execution.

"Captain, take the Arabs," Perrot begged with mounting desperation. "I'll testify against them. I'll push through a promotion for you."

"Close your blowhole or I'll push a bullet through your fat guts!"

Andrieux was relishing the spectacle. His intelligence colleagues feared Henri Perrot. They refused to listen to his suspicions about the colonel and had left him to conduct the investigation entirely on his own. They were imbeciles and cowards, Andrieux sneered to himself.

Unfortunately, he hadn't yet learned what Perrot was selling for the gold. No matter. *Spécialistes* at the depot could make the mute sing arias. Let Perrot and the Arabs squat naked, rectums just clearing upright bayonets or broken wine bottles. They'd tell everything, before or after their leg muscles gave out and sharp steel or jagged glass rammed up into their bowels.

There was a problem, Andrieux reminded himself. He was alone. The warehouse had no telephone. How to get the three prisoners and the evidence—six heavy crates—to the depot intact?

"You, boy!" he barked to Jemel, hitting on a solution.

Jemel's belly froze. *"Oui, m'sieu."*

"The port fire station is four hundred meters distant. Go there and telephone the depot. Say that Capitaine Andrieux wants a motorized patrol here immediately. Then return. All inside fifteen minutes, or I shoot your father. Understand?"

Jemel wet his lips, glanced at Hassan.

"Do as he tells you," Hassan said. His voice was shaky, but he had hope. He was rich, richer than Perrot or the dog-fucker, Andrieux, dreamed. He could buy even generals and cabinet ministers. He needed only to reach the right person.

Jemel's mind raced. The captain was sending him to call the depot, which meant he was alone, and no one at the depot knew his whereabouts.

"Allez!" Andrieux snarled.

The boy edged out into the aisleway. His armpits and crotch poured icy sweat. He forced himself to run toward the warehouse office.

He got as far as the tool rack, saw them and stopped, a spasm twisting his stomach. Baling hooks. Hanging in a row. Primitive tools—and deadly weapons. Forged from heavy, tempered steel with solid ring handles and needle-sharp points. They offered a chance, a hope.

Yes, Jemel bit blood from his lip, took down one of the baling hooks. He moved on to the door that led outside, opened it noisily and, without taking another step, slammed it shut. Remembering Andrieux's felt-soled slippers, he removed his own shoes.

Hassan had made his son spend numberless hours working in the warehouse, taking inventories, tallying merchandise. Jemel was familiar with every centimeter of the storage area, could find a dozen concealed routes through the maze of stored goods.

Creeping noiselessly on stockinged feet, he returned to the storage area, dodged behind a jumble of packing cases and paused there. He was holding the baling hook too tightly. Sweat from his clenched hand made the handle slippery. He wiped the metal dry with his shirt, rubbed his palm hard against a trousers leg. Better.

He started moving again, making slow progress that seemed infinitely slower. Blood pounded in his veins. Rats scampered; the sound was amplified to a terrifying pitch by his ears. He crouched low, gave wide berth to some heaped steel-wire coils. A strand sprung loose from its bindings could trip him.

Flour barrels stood directly ahead. Four rows. He counted them off with each step, detoured to the right. He had to approach Andrieux from behind, without being seen by his father or Perrot, for any change in their facial expressions would warn the capitaine.

Jemel heard a metallic clank, froze, heart battering ribs.

". . . we'll make you eat these tins, you pig-turds . . ."

Six more meters. Then five. Now the worst was to come. An open space between piled bales that was within Andrieux's vision-field. Jemel braced, peered around a bale. Clear. He leaped across the gap, almost fell, fought back terror and recovered his balance.

". . . *le question extraordinaire* tonight, trial in the morning, and you'll all dangle from a noose by noon!" Andrieux was jeering.

The side of his head was almost near enough. Almost. Not quite. One more step. Jemel's muscles tensed, his breath stopped.

Now!

The baling hook flashed up—then down. Jemel felt the spiked point punch through skull-bone, sink deep into brain cavity. He jerked at the handle with all his strength, toppling Andrieux backward.

An already dead finger flexed, pulling the trigger of the Browning. The blast was deafening, but the bullet went high, tearing into the roof. Jemel's knees buckled. He swayed, but steadied himself.

Perrot panicked. "He's dead!" he shrilled hysterically. "You killed him!" Hassan spun, grabbed Perrot and gave him a head-jolting slap. The colonel sobered. With Andrieux dead, there would be no arrest for him. But for the Arabs? And what of the gold? "The patrol," he mumbled.

Jemel glared at him. "I didn't telephone. I never left the building." *Strange,* he thought, *I just killed a man and I feel nothing.*

"We must do something!" Perrot croaked.

"Yes. Dispose of your friend," Hassan said. "A simple enough *ouvrage*—provided you keep quiet." He spoke to Jemel rapidly in Arabic. They left Perrot, returning minutes later with a hand-truck, a large burlap bag, several metal lumps, and a length of rope. Jemel put the bag on the floor, opened its mouth and dumped the metal lumps inside.

"Help me!" Hassan barked to Perrot. Together, they lifted Andrieux's corpse, stuffed it into the bag. The baling hook remained embedded in the shattered skull. Hassan tossed the capitaine's automatic in after the body. After Jemel tied the sack with rope, Hassan and Perrot heaved the bundle on to the hand-truck.

Jemel unbarred and opened a sliding door leading to the dockside. He went out, checked the pier. It was deserted, he reported.

Perrot and Hassan pushed the hand-truck from the warehouse to the edge of the pier. Hassan tipped the weighted bundle off the truck, and it fell, splashing, into the water. It sank immediately.

"Ten meters deep," Hassan remarked casually. He told Perrot to shove the truck back inside. The colonel obeyed without a word.

Jemel started after him, stopped. The dock-front cat skulked near a pile of litter. He whipped off his jacket, sprang, flung the jacket over the animal. It screeched, tried to escape, but Jemel held it securely. He carried it into the warehouse to where Andrieux's body had lain. Picking up the crowbar, he released the cat—and struck it a murderous blow with the heavy tool.

"The rats will eat it and explain the bloodstains," he said.

"Wish to inspect any more tins?" Hassan asked Perrot coldly.

"No. I—I am satisfied." He wanted only to leave. And quickly.

"Merci." Hassan's smile was caustic.

Jemel replaced the lid on the opened crate. He found the gold pellets Perrot had taken from one tin he'd inspected, gave them to the colonel who pocketed them without comment.

"There remains the question of the passports and emigration permits," Hassan said quietly.

"You shall have all four in the morning."

"Five. Or do you forget my daughter's nurse?"

"Pardon. Mais certainement. Five."

"And we depart when?"

"A ship leaves for Istanbul tomorrow evening. I will requisition passage aboard her for you." "And the devil take you," Perrot added silently.

"Excellent," Hassan murmured. Once they were in Turkey, all would be well. Their American visitors' visas were already bought, stamped into their passports. They'd lacked only the almost-impossible-to-obtain exit permits from Lebanon, and these were what the gold *boutons* were buying from Colonel Henri Perrot. "The crates will be delivered to you as soon as we have the documents, *mon cher colonel.*"

They left the warehouse after Jemel had retrieved his shoes and put them on. A thought struck Jemel.

"Perhaps Andrieux had an automobile," Jemel suggested.

"He would have parked far from here," Perrot said with assurance.

They got into Hassan's Renault. After stopping by the café where the watchman waited and sending him back to the warehouse, Hassan took Colonel Perrot to his quarters. Then he started toward the Ras Beirut quarter and home. The dark-potholed side streets through which he drove were empty, and all house windows were tightly shuttered. The Foreign Legionnaires who patrolled Beirut after dark were notorious for making arrests—or opening fire—at the slightest provocation.

"How do you feel?" Hassan asked Jemel in English, the language they both preferred to speak.

Jemel did not reply immediately. He was trying to organize and assess the thoughts that whirled through his brain.

All his life, Jemel had been his father's creature and creation. Hassan laid down the rules, insisting that whatever he said be accepted as dogma. Even minor shortcomings brought harsh reprimands and sarcastic sneers—and Hassan usually attributed them to the influence of the "weak French blood" Jemel had inherited from his mother.

It was a typical Arab father's way with his firstborn son, an obsessive desire to fashion the boy into what the father considered perfection.

It was all so stupid, Jemel reflected, staring straight ahead through the windshield. His father wasn't perfect —not by any means. Hassan was old-fashioned, behind the times—at heart the prototype of the arch-conservative Levantine merchant rather than the modern businessman he fancied himself. He always shunned risks, preferring lesser returns that were certain.

That won't be my way when I'm on my own, Jemel assured himself. *I know the biggest successes come when one takes the biggest risks.*

He blinked as pieces fell into place and a sudden realization came over him. The relationship between him and his father had been greatly altered by what had happened less than an hour before.

I could have left the warehouse and kept on going, Jemel told himself. *I could have found any number of places to hide, and I would have been certain that I, at least, was safe. But I stayed and did what I did and because of that, my father is free and still alive—and he hasn't said a word in praise, nothing to acknowledge what I did.*

Risks? Jemel was caught up by a wave of wild elation and he smiled broadly. *I'm willing to take them. I proved that tonight. I took the biggest risk anyone can take. I staked my life—and won.*

Jemel could feel the baling-hook handle in his hand, saw himself wielding it, slashing down, spiking the point through bone and deep into soft pulpy brain matter . . .

Elation and smile vanished—and long-delayed reaction set in.

Jemel retched, all strength draining from him. He slumped sideways in the seat and sobbed.

Hassan understood what had happened. He slammed on the brakes, seized Jemel's shoulder, and shook it violently. He rasped out the first words that came to his mind.

"So! The boy who thought he was a man is really a woman!"

His intent was to help, to jolt his son out of the shock-state—and apparently he succeeded. The boy regained control over himself. He sat up straight, quiet and composed now, and stared at Hassan.

Jemel knew he would never forget what had been said—nor that his father had said it.

"Are you all right now?" Hassan asked.

"Yes," Jemel replied, forging a smile. "I feel like a new man." He did, but not in any sense his father could have imagined.

5

New York City's exclusive Plaza Hotel became a haven for the wealthy of the Middle East and Aegean who sought to avoid the dangers and rigors of war in luxury. Swarthy men congregated in the hotel's bars and lobbies. While their women shopped avidly in Manhattan's glossier stores, they discussed business—and a common dilemma.

However obtained, their U.S. entry permits were temporary. Visitors' visas. Normal avenues for obtaining permanent residence permits and American citizenship were closed. Immigration quotas for their "countries of origin" were oversubscribed for years ahead. Many who occupied $100-a-day suites thus faced the threat of eventual deportation. Some solved the dilemma more quickly than others.

Arriving in New York the week before Germany invaded Russia, Hassan Karami, his three children and his daughter's nurse settled into a six-room Plaza suite. Mademoiselle Claire Viete looked after Felicite, Nuri was enrolled in a private day-school. Jemel was left free to acquaint himself with his new environment. They, too, had only temporary, visitors' visas—a deficiency Hassan was determined to correct without delay.

Over the years, Hassan—and his father before him —had transferred most of their profits to the Palmer National Trust Co., a leading New York banking firm. The accumulated total was nearly a million dollars, enough for the bank's head, Aubrey Palmer, to treat Hassan Karami with deferential consideration, and for his son, Miles Palmer, to service the account personally.

Soon after his arrival in New York, Hassan was invited to have lunch with Miles Palmer at the Harvard

59

Club. Toying with the pallid food, Hassan bluntly broached the subject foremost in his mind.

"I need your help in obtaining immigration visas," he declared.

Miles Palmer was startled and his cheeks, at thirty already flaccid, quivered. He sipped ice water before speaking.

"We're bankers, Mr. Karami. Not—ah—the federal government. Of course, we can recommend excellent attorneys who specialize . . ."

"Come, now," Hassan interrupted. "I am aware these matters are often arranged through private members' bills passed in Congress. Surely the Palmer National Trust has cooperative legislators among its friends."

Palmer saw it was useless to pretend ignorance. "Yes, we can introduce you to a—ah—a helpful senator." He cleared his throat. "However, I think I should warn you . . ."

"The senator is not an altruist?" Hassan smiled. "There are five of us," he said, raising and lowering his shoulders. "Perhaps the Senator allows discounts on quantity orders."

The voters in his midwestern state cheered whenever Michael "Iron Mike" Ferrenbaugh thundered his campaign slogan: "What this country needs is more God in government and less goddamned government meddling in your business!" In 1940 they elected him to his second consecutive Senate term by a landslide majority.

Ferrenbaugh's detractors ranked him somewhere between Bilbo and Byrd, but Iron Mike ignored them. He listened to other voices. Voices like that of Miles Palmer, who was telephoning Ferrenbaugh's Senate office from New York City.

". . . I understand, Miles," Ferrenbaugh was saying. "Only I'm a mite worried about him being an A-rab. Too many Christers in my state. They figure Mohammedans, Jews, Buddhists are heathen—worse'n niggers. . . ."

"Mr. Karami is a Lebanese Christian," Palmer told him stiffly. "A Protestant, I might add."

"That does make a difference, Miles."

"I promised Mr. Karami you'd come up here next Thursday. Go to the Plaza. He'll have rooms reserved for you there."

"I'll take the noon train," Ferrenbaugh said. He received several thousand dollars a year from the Palmers. "Always glad to oblige."

Plush, Iron Mike Ferrenbaugh thought, looking around the two-room suite. Liquor bottles, cigars and cigarettes were arrayed on a sideboard.

"Everything but orchids," he mused aloud, opening a bottle of rye. He poured two fingers into a glass, added ice, and drank. Good. He picked up the telephone, asked for Hassan Karami, was put through immediately. After greetings were exchanged, Ferrenbaugh asked when they could "get together and have a chat."

"My son Jemel and I will come right down, senator."

Mike would have preferred a meeting without witnesses, but . . .

A large man with a broad, homespun face, Michael Ferrenbaugh exuded his professional politician's cordiality when Hassan and Jemel arrived.

He pumped Jemel's hand. "How old are you, young fella?"

"Sixteen in a month."

"The kid looks and acts older," Mike thought. "Miles Palmer mentioned you have three children, Mr. Karami."

"Yes. Another son, Nuri, who is twelve, and my daughter, Felicite, three." Hassan and Jemel seated themselves on a long divan.

"I've got a daughter, five," Ferrenbaugh said. "My wife insisted on naming her Michele, after me. Only I call her Mickey." While he talked, he studied the Karamis, sizing them up.

New York was in the midst of a record heat wave, but they were fresh and crisp. Hassan in a hand-tailored blue suit—pure silk and worth $200,

Mike estimated. Jemel wore a light gray tropical worsted. Ferrenbaugh moved to the sideboard and commented dolefully on the weather, observing that his guests seemed unaffected by it.

"We're Arabs, senator," Jemel grinned. "Accustomed to heat."

Arabs, Ferrenbaugh reflected. Yep. Corny as it sounded, they had the exotic look of desert sheikhs in the movies. Both swarthy and ramrod straight. Hassan ropy-lean, Jemel lithe and solid muscle. Arabs—in hand-tailored suits and living at the Plaza . . .

"Care for a drink?" he asked.

"Scotch-and-water, please," Hassan said. "The Crawford's. Without ice."

Jemel had drunk wine since childhood, cognac and liqueurs since he was thirteen. But he knew how Americans felt about minors and alcohol. Although he loathed American soft drinks—they reminded him of a citrate of magnesia, a laxative favored for children by upper-class Lebanese—he asked for a ginger ale.

Ferrenbaugh served their drinks, sat down in a wingchair facing them and raised his own glass. "Welcome to the U.S.A!" he boomed.

"Oh, I was here before the last war," Hassan said. He drank. "I should have stayed. There were no immigration restrictions then."

Jesus, this bird doesn't stall around, Mike thought and said, "That's right. Congress didn't pass an immigration law until 1917."

"The first of a series," Hassan said, draining his glass.

I'm not rising to the bait that fast, Mike decided. "Another?"

Hassan said yes. Jemel declined. Ferrenbaugh poured Hassan's and his own drinks slowly, pondering how far he could trust the Levantine, realized he had no choice. *Miles Palmer had given the word,* he reflected, *so I take the hook.* He handed Hassan his fresh drink.

"Immigration laws are tough," he declared. " 'Course, exceptions *can* be made." Your ball, Mr. Karami.

"Permit me to be specific, senator."

Iron Mike rubbed his jut jaw and said, "Sure." Then he remembered Jemel and fixed him with a sharp, appraising look. Hassan smiled.

"My son is hardly an unlicked cub," he said.

No, not by a hell of a shot, Ferrenbaugh agreed, studying Jemel's impassive—and mature—aquiline face. "Sure," he repeated.

Hassan's almost-black eyes narrowed. "I understand a gentleman's agreement permits senators to introduce private immigration bills on behalf of individuals, and these pass without debate or dissent."

Iron Mike poured himself another rye. "Unfortunately, an unwritten law limits the number a senator can toss into the hopper—and I've used up my ration. However, there are other angles."

A top Immigration and Naturalization Service official owed his job to Senator Michael Ferrenbaugh. He'd backdate and double-shuffle papers, doctor the Lebanese quota lists. Easily done—if the price was right.

"Your immigration-visa applications would be given—well, special processing." Mike went on. "You'd be assigned numbers near the top of the Lebanese quota list." He sipped whisky. "There's just one catch. You'll have to go up to Montreal, reenter from there. It's a crazy law, but . . ."

"Yes, I'm familiar with it," Hassan said. He knew about the quota-numbers hocus-pocus, too. A Greek shipowner and his family had recently returned to the Plaza after a brief trip to Montreal—suddenly at the top of a list that was filled for the next seven years. "How long do you estimate it would take before we could go to Canada and reenter?"

"I can probably swing it for you by the end of September."

Hassan made his opening bid. "The visas would be worth forty thousand dollars to me, senator."

Ferrenbaugh stared into his glass. "Considering the war and all, that's kind of low, Mr. Karami."

"The sum is large."

"Not when you consider how many people want the same thing."

"Perhaps you can suggest a more appropriate figure."

"Oh, seventy-five would be closer."

"Sixty," Hassan countered. "A third in advance, tomorrow."

"In cash?"

"In cash. The balance on delivery. Also in cash."

Ferrenbaugh raised his glass. "We're in business, Mr. Karami."

"No," Hassan shook his head. "We've simply reached a single understanding. Once I have the visas, we can discuss going into business."

"Huh?"

"The war will last for years. I'm convinced America will be drawn into it. A businessman with influential friends in Washington will profit—and so will his friends."

Iron Mike beamed. To his surprise, his visitors stood up.

"I shall stop by for you at eight," Hassan told him. "I have arranged for two attractive and accommodating young women to accompany us to a nightclub."

Ferrenbaugh rose from his chair, leering happily. "I'll be ready and rarin'." He thrust out his hand. The Arab was a great guy.

Hassan was pleased.

"Ferrenbaugh is for sale like most politicians," he observed to Jemel as they walked down the corridor to the elevator bank. "But he is the type who gives value for value received."

"An honest grafter." Jemel's instinct told him that Ferrenbaugh remained "honest" because he lacked the imagination necessary for successful duplicity.

"He'll be valuable to us later. He can open doors, help me obtain government contracts."

Jemel started to speak, thought better of it. Hassan Karami would never change. He'd always choose the smaller, safer returns—which were what Michael Ferrenbaugh would deliver. The senator was a reliable, plodding workhorse—but to win large sums, one bet on thoroughbreds, not workhorses.

They took an elevator up to their own floor.

"What are you doing tomorrow?" Hassan asked when they left the car.

"I am meeting a girl at noon."

"A liaison?"

"With luck, yes. She is here at the hotel with her parents. If they leave her alone in their suite, or I . . ."

"Take her to the room I use as my *garçonnière*," Hassan said, stopping in the corridor. "It is on the third floor. I will tell the desk to let you have the key."

Hassan felt relieved. He'd detected a subtle change in Jemel since their departure from Beirut and had been afraid the Andrieux episode had left some deep mental or emotional scars on the boy. But his evident eagerness for sexual adventure was an encouraging sign there were no lasting aftereffects.

"Is she an American girl?" Hassan inquired.

"Yes."

"Then I trust you will exercise care. American women are inept. I have no desire to become a grandfather."

"I am careful," Jemel said. "And they are inept —at first. Then they act as though they wanted to spend the rest of their lives in a brothel. I've already discovered that."

They continued on to their suite.

Michael Ferrenbaugh settled himself into the seat of the taxi.

"Where to, gents?" the driver asked over his shoulder.

Hassan gave him an address in the East Seventies. "We're stopping there to call for someone, and then we're going on to the Caravanserai," he said. The hackie nodded, shoved down his flag, and pulled away from the Plaza entrance.

"I hope these dames are smart enough to keep their mouths shut, Hassan," Ferrenbaugh said. They had been on a first-name basis since Hassan collected him a few minutes earlier. "I have a wife and a half million voters to worry about."

It was the opening Hassan wanted.

"You have nothing to worry about, Mike. They were provided by a friend, Nicholas Varnum—who also owns the Caravanserai."

Ferrenbaugh's jaw dropped. Nicholas Varnum was a near-legend built on many myths and few known facts. He reputedly financed Prohibition-era bootleggers and was now outwardly legitimate, owning several expensive New York nightclubs.

"You know Varnum?" Ferrenbaugh asked.

"Very well. We were friends in Beirut long ago."

"I thought he was a Jew-boy who changed his name."

"He did change his name—it was originally Nadim Vehouni—but he is a Lebanese Arab and a Christian."

"I hear he's still the money-man behind the wop syndicate."

Hassan stared coldly at his companion. "I would not like to be the person who suggested anything like that to Nicholas Varnum's face," he said, his tone sawtoothed.

Mike recognized his blunder. "Sorry, Hassan. That was a damn-fool crack." He'd have to tread carefully with Hassan Karami. Any man whose friends ran the gamut from Aubrey and Miles Palmer to Nicholas Varnum . . .

Hassan chuckled inwardly. The point had been made. Senator Michael Ferrenbaugh was learning.

6

Jemel was arched over the girl, supporting himself on his knees and elbows. The only contact between their bodies was the gentle friction of his slow, shallow

movements inside her. He saw the wild look come into
her eyes again, and her hips began to undulate.

"Don't move yet!" he ordered.

"Please!" Lois Endicott begged. "Let me!"

"No. Wait." He continued his rhythmic thrusts.
Her fingers dug convulsively at the bedclothes. "Caress
your breasts," he said.

"What?" Lois failed to comprehend. She could
only feel, was once more almost to the peak, but he
held her maddeningly short of it.

"Put your hands on your breasts!"

"Jemel—I can't hold off any longer. Go on—
faster!"

Instead, he stopped entirely save for a flexing of
muscle that made the girl gasp with each throb. He
shifted an arm, seized her blonde hair, causing her to
whimper, pulled her head down into the pillow.

"Do as I tell you!"

"Yes. Yes, Jemel." Lois's hands went uncertainly
to her small, hard breasts. He resumed his movements, gradually increasing their tempo.

Her frenzy mounting, the girl crushed and
kneaded her breasts, lacquered fingernails clawing into
firm white flesh. Her blue eyes were wide, frantic, seeing yet not seeing, staring up into Jemel's face. Her
tongue stabbed and licked at empty air as though even
that has taste and texture to heighten sensual pleasure.
Tremors, violent and uncontrollable, coursed through
her body.

She was ready.

"Now!" Jemel rasped, suddenly speeding the
rhythm, driving himself deeper and deeper into her.

The girl moaned, flung her legs around him,
locked him to her, hips grinding. She still clutched her
breasts and strained to rub the taut points of her nipples against the pressing weight of his chest.

"Oh, Christ! Oh. . . !"

Jemel cupped a hand over her mouth to muffle
the loud cry he knew would follow. Her tongue licked
wetly at his palm, her teeth pressing into its flesh.
Then all other feeling was lost in the flooding rush of
his own gratification.

Minutes passed before he withdrew. The girl protested, tried to hold him. He pulled away. "It's getting late," he said. Lois Endicott's mother believed they had gone out together for lunch and expected her daughter back at two. It was almost that time now, and Jemel didn't want to arouse any parental suspicions. Still, he thought, he would enjoy another—just one more. His dark eyes swept from Lois's pretty, if vacuous, face along the length of her fresh and delightful body. It was enough to cause him partial erection.

"How can you fuck like that, Jemel?" A featherbrained almost-seventeen-year-old, Lois Endicott revelled in using forbidden words.

"I've told you before," Jemel said. "I learned in a sort of school."

Sons of wealthy Arab families receive elaborate sexual education. As tradition demanded, when Jemel reached thirteen, his father placed him in the care of a Beirut *hakim* for a month. The doctor taught Jemel about the physiology and psychology of sex. He provided women who initiated the boy into the "101 postures and 1,010 delights of *jima"*—sexual intercourse. Jemel also learned the disciplines of *msik,* the technique that enables Arab men to maintain erection and continue coitus for hours, to control ejaculation and intensify and prolong orgasm.

Jemel had tried to explain this to Lois previously, without avail.

"I don't believe it," she said. "There can't be schools for fucking." She extended an arm, reached for his penis and fondled it. Jemel noticed she caressed her breasts with her other hand. She'd learned something new today, he mused. Next time, he would show her how to . . .

"Let's fuck again," she murmured. "Look. Your dick's all hard and ready." He would have agreed, had she not spoken again. "Come on! Give my pussy more meat and make her purr again!"

The imbecile remark guillotined his desire. "I said it's late." He swung his long legs off the bed. "Your mother . . ."

"I can talk her out of anything."

"Her. Not me."

Realizing he'd made up his mind, Lois flung herself from the bed. "You don't like me!" she exclaimed, pouting angrily.

"You'd better shower and fix your face and hair," Jemel said.

"You don't even like my looks!" the girl wailed. "What's wrong with me?"

He pretended to study her intently. "I know!" he exclaimed at last. "You look like somebody who's been fucking for two solid hours!"

Lois stormed into the bathroom, slammed the door behind her.

Jemel chuckled, lit a cigarette.

Jemel escorted a sulking Lois Endicott from the third-floor room that served as his father's *garconnière* to the suite where she was staying with her parents. He then continued up to the Karami suite on the ninth floor. As he expected, no one was home. Hassan had gone out to complete his business with Senator Ferrenbaugh. Nuri was in school. Mademoiselle Viete had taken Felicite to Central Park for her daily afternoon airing.

Jemel debated whether to lunch in the hotel restaurant or have something sent up when the telephone rang. He picked up the sitting-room extension. A man's voice asked for "Mr. Hassan Karami." Jemel said his father wasn't expected until later. The caller then identified himself as the headmaster of the private day-school Nuri attended.

"We are sending Nuri home," he said. "He has been expelled."

"Why?" Jemel wanted to know. "What has he done?"

"I'll have to explain that to your father. Can you meet the school car at the hotel entrance in about fifteen minutes?"

Jemel said yes and hung up, frowning. Whatever Nuri's offense, it had to be serious. The high-priced school was unlikely to expel a paying pupil except as a last resort.

Odd, Jemel thought. He often found it difficult to realize that he and Nuri were brothers. Only four years separated them in age, but it might have been as many centuries. Of course, much of the gulf had been created by their parents. Hassan had always kept Jemel at his side. While their mother was alive, she held Nuri to her; they were inseparable. After her death, Nuri had been cared for by governesses.

Few of the governesses ever stayed very long. Most were unable to manage Nuri. The boy was willful, selfish and disobedient, usually whining for something, shrieking if he did not get it instantly. Unfortunately, Hassan took little notice of Nuri, leaving the boy's training in the hands of first his wife, then the governesses.

Jemel recalled the voyage from Lebanon to America. It was the first time he'd had close contact with Nuri for any long period. They had gone from Beirut to Istanbul, where they stayed almost three weeks, until Hassan managed to book passage for New York aboard a Swedish liner. That leg of the trip took another sixteen days. Nearly a month altogether.

Nuri had seldom shown anything but a negative, unpleasant side of his character. He frequently sulked—or raged. If any attempt was made to discipline him, Nuri would become ill—or feign illness. Jemel had decided that he didn't like his younger brother very much—and he sensed the feeling was mutual.

Jemel waited at the Plaza's Central Park South entrance until a blue-and-white station wagon pulled up to the curb. Nuri sat beside the driver. Jemel went to the car and opened the door.

"You the brother?" the driver asked. Jemel said he was. Evidently the man had not been told to keep quiet the reason for Nuri's expulsion; for he glared at Jemel and spoke angrily.

"If it was up to me, this punk would be in jail!" he snarled. "My God! Him—beating his meat and trying to grab another kid's prick so he could give him a blow-job! Why, the little . . ."

"Where did all this happen?" Jemel interrupted quietly.

"In the boys' can during recess."

Jemel said nothing. He pulled Nuri from the seat and closed the door. The car drove off. Jemel prodded Nuri towards the hotel entrance.

When they were inside the suite, Jemel seized Nuri's arm.

"What did you do?" he demanded.

"Nothing. The man lied," Nuri whined.

The brothers bore little physical resemblance to each other. Nuri was short, lumpy, his eyes and hair a nondescript light brown. He was a bad mixture of smudged characteristics haphazardly inherited from both his parents.

"What did you do?" Jemel repeated, shaking Nuri.

"Leave me alone!" Nuri yowled. "They all lied!"

Only Nuri had lied. Jemel saw that in the boy's gummy, guilt-ridden face. He reflexively drew back his hand and struck Nuri, who flung himself down on the carpeted floor and lay there screaming.

While Mademoiselle shared a bedroom with Felicite, Hassan and his sons each had his own. Jemel pulled Nuri to his feet. "Go into your room and stay there!" he ordered. Nuri slunk off, raw hatred burning in his eyes.

Hassan came home half an hour later, before Mademoiselle and Felicite had returned from the park. Jemel told him of what had happened. Hassan telephoned the headmaster. Their conversation left him stunned.

"There were many witnesses," he told Jemel, "and several boys say Nuri made homosexual advances to them in the past." He paused, nervously took a tipped Turkish cigarette from his case. "Two others have been expelled after admitting they let Nuri perform fellatio on them." He lit his cigarette with shaky hands.

"Then Nuri needs treatment," Jemel said. "Maybe he should even be sent to some sort of clinic."

"Impossible!" Hassan snapped.

Jemel blinked astonishment. "Why?"

"We dare not risk any scandal before we have our immigration visas—in late September or early October. Tomorrow I will bribe the headmaster and whoever else necessary to insure secrecy."

The corners of Jemel's mouth tightened. "Late September? That's two months away. What happens with Nuri in the meantime?"

"He cannot be sent to another school. Mademoiselle will have to look after him," Hassan said. "And I will watch him more closely," he added, almost as an afterthought.

He stabbed his cigarette into an ashtray. "Where is Nuri now?"

"In his room," Jemel answered.

"Did you whip him?"

"I hit him just once."

"Then I will finish the task," Hassan declared. "Later this evening, I will talk to Mademoiselle and contrive some plausible explanations for her."

"Those aren't solutions," Jemel thought sourly, but he nodded and held his tongue.

Hassan Karami had made a wise choice when he employed Mademoiselle Claire Viete. A plump, homely spinster with iron-gray hair, she was better educated and trained than most French nurses who found their way to Lebanon. She possessed a good working knowledge of English and Arabic. She had a gentle, patient and good-natured disposition. And, from the very start, Mademoiselle was devoted to Felicite Karami.

Mademoiselle cared for the baby as if she had been her own—and Felicite thrived, developing into a sweet-tempered, lovely child who gave promise of someday being a great beauty. She had inherited her father's large, liquescent dark eyes and her mother's fair hair and skin—a striking combination that drew gasps of admiration from all who saw her.

When, in Beirut, Hassan confided that he intended going to America and asked Claire Viete to accompany the family, the nursemaid had agreed immediately. There was nothing to hold her in Lebanon, and she could not bear to be parted from Felicite.

During the voyage, Mademoiselle had also taken care of Nuri. She'd had almost nothing to do with the boy before. In Beirut, he'd always had his own governess, and the nine-year age difference between he and his sister was too great for the two children to play together.

Claire Viete noticed that Nuri often teased and tormented Felicite. Being a simple person essentially, the nursemaid at first accepted this as more or less normal. After all, young boys did have a habit of teasing their much younger sisters.

Then, gradually, she began to sense there was a sullen resentment—even a cruelty—underlying Nuri's behavior. It troubled and baffled her.

Mademoiselle was hardly overjoyed when Hassan informed her that he had withdrawn Nuri from school, and that she would have to take care of him as well as Felicite for two or three months. However, she raised no objections and determined to do her best.

A week or so went by and everything seemed calm and smooth. Then one afternoon Claire Viete learned the truth behind Nuri's outward shows of aversion for his sister.

Mademoiselle was alone with the two children in the Karami suite. Felicite was taking her after-lunch nap, a golden-haired cherub tightly hugging a stuffed-toy kitten in her bed. Nuri puttered in his room.

Claire Viete remembered she had run out of Kleenex. Mistrustful of telephones, as most French are, she went downstairs to the hotel pharmacy. She made her purchase, returning in less than ten minutes.

The moment she stepped from the elevator on the ninth floor, she heard Felicite's cries. Rushing down the corridor, she burst into the suite and went to the bedroom she shared with the child.

"Mon Dieu!" she screamed, horrified by what she saw.

Nuri was bent over Felicite's bed, jabbing at her

flesh with a letter opener. Mademoiselle lunged at Nuri, dragged him away from the bed, twisted his hand until he dropped the letter opener. Luckily, it was made of plastic, not metal. The baby's skin wasn't broken.

The nursemaid whirled, slapped Nuri.

"Vache!" he spat, hysterical. "You protect her— and she killed my *maman!"* He spat at her again, turned, and fled from the room.

Mademoiselle let him go. She went to the bed, picked up Felicite, kissed and comforted the child.

Now, the nursemaid began to comprehend. Nuri's attachment to his mother had been obsessive, unnatural. In his warped mind, he obviously believed that she had died because she gave birth to Felicite, and thus Felicite had killed his mother, depriving him of his doting, permissive parent.

Claire Viete pondered whether or not to tell Monsieur Karami. No, she decided. He had more than enough to worry about. The children were her responsibility. She would simply make certain that Nuri was never again alone with Felicite—not even for a minute.

7

Room service delivered breakfast to the Karami suite promptly at eight. One portable table was wheeled into the sitting room for Mademoiselle, Nuri and Felicite, another taken to Hassan's bedroom, where he and Jemel ate their first meal of the day.

On this third Wednesday in September, Hassan sat at the table and scanned *The New York Times* while he waited for Jemel, who was a few minutes late. The headlines told of further German victories in Russia, more British retreats in North Africa and mounting apprehension in the United States. Hassan's smile was wolfish as he read. America's entry into the war was only a matter of time.

Jemel entered. He mumbled a greeting to his father, sat down at the table and stifled a yawn. The breakfast was Continental style, augmented by a liberal portion of *labeneh,* a creamy white cheese made from ewe's milk much favored by Levantines in general and Jemel Karami in particular. He reached for a roll, cut a slice of the *labeneh* with his butter knife, and smothered another yawn.

Hassan put the *Times* aside, poured coffee and hot milk into his cup and asked, "When did you finally come home last night—or was it this morning?"

"It was this morning, a little after five," Jemel replied, spreading *labeneh* on the roll. "A young wife whose husband leaves her alone too often. Once started, she didn't want to stop."

Hassan chuckled. As with most Arab fathers and sons, he and Jemel became comrades, equals when they discussed sex or traded accounts of their sexual experiences. "How much of your allowance is left?" Jemel received $25 each Monday.

"About twenty-two dollars."

"Remarkable! You would have spent more in a Zeitouni brothel."

"She wanted to give *me* money," Jemel smirked. "She told me her husband can't hold himself for more than five minutes."

"The great malady of the American male," Hassan said with a broad leer. "Only last week a woman asked me if I was impotent because I rode her for a half an hour without ejaculating."

Jemel swallowed coffee. "That's happened to me, too," he said and then spoke in a high, mimicking falsetto: "Darling, you're marvelous, but what's the matter? Can't you come?"

Hassan laughed, then grew serious. "Senator Ferrenbaugh has delivered," he announced. "We leave for Montreal next Monday—to return in a week or two as bona fide immigrants, eligible for citizenship."

"That's good news," Jemel said, but wanted to know more. "And afterward?"

"I should start doing business again—as Karami and Company, Incorporated—before the end of October." Hassan poured himself more café au lait. "We will move from here to an apartment with an address that confers *ton* and prestige." He drank some of his coffee.

Jemel finished the last of the *labeneh* and asked, "What about Nuri?"

"Nuri will be examined by doctors and psychiatrists and undergo whatever treatment they recommend," Hassan replied. "I imagine a private institution would be best for him." Unless Nuri's condition was greatly improved, he would be a constant potential embarrassment and hazard.

Hassan had finished his breakfast. He placed his napkin on the table and looked at his oldest son. "As for you, Jemel, you will have to start school again."

Jemel had almost forgotten about that. "And be done with it as fast as possible," he responded, and immediately realized he'd said the wrong thing. Hassan's look turned into a glare.

"Among your other weaknesses, you lack patience." The sarcasm was corrosive. "A typical French trait."

Jemel lit a cigarette as an excuse to avert his eyes for crucial seconds until a sudden surge of anger passed. He had not been very deeply attached to his mother, and his nature was anything but sentimental. However, she had been French—and his mother. Exhaling smoke through slit-narrow nostrils, he managed to speak calmly, casually.

"I'm impatient to prove myself," he said. "I want to begin making money."

"Why?" Hassan demanded, using familiar goading ploys to obtain answers he wanted to hear. "I am not a poor man."

No, not poor, Jemel thought. *You're worth around a million dollars. But that isn't real wealth. Not the kind of wealth that shapes events, makes things happen—or prevents them from happening. A man with a million accumulated dollars is rich—but he is still vulnerable, still a merchant-cog in an ap-*

*paratus controlled by those who had the imagination
and nerve to pyramid.*

He said, "I know you are rich, but I hope to become richer."

"Again why? To show you are wiser and more
able than I?"

That's part of it, Jemel agreed silently. *But then,
it's your fault. You whetted my appetite for money,
force-fed me with your ideas about "business" since
I began to crawl. I practically learned to read from
bills of lading and ledgers. Only, somehow. I got
ahead of you, realized that there are no limits to the
stakes.*

Aloud, he said, "No that's not the reason. I guess
the best explanation is that old Arab saying I heard so
often in Lebanon. "When money whistles, all dogs
come running to do their tricks. If I'm to have dogs,
I'd just as soon have entire kennels of them."

The reply satisfied Hassan. He was once more reassured that his son had learned the lesson taught
for centuries by the Levant. Money was the only reality
—and it could buy everything else. He stood up, went
to the mirror hanging over his bureau, and straightened his necktie.

"Your schooling will not begin again until next
February," he said to Jemel over his shoulder. "Until
then, gorge yourself. The supply of lonely wives in this
city is inexhaustible."

8

Hassan Karami and his household encountered no
difficulties in Montreal. On October 6, 1941, they reentered the United States with valid immigration visas.

Hassan moved swiftly to carry out his plans. He
filed declaration of intent papers as a preliminary to
eventual naturalization. Karami & Co. was incorpo-

rated, and he leased offices in the Lincoln Building on 42nd Street to begin his American business activities as a trader and general broker.

Psychiatrists—with some subtle proddings from Hassan—concurred that Nuri required long, intensive institutional care and treatment. Nuri was sent to a private clinic in upstate New York.

In the middle of November, Hassan Karami bought a seven-room, fully furnished apartment on Sutton Place, near 58th Street, and established his household there.

Until the next school term started in February, Jemel was to work with his father, and he was placed on the payroll of Karami & Co. at a $60-a-week salary.

Jemel stirred, rolled over on his back and recalled it was Sunday. There was no need for him to get up and, besides, he had a slight hangover. The girl he'd been with most of the night—Irene, was it?—had taken the cognac bottle to bed with them at her apartment. She had been very good, though, he reflected drowsily and went back to sleep.

The hangover was gone when Jemel woke again. He looked at the clock beside his bed. Twelve-thirty. Lunch would be served at one. He leaped from bed and raced through his bathing and dressing ritual.

Brenda, the Irish maid, told Jemel his father was in the study and said lunch would be served in ten minutes. Jemel went to the study. Like the entire apartment, it reflected the previous owner's taste for rather florid furniture of the rococo period. Hassan was reading the Sunday newspapers.

"Another large night?" was his greeting to Jemel.

"The night large, the girl small—and lunch is almost ready."

"Very well. I'll be along in a moment."

Mademoiselle Viete and Felicite entered the dining room seconds after Jemel. Felicite ran to her brother and hugged his legs. Jemel gave her long, honey-hued hair a fond tug. He leaned down, picked up the little girl, and raised her high above his head before plumping her down into her chair.

"More!" she pleaded. "Please, more."

Hassan appeared, spoke to his daughter, and Mademoiselle and seated himself. Brenda began serving soup from a silver tureen.

Jemel ate heartily, as usual substituting *labeneh* for butter on his bread. He made casual conversation with his father and Mademoiselle, paid his tiny sister the broad compliments her already evident feminine vanity demanded. They were almost through the meal, finishing their cremes caramel when Brenda burst into the dining room, sobbing.

". . . Holy Mother of God! Mr. Karami. . . !"

"Stop that!" Hassan commanded. "What has happened?"

"Cook and I just heard it on the radio!" the maid blubbered. "God save us all! We'll all be killed. . .!"

"Try to calm her, Mademoiselle," Hassan said. "Jemel, come into the study with me."

Moments later, they were hearing the initial, confused newscasts about the Japanese attack on Pearl Harbor. Hassan listened for only a short while, then told Jemel to turn off the radio.

"Don't you want to hear more?" Jemel asked in astonishment.

"I've heard enough," Hassan said, a leer cracking across his hawklike face. He reached for the telephone on his desk. "Right now, it's more important that I talk to Mike Ferrenbaugh."

Senator Michael Ferrenbaugh was one of the very few legislators who ventured away from Washington in the days immediately following Pearl Harbor. On the evening of December 9th, he came to New York and to the Karami apartment.

Hassan, his Lebanese-American attorney, Halim Chalhoub, Jemel, and Mike Ferrenbaugh closeted themselves in the study for an hour. When their meeting was over, Senator Ferrenbaugh owned one-tenth of the capital stock in Karami & Co., Inc.

Ferrenbaugh remained in the study with Jemel while Hassan escorted Halim Chalhoub to the front door.

"How does the war look, senator?" Jemel asked.

"Afraid it might be over before you can get into uniform?"

Jemel stared at him. "I can wait," he said. "Forever," he added to himself.

Hassan returned. "We're finally in business, Mike," he smiled. "It's only ten-thirty. We can have some supper before you go back."

"Sounds fine, I'm hungry." Ferrenbaugh made an expansive gesture with his large hands. "Be sure you come down to Washington next week," he said. "Believe me, Hassan. They'll be tossing purchase orders out the windows by the bale. We'll grab some."

But not the really big, important ones, Jemel thought as he followed Ferrenbaugh and his father towards the dining room.

Hassan suddenly stopped. "By the way, Mike, what are your plans for the holiday? You won't have much chance to get home, will you?"

"Absolutely none," Ferrenbaugh replied morosely. "I'll spend them alone in Washington. My wife Dot hates the place—and I wouldn't want her coming out in any case, not the way things are."

"Does Mrs. Ferrenbaugh hate New York, too?"

"Nope. 'Course, she's only been here twice, but she loves it."

"Then bring your wife and daughter to New York at Karami & Co.'s expense. They are welcome to stay with us—we have ample room—and surely, you can come up and be with them occasionally," Hassan urged.

"Sounds great, except we'd be putting you out and . . ."

"Nonsense. I consider the matter settled. Shall we see what the cook has prepared for supper?"

Hassan foresaw that the war would cause acute shortages in basic metals, especially copper and aluminum. Karami & Co.—which had as its entire staff Hassan, Jemel, and a secretary—bought up whatever stocks of these metals could be found available in the New York area.

It was Jemel's task to check sellers' warehouse

receipts and invoices against actual quantities. If all
was as represented, the seller was paid, and Jemel arranged for further storage of the metals. By Monday,
December 15th, Karami & Co. owned over 300 tons of
aluminum pigs and a hundred thousand pounds of
domestic refined copper.

"In six months, we'll double or triple what we've in-
vested," Hassan predicted to Jemel that evening in their
Lincoln Building office. "And tomorrow I am going to
Washington, where Mike will provide us with more prof-
itable business." He straightened the papers on his desk.
"Keep a careful eye on the office while I am gone."

Jemel yawned. It was almost seven, and he'd spent
a wearying day. "I think I'll go home and turn in
early," he said.

"You have no rendezvous?"

"Not tonight."

"I have," Hassan said. "We'll take a taxi, and I
will drop you off at the apartment."

"I'd rather walk. I spent hours breathing dust in
warehouses today. The air will do me good."

Jemel had not ceased to be fascinated by Manhattan. He marvelled at the city's size and its electric
vitality. It was the symbol and the expression of wealth,
power, sex—at once a challenge and a gratification. It
was in New York that men made great fortunes, where
they spoke in millions and tens of millions and there
was substance, actual money that was made and then
used to make more behind their words.

Jemel walked up Madison Avenue. The rush-hour
peak was long past, yet the stream of automobiles continued. There were more of them on a single avenue at
any given hour than there were in all of Beirut, he
thought. Possibly more than in all Lebanon.

His attention was distracted by the window displays in the shops and stores. They made him laugh
with cynical amusement, even contempt, at the gauche
incongruities that had resulted from America's entry
into the war.

The shop windows appeared to have been decorated by imbeciles who did not know whether it was

the Christmas season or the Fourth of July. Gaudily bedecked trees, holly wreaths, gaily wrapped packages were implausibly jumbled together with American flags, miniature Statues of Liberty, and bunting-draped portraits of George Washington, Abraham Lincoln and Franklin D. Roosevelt.

Tinseled placards wished passersby "Merry Christmas" or "Season's Greetings." Others, hasty improvisations in red-white-and-blue, exhorted the public to "Remember Pearl Harbor" or proclaimed "We're In to Win!"

Strange people, the Americans, Jemel thought. *They had wealth—enormous wealth—and yet they were naïve, credulous, gullible.*

Merry Chrismas, he said to himself. *We're In to Win!*

It was so easy to take their women, Jemel mused. He was certain it would be just as easy for him to one day take their money.

"Merry Christmas," he repeated, this time aloud, "We're In to Win." He laughed heartily.

9

Hassan returned triumphant from Washington on Friday evening.

"Look at these!" he exulted to Jemel. He brandished a sheaf of government purchase orders. "In wartime, all governments are alike. Turk, British, French, American—it makes no difference!"

Jemel scanned the documents. They called for a wide variety of items, none of which Karami & Co. owned. He noted that the prices were inflated, but the quantities ordered were relatively small. Twenty tons of lard here, fifty 60-inch wooden desks there, 200 folding steel cots for "immediate shipment" to Fort Jay . . .

"In effect, we are merely brokers," his father explained. "We buy these things cheaply, repack and ship the merchandise, and wait for the Treasury Department to send checks against our invoices. We take no risks. None!"

"I see," Jemel murmured. He read from an order form: " 'Socks, men's, medium weight, wool, white' and so on—sixty-seven cents per pair. They sell for less at retail."

Hassan clapped sinewy hands over his ears. *"Ma smi't shi*—I heard nothing!" he cried out in Arabic, feigning alarm, then bared his teeth in a grin. "Imagine the prices for which we can buy them from dealers in job-lots and seconds. We can send the poorest quality. A thousand-dozen-pair order will never be noticed. The army is ordering such socks by the millions of pairs."

"Yes, and that was the trouble," Jemel thought. Karami & Co. would get the thousand-dozen-pair orders. The million-dozen-pair contracts would go elsewhere. Senator Michael Ferrenbaugh could deliver only second-rate orders—and his father would never change.

"I estimate a three-thousand-dollar profit on that order for the socks alone," Hassan went on jubilantly.

"It looks as though business will be like it was in Lebanon," Jemel said.

"Better!" Hassan exclaimed, the irony of the remark eluding him.

Mike Ferrenbaugh's wife and daughter arrived in New York on December 23rd. Unable to leave the capital, Ferrenbaugh telephoned Hassan, asked him to meet their train from Chicago at Pennsylvania Station.

Jemel went to the station with his father. Dorothy Ferrenbaugh proved to be a handsome, chestnut-haired woman in her early thirties. The attractiveness of her face was further enhanced by a splash of freckles and uptilted nose.

"Please call me Dorothy—or Dossie or Dot!" she insisted and presented her daughter, a little girl of five who had her mother's hair and pert features. "And this is Michele."

"Mickey!" the child protested. "My name is Mickey."

"And mine is Jemel, Mickey." Jemel picked her up to carry her out of the station. A blissful look came over the child's face. "I like you," she said. "Can I call you Jimmy?"

"Jimmy? Sure you can," Jemel told her. Jimmy, he thought. It was good, had an All-American ring. Jimmy Karami. "Jimmy it is, Mickey."

Mike Ferrenbaugh appeared at the Karami apartment the next evening.

"I have to go back in the morning," he announced. "The war situation's so bad, we're working straight through Christmas Day."

"You'll be back of course?" Hassan asked.

"No telling when. Dot and Mickey will have to do their sightseeing on their own, I'm afraid."

"We could go down to Washington with you," his wife offered.

"Hell, honey, it's a madhouse. If Hassan doesn't mind having you and Mickey around his neck, stay in New York and have fun."

"I'm delighted to have your family here," Hassan interjected. "I'm sorry you can't be with them. I've obtained theater tickets, made plans."

"I love the theater," Dorothy sighed. "But I don't know a soul . . ."

"Perhaps Jemel—or even I . . ."

Jemel, detecting a note in his father's voice, pricked up his ears.

Mike broke in, "You've done too much for us already, Hassan."

"Nonsense! I would be honored." Hassan was the polished Continental host. "Mrs. Ferrenbaugh—oh, sorry, Dorothy—with Mike's permission. . . ."

Jemel applauded silently. The "Mrs. Ferrenbaugh —oh, sorry, Dorothy" was a diversionary ploy worth filing for future reference.

Mike managed another visit three days later.

"The vacation is doing you a world of good," he told his wife. "You look great." She did. She was radiant.

"I—I suppose it's just that I'm having a vacation," she said.

It never occurred to Ferrenbaugh that Dorothy chose that moment to examine her cuticles because she wanted to avoid his eyes, and he thought she was blushing because he'd made a complimentary remark.

Going into the sitting room, Mike found Jemel wedged between Mickey and Felicite on a divan, reading to them from a children's book. The little girls gazed at Jemel adoringly, attentive to his every word.

"Appears my daughter is stuck on you," Ferrenbaugh grinned.

"I don't know about that," Jemel said, "but she's certainly stuck me with a new name. Everybody's started calling me 'Jimmy.'"

On January 2nd, with headlines telling of the loss of Manila, Hassan and Jemel put Dorothy and Mickey aboard their homeward-bound train.

"Thank you—for everything, Hassan," Dorothy murmured.

As they left the station, Jemel asked his father, "Was she good?"

"Inexperienced at the start—I'm afraid the senator must lack imagination . . ."

"I could have told you that long ago," Jemel said to himself.

". . . but she was eager to learn." Hassan's tone changed. "Speaking of learning reminds me. Monday, you take school entrance examinations."

"Oh? You've decided where I'm to go?"

"Yes. There's an Ebury School in Connecticut. It is said to be among the best in the country for college preparation."

Jemel had completed the equivalent of the tenth grade in Lebanon. However, he scored very high on his tests and was admitted to Ebury as an upper-eleventh-grade student. By working exceptionally hard, he completed three semesters in a single year, graduating in February 1943.

He had already decided on the college he wanted to attend.

"I'd like to go to Dunhill College in Boston," he'd told his father while still at Ebury. "It's really a business school, more highly rated than Harvard or Wharton."

Hassan investigated and found this was true. Jemel made his application and was accepted as a freshman for the Spring 1943, term.

Jemel glanced at the slip of paper a clerk had handed him. It read:

> North Dormitory, Room 38:
> Jacobs, Marvin
> Karami, Jemel
> Stanton, Russell T.

The Dunhill College campus was small—the entire student body numbered only some 300—with mainly turn-of-the-century buildings ranged around a grassy quadrangle. He easily found the ornately colonnaded North Dorm and went inside to search for Room 38. He discovered it was on the third floor, in the rear, and that his assigned roommates were already there, glumly surveying the cell-like room and its dismal furnishings. Sagging cots, gaunt metal lockers, battered wooden chests of drawers, rickety chairs—

all triplicated. A scarred table. Some shelves. Two lamps, one broken.

"I'm Jemel Karami. Jimmy."

"Russ Stanton." He topped Jemel's six feet by two inches, his 159 weight by at least twenty pounds. About nineteen, his face blended New England Patrician with pro-football player, an nth-generation American from brush-cut sandy hair to the soles of his size ten-and-one-half loafers.

"I'm Marv Jacobs." A little younger than Stanton, but a sharp, incongruous contrast. He wasn't over five-eight—and so thin he appeared to be roaming loose inside a brownish sack-suit. His face was intelligent, but rather melancholy and sallow, with a nose even more Semitic than Jemel's.

"We're an oddly assorted lot," Jemel thought, "and we'll have to share this miserable cubicle for an entire semester."

"So this is what they mean by the ivory towers of academic life," Russ Stanton laughed. He flopped down on the nearest cot. "Somebody else better get prone. There isn't enough space for more than one of us to unpack at a time."

"I might as well stretch out," Marvin Jacobs said and took another cot. Jemel politely protested that since he had been the last to arrive, he should also be the last to unpack.

"Oh, hell, Jimmy," Stanton said. "Go ahead. Marv and I'll be the nosy neighbors peeking to see what kind of furniture the new family next door is moving into the house." He grinned. "We're stuck with each other, so we might as well get acquainted. Where you from, Jimmy?"

"Lebanon—Beirut—originally. More recently, New York . . ."

For obvious reasons, Jemel blurred or drastically censored parts of his life story. However, before long, he had fairly complete biographies of his roommates stored in his mental files.

RUSS:

In 1897, Boston industrialist John C. Dunhill donated half the money to establish a college that would "train young gentlemen to be leaders of commerce and industry." Among the three other Bostonians who provided the remainder of the needed funds was Roger Williams Stanton.

The endowing founders wrote into the college charter that any of their lineal male descendants would be thenceforth eligible for free Founders' Scholarships. Roger Williams Stanton's son, William, attended Dunhill on such a scholarship and later inherited $2 million from his father. He steadily increased his fortune until 1929, when he was wiped out by the Wall Street Crash.

A year later, William Stanton contrived to fall off a local-stops-only station platform just as a Boston & Maine express thundered through. He left a widow, Frances, and a six-year-old son, Russell.

Frances and her son moved to Rutland, Vermont, where she had relatives and she obtained a clerical job. Russell Stanton adjusted to the change easily. Memories of his father were vague. Vaguer still were memories of a large townhouse staffed by numerous servants. He accepted that he and his mother had to live in a four-room frame cottage, and that she had to work. He developed into a hardy, self-reliant individual. At ten, he sold magazines after school. The next year, he had a paper route. Later, he took varied after-school and vacation jobs.

During his sophomore year in high school, Russell Stanton told his mother he intended going to Dunhill College on a Founders' Scholarship. Vacation jobs in the woods or with construction gangs would provide him with spending money.

"Won't it embarrass you?" his mother asked. "All the students at Dunhill are rich."

"I couldn't care less, Mom," Russ laughed. "The last of the Stantons is a Depression brat, remember? I'm after security, a good job with some big corporation? A degree from Dunhill will get both for me."

Russ graduated from high school with a fine academic record. However, he would have been accepted at Dunhill regardless of his grades. As Roger Williams Stanton's grandson, he had to be admitted automatically—and he needed to pay neither tuition nor dormitory fees.

MARV:

Jews applying for admission to Dunhill College had to possess both outstanding academic records and money. Marvin Jacobs achieved the first at Brooklyn's Abraham Lincoln High School. The second was provided by his father, Pincus Jacobs, a successful clothing manufacturer.

Pincus and his wife Ida fled from Russian pogroms to the United States in 1911. He worked in a Lower East Side sweatshop, saved a few dollars, opened his own tailoring shop. His business grew.

The Jacobses had two daughters, then somewhat later a son, Marvin. The daughters married. Marvin proved to be a brilliant scholar with a particular talent for mathematics and a desire to become an accountant. Pincus, dismayed, pleaded with his son to become a doctor, an attorney, a dentist—anything but a "glorified bookkeeper."

Marvin finally thought to explain his reasons. "Business is getting to be almost a science, Pop. Anyone who wants to make a profit has to know cost-accounting, tax-accounting . . ."

Now Pincus understood and agreed.

There was another squall when Marvin indicated a desire to attend Dunhill, which limited Jewish students to a strict 5 percent quota.

"Why pick some two-by-four *anti-semiten* college?" Pincus groaned.

Marvin had his answers ready. "Size isn't anything, and Dunhill is the best business school. Besides, the more Jews who go to *anti-semiten* colleges, the more chance they'll become less *anti-semiten*."

Pincus surrendered, and his wife Ida was happy.

A total of twenty-seven Jewish students applied for admission to the Spring 1943 freshman class at Dunhill. Of these, two were chosen. Marvin Jacobs, because of his grade average, was the first.

Dunhill clung to the stern precepts laid down by its founders.

Students were expected to learn, not to play.

At Dunhill sports were intramural and kept to a minimum. Freshman hazing was unknown. Social fraternities did not exist—on the grounds that admission to Dunhill in itself constituted entry into the most select society of all.

Courses were difficult. Most students slaved to maintain their scholastic averages. Marvin Jacobs, Jemel Karami, and Russell Stanton were exceptions. They found it all a breeze because their respective aptitudes and stores of knowledge complemented one another.

Mathematics and the exact sciences were child's play for Marvin. Russ was the authority on American history and literature, and he had the type of mind that quickly broke the complex down to essentials. Jemel knew languages, European history and literature—and, of course, he'd had practical business experience.

The three made studying a cooperative enterprise. In effect, each enjoyed the services of two specialized private tutors. Evening study periods in their room were more bull than skull sessions.

This led to unforeseen difficulties.

They attended all their classes together and invariably scored the highest grades on quizzes and examinations. The order in which they placed varied, but some combination of Jacobs, Karami, and Stanton always topped the list.

Their classmates grew envious, resentful, angry. Ugly whispers became audible grumbles.

". . . smart-assed kike . . ."

". . . goddamned greasy Arab . . ."

". . . that fucking freeloader . . ."

Now it was clear why such an oddly assorted trio had been assigned to Room 38, North Dormitory. They were pariahs—a quota-Jew, a swarthy Arab, and a penniless nobody with a free Founders' Scholarship who had been lumped together, segregated in the seediest, least desirable dormitory room.

That these three received the highest marks infuriated Dunhill students who were Christian, native-born, pure-white Americans and whose parents paid the full, high tuition and other fees. Their rancor and hatred boiled into the open one afternoon shortly before the Easter vacation began.

Jemel, Russ and Marv entered their room.

Russ was the first to notice anything unusual.

"Now what the hell is this?" he growled, going to his cot. He bent over it and his face turned purple. "The motherfucking sons-of-bitches!" he roared.

Someone had placed a tin cup, of the kind used by sidewalk beggars, on his cot. In it were a few dimes, nickels, and pennies—and a note that read: "Here's carfare and coffee-money, bum. Now move on!"

Jemel and Marvin each looked at their cots.

On Marvin's pillow was a cardboard cutout six-pointed star with a strip of bacon stapled to it. Across the face of the cardboard were scrawled the words: "Hitler has the right idea." Marv picked up the cardboard, and his pale face became almost transparent.

Both he and Russ turned around astounded when they heard Jemel laugh loudly.

"The stupid bastards!" Jimmy snorted. He held up what looked like a circlet of beads held together by a colored tassel, and there was a strip of bacon attached to it, too. " 'Mohammed eats pig-shit,' " he read aloud from a piece of paper that had been on his pillow. "They think because I'm an Arab, I must be a Moslem." He pulled the bacon away from the beads and tossed it into a wastebasket. "This is a *sibah*—a Moslem rosary."

Russ Stanton angrily flung the tin cup and its contents into the wastebasket after the bacon.

"The natives are growing decidedly hostile," he rasped, trying to make light of the situation. "We may have to take down our muskets and sharpen our bowie knives."

He saw that Marvin was still holding the cardboard star and staring at it, his hands trembling. He took it gently from Jacobs and crumpling it, hurled it after the tin cup.

"Maybe—maybe I'd better start flubbing," Marv stammered. "I'll throw the exams from here on . . ."

"What?" Russ demanded. "And admit the cruddy pricks are scaring you?"

"Look, Russ. There are forty-three freshmen. Only two of them are Jews . . ."

"So? Shake off that ghetto-complex!" Stanton's tone was stern, yet somehow very gentle. "If I can stand being called a freeloader and a bum, you can swallow their cracks about your being Jewish."

Marvin ran his fingers through his thick thatch of brown hair. "It's not the same. You can't tell how different it is unless you're a Jew."

"What do you say, Jimmy?" Russ asked.

Jemel was carefully wiping the last traces of bacon fat from the *sibah* with a handkerchief. "I'm going to ram it further up their asses," he muttered. He fingered the prayer beads as he had seen Moslems do in Lebanon.

Stanton put a big hand on Marvin's shoulder. "See, kid," he said. "We'll stick together. We've just begun to fight."

Jimmy Karami wasn't listening. He slipped the Moslem rosary into his right-hand trousers pocket. He had decided to keep it. It would bring him luck. No, not luck. Protection. From himself. He'd never had any illusions about ethics or scruples. But anytime he found himself in danger of falling for talk about sportsmanship and fair play, the *sibah* would serve as a reminder, bring him back down to earth.

"My God, Jimmy, you look like you're ready to cut somebody's throat!" Russ Stanton exclaimed, seeing the sinister, brooding scowl that made Jemel's face more like that of vulture than falcon.

Jemel gave a start, forced a smile. "Oh, I'm always ready to do that—literally or figuratively," he said. He slid his hand into his pocket, touched the *sibah,* and his mind was off on a tangent again, leaping ahead to some as yet undetermined future when, by one means or another, he would make himself invulnerable.

BOOK TWO

One Week
April 30th—May 6th

1

Rome, Italy. Tuesday, April 30th.

Michele Hayworth set her glass carefully on the washbasin rim. Nice, fresh drink, she mused. The ice cubes free-floating in scotch were still square, sharp-cornered.

It was almost eight o'clock and the evening's schedule teetered on the brink of total disintegration. Mickey should have leaned close to the mirror and begun applying eyeliner and mascara.

Instead, she winced, pressed a hand against her groin, eased herself down on the bidet. When the knifing ovarian stitch faded, it would be followed by two or three more. She might as well wait for them to pulse and pass. Mickey stared at the glass of scotch and ice. It had already fogged opaque with condensation. Things could change much and quickly over a comparatively short time span. Not long ago—five years? six? no, not quite six—when she was still Michele Ferrenbaugh and not Mrs. Frederick Hayworth, a fresh drink had been a two-or-three-of-an-evening thing, friendly and congenial.

Now, fresh drinks came off the assembly line. "Christ," she said to herself, "I couldn't even start to guess how many because I lose count before the average evening is halfway through."

Mickey reached for the glass, stopped, jolted by another twinge, stronger than the first. She gasped and dropped both her hands down towards her pelvis as if to push back the stabbing pain.

The bathroom door opened abruptly. Senator Frederick Hayworth, a million women voters' togetherness-symbol in shorts, undershirt, socks, and EZ-Pak slippers, entered. He looked only at her hands and where they were.

"Playing with your snatch?"

"I'm ovulating," Mickey replied automatically, and then she lashed back. "I don't masturbate in the john, Freddie-boy." The pain passed. "I save that for later. At night. When you're asleep." Hayworth had gone on to the toilet. He kicked up the lid and seat and began to urinate. "It's more like cheating on you that way."

"Why not sneak a bellhop into the room?" he sniggered above the splashing. "Get yourself some real kicks." She didn't turn around. He'd spit into the toilet before flushing it. He always did, and it revolted her. He moved past her, a reverse image of his surly-sneering face briefly reflected in the mirror.

"Who do you think about when you diddle your twat?" He went into the bedroom. "Jimmy Karami, maybe?"

Mickey held an eyeliner brush. She put it down, took another long swallow of scotch. "Sometimes." She spoke into the mirror. Thank God they'd be returning to the States in a few days. Then she could go home, and he'd be in Washington.

Fred Hayworth had paused only to take a clean shirt from a drawer. He banged the drawer shut. "Glamor-prick Karami!" he jeered. "You think your Arab wet-dreamboat's pretty smart, don't you?"

Michele snapped alert, but said nothing. Fred was drunker than he realized. Silence would irritate him, goad him into talking more in an effort to get a rise out of her. Since his mind was on Jemel Karami, he might blurt out something that would explain their trip to Beirut and visit to Incombank the previous week.

"The wise-ass thinks he's pretty smart, too!" Hayworth rasped.

Mickey listened intently.

"Shit!" Fred Hayworth was fumbling with cuff-links. "Well, have yourself a surprise. He's not so fuck-ing bright."

She laughed loudly. "But you're brighter than Jimmy—brighter than anybody, aren't you, Freddie?"

"God—goddamn right I am. I'm brighter'n Karami."

"Yes, indeed!" Mickey jibed. "That's why he's a multimillionnaire and you beg for any graft he'll throw at you."

"You're one to talk about begging and graft, you cock-happy bitch!" Hayworth flung open a closet door, jerked a pair of trousers from a hanger. "You beg to get laid, and your old man was the biggest thief in the Senate!" He missed a first attempt to thrust a leg into his trousers, lurched, slammed against a wall. He cursed and regained his balance.

"Lemme tell you!" He was slurring his words bad-ly. "I outsmarted Karami. Why'n hell you think I went to Beirut?"

Now push further, Mickey thought, make him brag. "Sure, Freddie," she scoffed. "I believe every word you say."

"Got my dough outta his bank—plus! Karami 'n' that Engish shit, Lockhart, can't affort to have me blow—have me blow the whistle . . ."

So that was the answer—or part of it. Fred had drawn money out of Incombank in a hurry, and he'd evidently managed to squeeze out more than was le-gitimately his. Why and how, Michele wondered, wait-ing.

". . . I scared Lockhart so bad he pissed in his pants . . ."

"That, I doubt," Mickey said to herself. Brian Lockhart had impressed her as being anything but the sort of man who could be scared. Unless . . .

". . . all I'd have to do is pass a few tips to the right people . . ."

Michele frowned. Could Jimmy be in trouble? She doubted it.

". . . I'm telling you." Hayworth sat down heavily

on one of the twin beds. Maybe he could manage the trousers easier if he slowly worked in one foot, then another. "I have Karami over a barrel . . ."

His voice cut off. Fred Hayworth had passed out. His jaw flopped open, saliva dribbling from a corner of his mouth.

Mickey's reaction mingled disappointment with relief. On the one hand, she would have liked to learn whatever Fred knew or thought he knew about Jimmy. On the other, she was grateful he'd passed out. Now there was no going to the party, which was certain to be a deadly bore, a horror.

Mickey smiled at herself in the mirror. Thank God! She reached for cleansing pads, removed what makeup she'd already put on, studied the results with satisfaction. Her face was still good, youthful. Not a strand of hair that wasn't lustrous deep-brown.

The sense of being liberated grew. Impulsively, she unhooked her brassiere, took it off, tossed it in the general direction of the bathtub. She really didn't need a bra. Not for support. Her breasts were full, tipped with pink cones—without a hint of sag to them. Mickey cupped her breasts in her hands, lightly brushed thumbs across nipples. She watched with the same delighted wonder she'd always felt when they responded instantly, springing into erect points.

She turned, hurried into the bedroom. She went to the empty bed, pulled back the covers. Kicking off slippers and removing her panties, she got into the bed, pulled up the top sheet to cover her body.

The room was dark. Outside the heavily draped windows, the Via Veneto evening traffic din provided counterpoint to Fred Hayworth's snores. Mickey mentally shut out the sounds and closed her eyes.

Her right arm was under the sheet. She slid her hand along her smooth belly until it rested at the juncture of her thighs. Parting the pubic hairs, her fingers found the moist mound of her clitoris.

"Jimmy," she whispered.

Her fingers began their caressing motion, and her hips stirred and rose and fell against their urgent pressure.

New York City. Tuesday, April 30th.

Jemel Karami sat at his desk in Karamcorp's Rockefeller Center offices. The Weisler chronometer on the desk top silently whirred off time in hundredths of seconds: 13:59:98, 13:59:99, 14:00:00, 14:00:01, 14:00:02 . . .

Two o'clock. The telephone call should come in soon. Very soon.

He picked up a fountain pen, printed FRIDAY in block letters on an embossed memorandum pad, drew a heavy line under the word.

The loss of the Pan-Arab Airways Caravelle had been officially confirmed on Friday morning, New York time. Jemel knew that because Abdul el Muein had been aboard and killed, there would be reaction from the Kuwaiti government. Being familiar with Arab psychology in general and Kuwaiti bureaucracy in particular, he had calculated it would take from three to five days.

He wrote "Sat. Sun. Mon. Tue." under the line on the pad. Today was the fifth day.

Jemel had kept busy during the interim. He'd presided over the opening of Incombank's second Manhattan branch. A host of details required follow-up after Miles Palmer's syndicate transferred the $50 million to Beirut. Questions concerning Karamcorp, the American mainstay of the Karami empire, demanded his personal attention and decisions.

Nonetheless, when four days passed without any reaction from Kuwait, Jemel began to spool up inside. If Brian Lockhart made his daily transoceanic call and still had nothing to report, it would be an abnormality that could imply almost anything.

Jemel's telephone rang minutes later. He reached for it with his left hand. Although he felt self-conscious and not a little foolish, he thrust his right hand into his trousers pocket, touching the smooth beads of the Moslem *sibah* he'd carried as a talisman since his brief college career.

The call was from Brian Lockhart in Beirut, and his voice was clipped, efficient and serious.

"I've been informed His Excellency, Sheikh Nasib-al-Harith will be in Beirut tomorrow, Jimmy. He wishes to see you personally."

Sheikh Nasib-al-Harith served as assistant finance minister to Kuwait's ruling Sabah family.

Jemel's face reflected satisfaction, but his tone was ponderously grave and meditative when he spoke into the mouthpiece.

"I'm afraid I can't possibly pull free from here today, Brian. I can fly tomorrow, though, arriving in Beirut early Thursday, Lebanese time. You'll have to make my apologies to His Excellency and make certain he's properly entertained until I . . ."

"We've been asked to dispense with all ceremony," Lockhart broke in. "Sheikh Nasib's visit is purely business."

"Oh?" Jemel sounded concerned and a little uneasy. "I hope no one at Incombank has given His Excellency reason to take offense." He paused and his tone next emerged quick-frozen. "Because if anyone has, he starts job-hunting thirty seconds after I land at Khaldeh!"

"It's nothing like that!" came the hasty assurance. "As I told you during our conversations since Friday, Abdul el Muein carried copies of documents he and I prepared. And—ah—there's no trace of them."

"Of course." A relieved sigh. Then puzzlement. "Wait a minute. Didn't el Muein keep Kuwait informed on the progress of negotiations?"

"Afraid not, Jimmy. I urged him to, but he insisted otherwise. Wanted to take the final agreements to Kuwait City himself." Brian Lockhart dropped his voice. "He—um—hinted he'd get high marks, shall we say—if he hand-delivered everything in a tidy package. Since he had absolute authority from the emir himself, I couldn't . . ."

"No, you couldn't," Jemel interrupted. His lips flicked an on-and-off smile. The 5,500-mile line to Beirut was completely static-free, sure proof that power boosters were compensating for the drain caused by any number of electronic eavesdropping devices. "But you have duplicates of all the material, haven't you, Brian?"

"Naturally. In both Arabic and English. Properly signed."

"In that case, simply show them to His Excellency."

Lockhart coughed, then: "We must allow for the possiblity that Sheikh Nasib might want to invalidate the agreements. If he does . . ."

"Funds belonging to the Sabahs are at their disposal!" Jimmy said sternly. "We hold, transfer, or pay out as His Excellency directs." He held off a beat, added, "In any currency, at preferential exchange rates. Is that clear?"

"Yes—and sorry. Just thought it best to ask."

"No harm done." Jimmy's tone was relenting. "All right, Brian. Someone will Telex you my Beirut ETA. Have my car meet me at Khaldeh airport. I depend on you to show Sheikh Nasib every courtesy until I arrive."

When the conversation ended, Jemel indulged in a critique of the dialogue. On the whole, excellent, he judged. Sheikh Nasib would, of course, hear a taped replay before meeting with Lockhart. It would sound spontaneous. Brian would further palliate with documents and data, masses of figures and stacks of financial statements.

At that point, I'll make my entrance, Jemel mused, and that should complete the job of keeping the Sabahs and their money safely in the Incombank fold.

But suppose it didn't?

The possibility was far from pleasant to contemplate. However, Jimmy Karami reflected, that was another of the calculated risks—and he conquered the queasy feeling elicited by the thought.

2

Jiddah, Saudi Arabia. Wednesday, May 1st.

Midmorning sunlight seared into the foyer of Russell Stanton's VIP bungalow when the *khaddam* opened the door. Lloyd Emmerick stepped inside and blinked to accustom himself to sudden dimness as the door was closed behind him. Russ was waiting for him in the living room.

"Lead off, Lloyd," Stanton said.

Emmerick quickly reviewed what he'd learned in Beirut and recounted his Monday telephone conversation with Whitehead MidEast Oil Co.'s president, Quentin Yeager.

"Yeager said he'd go see the boss," Emmerick concluded.

Stanton's blue eyes narrowed. "R. D. Whitehead himself?" Receiving an affirmative grunt from Emmerick, he said, "Then it must look bad to Quent, too, even from his distant and detached perspective. He doesn't panic easily—and he sure as hell doesn't barge in on R. D. Whitehead unless he's sure it's something serious."

Lloyd Emmerick fired up one of his black cigarillos. "One or two things I didn't find out until after I'd talked to Yeager," he said. "Like the stories about what Abdul el Muein was supposedly doing in Beirut."

"What was that?" Russ asked with keen interest.

"He was there almost a week, holding confabs with Incombank. Most people think he was lining up some giant-sized deal for the Sabahs."

"That's possible. Any rumors who sabotaged the plane?"

"The theories go in all directions. One version

blames it on dissident sheikhs. Another holds it was
the Iraqis. Then, there's a lot of talk that tries to
hang the crash on the Israelis."

"Oh, shit! None of those make sense."

Emmerick puffed great clouds of smoke. "What
does make sense out here?"

Stanton lit a mentholated cigarette in self-defense.
"Nothing," he grunted after taking several deep drags.
"I did a little checking myself. I used the company
Comanche and pilot and took a couple of quick flights
out into the field while you were gone. I made it seem
all ordinary and routine—like fast once-over checkups.
But I got around to talking to a few sheikhs."

"And?"

"The feel was all wrong. I didn't get a straw of
information, but they were overly ingratiating, practically smothered me with courtesy."

Emmerick chewed his cigarillo. "The *alf ahlan
wasah'lan* bit?"

Arab etiquette demands a host bid his guest *"mit
ahlan wasah'lan*—a hundred times welcome." Substituting *"alf"*—a thousand—for *"mit"*—a hundred—lam-
inates extravagance onto the courtesy, makes it egre-
gious, ironical, as all of old Middle East hands are
aware.

"Exactly," Russ Stanton replied. "The smiling
sneer treatment. Laughing up the sleeves in which
they've hidden the knives they're going to shove in your
back." He extinguished his cigarette. "And, Lloyd,
not one of them said a word—not a word—about
money. Which is suspicious in itself."

"Suspicious? It's a dead-sure sign trouble's coming."

Stanton nodded. He was certain now that trouble
was brewing—but clues as to what kind and from what
directions eluded him. Were the Saudis and Kuwaitis
thinking of nationalizing oil company properties? Was a
Ba'athis or Nasserite coup in the making? Revolt and
rampage by dissident tribes? Rebellion or open revolt?

"Conjure up your own calamities, Lloyd," he said
wearily. "My nightmare locker is overloaded."

Emmerick shared Stanton's pessimism. There was a heavy smog gathering, no less ominous because it could only be sensed, not seen.

"You're the only Whitehead MidEast vice-president we have over here at the moment, Russ," he said. "So make dynamic executive noises and tell me what we do next."

Stanton stood up, stretching his powerful six-two frame. "We need instructions from the home office. If nothing comes in by this evening, I'll send Quent Yeager a fable-cable and light a fire under him."

Saudi laws requiring all cables to be sent *en clair* leave foreign oilmen only one alternative when they find it necessary to use cable-communications. They devise interminable messages apparently dealing with routine matters. However, while not in code, these are fictions, the mass of wordage covering the real, pithy meaning. They are thus analogous to Aesop's tales, which carry a short, sharp moral—and it is for this reason oilmen call them "fable-cables."

"Then you're not going back to New York, Russ?" Emmerick asked hopefully.

"Not until things are a lot clearer than they are now—or I get orders from topside."

Lloyd Emmerick grinned. If there was going to be trouble, he could think of no better man to have around than Russell Stanton.

3

Beirut, Lebanon. Thursday, May 2nd.

Jemel Karami, Brian Lockhart, and Sheikh Nasib al-Harith conferred in Jemel's executive suite on the top floor of the towering Incombank Building.

Ledgers and papers were arrayed along Karami's

desk. Sheikh Nasib, financial adviser to those who ruled and controlled Kuwait and its incalculable oil wealth, sat quietly, sleek in his Brioni-tailored Western suit, and listened while Jemel spoke.

". . . when Abdul el Muein was sent here to investigate rumors regarding Incombank's solvency, I gave the matter no thought. The rumors were baseless, and I was confident that Brian would be entirely capable of demonstrating the solidity of our position to el Muein."

Jemel allowed a note of boredom to shade his tone. "Quite obviously, I was correct." He waved a careless hand at the documents on his desk. "El Muein found everything in order and formally extended existing agreements. I regret he did not notify you, but Brian tells me he wished to maintain secrecy and deliver his report and his copies of the papers that were signed to Kuwait personally."

Nasib al-Harith fingered his rosary. Yes, he told himself, the bank's records and financial statements showed it to be in excellent condition, and the copies of the documents signed by Abdul el Muein were in order. Yet, the original rumors had come from reliable sources and the midair explosion of the aircraft had raised further doubts.

He quoted to himself from abu-Hanifah: a zephyr may momentarily part the mists of suspicion, but a strong wind is needed to clear them entirely. Aloud, he murmured politely, "I fear this unfortunate affair has caused both of you gentlemen much inconvenience."

"No inconvenience," Jemel said. "Deep concern. Need I say that Emir Sabah, his families, and his aides are our most valued clients? It is our duty as bankers to serve and satisfy them." He threw a sharp look at Brian Lockhart, who sat on Sheikh Nasib's left. "You informed His Excellency that we stand ready to disregard the el Muein agreements and do as he directs with the funds?"

"Yes," Lockhart replied. "I've signed a letter to that effect."

Jemel redirected his attention to Sheikh Nasib.

"If, for any reason, you are not satisfied, I assure you that we would much rather lose Kuwaiti business than lose Kuwaiti goodwill and friendship."

The knife is double-edged, Sheikh Nasib reflected. Incombank paid high returns and performed many valuable services. The leading families of Kuwait could afford to lose Incombank's "goodwill and friendship" only if there was real danger to their invested and deposited funds.

"The destruction of the Caravelle," Nasib al-Harith said. "Have you formed any theories as to who sabotaged the craft?"

Jemel's generously proportioned mouth tightened and his eyes grew black. "Do you have the account book, Brian?" he asked.

"Yes." Lockhart took a thin, slender book bound in green morocco leather from his inside breast-pocket and gave it to Jemel, who opened the book, leafed through its pages until he found the one he sought.

"If Your Excellency will be kind enough to look at this." He extended a long arm across the desk, held the book so Sheikh Nasib could see the open page, which was headed "Damascus and Cairo Export Co." A series of dates appeared in a left-hand column. Opposite them were dollar-sums ranging from $5,000 to $10,000.

Sheikh Nasib felt a puff of mist-clearing wind and nodded. The Damascus and Cairo Export Co. was familiar to all *au courant* Arabs as the fund-gathering agency for the Lebanese-based anti-Israeli terrorist organization, the PFL—Popular Front for the Liberation of Palestine.

"The Jews know Incombank owns Pan-Arab Airways," Jemel said, closing the account book and returning it to Lockhart. "They doubtless learned Incombank has been making large monthly contributions to the PFL. The Israelis sabotaged the Caravelle as warning and revenge."

He leaned forward, arms on desk. "The Jews were clever. They timed the explosion to occur over uninhabited and almost inaccessible Saudi territory. We can prove nothing, and the Israeli agents are safe."

Nasib al-Harith saw the mists of suspicion vanish. All was as Karami said. The bank's balance sheets withstood the closest scrutiny; Sheikh Nasib had studied them the day before. He had also inspected Lockhart's copies of the papers signed by Abdul el Muein and could find no irregularities. Both Lockhart and then Karami had offered to let him withdraw all Kuwaiti monies, in full and immediately. As for the destruction of the aircraft, Karami's explanation was logical—indeed, the only satisfactory answer.

It verified what Sheikh Nasib had already learned. Kuwaiti agents had traced Abdul el Muein's movements. He'd spent the night before the flight with a young male prostitute. If Karami or Lockhart had wanted to remove el Muein for any reason, they could have done it far more easily than by blasting an airliner to bits. Beirut swarmed with professional assassins perpetually seeking employment. A hired killer, a faked robbery, the corpse thrown into a Zeitouni alley or into the sea—and it would have been done.

Jemel Karami spoke. "It might please Your Excellency to know that the first retaliatory measures will be taken against the Jews tomorrow."

"*Inshal'la!* They will be made to pay?"

"Only an instalment on the debt—and not in money."

"Would it be possible for me to observe this?"

"It shall be arranged, Your Excellency."

Sheikh Nasib inclined his head a fraction of an inch. "I am satisfied with what you have shown and told me," he declared. "The agreements Abdul el Muein made with Mr. Lockhart will remain in force. No Kuwaiti funds shall be withdrawn. We need only to countersign the documents. I shall take a set of copies with me to Kuwait."

Jemel and Brian Lockhart were alone.

"Another step forward," Lockhart observed.

"A very large step, entirely thanks to you, Brian."

"Not at all. Honors divided, I'd say." Lockhart ran the tips of his fingers over his impeccably trimmed moustache. "Mustn't forget our assorted coolies, either.

Especially the penmanship chap." No need for mentioning the Pan-Arab copilot who'd so willingly agreed to take a bulky package aboard with him and take it personally to Kuwait City. "Our scribe proved a dab hand with friend Abdul's signature."

"He didn't see any of the texts, did he?"

"Lord, no! Practiced his squigglings on blank sheets. I filled 'em in afterwards."

"And the originals?"

"Burned. We couldn't very well have orders directing payment of ten million pounds sterling of Kuwaiti money to other banks lying around, could we?"

The question needed no reply.

Lighting a cigarette, Jemel blew smoke toward the high ceiling. "I still have a full day ahead of me," he said. "I must see the Damascus and Cairo Export people—and then clear things with Cousin Rashid."

"Ah, yes. Tomorrow's pyrotechnics."

"We call them "fireworks" in America, Brian. In this instance, kosher-style."

4

Ramim, Israel. Friday, May 3rd.

The residents of Ramim, an Israeli town located only a few thousand yards from the Lebanese border, went about their Friday-afternoon activities. They looked forward to sundown, which would mark the end of the work-week and the beginning of the Sabbath.

Housewives made their purchases in the shops. Shifra Hirshon selected a plump roasting chicken and after the poulterer had weighed and wrapped it, she paid him and started on her way home.

Men did their work. David Stern, a twenty-three-year-old *sabra* truck driver, backed his vehicle up to the rear loading platform of a small furniture factory. Stern had every reason to feel good. It was his last delivery for the day, and he would be going to his current girlfriend's house for dinner—and staying the night.

In the Ramim hospital's maternity wing, Nahum Grossman sat entranced by the bedside of his wife, Miriam, watching her nurse their child, born only two days before.

No one in Ramim heard the distant, hollow cough of the 82-millimeter mortars or the tremolo whisper of the shells that spewed from the tubes.

The mortars had been laid with deadly accuracy. The initial salvo of four shells dropped squarely into the town.

Shifra Hirshon was crossing the street. An explosion flung her into the air, steel fragments dismembering her body. Oddly, the parcel she had been carrying was blown from her hand and rolled against a curbstone intact.

Dismounting from the cab of his truck, David Stern heard an onrushing whine—and then a roaring sheet of flame blotted out his consciousness forever.

Nahum Grossman heard nothing, and the half-pound shard of shell-casing that split his skull in half mercifully prevented him from seeing his wife and child instantly transformed into ghastly lumps of raw, blood-soaked flesh.

Twelve more salvos were fired by the mortars emplaced in a deep ravine near Houle, two miles away in Lebanon. Forty-eight more shells rained down on Ramin.

The gunners were experts. It all took less than fifteen minutes. But the sudden storm of high explosive left Ramim a rubbled charnelhouse. More than a score of the town's residents were killed, over a hundred wounded. Homes and buildings were blasted, smashed—and since a third of the mortar rounds fired were thermite shells—incendiaries that would melt even steel and could not be extinguished with water—much of Ramim was left burning.

Jebel Haroun, Lebanon. Friday, May 3rd.

Food, iced nonalcoholic beverages, a shade umbrella, a comfortable folding chair and tripod-mounted binoculars had been brought to the hillside.

Sheikh Nasib al-Harith nibbled at the food, sipped cooling drinks, and then, at the appointed time, settled into the chair under the umbrella and watched the spectacle through the binoculars.

He was fascinated by what he saw. He kept his eyes glued to the binoculars, occasionally swiveling the powerful glasses from left to right and back.

At last the display was over.

"Remarkably accurate," he said approvingly, nodding toward the mortars in the ravine. "The Jews have been taught a lesson," he added, giving a final glance at the great clouds of smoke billowing from the ruins of Ramim.

Sheikh Nasib rose from the folding chair and walked to the Land Rover parked a few yards away on the hillside.

Beirut. Friday, May 3rd.

Reports that Ramim had been shelled from Lebanese territory spread through Beirut within an hour after the last shot had been fired.

Foreign correspondents guessed it to be the work of the PFL and knew it could not have been carried out unless the Lebanese government had given at least tacit approval. The journalists converged on the office of Premier Abdul Kamal.

"The premier is unavailable to the press, and he will issue no statements regarding the incident," they were informed by a minor official.

When the correspondents stubbornly persisted in asking questions, soldiers wearing red berets and carrying submachine guns "escorted" them to the nearest exit.

New York City. Friday, May 3rd.

R. Daniel Whitehead came to New York City from his Oceanside, California, home on Thursday. He thought it advisable to headquarter himself temporarily in the Whitehead MidEast Oil Co. Building on Lower Broadway.

"Don't get any idea I intend meddling in normal company operations," he'd told Quentin Yeager. "You're the president, and it's your baby. But you and I can play field marshals a lot better for the duration of the Karami campaign if I'm in New York. And," he added, "there are some nasty pieces of work I can't ask anyone else to do. I'll have to take care of 'em myself."

Quentin Yeager's built-in seismograph was sensitive to home-office vibrations. He correctly surmised that Whitehead's arrival might unnerve company personnel, make them afraid that R. D.'s presence meant top-to-bottom reorganization and wholesale firings lay ahead. He countered the rumors before they could start by passing along confidential hints that the big boss was contemplating a large expansion program. The good word flashed along the organizational grapevine—and, as Yeager expected, spread beyond company walls. This was a bonus benefit. It diverted oil industry and financial-circle attention from their real aims.

Among the people Dan Whitehead could trust implicitly was the head of the brokerage firm through which he had been dealing for decades. He allotted a round-sum million dollars, gave instructions the money be used to buy 1,000- to 5,000-share blocks of stock in various public corporations controlled by Jemel Karami.

"Buy on my personal account—but in street names," he directed. "No one is to know I own a share of Karami stock."

It was a small, albeit expensive, extra safety measure. There was no telling when a minority stockholder's suit against this, that, or another Karami company might prove a useful delaying or hampering tactic.

"First time in my life I ever bet against myself," Whitehead remarked to Yeager. "If we lick J. Karami, his whole structure folds—and I'll be surprised if I salvage ten cents on the dollar."

"You can always write the difference off as capital loss," Yeager grinned. "That's some consolation."

"Not much." The oil magnate's weathered-granite features contorted into a simian grimace. "You have to hold for six months to take a long-term capital loss. We'll win or lose in a lot less time than that. I'll have to take the short-term loss—and consider it a bargain."

The million was a fraction of what he anticipated spending before the "campaign" was over, Whitehead thought, and it was an insignificant petty-cash item compared to what would go down the drain in the event Karami emerged the winner.

On Friday morning, Quentin Yeager received a cable from Russ Stanton. Like most cables sent from Saudi Arabia, it had been delayed. On its face, the message was a long-winded narrative of everyday commonplaces in the company's Middle Eastern operations. Between the lines reading by Yeager and R. D. Whitehead pared away the Aesopian padding. Stanton was gravely concerned over the developing situation and asked for specific instructions.

"I suggest we tell him to stay in Jiddah until further notice and give him a free hand," Yeager recommended. "He and Lloyd Emmerick are a good team—the best."

"Nope," Whitehead rejected the suggestion. "Stanton has to be ordered home. He's seen only a narrow aspect of this thing. He doesn't know what we know and would be operating in the dark."

"Then let's bring him over, fill him in, and send him right back."

Mild amusement flickered for a moment in Dan Whitehead's gun-metal eyes. It was reassuring to know that at seventy-three, he could still think several moves ahead of a whip-smart executive two-thirds his age.

"You read the digests of my Karami files in Oceanside, Quent. We assayed our hole-card values, agreed we had a fair stack—some kings, some queens and two trump aces. Right?"

"Yes," Yeager replied.

"Being as how this is a cockeyed world, the aces turned up to be a one-armed Jewish cloak-and-suiter —and Whitehead MidEast's most promising vice-president, Russell T. Stanton, no?"

"Yes again."

All levity vanished from Whitehead's face and tone.

"We order Russ Stanton to return," he said. "I'll give him all the information we have—including the details of what Karami did to him behind his back."

"That's going to hit Russ hard," Yeager murmured.

"The shock will wear off," Whitehead declared coolly, yet not without compassion. "In the long run, the truth will probably help Stanton, ease that ten-ton guilt-load he's been carrying around far too long." He cracked his knuckles. "Sure, it'll hurt when he discovers that his most cherished illusions and memories are delusions and horse manure—but at least he'll stop bleeding inside."

"I hope that's how it works out, anyway," he added to himself, "and even if it doesn't, Stanton has to be told." That would be the catalytic factor. He drew a deep breath, continued.

"When Stanton is primed, and I've convinced him he'll accomplish more by following orders than by pulling some goddamned fool stunt that'll get him a life sentence, we'll send him back to the Middle East. Then. Not before."

"And the other man. The garment manufacturer. Marvin Jacobs?" Quentin Yeager inquired. "What about him?"

"Same basic formula. I'll arrange to see Jacobs soon, let him soak up the pertinent facts from the secret life of Jemel Karami—and stand by while the volcano erupts. Naturally, I can't *send* Marvin Jacobs anywhere or give him any orders. But once he's cooled

down a bit, I'll talk reason to him and *ask* him to go
where he'll do the most good."

"Think he will?"

"You've read the record I have on Jacobs,
Quent. The man, his nature, beliefs and convictions
are all clearly defined. Toss the truth at him, and
there's motivation to spare."

Quentin Yeager grimly nodded agreement. When
they knew the facts, the two men who considered themselves to be Jemel Karami's best friends would become
his deadliest enemies. They'd go anywhere—do anything—to square accounts.

5

Beirut, Lebanon. Saturday, May 4th.

Jemel Karami readily admitted that the house near
the Corniche on the rue d'Australie was a garish
chrome-and-heat-resistant-glass jukebox in the height
of Lebanese neo-monstrous architectural fashion.
Luckily, since his visits to Lebanon were intermittent
and brief, he rarely stayed there. He considered it less
house than mid-twentieth-century version of a viceregal palace built to overawe the natives whose money
had paid for its construction and continued to pay for
its upkeep and operation.

Junoesque, brunette Renate Zeitzler was hardly a
native. The young wife of a new-rich German industrialist, she was vacationing in Beirut, staying at the
Phoenicia with her sister-in-law and a personal maid.
However, Renate was greatly awed by Jemel's house
when he brought her there a little after midnight—
and, it was the awe that finally overcame her reluctance
to go to bed with him.

She had ample reason to hesitate. She'd attended

a party at the West German embassy and met Jemel there. Although she found him charming, she felt no particular sexual attraction to him. Then, of course, she would be taking serious risks. Her husband, Gerhard Zeitzler, was extremely jealous. Her sister-in-law or maid might inform Gerhard that she failed to return to the hotel until very late.

Then Jemel showed her through the house. Evidence of wealth had always aroused Renate. Now she saw proofs of wealth far greater than what her husband possessed.

"And you own the Incombank, too?" she asked.

"Yes."

They had drinks in a room outfitted like a cocktail lounge. Jimmy's barman served Renate with the large Steinhager she requested. Jemel had a Crawford's scotch. He'd acquired a taste for the brand from his father, who had seldom drunk any other.

"I suppose I could tell my sister-in-law the party lasted till late, and that I had supper at someone's house afterward," Renate said as she sipped her drink.

Jimmy felt something almost akin to gratitude. The events of the last two days had created inner tensions and an imperative need to release them. None of the innumerable girls in Beirut with whom he'd had affairs and whom he could take to bed easily at any time would serve. Renate's newness, her initial resistance and now, finally, her acquiescence provided the ideal ingredients. They were reassurance, confirmation —psychological refractions of the want-strive-attain equation Jemel recognized as expression of his fundamental drives.

He led her into the florid immensity of the master bedroom suite.

"But I must leave by five and return to my hotel!" Renate said.

He gave no sign of hearing. He lifted her bodily, all but threw her on to the bed.

He knelt, thrust the folds of her dress above her thighs and hips. His fingers groped, encountered filmy material already soaked with moisture, tore it away.

Moaning, Renate drew her feet—still encased in evening-slippers—up, and, her thighs spread wide, Jemel's lips and tongue searched between converging walls of soft, musky flesh, found the swollen mound they sought.

Later they undressed. Still later, with scents and tastes still lingering strong, they lay silently, Renate on her side with her head on Jemel's shoulder, sleeping.

Jemel remained awake and motionless for perhaps half an hour. Then he reached around with his right hand, touched the small of Renate's back and began tracing a circular pattern with his fingertips. Within moments, the sleeping girl's muscles twitched. He gradually increased pressure. Her muscles quivered, she stirred in her sleep, pubes straining in unconscious reflex against his thigh.

She was ready. Jemel ceased the caressing, stroking motion, pressed his fingernails with abrupt force into the flesh surrounding the base of her spine.

Renate awoke with a convulsive spasm. "My God!" she gasped, her eyes huge, filled with wonder. "I—I had an orgasm—or did I dream it?"

"You didn't dream it," Jemel laughed. The technique, requiring absolutely controlled rhythm and precise timing, never failed. "That's called *yfik*—literally 'to awake.' Are you awakened?"

"Try me!"

She suddenly turned over on her stomach. Her legs veed out and her hands reached behind her, parting her buttocks. There was sufficient light for Jemel to see the glint of the huge square-cut diamond solitaire and the diamond-encrusted wedding band she wore, and this further heightened his desire.

"Will you do it like this?" she asked. "My husband, Gerhard, never will . . ."

Jemel sat up, turned, pivoting on one knee, and straddled her. He slid his hands between her body and the mattress, gripped her breasts. He eased himself down on the girl, slowly forcing his tumescent penis into the constricted sheath. "So your husband never will," he thought. That, too, was a form of triumph that amplified his pleasure.

Jemel sent Renate Zeitzler to the Phoenicia in his limousine and slept for a few more hours. He was up at eleven when his majordomo ushered Brian Lockhart into the dining room that looked out over the Mediterranean.

"On the dot, as usual, Brian," Jemel said. He was breakfasting on freshly baked, crisp-crusted bread spread thickly with *labeneh,* and coffee. "Your tea is being brewed." He looked up as a servant entered from the kitchen. "My mistake. It has been brewed."

Lockhart despised both Arab and French coffee, clung tenaciously to his English tea-drinking habits. He seated himself at the table facing Jemel. The servant placed cup, saucer and the other impedimenta of an English tea service before him.

"You have a sleek look this morning, Jimmy," he observed, deftly manipulating strainer, tea and hot-water pots.

"I had a successful night."

"Mm," Lockhart murmured, pouring from the cream jug with the precision of a chemist mixing a formula. "Fancied as much."

Lockhart's own sex life followed a set pattern. He would take a mistress, live with her for several months, then discard her and acquire another.

"Any late news?" Jemel inquired.

"Only the expected. The Israelis are howling. The Arab nationalist press is crowing. Cairo is claiming the credit. That's roughly the sum."

"Speaking of sums. Is the extra one hundred and fifty thousand dollars you promised Fred Hayworth blocked so he can't touch it without your approval or mine?"

"Never bothered opening the new account. He's not entitled to a penny until everything is done. Then we can pay him."

"Good." Jemel played with his cup and saucer. When he spoke, his tone was elaborately casual. "How was Mickey—she was probably introduced to you as Michele, or did you not have much chance to talk to her?"

"Chatted with her a bit." Lockhart finished his

tea, prepared to concoct another cup. "She was most attractive. Maintained a patina of wifely good cheer. Something rather different showed through to my critical eye, however." Brian Lockhart knew of Jemel's long, intermittent affair with Michele Hayworth. "Ah—when did you see her last?"

"Some months ago." Jemel abruptly shoved his cup and saucer aside. "Let's talk business," he said impatiently. "Received the confirmations yet?"

Lockhart gave an affirmative nod. "Yesterday. Cummings was only waiting to get our cash in hand. The hardware is being shipped. It'll arrive so we can have our planes loaded and ready on the night of the twenty-fifth."

Jemel nicked at the linen tablecloth with his thumbnail. Excellent, all around. The dike was adequately shored. No sweat there for the next three weeks. Brian had performed magnificently, lopping two entire months from the original schedule. They had all the elbow room they needed—and more.

Lockhart leaned down from his chair. He opened the attaché case he'd brought with him and laid it on the Isfahan-carpeted floor. He straightened up, a sheaf of papers in his hand. "I've had the shipment broken down into self-contained units. Eliminates the need for sorting and shifting. Everything that's to go aboard the first plane is marked 'One' on the crates, 'Two' for the second and so on." He gave the papers to Jimmy.

Jemel flipped through the documents, reading at his accustomed lightning speed, and stopped at one point. "Rather high on the proportion of plastic charges consigned to Abqaiq, aren't we?" he asked.

"No. They're needed to blow the Trans-Arabian Pipeline storage tanks there. Something will have to be blasted as a dramatic symbol, and those tanks are ideal. They'll burn for days, draw off enormous manpower to save the other installations at Abqaiq."

Brian was right. Jemel gave the papers back to him without reading further. Lockhart was the logistics expert and tactician, Jemel the overall strategist. Each had his own functions. One had to trust the other implicitly.

What they stood to gain defied calculation, Jimmy mused. Their losses if anything went wrong? Simple to measure. Everything. Including their necks.

*

6

Jiddah, Saudi Arabia. Monday, May 6th.

Russell Stanton stared at the text of the cablegram:

STANTON NEWYORKWARD UNDELAY
DANIEL WHITEHEAD

"Now what the hell does this mean?" he growled, his expression and tone baffled, cheerless.

"Means the old man doesn't believe in wasting money on cable charges," Lloyd Emmerick retorted, hiding his own sense of disquietude. The curt summons caused him to worry for Russ Stanton. It was the kind of message sent as a prelude to a "request" for a resignation.

As for himself, Emmerick didn't relish the prospect of being left to direct operations alone—not with every barometer indicating the approach of a gale-force storm.

Russ activated muscles to produce a facsimile grin, let them go slack. "This says whole volumes that make no sense, Lloyd. How often have you received cables from R. D. himself over here?"

"Never." Emmerick admitted glumly. "I get plenty of cables—but they're signed by you or Yeager or some department head."

"And the damned thing is datelined New York City," Stanton went on. "I doubt if R. D. has been in New York twice in the last five years—and then he shot in and shot right out again. He'd rather break both his legs than stay around New York."

"The cable's legitimate," the resident superintendent said glumly. The authenticating number for May was incorporated in the address:

STANTON 37 WHITEHEADCO JIDDAH
SAUDI ARABIA

"So what now, Russ?"

Stanton shrugged his broad shoulders. "I follow orders—and book myself out for the States."

New York City. Monday, May 6th.

Miles Palmer habitually read his morning *New York Times* while being driven downtown to the Palmer National Trust Building.

He was going over the front page, and a medium-sized headline caught his eye:

LEBANESE EXPECT
ISRAELI REPRISAL

Palmer read the first few lines of the Beirut-datelined story:

> Widespread fears are being expressed here that Israel will soon take retaliatory action against Lebanon for last Friday's shelling of Ramim, an Israeli town situated near the Lebanese border. Although government sources in Beirut now admit the mortar shells that bombarded Ramim and caused heavy casualties were fired from Lebanese territory, they maintain the attack was made by unknown terrorists . . .

Miles Palmer folded the paper and put it down on the seat beside him. He stared at the back of his chauffeur's head. He sensed that Jemel Karami was mixed up in the Ramim incident somehow.

He wished he knew more about Karami's plans. He and his associates had $50 million invested in whatever it was Karami intended doing—and the details were complete mysteries to them.

Palmer's colorless lips set into a hard line. It was too late to change anything now. The money was committed. He picked up the newspaper again and turned to the financial pages.

Marvin Jacobs had arrived at his office late, and he was winnowing the telephone messages he'd found on his desk. The first four or five were unimportant, then:

"9:45. Miss Rogers for Mr. R. D. Whitehead. Urgent," and a downtown telephone number Marvin recognized. He'd called Russ Stanton there often. Marvin's thin face beamed. Russ was back in town and making with gags. The last was a good sign, perhaps an indicator that Russ was finally coming out of the emotional tailspin he'd been in for a couple of years, ever since his wife died.

Jacobs hitched the shoulder muscles that worked his artificial left arm, bringing the hand up on the desk. He transferred the message slip to the artificial fingers, used his normal right hand to reach for the intercom key and depress it.

"Ethel, call Whitehead MidEast Oil and ask for Russell Stanton," he told his secretary. Might as well add more corn to the load, he thought. "Say it's David Dubinsky calling."

He released the key, crumpled the message slip and dropped it in a wastebasket. He picked up the stack of already-opened morning mail—carefully, to avoid disturbing the framed picture of his wife and two children that stood on the desk.

The topmost letter was a request for price quotations from a retail clothing chain. He was poring over it when his secretary's voice spoke from the intercom.

"Mr. Stanton is in Saudi Arabia, Mr. Jacobs."

Marvin frowned, scratched at his gray-streaked mop of brown hair. Russ Stanton was the only person he knew at Whitehead MidEast. Who in hell could have called? R. D. Whitehead, one of the world's richest men, wouldn't even be aware that Marvin Jacobs or the firm of Pincus Jacobs & Son existed.

"Mr. Jacobs?"

"Yes, Ethel."

"I remember the call. Miss Rogers sounded like it was really important. Shall I ask for her?"

Marvin hesitated before replying. "Okay, but don't be surprised when you're told there is no Miss Rogers —or that you're crazy."

He returned to the letter. The telephone rang. He lifted the handset, wedged it between raised left shoulder and ear, absently said, "Yes?" and continued reading.

"I have Mr. Whitehead on the line."

"Huh?" he gave a start, almost lost the handset, secured it again with his right hand, and his slightly myopic eyes grew wide. "Please put him on."

Click, pause, click—followed by a strong, pleasant-gruff bass: "Mr. Jacobs? Good morning. I'm R. D. Whitehead."

Marvin Jacobs's own net worth hovered close to the million mark. He knew many businessmen who were bona fide millionaires. His college classmate and friend, Jimmy Karami, could probably cash in for ninety or a hundred million. But, Marvin reflected, he'd never before talked to a genuine billionaire—rated as being one of the wealthiest men on the face of the earth.

"Uh—good morning, Mr. Whitehead."

"Thank you for returning my call so promptly."

Marvin smiled. "To tell you the truth, I almost didn't. I thought it was a joke."

"I'd have kept on trying, Mr. Jacobs. I'm a persistent cuss when I have favors to ask. I'd like to speak with you privately. I wonder . . ."

"Excuse me, Mr. Whitehead. Are you sure you have the right Jacobs?"

"Certain. You're Russell Stanton's friend."

Marvin felt a jolt of anxiety. "Has something happened to Russ?"

"No. He's fine. He should be in New York day after tomorrow. I used his name only for identification purposes."

Now Marvin's features registered consternation. "R. Daniel Whitehead wanting a favor from me," he thought.

"Could you possibly spend a few hours with me Wednesday, Mr. Jacobs? I'd come to your office and save you trouble, but there's a mountain of reading matter down here I'd like you to wade through."

There was only one answer. Yes. If for no other reason than to meet a man whose name, fortune and power were legendary. Still . . .

"I don't want to sound rude, Mr. Whitehead, but could you . . ."

"Sorry for anticipating the question, Mr. Jacobs. Unfortunately, I can't explain anything over the phone. I can only say that it's important. Not just to you and me. To a lot of other people, too."

Was the old boy wacky, Marvin wondered. He racked his brain. No, he'd never heard anything to suggest that Whitehead was a nut. There weren't any rumors about him like those that made the rounds concerning H. L. Hunt, Howard Hughes, and others of the super-rich genre.

"All right, Mr. Whitehead," he said. "My curiosity alone would be enough to compel. Be glad to oblige. What time would suit you?"

"I'm imposing on you. At your convenience."

"Nine o'clock too early?"

"Not at all. There's an elevator marked 'fiftieth floor only' in the Whitehead Building lobby. I'll have someone waiting by the car to bring you right up. Thank you, Mr. Jacobs. I'm looking forward to meeting you."

"That, Mr. R. D. Whitehead, goes like double or triple," Marvin said to himself. They exchanged good-byes, and Marvin hung up. Lucky I'm not a nail-biter, he mused. With only one good hand, I'd be gnawing on bloody stumps before 9:00 A.M. Wednesday.

He couldn't figure the invitation. Invitation? It was more like a command performance.

"Beats me," Marvin muttered and pressed a button to summon his secretary.

"Cancel everything I have scheduled for day after tomorrow, Ethel," Marvin said when she came into his office. "I'm spending the morning with none other than

R. Daniel Whitehead—and I'll need whatever's left of the day to recover."

She stared at him as though she couldn't believe it, either. "He really wants to see you?"

Jacobs mimed supercilious hauteur. "My dear young lady. You've never fully appreciated your boss. I'm a big *macher*. The world's third—or second, is it? —richest man calls on *me* for help. He needs my iron will, steel nerves, tin arm—and lead ass—to stave off disaster."

Ethel grinned at her employer.

"Actually, I think he's just looking for bargains in two-pants suits," Marvin rattled on. "Probably figures that since Russ Stanton and I are friends, I can get them for him wholesale."

I wish to God I knew why he really called me, he added silently. He felt an inexplicably ominous premonition.

"Add Marvin Jacobs to our calendar," Daniel Whitehead remarked with satisfaction to Quentin Yeager. "He'll be here at nine sharp Wednesday morning. I'll see him first thing."

"Russell Stanton is due in on Wednesday, R. D. At best, you'll have a busy day. At worst, the schedule might get fouled, and there could be conflicts."

"There won't be. Each of them is going to get a bad jolt—without any anesthetics—from me. The effects of what I'm going to tell and show them about Jemel Karami will leave each of them in a state of shock—until they get together."

"And then?"

"Then one of two things. They say yes with a vengeance—or tell me to shove it up my behind. It's like everything else about this whole deal. Quent. All or nothing. No consolation prizes." He grunted. "Those are the rules Karami himself has been playing by all his life."

Protasis II

1

"Win, place and show!" Russell Stanton chortled to Jemel and Marvin. It was June 1943. Final academic ratings of first-term freshmen had been posted on the bulletin board:

1. Jacobs, M.
2. Karami, J.
3. Stanton, R. T.

They didn't bother reading further.

"Come on A-rab and Jew-boy, we've got to pack," Russ said.

Marvin grinned. It no longer surprised him that he'd ceased to be self-conscious about being Jewish. He had his roommates to thank for that. Especially Russ. Stanton's friendly encouragement had chipped away the walls of his ghetto-complex, replaced them with unassuming self-confidence.

Summer vacation began the following day. Russ had a $1.50-an-hour construction job lined up with a contractor building a war plant near Rutland. Pincus Jacobs had agreed that his son could try to bring order out of the muddle wartime substitute bookkeepers had made of his company's accounts. Jemel was to spend his vacation working for Karami & Co.

Nuri had been released from the clinic in May. Psychiatrists had recommended "an experiment in integrating the boy into the family unit." Hassan en-

125

rolled the boy in a year-round day school for "children requiring specialized guidance" and employed George Rickard, a middle-aged tutor-companion, to look after Nuri at home.

The meeting between Jemel and Nuri was strained. His brother had grown, Jimmy observed, but his face still seemed molded from lumps of discolored rubber, and envy and resentment glinted behind the otherwise listless expression in his eyes.

"Glad to see you home, Nuri," Jemel said.

"It's better than where I was," Nuri responded sullenly.

"I—uh—I can imagine."

"I doubt it."

George Rickard, obviously more keeper than companion, stepped forward. "Let's take our afternoon walk now, Nuri," he said.

"See you later," Jemel said uncomfortably. Nuri made no reply.

Jemel directed his attention to his little sister. Felicite was being very much the coquette.

"Got any new girlfriends?" she asked, giving Jimmy the full treatment with her great dark eyes and needlessly adjusting the crinkly-fresh ribbon-bow tied in the back of her long, tawny-blonde hair. Mademoiselle Claire Viete stood nearby, watching it all and beaming.

"A few," Jimmy replied.

"Are they pretty?"

"You wouldn't want me going around with ugly ones, would you?"

"Prettier than me?"

"Oh, no!" Jimmy assured her, and she relented, allowing herself to be picked up and fondly nuzzling his cheek. My God, he thought, Felicite was only six —what would she be like in another ten years? He laughed. Jemel and his father retreated to Hassan's study and talked.

"I'll have to register for the draft next month," Jimmy reminded Hassan.

"Mike Ferrenbaugh guarantees your permanent

exemption," Hassan said. "He'll come to New York and personally see you through the routine."

"I hope there won't be any slip-ups," Jemel said. He had taken out his Moslem prayer beads.

"Since when have you carried a *sibah?*" Hassan asked in surprise.

"For months. I guess I never got around to showing it to you when I was home for spring vacation or on weekends. It's a token of esteem from my classmates." He related how he, Russell Stanton, and Marvin Jacobs had found *sibah,* tin beggar's cup, and six-pointed cardboard star with their accompanying messages on their beds one afternoon.

Jimmy's sharp-cut features had turned glacially cynical. "In case I ever get giddy and feel any patriotic spasms coming on, the *sibah* will cure me."

"Yeah, we do lose out on some good deals," Douglas Ford told Jemel. A stocky, ruddy-faced man in his mid-twenties with a heart murmur that exempted him from military service, Doug Ford was one of Karami & Co.'s two "expediters" who searched the black market for scarce items.

"Your dad believes in playing it super-safe," Ford said. Only after a bona fide order had been received did Karami & Co. scour the market to obtain the goods or items to fill it. "So, instead of grabbing stuff when it's offered comparatively low, we usually have to buy pretty high."

Consequently, Karami & Co. often had to settle for slender profits when, by having purchased earlier, it could have made much more. True, it was all profit, Jimmy conceded, steady and safe, but his father's caution was excessive under prevailing conditions. He tried to convince Hassan.

"When the war started, we bought copper and aluminum outright," he argued. "You held on and more than doubled your investment later. Why not do the same now? Prices fluctuate. Buy what comes on the market when prices dip, hold, then sell when we get a peak-price order?"

It had been different at the start of the war, Hassan countered. Then, there was absolute certainty that shortages would develop and prices would soar. The situation had changed.

"New productive capacity is increasing at a fantastic rate. Anything that's in short supply could become plentiful at any time."

"Not until the war ends," Jemel protested.

Hassan remained adamant. It *could* happen. If he bought something outright and it became available through normal channels, the black-market price of the item would plummet. Karami & Co. would lose heavily.

"I refuse to take any risks," he declared. "Not with money. I am a merchant, not a plunger."

Jimmy was certain the policy was shortsighted. However, he recognized that further argument would be futile.

Going through the Karami & Co. files, Jemel noted a gradual dwindling of government purchase orders over the preceding six months. He said nothing to his father, waiting until Senator Michael Ferrenbaugh arrived in New York, to arrange his draft exemption. He found a chance to speak with Ferrenbaugh alone and casually mentioned the subject of the purchase orders.

"I've been trying to make Hassan see the light," Iron Mike grumbled. "The wild buying is almost over."

"Somebody's getting contracts, though," Jimmy said.

"Sure, but not brokers. I've been telling your father he should invest half a million or so, start any kind of war plant. Then I could get him additional capital in government money plus big long-term contracts."

Jemel had new respect for Ferrenbaugh; he wasn't such a dull, plodding workhorse after all. But Hassan could never be made to invest—to "risk," by his definition—even a fraction of half a million dollars.

They chatted about other things—including Ferrenbaugh's family.

"Y'know, my daughter's never forgotten you," Mike said. "Mickey is always asking about you. She'd

be in seventh heaven if you found time to send her a
postcard, Jimmy."

Jemel went through the motions of registering for
the draft just like any other eighteen-year-old male in
the country. Then, after Senator Ferrenbaugh pulled his
backstage strings, Jimmy was given a travesty of a
medical examination.

A draft-board doctor placed a set of X-ray negatives into Jimmy's Selective Service medical file. They
were chest X rays. The doctor hadn't the faintest notion whose they had been originally. Now they were
labeled "Karami, Jemel," and proved at a glance that
his left lung had already resigned its functions and the
right would soon follow suit.

Jimmy was issued a draft card that declared him
4-F, permanently disqualified from any form of military service. The same day that he received the card,
Jimmy went to F.A.O. Schwarz, bought the most
splendid doll he could find, wrote a short note that began, "Dear Mickey," and had both airmailed to "Miss
Michele Ferrenbaugh."

2

When Jimmy returned to Dunhill College in September, Russ and Marv accepted his announcement of
4-F draft status without question. That was how the
ball bounced. A little luck, and maybe the war would
be over before their own draft boards sent them greetings.

Jemel Karami's memories of his second semester
at Dunhill would always remain somewhat blurred.
He'd spent the summer working, active in the market-
place, which he recognized as his natural element. He
found himself increasingly exasperated by those who
taught him and by what they taught. His instructors

sermonized theories of how things should be, and these contradicted what he knew from experience to be the realities of practice.

Nevertheless, he kept up his studies. Studying together with his two roommates was easy—and a source of laughs and of malicious satisfaction. They continued to maintain the highest averages, further increasing the envy and animosity of their fellow freshmen—who had virtually ostracized them.

Ambition gnawed at Jemel and ideas formed in his mind. He daily scanned the *Wall Street Journal,* the *Journal of Commerce* and other business publications, searching for the sure-fire opportunity he felt he must inevitably find.

At the end of the second freshman term, Marvin Jacobs again held the number-one position in academic averages. Russ was next, Jemel third.

Their sophomore year began under what Russell and Marvin considered promising auspices. The February 1944 national draft call was only for 75,000 men, the lowest monthly quota since December 1941.

"Maybe none of us will have to play soldier," Russ ventured hopefully.

He spoke too soon. Heavy battle casualties created a demand for more healthy bodies. In March 1944, the draft call leaped to more than 233,000— the highest monthly quota in a very long time.

Russell Stanton received his induction notice on March 9th. Marvin Jacobs's arrived less than a week later.

Jemel, in the meantime, believed he had found his opportunity. He remained, doing some additional private research until the spring vacation began. Then he packed all his things and returned to New York, firmly determined to stay and fully prepared for the clash with his father.

Jimmy bluntly stated he did not intend going back to college.

"I'm sick of hearing professors who couldn't run a hotdog stand spout horseshit like lectures on 'The

Internal Dynamics of the Organization Chart,'" he declared.

Hassan flew into a rage. "You must have a college education!"

"Why?" Jimmy shrugged. "You can buy men with college degrees—and cheap. Look at George Rickard. He has a bachelor's, and you pay him what? Fifty a week plus room and board to be Nuri's nursemaid?"

The storm reached its peak one evening in Hassan's study.

"By God, you'll obey me!" Hassan roared. "Until you reach twenty-one, I'll make all the decisions for you!"

"Not all," Jemel said quietly. "I can go to the draft board anytime and request reexamination and immediate induction." It was an empty threat he would never carry out, but it stunned Hassan into silence. Jimmy's next lines were rehearsed, conciliatory to permit Hassan to save some face.

"Let me make you a business proposition. I think I've discovered a gold mine. Suppose I work for Karami & Co. until the fall term starts. If I haven't made the company fifty thousand dollars in gross profit by then, I'll go back to college. If I go over the mark, I stay out for good."

Hassan parried with sarcasm. "You talk big. How much of my capital do you expect me to pour into your venture—whatever it is?"

"None. I'll buy only against firm orders—*and* get same-day payment on delivery. I want only the same commission deal as Doug Ford has—twenty percent on the gross profit I bring in."

"What is this 'gold mine?'" Hassan's tone was gruff, grudging.

"Newsprint."

"The paper on which newspapers and cheap magazines are printed?"

"Yes. I've checked this through carefully. Listen..."

The War Production Board severely limited newsprint output and consumption; the Office of Price Administration set a $48-per-ton ceiling on its mill-price. But demand was skyrocketing. Daily newspapers were paying $250 a ton and more for every extra scrap they could feed into their presses. A newsprint black market was emerging, with Manhattan as its trading center.

"Where would you buy tonnage?" Hassan asked, his interest kindled.

"It can be found." Some newsprint mills produced more than their legal quotas, sold the excess through middlemen at inflated prices. Some marginal magazine publishers and others with WPB allotments were side-dooring part of their tonnage into the black market.

Hassan capitulated. "You have until September." He didn't believe Jemel could reach the $50,000 goal, and failure would bring him to heel.

3

Jimmy was painfully aware that his father's smile grew more knowing and ironical with each passing day.

By the middle of June, Jemel had earned some $8,000 in gross profits for Karami & Co.—a very long way from the $50,000 minimum—and he was plagued by the knowledge Hassan was convinced he'd never make the grade.

Then, one morning, the telephone rang in the cubicle that served as Jimmy's office. The publisher of the Pittsburgh *Herald* was calling. He'd heard from some source or other that Jemel dealt in newsprint.

"We need four hundred tons in seventy-two-inch rolls."

Jimmy almost whooped. Here was a really big order. A coup. He'd never heard of 72-inch-wide rolls before, but he confidently said, "Cost you two hundred sixty dollars a ton, f.o.b. shipping point. Establish a credit with a New York bank for one hundred four thousand dollars payable against shipping documents, and you'll get your paper."

The publisher was cagy. "We can't print on telephone promises," he said. "I'll establish a thirty-day credit if you confirm the order on your corporate letterhead and state that you'll pay a ten thousand dollar penalty in the event you fail to deliver before the credit lapses."

Jemel swallowed. "The letter will go out today." He hung up, chewing worriedly on his lower lip. Hassan would never agree to the penalty clause. But damn it, the order meant anywhere up to $25,000 in profit!

He locked his office door, pulled his typewriter table closer to his chair. He was nervous, jumpy and his lower lip took hard punishment while he typed out a letter to the Pittsburgh *Herald*. When it was finished, he stared for several minutes at the space above the typed lines reading: "Hassan Karami, President, Karami & Co." Then he uncapped a fountain pen and signed his father's name. He mailed the letter himself. He told his father only that he'd taken a telephone order, and that a credit would be established by the customer.

The Pittsburgh *Herald* established a 30-day, $104,000 credit on June 28th.

Now Jimmy could start shopping around. He began telephoning his sources—paper merchants, brokers and all-around black-market operators. The answers he got to his inquiries were not very encouraging.

"What width rolls? Seventy-two-inch? Don't have a one . . ."

"Hell, Jimmy, that's a bastard size for a limited-series-model Scott press. Tough to find . . ."

"I haven't heard of any seventy-two-inch newsprint in God knows how long . . ."

Just have to keep trying, Jimmy thought at the end of a fruitless day.

FRIDAY, JULY 20th. The date screamed up at Jemel from the desk calendar, and his stomach knotted even tighter. Eight days—no, six working days—left to pull 400 tons of rabbit out of the hat, and he'd tried everything. Many times.

Jemel hadn't been able to locate an ounce of newsprint in 72-inch-rolls, and July 27th was the deadline. With emphasis on the dead, he told himself grimly. If he couldn't deliver, Hassan would find out about the $10,000 penalty—and that Jemel had forged his signature to the letter confirming the order.

Jimmy racked his brains. Nothing new. Nothing but to make the same old telephone-tries again. He started through his list.

"I've told you before, Mr. Karami. We never have any seventy-two-inch . . ."

"Could sell you sixty-six- or sixty-seven-inch, but not the width you need . . ."

Same tries, same results, Jimmy thought with gut-wrenching despair. He dialed yet another number, dully recited his unvarying inquiry.

"Seventy-twos? Only outfit I know with presses using that size is Corley up in Springfield, Mass."

"Who?" Jemel, tensed to lunge at any straw, hadn't heard the name before.

"Corley Press. Prints for Bice and for Decker. Both duds. Neither of them will side-door. Well, sorry . . ."

Jimmy knew of Bice Periodicals, a subsidiary of a company far too big for it to engage in any black marketing. But Decker was another name new to him. He referred to his magazine publishers' directory. Decker Publications. A Madison Avenue address. Alfred Decker, president and publisher. Comic books, confession, and detective magazines. Jemel thought hard, hoping against hope, acutely conscious that whatever he did, it would have to be done fast. He didn't have time to make tentative approaches, to haggle—or to chance a turndown if there was any possibility at all.

He made another phone call, to the Palmer National Trust Co. Miles Palmer had been appointed to a

"War Economic Planning Board" and spent much of his time in Washington. Jemel asked for Palmer's assistant, Charles Stewart.

"I'm calling for my father," he said. "We need some information . . ."

Bankers easily obtain meticulous credit-data from a multitude of sources. By 4:00 P.M. Stewart had a complete report on Alfred Decker and his company Jemel listened intently, making notes while he did.

"Thanks," he said when the banker was finished. "That's a help." It was more than that, Jimmy told himself. It was a glimmer of hope—but only if he did a dangerous tightrope walk. He had to. There was no choice.

Early Monday morning, Jemel took a train to Springfield, Massachusetts.

The Corley Press was housed in a complex of old red-brick buildings laminated with grime. Jemel sat in a cluttered office that smelled of printer's ink, opened a notebook, glanced at it and spoke.

"I'm here to see you about $73,209, Mr. Corley. The amount of a past-due bill owed you by Decker Publications."

Howard Corley, a moonfaced man, flushed angrily. That was the correct—the exact—figure, but how did his visitor know and what affair was it of his? "You have a damned funny way of starting a conversation!" he growled.

"Funny? Mr. Corley, Decker Publications owes more than three hundred and seventy-five thousand dollars—with actual assets of less than one hundred fifty thousand dollars. Did you know that?"

Corley stared. Decker was an old client who usually dragged on payments, but he'd never suspected Alfred Decker was that bad off—and this Karami bird appeared to have accurate information. "No, I didn't," he said.

"Would you sell Karami & Co. Decker's bill for face value?" Jemel asked. It was pure bluff.

"What in hell would you want with it?" Corley snapped back.

The tightrope swayed a little. Jemel steadied himself. "Leverage," he said and took another step. "Consolidated Paper ships in three hundred tons of WPB allotted tonnage for Decker's account each month. Right?" Howard Corley was dismayed by the details Karami knew. "What does he have stored up?" There had to be some reserve against delayed shipments or other contingencies.

"Around five hundred, five hundred fifty tons," the printer blurted—and saw a look that reminded him of a buzzard closing in to feed come over Jemel Karami's face.

"We want to buy four hundred tons of Decker's seventy-two-inch newprint—at two hundred dollars a ton," Jimmy said smoothly.

"He won't sell," Corley declared. "He'd be crazy to sell his reserve."

Jemel gazed at the ceiling. "How much do you think you'd collect if Decker Publications went bankrupt, Mr. Corley?" he inquired softly. "With the debts-versus-assets picture being what it is, that's not an impossibility. Now, if you sold his obligation to us, we would demand immediate payment—and Decker can't raise the cash." At least I hope he can't. "He'd be forced to sell us the newsprint."

He couldn't afford to lose $73,000, Corley admitted to himself. Who could?

"It would be a rotten trick," he said. "Decker's an old customer."

Jimmy's feet were secure on the rope. "I'll see Decker in New York tomorrow and offer him eighty thousand dollars on the line for the newsprint. Seventy-three of that will be yours—if you play along. I'll tell him frankly I was here and offered to buy his printing bill. He'll be sure to phone you and check up on me. When he does, just say whatever you think best."

"I'll have to say I want my money," Corley thought. He wet his lips.

"When would Al get the eighty thousand from your company?"

"As soon as he has the warehouse receipts covering four hundred tons of newsprint ready to sign over to Karami & Co.," Jimmy replied.

"He'll have them by Wednesday afternoon if he can't cover my bill otherwise," Corley declared. "I'll bring them down to New York myself."

4

Elinor Randolph was fed up. Her job as an editor for Decker Publications had proved to be a dismal dud. Then Alfred Decker had just fired the receptionist, forcing Elinor to do double-duty until a replacement could be found.

She sat at the receptionist's desk, proofreading a confession story galley. "Christ, what ghastly tripe," she thought. The outer door opened.

"Good morning." A deep-timbred voice. A young man, tall and offbeat handsome. Not a usual salesman or bill collector type. "I'm Jemel Karami. I have a noon appointment with Mr. Decker."

The girl called an inner office. Jemel made a quick inventory. She was a beauty. Red hair. Green eyes. Silk-print dress generously filled at the bustline. Engagement and wedding rings on left hand . . .

"He'll see you. I'll take you to his office." She stood up.

. . . . shapely legs. A delightful, ungirdled *derrière* . . . plus an air . . .

"Thank you, Mrs. . . ?"

Observant man, she thought. "Randolph. Elinor Randolph."

"For you, Mrs. Elinor Randolph." He'd taken something from his briefcase.

"What is it?" Elinor was disappointed. He was a salesman after all.

"A Longchamps menu. You can decide what

you'd like to have when we go to lunch after I've talked with your boss." If he succeeded with Decker, he'd want to celebrate. If not, the girl would briefly divert his mind from thoughts of the onrushing disaster.

Elinor's laugh was throaty. "That's the smoothest approach of the year." She put the menu on her desk, gave Jemel a long look.

Alfred Decker, lanky, fortyish, and with the raddled complexion of a heavy drinker, reached across mountains of paper to shake Jemel's hand.

"Take that chair, Mr. Karami," he said. "What's on your mind?"

"Newsprint."

"Shit!" Decker said, yawning. "That's bothering a lot of people these days. Not me, though. I don't need any more, thanks."

"I'm not selling, Mr. Decker. I'm buying. You have some excess in storage. Karami & Co. will buy four hundred tons of it—at two hundred dollars a ton."

Decker snorted. "Sell my reserve and have the WPB and OPA hit me with a year in the federal pen? You've got the wrong sucker, friend!"

"There's no risk the way we work."

"Oh, no?" It was a belligerent sneer.

"No. Your paper is wound on nonreturnable cores. Serial numbers on the wrappers only. We cut the numbers out of the wrappers. We ship the rolls from your printer's to Camden, reload there into different freight cars consigned to a dummy, say, in Ohio, and divert to our customer en route. Impossible to trace the paper back to you."

"Balls!" Decker snarled. "I'm not selling—so beat it, huh?"

Jemel remained seated. "Would you rather we bought your printing bill and demanded immediate payment?"

The publisher leaped to his feet, booze-scarred face livid. "What the hell are you trying to pull, you hook-nosed bastard?" he shouted.

Jimmy's manner was placid. "I was in Springfield yesterday and offered Howard Corley $73,209 for your overdue bill."

"And he told you to go fuck yourself!" Decker rasped.

"Not exactly. He'd rather not sell the bill, but I think he's about to demand his money. Why not give him a call?"

Alfred Decker hurled himself back into his swivel-chair, grabbed his telephone. "Get me Howard Corley!" he barked and slammed down the handset.

Jemel felt jagged icicles sawing at his spine. Corley could have had second thoughts, or Decker might have money squirreled away against just such an emergency. Jimmy knew the next few minutes would make or break him.

The telephone rang. Decker snatched it up, clamped the instrument to his ear. "Howie? Al Decker. There's a prick in my office by the name of Karami. He claims he talked to you yesterday, and ..."

Decker's voice trailed off. He listened. His face turned grayish.

"For Christ's sake, Howie, you know how it is in publishing. I'm a little tight on cash at the moment, but ..."

He fell silent again and listened—for two, perhaps three minutes. They must have seemed long to Decker. To Jemel, they were endless.

"Yeah, I see, Howie," Decker said finally, his voice hoarse, uneven. "You need the dough. Okay, Howie," He replaced the handset slowly.

The thousand springs coiled tight inside Jemel uncoiled simultaneously. He met Decker's helplessly malevolent glare.

"Corley will be here tomorrow at one with the warehouse receipts," the publisher grated.

Neither of them thought of shaking hands when Jemel left.

Jimmy's pulse pounded. He was in the clear. No penalty payment—and Hassan wouldn't learn of the forgery. He felt pressure building in his loins.

"Hungry?" he asked Elinor Randolph when he reached the reception room. She nodded, set up the switchboard.

"We'll go to the Plaza," he said.

"The Plaza? I thought we were going to Longchamps!"

"I'm in an expansive mood." Their eyes met and held for a moment.

Jemel ordered a daiquiri for Elinor, a Crawford's scotch sour for himself.

"To the Longchamps menu!" Jimmy toasted, raising his glass.

Elinor gave him an amused glance. "Does it always work?"

"Almost always." Feminine vanity would have to respond. It did.

"And do you always come here instead?"

"No. Only on special occasions." Their eyes met again—and he was certain the chemistry was working both ways.

Elinor saw that Jemel was very much at ease in the Plaza. He spoke flawless French when ordering lunch and wine. Then he turned his attention to her.

Elinor came originally from Baltimore. Her parents were alive, her father a prosperous insurance agent. She was twenty-two, a Goucher graduate. She had majored in English Lit and wanted to be a writer. The Decker Publications job was her first. She'd had it a few weeks and didn't like it.

". . . but it's too much trouble to quit and look for another," she sighed between *foies* and *tournedos*. "What with Bob in Australia . . ."

"I'm sorry," Jemel interrupted. "I take it Bob is your husband?"

"Oh! Yes. We were married last January, just before he went overseas."

The feeling in Jemel's groin became painful. Some of the intensity of his desire communicated itself to Elinor, heightening that which she'd found growing within herself.

"Bob and I had one weekend together," she

thought, avoiding Jimmy's eyes. "Now I'm a second lieutenant's wife. I write a V-mail letter each day, get one occasionally from Bob—and at night I'm so lonely I want to scream." She sliced into her *tournedos*.

"So," she said. "I'm in a state of animated suspension—oops, that's a fine Freudian slip—a state of suspended animation until Bob comes home."

She looked up. Her gaze locked with Jemel's. He touched her hand. The sensation was galvanic. Suddenly it was all there, implicit, potent. For an instant, she fought it. But why? Bob Randolph was a physical-training officer who gave cooks and clerks their setting-up exercises and spent his weekends in Melbourne. Elinor tried to eat. It was useless. She was burning.

Jimmy signaled a waiter, told him to bring a telephone.

"This isn't an afternoon to be cooped up in an office," he said.

"No," Elinor agreed in a whisper. "No, it isn't."

The telephone appeared on the table. Jemel picked up the handset, gave the operator the Decker Publications number, and placed the handset in Elinor's unresisting fingers. She spoke to someone, said something about having become ill and being unable to return that afternoon.

Elinor sat close to Jimmy in the taxi. He was conscious of the hard press of her breast against his arm, the brush of her flame-colored hair against his cheek. He touched her face, traced his fingertips over her lips. They parted, and she caught his fingers between her teeth, bit them gently. Jimmy pressed the ball of his thumb against her chin, then drew his hand away.

"My God!" Elinor murmured. That alone had brought her almost to orgasm.

They entered her apartment, went directly into the bedroom.

Jemel took her in his arms, kissed her, his tongue probing. He eased down the zipper of her dress, slipped the dress off her shoulders, let it fall. She responded wildly, crying protest when he took his mouth from hers, moaning with pleasure when he kissed her throat, removed her slip and bra and moved his mouth to her breasts, his tongue lingering on the nipples.

His hands slid her panties down past her hips, and they, too, fell to the floor. She tore open the zipper of his trousers, grasped his erect sex. She pressed it against herself, rubbing it against her smegma-drenched labia and clitoris. Within seconds, she gasped, every muscle taut and climaxed.

"Here," Jemel murmured, leading Elinor to the bed. He watched her kick off her shoes and lie down without even bothering to remove the bedspread. He took off his clothes quickly, gazing at her while he did, savoring the perfection of her body, the glint of the fiery red swirl of the hair loose around her head and its fine, silky counterpart that formed a triangle at the juncture of her thighs.

"Jimmy," she called to him. Naked, he went to the bed. He was beside her, hands and mouth moving over her body. They coupled, and her arms and legs gripped him.

Elinor lay, euphoric and unbelieving, gazing at Jimmy Karami's classic-sharp profile. She had lost all concept of time. She had not been to bed with very many men, but she had thought that most of them had satisfied her. Now, she told herself, I know they were clumsy, awkward, callow.

"Jimmy?" she asked on sudden impulse. "How old are you?"

"Nineteen in a few weeks." He saw no reason to lie.

"What?" She raised her head, incredulous. "You *can't* be that young!"

"I am. Does it make a difference?"

She repeated the question to herself, and said, "No. Not anymore."

"That could mean almost anything."

"It means I don't care how old you are. If you want to make love to me again tomorrow or next week or . . ."

"Even right now?"

He couldn't be serious. "Jimmy, it isn't possible so soon after . . ."

Then she saw his sex, rigid and straining.

"Yes, even right now!"

When he stirred to raise himself, Elinor pressed her hands against his shoulders and covered his mouth with hers. Elevating her own body, she twisted, shifting her left leg until she was astride his hips and sank down, swallowing him inside her.

5

The "Decker deal"—as he would always call it in his mind—was the first major turning-point in Jemel Karami's business career. The newsprint he coerced Alfred Decker into selling enabled Jimmy to meet the Pittsburgh *Herald* order less than forty-eight hours before the crucial deadline.

The success added immeasurably to his self-confidence and further fuelled his drive. He knew he had turned the corner—and by the end of August 1944, he had exceeded the $50,000 gross-profit minimum by several thousand dollars.

Hassan grudgingly lived up to his end of the bargain. Jemel would not return to college, but would continue to work for Karami & Co.

Jimmy saw Elinor Randolph frequently after their first afternoon. The girl was not only wonderful in bed, but a good companion. They had much (but, thank God, Jimmy thought, not too much) in common. They both enjoyed dancing, swimming, horseback riding, tennis, the theater. Their moods seldom clashed, and they laughed at much the same things.

Elinor quit Decker Publications and obtained a job as a bottom-rung employee in the editorial department of the New York *Daily News*.

"You've brought me luck, Jimmy!" she said the

evening after she was hired by the *News*. "I've got my start! I'll write yet one of these days!"

Although he congratulated her warmly, Jemel failed to recognize that Elinor Randolph's ambitions were hardly less powerful than his own.

Their relationship developed into a continuing affair. Jemel found it more gratifying than any he'd ever had before. He knew Elinor had fallen in love with him, but this caused him no great worry. Her absent husband provided the protection factor.

Jimmy branched out, dealt in other things besides newsprint. He shared a spacious office with Douglas Ford. He and the short, rather beefy Ford had always got on well, and they entered into friendly rivalry, vying to see which of them could make the biggest and best deals—and, naturally, earn the largest commissions.

This led the third "expediter" working for Karami & Co. to complain that Jimmy and Ford were "hogging the best propositions," and, finally, to leave. He was not replaced, and Jemel's work pace grew even more hectic.

Aside from work, the months that followed were marked by several incidents that were to have varying degrees of aftereffect on Jimmy's life—and on his business career.

Russell Stanton stopped off in New York during the first week of November. He sported corporal's chevrons and was going to spend a seven-day leave with his mother in Rutland before embarking for service in Europe.

Russ wasn't surprised to hear that Jemel had no intentions of ever completing his college education.

"I never really figured you'd stay the whole four years, Jimmy," he said. "You've got the touch—and you'll probably be a millionaire."

"I hope so," Jemel said.

"So do I," Stanton grinned. "I may have to come around and ask you for a job when I'm in civvies again." Russ was only joking, but his remark gave

Jemel an idea to be held in suspense for future reference.

A few weeks later, Marvin Jacobs telephoned Jemel from Fort Ord in California. He was being sent overseas. Somewhere in the Pacific theater.

"No furlough to see your family before you go?" Jemel asked.

"Only five days. Not enough for the round trip by rail, and I can't get airline reservations. No priority."

"Crap! Sit tight and call me again in three hours. I'll fix it."

"If you can, I'll be grateful to you for the rest of my life, Jimmy."

"I know you will," Jemel thought, and an easy favor that earned undying gratitude was always a gilt-edged investment. He contacted a bureaucrat Karami & Co. carried on its bribe-rolls. "I want air-travel priority for a Private Marvin Jacobs. San Francisco to New York and return."

Everything was arranged before Marvin telephoned again.

At the year's end, Karami & Co.'s commission statements showed that Jemel had earned just under $20,000 as his share of the gross profits he'd produced for the company. When money he'd drawn in advance was deducted, he still had an $11,000 balance due to him.

He used part of the money to buy an Oldsmobile convertible, a 1942 model, one of the few produced before all civilian auto manufacture had been halted by government order. Although used, the car was in excellent condition—and, of course, cost an astronomical sum.

One evening in February 1945, Jimmy drove Elinor Randolph out to the Long Island North Shore for dinner. He sensed that she was excitedly holding back something she wanted desperately to tell him.

"Something good happen on your job today?" he asked.

"No. That is, yes. Everything's fine there."

Jimmy took a hand from the steering wheel and tugged at her red hair.

"Come on, out with the big news before you bust."

"It's Bob. . . ."

Jimmy dropped his hand.

". . . He's met a girl in Australia. He thinks we made a big mistake getting married and wants a divorce!"

Oh-oh, Jemel warned himself.

He saw her much less frequently, soon stopped seeing her altogether. Elinor called him several times at both his home and office, but he avoided speaking with her. After a time, the calls ceased.

An afternoon mail in March brought a V-mail letter from Russell Stanton. Russ had been given a battlefield commission for something or other he'd done during the 94th Division's assault crossing of the Saar, Jimmy read.

". . . and I'm thinking of staying in the army for a while," Russ wrote. "I'll try for a transfer to AMGOT after the shooting stops . . ."

Jimmy buzzed for the secretary he shared with Doug Ford. "Take an extra hour for lunch today," he told her. "Go someplace that sends food parcels overseas. Have the best there is sent to Lieutenant Stanton."

"I think you can enclose personal notes with the parcels," the secretary said. "Would you like to write one? I can take it with me."

Jemel's phone rang at that moment. He answered. A broker was offering 200 tons of cold-rolled steel. Jimmy cupped his hand over the mouthpiece. "You type something up and sign my name," he instructed and turned his attention back to the telephone. "Okay," he said. "What are the specs and price?"

There was, of course, a very frantic period right after the European war ended. Karami & Co.'s business dipped, but quickly recovered. American political and military leaders agreed that another year—maybe much longer—would be needed to defeat the Japanese in the Pacific. Most commodities remained in short supply. While a few prices softened, most remained steady. Some rose even higher.

In the midst of this confusion, Jemel received a letter from Marvin Jacobs. It was written in a shaky script. A staff sergeant in the 305th Infantry Regiment, Marv had lost his left arm while leading a combat patrol on Okinawa. He begged Jimmy to visit his parents.

". . . just for a few minutes. Tell them I'm okay except for the arm, and not in any neurotic tailspins. It'll reassure them if they hear it from someone besides me, especially since they know we're friends . . ."

Jimmy told himself he'd drive out to the Manhattan Beach section of Brooklyn, where the Jacobses lived. But he was in the midst of an involved deal. He put the visit off from one day to another. Finally, Marvin's request slipped his mind completely.

6

Atom bombs blasted Hiroshima and Nagasaki—and Japan surrendered.

There was reason for Jamel to go to Europe. Mike Ferrenbaugh slashed red tape, and Jemel received passport, special travel permits required for occupied areas, and letters introducing him to American officials on the Continent. He went first to Zurich, Switzerland.

Jimmy Karami's taxi turned into the Bahnhofstrasse, aorta of the awesome Swiss banking industry. The rectangular trolleys of trim, freshly painted and tandem-coupled tram cars sparkled against overhead wires. Stolid, overfed Swiss pedestrians bustled along antiseptic sidewalks lined at precisely spaced intervals with identically clipped trees. Walling the Bahnhofstrasse were the somber, bastionlike buildings that housed the central offices of the more important among Switzerland's 40,000 banking outlets.

Banks, Jimmy thought. *Perpetual-motion machines that generate money from money. The ultimate business, banking. Now, if someday . . .*

The taxi had stopped before the staid entrance to the Bauer Kreditbank. Jimmy paid the driver, wrestled a locked satchel out of the cab and went into the bank. Inside, the hushed, reverential atmosphere of a chapel royal. Jemel gave his name to a gray-suited sacristan who bobbed his head and said yes, the Herr Direktor was expecting Herr Karami and offered to carry the satchel, but understood instantly when Jimmy said no, and led the way.

The Herr Direktor was paunchy, pompously deferential. An older Miles Palmer, Jemel reflected with amusement as he hoisted the satchel up on a sturdy darkwood table, unlocked and opened it, exposing neatly-banded packets of American currency—$800,000 worth. The unreported wartime net profits of Karami & Co. The portion about which the U.S. Internal Revenue Service had been kept in ignorance.

"I imagine you will want to have someone make a count," Jimmy said in good school-learned German. He and the bank director chatted and sipped sweet hot chocolate while clerks counted and double-checked the money. Within half an hour, all the formalities were completed. The $800,000 had been deposited in a secret Bauer Kreditbank account Hassan Karami had arranged to have opened in his name. Jimmy's first chore was done.

The next morning, Jemel was in Vaduz, Liechtenstein. He left the Hotel Real and walked a few hundred yards to a modest, shingle-roofed three-story building. He climbed a flight of stairs to the second floor, stopped outside a frosted-glass-paneled door. He grinned. The names of some sixty different companies were painted on the panel in minuscule letters.

The attorney heard Jimmy out, adjusted his pince-nez, and said, "Yes, our laws permit *foreign* businessmen the utmost—ah—flexibility."

Flexibility? Jimmy smiled to himself. Liechtenstein gave foreign businessmen a year-round, no-limit shooting license. Dummy companies established there could conduct any form of business in absolute secrecy and enjoy absolute freedom from all taxes. No government—American or any other—could tax a corporation its citizens organized in Liechtenstein. Forming such a company required only $4,600 in founding capital, payment of a $115 fee to the principality and the appointment of a Liechtenstein attorney as "resident director."

Jemel glanced around the attorney's austerely furnished office again. A desk, some chairs, several filing cabinets, a coat stand.

"And what are your fees as resident director?" Jimmy asked. "One-half percent of the monies that pass through the company," the lawyer replied. A bargain, Jimmy thought, then remembered the sixty or so company names on the door. He wondered how many millions were channeled through the spartan office each year. The attorney must make a fortune with his half-a-percent. However . . .

"That is entirely satisfactory," he said. "I would like to retain you to organize the HJK Trading Corporation."

The lawyer was already taking printed forms from a desk drawer.

Jemel had convinced his father that Karami & Co. must sooner or later acquire a patina of respectability. He recommended they hire Russell Stanton and install him as a figurehead, an idea sparked originally by Stanton's casual remark about "coming around to ask for a job" when he was "in civvies" again. Russ would be an ideal figurehead. He had an impeccable WASP lineage and an outstanding war record. His concepts of friendship would make him fiercely loyal, reliable—and manageable. All these qualities would be invaluable assets as window dressing for peacetime Karami & Co. operations.

Jemel went to Munich from Vaduz.

He located Captain Russell T. Stanton's office in a Quonset hut erected on a bombed-out site near the gutted Rathaus on Adalbertstrasse. Russ, looking bigger and more athletic than ever in an Ike jacket decorated with rows of colored ribbons and a combat infantryman's badge, pumped Jemel's hands and pounded his back.

"What the hell are you doing in Munich?"

"I had business in Europe and thought I'd look you up."

"Where are you staying?"

"The VIP billets." Jemel carried Pentagon accreditation letters, courtesy of Senator Mike Ferrenbaugh. "Let's go over there and have a drink."

They took a corner table in the VIP billets club bar, ordered drinks, toasted each other heartily and periodically called for refills as they talked, bringing each other up to date.

Jimmy waited for a logical opening.

". . . and I heard from Marv last week," Russ said. "He's out of the hospital and the army, trying to get used to his tin arm."

"I'll call him soon as I'm back in New York," Jimmy said, and used this as his cue. "I'm glad to hear he's out of the army—but how about you? You're not going to make it a career?"

Stanton signaled a waiter for another round. "I'll stay in a couple more years and kill two birds. Draw captain's pay and work for my B.A. through USAFI —the Armed Forces Institute—at the same time. Earn while I learn."

He sounded content, Jimmy thought, but how could he be? An Army captain made slightly more than $300 a month. Russ would never be able to turn down the offer.

"Why waste the time?" he asked. "Get out now. There's a ten-thousand-a-year slot open for you on the Karami & Co. payroll." The figure alone should do it, but to make sure, use the friendship clincher. "We got along fine at college. We'll make a great team in business."

Russ stared into his glass. He didn't doubt Jimmy's sincerity for a moment—hell, Jemel Karami was one of his two best friends—and the offer was tempting. Almost irresistible. Almost. Only he wouldn't make that good a team, he mused. Russell T. Stanton, U.S. Army officer *pro tem,* was a Depression brat. He couldn't forget the story of his father's financial ruin and probable suicide, and he vividly remembered the tough times his mother and he had known. He wanted security. The thirty-year-climb sort of job with some rock-solid corporation. Dull, maybe, but assured and insured. No, he'd never fit into Jimmy Karami's free-wheeling kind of operation.

He looked up and said, "Thanks, Jimmy—but no. Wish I could accept—there isn't anybody I can think of I'd rather work with or for. But I've got my future planned about as far as it can be planned. I'm getting good experience in the job I'm doing here with Amgot, and I want that B.A."

It was clear that Stanton was determined, and it galled Jimmy. He'd been certain Russ would jump at the chance, had counted on it.

"The offer stands," he said. Stanton would always be useful window-dressing, and someday he might be more amenable. "If you ever change your mind . . ."

"I'll let you know, Jimmy. Believe me."

Russ leaned forward. "In the mood for wassail and saturnalia tonight?"

Jemel returned his mind. "What? Oh. Why not. What's available?"

"Grade-A nurses. Slightly shopworn WACS. *Schatzies*—any size and shape, all fairly well denazified. No swastikas on their moving parts, anyway."

"Find me something raw and way-out—and while you're at it, get me two."

The rough-scrub sex-bath helped ease some of the disappointment that rankled inside him.

The week after he returned to New York, Jemel arranged to have lunch with Marvin Jacobs. Marvin came to the Karami & Co. offices in the Lincoln Building. He looked gaunt and haggard, but he beamed when he shook Jimmy's hand.

"Been a long while, A-rab. Still lugging those prayer beads?"

Jimmy took the *sibah* from his pocket and exhibited it. "About the only memento I've kept from our dear old college days." He put the rosary back into his pocket. "And how are things going for you, Jew-boy?"

"I'm in fair shape—except for this," came the reply. Marvin tapped his artificial left arm with the fingers of his right. "I'm working hard, running Pop's garment business. It's Pincus Jacobs *and Son*, Inc, now."

"Has your father retired?"

"Yes and no. He's a typical Jewish father. My losing an arm hit him hard. Ulcers, nerves, high blood pressure. The *ganze tzimmis,* as we say in Yiddish."

Jemel studied Marvin's face uneasily. No, there was no sign of reproach. He's either forgotten that he wrote and asked me to see his parents or thinks the letter went astray, Jemel decided. He expressed his sympathies, and they spoke of other things for ten or fifteen minutes. Then, Jemel casually asked, "By the way, are you looking for more business?"

"Can't touch any," Marv said. "We're back-ordering eight months."

"Oh," Jimmy said, looking crestfallen and surprised—even though he knew every garment manufacturer in the country was in the same position. "Okay . . ."

"Hey, wait a minute. What do you need?"

"Look, if you're all booked ahead . . ."

Jemel finally allowed himself to be talked into confessing he wanted to order 4,000 dozen pair of men's work pants and as many shirts, and that he needed them within thirty days, for export.

Anyone else, and I'd tell him to come back and see me in a year, Marvin thought, and said, "No sweat. I'll bust into the production schedule. You'll have the stuff." He quoted Jemel a price that was exactly Pincus Jacobs & Son's cost. It was the least he could do for the friend who'd made it possible for him to get home before being shipped overseas.

That was how Jemel had anticipated it would be

when he took the order in Paris after seeing Russ
Stanton in Munich.

"Let's go have some lunch, Marv," he said.

7

The long-pent-up demand of war-ravaged European countries for every conceivable variety of merchandise was insatiable. European buyers and importers seemed to want everything, and they asked few
questions about quality or price.

Karami & Co. began concentrating heavily on export business, straining its deals through the profit-
catching colander of the HJK Trading Corp. Jemel
had established in Liechtenstein. The process was
simple, the results astounding. European customers
gave orders to HJK Trading Corp., which charged
them whatever the traffic would bear. Then, the dummy HJK Trading Corp. in turn ordered from Karami
& Co.—at prices that allowed Karami & Co. only
the most slender profit margins.

The large sums were netted by HJK Trading and
transferred into the secret Bauer Kreditbank account.
Both dummy Liechtenstein company and Swiss bank
account were beyond the reach of American tax authorities. Karami & Co. did, of course, pay U.S. taxes
—on its relatively small net profits. Tax agents could
ask no embarrassing questions. After all, if Karami &
Co. chose to sell to some European concern called
HJK Trading Corp. at much below the going market,
that was Karami & Co.'s affair.

Still, it would look better if Karami & Co. appeared to have a number of different overseas customers on its books, and Jemel made another trip to
Europe, organized several additional dummy corporations in Liechtenstein.

Hassan unbent sufficiently to indicate he was at last satisfied with Jemel's showing as a businessman.

"You are a Karami," he told Jimmy. "A merchant. I trained you well."

Jimmy didn't feel flattered. True, Hassan had taught him fundamentals, but his own aims and abilities far exceeded those of any "merchant." And, he rejected the thesis that all positive qualities stemmed from the Karami side of the family. He hadn't been very close to his mother, Annette, but he remembered her fondly enough and felt he'd inherited several qualities from her French blood—imagination and finesse among them. In Jemel's opinion, these were not traits that Karami "merchants" had ever possessed in any great abundance. However, he accepted Hassan's tossed-bone praise silently. There were other issues—large and small—over which he could better spend time and energy in arguments.

Among them was his conviction that Karami & Co. should expand—and rapidly. He urged Hassan to obtain more elaborate offices, hire more employees, enter into diversified business enterprises. Hassan obdurately refused, for all this would involve heavy outlays of capital—and risk. Jimmy viewed this as the purblind philosophy of a mentality not far removed from that of a *soukh*-stall moneychanger. He continued his urgings, even while fearing the cause lost as long as Hassan lived or controlled company and capital.

Then, typical of the small issues, was one that arose when Mike Ferrenbaugh announced his candidacy for a third consecutive Senate term. Jimmy suggested they contribute to Ferrenbaugh's campaign fund.

"You want me to give him a gift of money?" Hassan fumed. "He brings us no more government business, yet he still holds ten percent of Karami & Co.'s stock, from which he receives dividends!"

Jemel knew the dividends were based on the company's reported net; Mike shared in none of the siphoned-off profits. He tried to reason with Hassan. While their final citizenship papers would come through very shortly, there was never any telling when they'd need some special favor. As a third-term senator, Mike would have much more seniority and influence than before. He could be very useful again. His arguments were unavailing. Hassan refused.

Jimmy had accumulated a very sizable sum from his trading commissions. He could easily afford the $5,000 he personally gave Ferrenbaugh—as an insurance premium on his own future.

Iron Mike won his third term. Jemel's guess that he'd have increased influence proved correct. In June 1947, Ferrenbaugh was among the leaders of the Senate group that overrode Harry Truman's veto of the Taft-Hartley Labor Act. Jimmy was in his office, reading the *New York Times* account of the final vote when his secretary came in and said Hassan wanted to see him.

The squint-eyed Bedouin, looking ill-at-ease in his Western suit, leaped to his feet and presented himself before Hassan could make introductions.

"You do me honor, sir! I am Abdul el Muein."

His stilted English was further mangled by the harsh laryngeals and exaggerated consonants found in Arabic. As Hassan had done earlier, Jemel tried to make things easier by speaking Arabic. Abdul el Muein pleaded that they converse in English.

"It is my striving to exercise the tongue, if it does not offend you, sirs," he said, practically cringing. "I am of the hope that I shall improve my fluency, and I pray for you to indulge me."

Jemel studied the man with distaste. About thirty, he was scrawny and had a servile, yet furtive, air. A *Taiya* Bedouin. The *Taiya* were a Transjordanian tribe notorious for producing shifty lickspittles. Jemel sat down.

"Mister"—Hassan laid heavy emphasis on the word—"el Muein represents certain Palestinian sheikhs to whom Karami & Co. was recommended by some old friends of mine in Beirut who know that we have European contacts."

Not much enlightened, Jimmy gave a noncommittal grunt.

"We are being asked to act as buying agents and purchase some rather specialized technical equipment in Europe," Hassan added.

Jemel understood. Palestinian Arabs were waging a merciless guerrilla war against the Jewish residents of Palestine. "They want guns," he said.

"I have given your most honorable father a list, sir," Abdul el Muein interjected. Hassan held up some papers, dropped them back on his desk.

"What do you think, Jemel?" Hassan asked, lighting a cigarette.

Jimmy shrugged. "Buying is simple. Europe is loaded with weapons—British, American, German—left over from the war. Shipping is difficult. Arms have to be repacked, disguised as machinery. Then, railroad officials, customs guards, God only knows who else—all have to be bribed."

"Oh, that is known, sir!" the Bedouin exclaimed. "Delivery is required only to a seaport. Those whom I am honored to serve will dispatch a ship to the port."

"Where will the stuff be consigned?" Jemel inquired.

"Beirut," Hassan replied. "The merchandise will be slipped across the frontier by my friends who recommended us to the sheikhs."

Jimmy raised an eyebrow. "What about money?"

"*Mister* el Muein is authorized to pay us one million dollars—in cash. Three-quarters of the money is to be used for buying arms, transportation expenses, and bribes. The remainder is our fee." He stubbed out his cigarette. "Naturally, the sheikhs are in a great hurry to obtain the weapons. How soon do you think you can leave for Europe?"

Jemel's face was that of a falcon about to dive on his prey. "Tomorrow," he said. "For two hundred fifty thousand in clear profit, I pack fast."

8

Hassan Karami suffered a stroke in January 1948, and Jemel of necessity became president of Karami & Co.

Hassan's stroke left him unable to walk any considerable distance, and the fingers of his right hand moved only with great difficulty. While his mental faculties were not impaired, the psychological effect was crushing. Hassan realized that, at fifty-six, he had suddenly become a very old—and crippled—man. He spent most of his waking hours in his study. Sometimes, he read. More often he simply sat, brooding, cursing his fate.

His attitudes towards his children took strange forms. He belatedly and desperately sought to compensate for his long neglect of Nuri. He summarily dismissed George Rickard and tried to win shows of affection from the boy. Nuri, almost eighteen, and a nondescript blob, had ample native cunning to take advantage of the situation. He made endless demands —for a car, money, whatever whim moved him to desire—and Hassan agreed to everything.

He'd always shown fondness for Felicite, but now Hassan had less patience with her. A crippled, embittered man of fifty-six can find little common ground with a lively, effervescent little girl of ten. Their topics of conversation were few and soon exhausted, and he was unable to play with her. After half an hour at most, their talk would trail off into a dismal silence that irritated Hassan and perplexed his daughter.

At first, Hassan's attitude towards Jemel turned almost hostile. Jimmy, worried over his own future, made a great, and eventually successful, effort to analyze the reasons behind his father's behavior toward him.

Hassan had always sought to mold his firstborn son into his own image, and had convinced himself he'd done just that. He now saw Jemel as a duplicate of himself—but young, vital, in perfect health and in Hassan's place as head of Karami & Co. It was the most corrosive of ironies that what Hassan had fashioned could not reciprocate and mold Hassan into *his* youthful, healthy likeness.

Jimmy also recognized what Hassan did not. They had long been in competition with each other, and Hassan had constant need to prove that he was superior, and Jemel could only function with his instruction and guidance.

Arriving at this analysis, Jimmy made a major strategic retreat. He did nothing at Karami & Co. on his own initiative. He cleared every detail first with Hassan, and made himself convincingly meek and submissive. Hassan gloated over what he felt was a triumph, and the pendulum of his relationship with Jemel swung back to normal.

Galling as they were, Jimmy knew the restraints were necessary. Although he held the title of president of Karami & Co., Hassan still owned 90 percent of the company's stock and held tight control of all capital—to say nothing of his personal fortune.

Jemel forced himself to be patient, but he was looking ahead.

Douglas Ford scratched his forehead where scalp met receding hairline.

"Sure. I'll stick with the company, Jimmy," he said.

Jemel had been outlining his plans for expansion —when he could prevail on Hassan to turn stock and capital over to him.

"We may have quite a wait, though," Ford continued, his deceptively innocent, ruddy face serious. "Your father is stubborn." His tone changed. "Got anything else in mind as spadework in the meanwhile?"

"As a matter of fact, I have," Jimmy replied. "A personal buildup to get my name known, establish a reputation for me as boy wonder of the business world."

Ford nodded approvingly. "That can't hurt. It'll certainly give you a big headstart. I suppose you'll hire a PR firm for the job?"

"Only as a last resort. Retaining some public relations outfit is too obvious, and sometimes it doesn't work out. The best way is to let it all come naturally—and I think I may just be able to swing it."

Although Jimmy hadn't seen Elinor Randolph in more than three years, he'd remained aware of her existence, for she had become something of a celebrity.

It began when Elinor made temporary substitute for a *Daily News* woman's-page writer who'd quit in a huff. Her saucy, irreverent style and talent for spicing copy with libel-proof innuendo caught on. The *News* made her a society-cum-bedroom-gossip columnist. The title of her now nationally syndicated column, "Busybody" was turned into an unmistakable *double entendre* by the photograph of Elinor that appeared regularly at its head. She beamed an openly erotic smile at the readers and wore a sweater scooped low to partially expose her breasts and emphasize their impudent thrust.

Jimmy pondering the problem of renewing the acquaintance he'd axed, hit on an answer. He obtained a Longchamps menu, wrote on its front: "Hoping the approach still works. Jimmy." He went to the Plaza—it had to be the Plaza—and bought out the hotel florist's orchid supply. He had flowers and menu sent to Elinor Randolph's office, returned to his own.

She called him a few minutes before five. "Hello, Jimmy." Civil, but no warmth. "The orchid jungle is overwhelming." A pause, then a slight thaw. "The menu. You have quite a memory." Another temperature drop. "Sometimes."

"We were getting in too deep, Elinor. By now, the emotional knots should be unsnarled. I'd like to see you again."

"Very pretty speech. Shall I applaud?" Feminine pride was giving its old scars a lick.

"I really would like to see you again," Jimmy said, a hurt edge to his tone. "But if you . . ."

"Don't ham it up, Jimmy. It wouldn't be like you." A pause. "I'll admit I'm curious, too."

"How about drinks now and dinner later?"

"Drinks, yes. Dinner, no. I have a date." With amusement: "I'll take you literally. Meet you at Longchamps in the Chanin Building at five-thirty."

Success had added poised gloss to Elinor's beauty. She studied Jemel appraisingly as he radiated charm and attentiveness and congratulated her on the progress of her career.

"You know," she said when their second drinks were served. "I came to a conclusion about you a year or so ago, Jimmy. You're one of the world's bigger sons of bitches." *And the world's greatest lay and you know it and that's one of the things that makes you such a son of a bitch,* she added silently.

Jemel winced inwardly, said, "At least you've thought about me."

That I have, my friend, Elinor reflected. *That I have.*

He saw her green eyes soften, leaped at the cue. "Do you really have a dinner date tonight?" His tone and manner were wistful.

Elinor laughed. "Just because I was dumped by both you and a husband doesn't mean I can't find anyone to take me out. Yes, Mr. Karami, I *really do* have a date tonight." *With a man who's fascinating across a dinner table but acts like a squeamish mortician's assistant poking around a corpse when he's in bed. Just the same, you're not going to find out so soon and so easily how much I still want you, friend. I'll mull this over for a while.*

They drank. Elinor said she had to go home and dress for dinner. Jemel called for the bill and squirmed uncomfortably.

"What on earth's wrong with you?" Elinor asked.

Jimmy gave her a long look she remembered—all

too well—then grinned sheepishly and glanced down at his lap. "I'm afraid it'll show when I get up."

You rotten bastard, Elinor thought. *My glands are pumping and I'm soaked. You goddamned magnificent satyr.*

"Throw that control of yours—wait, I'll think of it—that *msik* into reverse," she said, glib and casual, but looking at her wristwatch to avoid his eyes. "I *must* leave." *Run, not walk to the nearest exit before I start making animal noises.*

He held her arm as they went out, the back of his hand pressing against her breast. It was agony for her, and she insisted on taking a taxi alone.

"When can *we* have dinner?" Jemel asked, helping her into the cab.

"I don't know. I'll have to check my calendar at the office."

"I'll phone you there tomorrow."

"All right—but not before noon," she forced herself to say.

Elinor Randolph claimed she was booked solid for over a week and none of her engagements were of the sort she could or wished to cancel. The first was entirely true; her work required her to make the Manhattan café society rounds to see and be seen almost every evening. The last was a slight embroidery that had its calculated effect.

"I can make it for dinner a week from Tuesday," Elinor told Jimmy.

He seethed afterward, grew crankier as the days went by. This wasn't what he'd expected, and while at Longchamps with Elinor there were many indications that led him to believe she was eager to resume their affair. He uneasily wondered if his instincts had misled him and admitted to himself that, his other motives aside, having again seen Elinor, he would like very much to pick up where he'd left off years before.

Tuesday finally arrived. Elinor had moved to an apartment in Gramercy Park. Jemel, long since graduated to fishtail Cadillacs—his latest a black convertible with bleached-white top—drove downtown to pick her up. She wore a green dress that accentuated the luster of her fiery red hair and allowed her breathtaking figure to make its own exclamatory statement.

He took her to the Stork Club, then still at a peak of popularity with New York café society. Too late, he recognized it as an error. Billingsley was cordial enough to him, but fawned over Elinor, and they were constantly interrupted by people who stopped by their table to greet Elinor and exchange a few words.

Jimmy ordered another bottle of Krug's Private Cuvée.

"You're famous," he remarked, masking his annoyance.

"I'm not," Elinor replied smoothly, "but the publicity hounds think I can help them become famous." She was secretly glad for the interruptions. They put Jemel on the defensive and kept her mind off things she didn't want to think about—yet.

Jimmy raised his glass, and then someone else passing by the table paused and spoke to Elinor. "It's fun to be a sadist every now and then," she thought, sensing—and relishing—Jimmy's discomfiture. She stretched her conversation with the table-hopper well beyond her own boredom point.

It was more difficult when she danced with Jimmy. *Think about carrying out the garbage and chatter away about what other women were wearing,* Elinor reminded herself. *I must congratulate myself, she thought afterward. Aside from a trace of moisture —on the palms—I managed beautifully.*

The drive home was more difficult still. She was alone with Jemel—and with memories and sensory recollections. *Steady, gal, one last effort,* she warned herself when Jimmy saw her to the entrance of her apartment building.

She kissed him fondly on the cheek. "It's been a lovely evening," she said. "I'd invite you up for a nightcap, but I have a murderous day tomorrow." *And a murderous rest-of-the-night. All I have to do is touch myself, and I'll go through the ceiling—but touch myself, I will. And often.*

"Let's do it again soon," Jemel said, smiling through mentally gritted teeth, his frustration boiling inside him. *Damn it, she couldn't have turned that cold!*

"Mm. I'd love to." *How much longer can I play sadist when I already feel like Joan at the stake myself?* "I don't think I have anything on Friday night." *By then, my bedroom ceiling will be a shambles, but maybe it'll be a new kick to have loose plaster dropping down on both of us.*

Elinor's resistance evaporated Friday night, and Jemel could never be certain how much of it had been originally contrived with malice aforethought.

When he took her home, she asked him upstairs to her large, tastefully traditional apartment. They had one drink—and then they were in bed.

"On top of me first," she murmured. "I want to feel your weight on me."

That told him she was still in love with him. Much later, the near-savage hunger with which her mouth brought him to tumescence and climax seemed explicit reiteration. It was past dawn before they slept.

The raucous buzz of a bedside clock awakened Jimmy. Elinor had turned off the alarm and was sitting up in bed, stretching. The coppery sheen of her hair against creamy shoulders and the gentle movement of her lovely breasts as she stretched aroused him instantly. He reached for her.

"Good morning, Jimmy," she said, and to his surprise, eluded his touch and got out of bed. "Both of you will have to wait," she smiled, glancing at his upthrust sex. "It's nine o'clock."

"Hey, it's also Saturday!" Jimmy protested.

"I still have to make my morning calls." She had slipped into a dressing gown. She went to a desk at the other side of the room, sat down in the chair before it, and, after readying pad and pencils, pulled the desk telephone closer and began making calls—to the *News,* to various individuals, getting tips and items for her column. It took her an hour.

At first, Jemel thought the feeling of near-jealousy

was inspired by immediate sexual disappointment. Then, watching Elinor concentrating on telephone and notes, oblivious to his presence, he began to realize that her real love was her work, and that he and anything else were secondary to her career ambitions. Why he should resent this, he didn't quite understand.

"There," Elinor said finally, swinging around to face him. "I do that every morning to fill in the bits and pieces."

Jimmy shook his head dolefully, patted his now flaccid member, pretended to speak to it. "See what it's like to go around with a famous girl?"

Elinor grinned. "I told you before. It's not me. It's other people. They want to become or to stay famous. I just help ballyhoo them."

The remark suddenly reminded Jemel he was only halfway home with Elinor. Maybe it was a good time to drop a casual hint or two. He cupped his palm around his recumbent member, raised it.

"We're in the wrong business, my boy," he said sternly. "And sit up and listen when I talk." He removed his hand. His sex grew rigid, and stood erect. "That's better. Now, why don't you and I go into the fame-making business?" He flexed muscle. The blue-veined column of flesh appeared to bob in assent.

"The pair of you are famous already," Elinor said. An amplified echo of what she thought and said when she'd met Jimmy at the Longchamps came to her mind. It's his prick that helps make him such a prick. She burst out laughing—not at the line, but at the idea it generated, an idea that tickled her sense of the sardonic.

"Jimmy," she said, the laugh throttled down to a peculiar, cynical smile. "You'd like to be famous, wouldn't you?" She didn't dream it was a question he wanted to hear from her, but then, it hadn't been inspired the way he'd intended.

He stared at her, startled. Had he been that clumsy and obvious? No, while there was something in her tone, it wasn't accusation or recrimination. He combed fingers through his black hair to gain a moment.

"Yes, I suppose so," he said. "Who wouldn't?"

Elinor's smile remained unchanged. *At least he doesn't deny it,* she thought. "I'll help make you famous," she said. "Once I start plugging you in my column, the rest of the herd—Knickerbocker, Sullivan, Kilgallen, all the others—will follow like sheep. You'll be a celebrity, Jimmy."

He was unnerved. It had been much too easy. Something was wrong somewhere. "Why should you?" he asked, studying her face.

"I think it'll be fun to play God," she replied. She stood up, took off the dressing gown. *I'll do it because I know exactly what you are,* she said to herself—*and I deserve to play a dirty inside joke on myself for being in love with you.*

She walked toward the bed.

Elinor Randolph's "Busybody" column began to carry items about Jemel Karami at the rate of one every week or ten days.

"That Boy Wonder of the Business World, Jemel 'Jimmy' Karami lunched at '21' yesterday. A sharp-eared waiter heard him discussing a million-dollar deal with a top-flight financier as casually as a corner grocer quotes the price on a can of peas . . ."

"My confidential poll of glamor girls qualified to judge from sexperience gives suave Jimmy Karami a two-to-one margin over Aly Khan in the Best Man (and not at weddings) Sweepstakes."

Elinor was right about her colleagues. They followed her lead, each writing as though he or she had personally discovered the exotic, intriguing Jemel Karami.

Jimmy was acquiring the reputation and status on which he would build in the future, and he was already seeing some concrete results in the form of added business and profits. But they were still slow and to him minor.

The British evacuation of Palestine and the establishment of the Free State of Israel raised his hopes for quickening the pace. The guerrilla warfare that had raged for years erupted into full-scale war. Egypt,

Syria, Jordan, Iraq, Lebanon—the entire Arab world —were ranged against Israel.

It was an easy matter for Jemel to reestablish contact with Abdul el Muein. The *Taiya* Bedouin had advanced in rank and was able to give Jimmy—and the HJK Trading Corp.—larger orders than before for weapons to be shipped to various Arab forces battling the Israelis. The profits made from selling guns to Arabs were further swollen—from entirely different sources and almost by accident.

Jemel's secretary announced a Mr. Marvin Jacobs.

"Send him in." Jimmy wondered what Marvin would be doing at Karami & Co's offices at that time of the afternoon. He was hardly prepared for the exuberant Jacobs who burst into the room moments later.

"I dropped by to say good-bye, Jimmy!" Marvin's face glowed.

"Oh? Where are you going?"

"Israel."

"To Pales—to Israel? They've got a war going on there."

"That's why. I was a fair-to-middling infantry NCO, Jimmy."

"But you had one war and you . . ."

"Lost an arm?" Marvin laughed. "This is another war. You know we Jews are always supposed to try and get two of everything for the price of one."

Jemel stared at Marvin. "What about your business?"

"Pop will look after the store."

"Isn't he semiretired?"

"Jimmy, last May Fourteenth was some day. A *mitzvah*. You can't imagine how many Jewish ailments were cured. Snap, crackle, whoosh—and the doctors in New York lost two-thirds their Yid patients. Pop was no exception. I was braced for howls when I told him I wanted to go. All he said was 'I've been going crazy doing nothing. So you give me an excuse to start working again'—and brought out the *schnapps* bottle!"

Marvin prattled on. Jimmy toyed with a paperweight, pretending to listen. He was aware of how the American Jewish population had reacted to the establishment of Israel and the war—with almost fanatical support and immense sums of money. An idea formed. He examined it closely. It held up. Worth a try, anyway. He pushed the paperweight aside, produced a checkbook and took a thin gold pen from his pocket. He opened the book, began filling out a check, paused.

"Say," he interrupted Marvin Jacobs. "Know any outfit collecting money for Israel?"

"Do I?" Marvin exclaimed, and instantly flushed with embarrassment, became flustered. "Hey, if you're —damn it, I didn't come here to . . ."

"Stop stammering. Give me a name, not a hard time."

Marvin named an organization. The gold pen in Jemel's hand glinted as it moved across the check. He detached the check, handed it across his desk. "Deliver or mail it for me, huh?"

Marv's jaw dropped. "My God. This is for ten thousand bucks! Why. . . ?"

"Why not? It's tax-deductible. Besides, we both have hooked noses."

The letter arrived the following Friday:

Dear Mr. Karami:
   It is indeed difficult for me to express in words the extent of our entire organization's gratitude to you for your most generous contribution . . .

Jimmy dropped the letter into the "File" basket with a satisfied smile.

Word got around even faster than he expected.

On Monday, Pincus Jacobs called and asked if Karami & Co. would handle the import of some British fabrics his company needed. The Liebowitz stores sent a purchasing agent to the Lincoln Building—with a large order . . .

By Thursday, Doug Ford was marveling at the phenomenon.

"New business is pouring in over the transom!" he exclaimed. "All from companies owned by Jews. I don't get it!"

"Don't try," Jimmy grinned. "Accept all blessings —regardless of race, creed, or color. As long as the color is green. Like in money."

9

Hassan Karami suffered a second stroke and died on March 18, 1949.

Including the money deposited in the secret Bauer Kreditbank account, he left a total net estate of $4,200,000.

Jemel knew Hassan intended leaving Felicite a million dollars in a trust fund, and that he would be his sister's legal guardian until she reached eighteen, and the administrator of her trust until she was thirty or married, whichever happened first. He was unprepared for the shock of discovering that his father had left the same amount—a million dollars—to Nuri.

"A codicil drawn up after his first stroke," Halim Chalhoub, Hassan's attorney told Jemel. "Nuri . . ."

"Jesus Christ! Who's the trustee?" I am, I hope. I must be.

Chalhoub scowled. "A couple of guys Nuri wanted," he replied. "He had Hassan eating out of his hand toward the last. Didn't you notice?"

No, Jemel had been too busy to pay much attention. "Can we sue to break?"

"I don't advise it. Too much might be raked up about Karami & Co."

Jemel was left $2,200,000 cash, all Hassan's stock in Karami & Co. and the deed to the Sutton Place apartment—the last with a proviso that Felicite and Mademoiselle Claire Viete continued living there with Jimmy. The money was a million less than Jimmy had counted on—but he could start expanding Karami & Co. nonetheless.

Chalhoub cleared his throat. "Hassan tell you about Nuri's guardianship?" Jemel said he took it for granted it would be himself, or Halim, or perhaps even Miles Palmer. "Same two people who're his trustees," the lawyer said. "I tried to talk Hassan out of it." He spread his chubby hands wide. "He wouldn't listen. Said you were just like he was, and that you'd ignore Nuri the same way he had. I think you'd better brace yourself for a showdown with your kid brother."

The confrontation came two days later in what had been Hassan's study.

Nuri's close-set pale brown eyes were insolent, spiteful. "You have your ass planted behind the old man's desk already," he sneered. "It figures. You were two of a kind."

Jemel gazed at Nuri's weak-chinned face coldly. "You said you wanted to see me. Alone. We're here. Felicite and Mademoiselle are out. The servants are in the kitchen and the door is closed. Say your piece."

"In a hurry, Jimmy? Can't spare much time from your high-society fucking, can you?"

Jimmy grinned wryly. "Now I know you can read. Go on, Nuri, dump your load of shit in my lap without stalling around."

Nuri, about twenty pounds overweight for his five-seven height, pulled up a chair and sat down. "I want out," he said.

"You want out," Jimmy repeated. "Good. Out of what?"

Nuri's face contorted. "Out of here. This apartment. The Karami family."

Jemel shrugged. "Why tell me? You're free to go. You have your legal guardians and trustees. Presumably they'll administer your trust fund so that you'll have a five-figure income. I haven't any control over you."

"No, you haven't. For once in my life, I'll be living honestly alone."

"What does that 'honestly alone' line mean—if anything?"

The hatred came pouring out of Nuri.

"And you're supposed to be smart? Crap! I've lived alone in this family ever since *Maman* died. She was the only one who ever cared for me. All you and the old man ever cared about was money—and that spoiled little cunt, Felicite!"

Jemel's eyes narrowed; his full lips drew thin and taut. "You're begging to get the piss kicked out of you, Nuri," he said, his voice glacial, menacing. "Everybody did the best they could for you."

"Oh, yeah? You let me rot for years in a clinic. When I came home, who paid any attention to me? A keeper, that's who! I was treated like a freak . . ."

"Bass!" Jemel barked—in Arabic, for some reason unknown to himself. "That's funny," he thought, and went on in English. "You got sent to the clinic and needed a keeper because you were a freak—a fag and a cocksucker among other things." He saw a strange flicker in Nuri's eyes. "I'll be damned," he thought, "let's see if I'm right." "You were just a kid, and going down on the other kids in your school, taking their pricks and working them off in the crapper." "By God, I am right." His clinical descriptions and four-letter words brought unconscious response from Nuri. His eyes gleamed, giving him away. "So much for psychiatrists and clinics," Jimmy thought. "It was for your own protection," he continued, veering off. "I'm yet to be told why you wanted to talk to me."

Nuri thrust himself up on his feet. "So I could tell you to your face that I hate your guts. Yours and Felicite's. One of these days, I'll square off some old debts you two owe me."

Jemel yawned his contempt, "Get out of here right now—and be out of the apartment tomorrow." He tried a long shot. "You can suck your guardians' cocks without a care in the world."

Nuri's jaw dropped. Bull's eye, Jimmy reflected. And handy knowledge to have.

The door slammed as Nuri went out.

Major Russell T. Stanton, B.A.—in business and finance courtesy USAFI and Army University Study Centers—returned to civilian life at what, to Jemel's mind, was precisely the right time. Karami & Co. had moved to new, spacious offices in Rockefeller Center. Doug Ford had been appointed executive vice-president, more employees had been hired and the company was stepping up operations and venturing into new fields—including factoring.

Russ would add the final touch of respectability even while Jimmy could begin living up to his press-puffed reputation as a precocious entrepreneur.

Jemel renewed his offer to Stanton, made it even more attractive than before. "A vice-presidency and fifteen thousand a year, Russ."

Russ wavered. He could expect nothing remotely comparable from any large corporation, and Karami & Co. gave every indication of being on a sound footing. Still . . .

"Give me a few weeks to think it over, Jimmy," he said. "I'm not used to being a civilian yet, and I'd like to readjust a little." And look around the job market, he thought, do some comparison shopping.

"Of course." Jemel sensed that Russ was weakening and knew the offer wouldn't be matched by any of the big companies. Karami & Co. was bound to get its WASP war-hero window-dressing, he assured himself.

Russell Stanton sent out numerous résumés, filled out many applications, had several interviews. Few of the positions he was offered seemed very promising. American industry's big veteran-hiring spree was long over. Jemel Karami's offer looked better and better.

Then Stanton was interviewed by the personnel director of the Whitehead Oil Company, one of the largest in the petroleum industry. A new subsidiary— the Whitehead MidEast Oil Co.—was being formed to exploit oil concessions in Saudi Arabia and the Middle East. Whitehead MidEast needed young junior executives it would train from the bottom. The starting salary was only $7,500 a year, but all companies owned or controlled by R. Daniel Whitehead had a policy of promoting within the organization. Good men rose rapidly to middle-management positions; the better went higher.

As far as the personnel director was concerned, ex-Major Russell T. Stanton possessed all the necessary qualifications. From Russ Stanton's viewpoint, the job was perfect—even if it only paid half what Jemel had promised him. He went on the Whitehead Mid-East payroll.

"It's exactly the kind of corporate complex I've always wanted to work for," Russ explained to Jemel. "And the job sounds interesting. I won't just sit behind a desk. I'll be going out into the field."

Jimmy again found resentment creeping into his sense of disappointment. He thought he knew Russ Stanton and had taken his measure. Easy, he warned himself, don't make it final. Leave an opening.

"I wish you a lot of luck," he said—and made it sound sincere. "But take it from an Arab. American oil companies operating in the Middle East won't have it easy." He managed a smile. "If things don't work out for you with this Whitehead outfit, let me know. There's always a place for you with Karami & Co."

The world could use more friends like Jemel Karami, Stanton thought.

10

American troops were ordered into action against Communist armies in Korea. Jemel Karami—like countless others—was convinced the "police action" would lead to a World War III. Any doubts he might have had were dispelled after consultation with Senator Michael Ferrenbaugh who declared that the political and military consensus in Washington predicted Russian intervention within weeks.

"It's Pearl Harbor all over again," Jimmy told

Douglas Ford. "We buy and hold goods that are most likely to become scarce. When this fracas spreads, the government will impose controls and rationing—and prices will go to the stratosphere."

Ford's deceptively cherubic features mirrored Jemel's expression in their own broad-smiled idiom. "We'll clean up!" he exclaimed delightedly.

Karami & Co. bought basic metals and commodities in huge quantities, paying spot cash and often premium prices. The goods were to be held in storage until World War II-style black markets developed.

Torrents of cash flowed out—and were frozen into mountainous inventories. When Karami & Co's American resources ran low, Jimmy drained the Bauer Kreditbank account, then approached Miles Palmer for a million-dollar loan from the Palmer National Trust Co.

Palmer was glad to grant the loan. He'd remained a "Special Economic Adviser to the Treasury Department," and his sources, too, believed full-scale war was imminent. Miles considered Karami & Co's massive buying shrewd, certain to produce astronomical profits.

Weeks passed and few, if any, scarcities developed. Save for scattered—and minor—spurts, prices remained stable. No rationing or drastic controls were imposed by the federal government. The hopes of innumerable speculators—Jemel among them—dimmed when UN and American forces drove up the Korean peninsula to the Manchurian border. The hopes flared high again when the Communist Chinese intervened and sent U.S. and United Nations troops reeling back below the 38th Parallel.

Mike Ferrenbaugh flew to New York from Washington with the latest news.

"MacArthur wants to bomb Manchuria and A-bomb China," he revealed to Jemel and Doug Ford. "Truman and the Joint Chiefs are in a stew."

"America will have to declare war on China now," Ford said.

"And that'll bring Russia in," Jimmy nodded. "Eh, Mike?"

"I'd bet on it," Ferrenbaugh agreed. "The minute Truman releases MacArthur's reports to the public, we'll have a war-fever that won't quit. If he doesn't—well, MacArthur has direct lines to Bob Taft and Joe Martin . . ."

Miles Palmer shared the opinions. When Jimmy requested another million-dollar loan to make even more purchases, the Palmer National Trust supplied the money immediately.

By April 1951, all hope had faded. The Korean conflict remained localized. There were no government restrictions or rationing. Black markets had failed to materialize. Untold numbers of speculators were struck, jammed tight.

Jemel was at last forced to admit that he had made a monumental error. That others were in the same bind was no consolation. He'd suffered a major disaster. Karami & Co. had almost no liquid resources left.

"Start selling!" Jimmy instructed Doug Ford.

"It won't be selling. We'll have to dump."

"Goddamn it! Do you think I don't know that?" Jemel barked. "The only course we have is to pull what cash we can out of this fucking mess—and then try to make back what we lost!"

The huge inventories Karami & Co. had piled up around the country were sold off. As speculators were throwing hoarded merchandise on the market right and left, buyers demanded large price-concessions. These had to be granted. The need for cash was desperate.

Discounts, storage and freight charges, interest on borrowed money, and other expenses added up to staggering losses. A final balance was struck and Jemel learned the actual money-cost of his error. He was left with less than half the wealth he'd had before the Korean war began.

Jemel was severely shaken by the experience. He wasn't yet twenty-five, and he'd already managed to lose a fortune. He had to recoup, and quickly. But how?

He raged, tore his brains apart—and then calmed. The realization emerged that he had learned an invaluable lesson, perhaps the last major one he needed to complete his practical education. Hassan had been right—to a halfway point. It *was* foolish to take risks —but only if they were taken with one's own money.

That was the trouble with a family business, a closed corporation. When money was lost by the company, it came out of one's own pocket.

The formula began to take shape.

If Karami & Co. were turned into a public-stock company, thousands of faceless money-greedy stockholders would be taking the risks, suffering the losses. And, if the corporation was established and operated with a little finesse, precious little of the profits would have to go to those stockholders.

Jemel believed he had all the ingredients to fill the formula. To determine if it would work as well as he expected, he had to take one final risk with his own money—but it was a calculated risk, and he was certain it could be controlled.

Halim Chalhoub had remained the attorney for Karami & Co. for Jemel.

Chalhoub was the first person with whom Jimmy discussed his idea.

"I'll not only make up everything I've lost, but get ahead," Jimmy told the lawyer. "We set up a corporation, peddle shares."

Halim looked dubious. Karami & Co. did not have a very impressive earnings-record, he reminded Jimmy.

"Screw the earnings record!" Jemel retorted, his teeth flashing white. "Most of the money I salvaged from the wreckage is unreported—profits that never passed through the company's books but went to HJK and the other dummies, then to Switzerland. If I feed that money in, pick it up on slightly doctored books, do a little juggling, the new company can be made to look like a terrific 'growth' proposition."

"Um," the moon-faced Lebanese-American attorney grunted. "What about the SEC?"

The best specialists to doctor the books and Senator Mike Ferrenbaugh to grease things with the SEC, Jimmy told him, and continued to the next answer before Chalhoub could voice the question.

"Miles Palmer will know how to set up a front-syndicate or find some other gimmick for floating the issue."

Halim looked dubious. "Palmer can't afford to fool around with a boiler-room operation," he said.

"Boiler room?" Jimmy laughed. "This is going to be a legitimate venture—and Miles will jump at the chance to skim off some cream." "And it's always the bankers who get the most cream for the least effort," he reflected. However, that couldn't be helped now. Maybe if things worked out, he could later cut out the bankers—but not yet. "I have this thing figured down to the next-to-last details. I'll have the stock issue preheated before it goes on sale. You just start thinking how the corporate structure will be organized."

"What are you going to do in the meantime?"

"Work with you on designing the framework—and start seeing some people who'll do the rest for us."

11

Jimmy flew from New York to Chicago, thence on to Michael Ferrenbaugh's home town, an archetypal Border States metropolis of some 150,000 population.

It was Jemel's first visit to the place, and, of course, Mike Ferrenbaugh met him at the airport in a new, optional-accessory-cluttered Buick.

"The girls—Dot and Mickey—are dying to see you, Jimmy."

Iron Mike was gradually sagging into smug corpulence—and arriving at the Ferrenbaughs' house,

Jimmy saw that Dorothy had blurred into plump, cheerful and still attractive matronliness. As for Michele, for Mickey . . .

Great horny Jesus, Jimmy thought. Mickey Ferrenbaugh had been transmuted into a ravishing teenager. Her face was fine-boned, lovely with soft auburn hair and gold-flecked brown eyes. Darken the hair, and there would be more than a passing resemblance to Elizabeth Taylor. Her fresh young breasts were alive beneath her orange-colored cashmere sweater.

Dorothy Ferrenbaugh embraced him warmly. Then Mickey hugged him and kissed his cheek. Outwardly all very innocent and childish, but Jemel could have sworn . . .

"Mickey's still stuck on you!" Ferrenbaugh laughed loudly as they all went into the living room.

The gauche paternal remark failed to embarrass Mickey. "Oh, Jimmy's always been my only real boyfriend." She spoke with parent-dissembling casualness —but with a glance at Jemel that he was sure carried a message.

He was intrigued, aroused—and very much on his guard. Mickey was how old—fifteen? And she was Mike Ferrenbaugh's daughter. Start anything, and there could be serious trouble, he warned himself. She looked at him again. There was no mistaking the message now. Well, it couldn't hurt to do a little teasing in exchange for being teased.

"You've been my girlfriend, too, Mickey." Light, bantering. "You gave me a nickname. Remember?"

"And I still have the doll you sent me. Remember it?"

Jemel did—rather vaguely. Oh, yes. When Mike had got him out of the draft. He nodded and smiled.

"She keeps it in her bedroom like a trophy," Dorothy Ferrenbaugh said—and hurried on as she recalled her own memories of Jemel's father. "Why, Mickey has scrapbooks filled with every clipping she's seen that mentions your name."

"A lot of them came from Elinor Randolph's 'Busybody' column," Mickey said with elaborate nonchalance. "She must like you, Jimmy."

"Elinor and I are old friends." *So the girl was jealous. Should I push or ease. Oh, hell, ease. She's just a kid.* "I knew her ex-husband and all the fellows *she* has as boyfriends," he lied. Mickey's eyes, Jimmy noted, shone with happy relief. Her body, lithe yet surprisingly mature, seemed to strain towards him.

After half an hour, Jemel and Ferrenbaugh excused themselves and went into what Mike called his "den." Jimmy glanced around at wall-mounted deer heads, peg-hung rifles and shotguns, racked—but obviously seldom-smoked—pipes. "A real man's room," he said. Ferrenbaugh beamed pride, the subtlety eluding him completely.

Jemel folded himself into a leather armchair, his aquiline facial planes taking on a serious businesslike aspect.

"Care for a drink?" Mike asked. "I have some of that Crawford's scotch you and Hassan always liked. It's good, makes me wish I wasn't a bourbon drinker."

"Not right at the moment, thanks. I'd like to get my business cleared up first. I told you over the phone I was coming out to have a very private talk with you—and it shouldn't take long. I want to take a big step—and I'll need your help to take it."

"There isn't much I can refuse you, Jimmy." *Karami & Co.* had got into deep water partly because of the bum steers I got and gave, Mike thought. *If Jemel gets out, I'll make out, too.*

Jimmy explained that he wanted to go public. "Which leaves us with the problem of the SEC," he finished. He didn't need to go into further detail.

"The SEC doesn't have a very big staff," Mike said. "It can't check every registration down to where the t's are crossed and the i's are dotted—and where all the decimal points are." He studied his cigar ash. "Mostly, the registrations are kinda skimmed—and then one in every so many given the full treatment."

He slid a panatela back between his teeth. "It could be, Jimmy, that the papers you send in are given only a quick once-over. It could also be that I can make sure that's all they get."

"That's what I wanted to hear, Mike," Jimmy

said—and told Ferrenbaugh what he wanted to hear. About what he'd receive in return. That took another fifteen minutes, and the deal was made.

Mike looked at his watch, grinned wide around his cigar. "Last plane to Chicago left. You'll have to stay overnight. We got spare bedrooms all over the place. The maid'll fix one up for you."

"Thanks, Mike."

"Let's go join the girls. I'll mix up some drinks. It's Saturday night, so we'll have dinner at the country club."

Hearing that Jemel would spend the night Mickey proclaimed her intention to monopolize him for most of the following day.

"I'll borrow your car, Mom, and show him the local sights."

"Now, honey, that's up to Jimmy," her father drawled. " 'Course, you should see the lakes while you're here," he said to Jemel, proudly adding, "We have a summer place out there. Good fishing. Bass. Full of fight."

Dorothy was speaking to her daughter. "Don't be disappointed if Jimmy says no. After all, he's very busy."

"How can I refuse?" Jemel interjected. "I'll be a model rubbernecker—ask all sorts of dumb questions."

"You're spoiling her worse than she is," her father complained. "She always managed to have her way."

Jemel gave Ferrenbaugh a resigned-sympathetic look, slightly modulated for Dorothy's benefit. The glance that flicked between him and Mickey said something totally different.

"Another drink?" Mike inquired.

"Please," Jemel nodded. "I'll store up for tomorrow when I'll be on cola and milkshakes with my teenage tourist-guide."

Mike Ferrenbaugh was on a first-name basis with every middle-aged male in the Saturday-night country-club crowd, and it seemed necessary that he have a drink with each. By midnight, he'd become sufficiently fuddled to mumble acquiescence when Dorothy declared they should leave.

Jemel shared the back seat with a very drunken Mike Ferrenbaugh. Dorothy sat in front, allowing Mickey to drive back to the house.

"She really shouldn't after dark with her junior license," Dorothy clucked, "but you'll feel safer tomorrow, Jimmy, if you see how well she can handle a car."

Jemel lay awake in bed—thinking. About the millions to be gained if all the gears meshed. And about Mickey Ferrenbaugh. Her bedroom was at the other end of the hall. The knowledge excited him, and he looked forward to morning.

Mike's gargantuan hangover kept him in bed. Dorothy and the family's maid prepared and served breakfast. Jimmy was amused. Someone had even remembered his preference for *labeneh* instead of butter, and a comparatively nothing-tasting cream cheese had been provided as the only local substitute.

"Are you sure you won't be bored driving around with Mickey?" Dorothy asked him. "If you'd rather stay in and rest . . ."

It sounded a purely polite inquiry; he could detect no underlying note of suspicion. Safer to play safe, he reminded himself—and his memory-file produced the echo of a ploy Hassan had used. Jimmy modified it to fit.

"Having given your little girl—oh, sorry, I mean the young lady—my promise, I'll keep it," he said, and reached for another slice of toast.

Jemel guessed why Mickey borrowed her mother's car. It was a black two-door Ford—anonymous, while Mike's Buick was glaring, unmistakable. Clever girl.

They were several blocks from the house before either of them spoke.

"Like to know where we're going?" Mickey asked, her voice husky, tight.

"Yes."

"Our place on the lake. There isn't another house near it."

The air inside the shuttered lake-house bedroom was close, musty, but they weren't aware of it. They entered the room. Mickey opened a shutter sufficiently to provide light. Then, her eyes soft and misting, she turned towards Jemel, stepped close to him, and as his arms went around her, kissed him.

Her mouth humbled itself against his, at once offering and begging. She clung to him. His hands gripped her shoulders, moved slowly down, along her back, until his hands held the soft swell of her buttocks, drawing her closer.

The last-gasp warning alarms rang in his brain.

Jesus Chirst!

He gave a start, releasing her. Womanlike, Mickey read his mind. Her smile was tender.

"I'm not a virgin, Jimmy," she murmured. Her fingers moved swiftly, unbuttoning her blouse. "And no. I'm not sixteen."

Her gaze was level, peaceful with calm, yet intense at the same time. Jemel felt unidentifiable emotions start a whirl inside him.

Mickey spoke again. "I know what I'm doing, Jimmy." She removed her blouse and bra. Rose-pink nipples thrust themselves from fresh-ripened breasts. Her eyes continued to hold his. "I've always wanted to with you." She unfastened her skirt, let it drop. Her legs and thighs were perfectly tapered.

She reached for his hand, took it gently.

This is insane, Jemel thought. *She's fifteen, and leading me to bed. Leading me like a small child. And I'm letting her do it!*

"Take off your clothes, Jimmy." She pulled back the bedspread, took off her panties, sat on the edge of the bed, the auburn-hued wedge sharply defined against the whiteness of her belly and upper thighs.

Her eyes underwent transformation. The calm and tenderness faded from them. They smoldered, then blazed with hunger and this added savage depth to her beauty.

Jemel, nude now, bent down, slid an arm around her back, the other under her thighs and lifted her. He held her, kissing her lips, then her throat and breasts, then her lips again. Their mouths locked, tongues searching, and he lowered her and himself on to the bed.

"Jimmy—do anything! Everything!" Mickey begged, her body worshiping his touch. "Jimmy!" Her desire mounted to a level of exaltation. She sobbed, closed her eyes, held them shut tight in terror she might discover that the reality of which she had dreamed for so many years would once again prove to be nothing but a dream.

The dimension of her desire and emotion dismayed Jimmy, evoked feelings in him he could not identify.

"Jimmy!"

Her fingers clutched blindly, spasmodically at his flesh, at the bedclothes, at empty air. Then her hands seized his head, pulling it down until their lips touched.

"I love you, Jimmy! Oh, God, but I love you!"

Mickey lost herself in the ecstasy of orgasm.

12

Karamcorp, the successor to Karami & Co., was designed as a holding company, incorporated under the benign laws of the State of Delaware. This parent corporation would own or control an array of other holding and operating companies. Karamcorp's principal operating subsidiaries were to engage in general trading, brokerage, factoring, import-export operations, and varied other business activities. Included in the conglomerate would be the four smallish manufacturing firms that Karami & Co. had previously taken over when their owners were unable to repay money advanced them against accounts receivable or inventories.

Behind the elaborate facade would lie another, intricate apparatus. Its chief components would be overseas dummy companies, secret Swiss bank accounts. These would engage in activities about which American tax and regulatory agencies were best kept in ignorance, and siphon off and conceal income and profits Jemel Karami did not want to share with the U.S. Internal Revenue Service or minority stockholders.

Jemel was to own 60 percent of Karamcorp's stock and thereby retain clear-cut control of the parent company and its subsidiaries. Halim Chalhoub and Michael Ferrenbaugh were each to receive 2½ percent of the stock. The remaining 35 percent would be sold to the public.

Jemel presented the completed blueprint to Miles Palmer.

"An attractive package," Palmer commented after long study. "With Ferrenbaugh keeping the SEC quiet, it has a fair chance." He'd agreed to arrange for underwriting of the issue in his own mind, but wanted a high premium. "On the other hand, there's a great deal of air inside the bubble, Jemel. It could burst and leave the underwriters in a sorry state."

Jimmy had foreseen Palmer's reaction. "You'll get a free ride, Miles—and with no taxes on the profits," he said, and explained how a large block of stock would be shifted back and forth through a European dummy, with the profits deposited to Palmer's credit in a numbered Swiss account. "You'll have a big advantage over anyone else you pull in on the underwriting."

Palmer had one more question. "The issue has to be alluring to the—ah—investing public. This is something . . ."

"Don't worry, Miles. It'll be a hot issue. The hottest in many years."

Jimmy relied on Elinor Randolph to kindle the first glows.

"Latest rumor among Manhattan's money-minded: Jimmy Karami's private corporation won't be private much longer . . .

"Karamcorp is the name of the new company that glamor king Jemel Karami has been quietly forming . . ."

A few such quips slipped into her column, and other columnists fanned the glow into flame. To build the needed bonfire, Jemel paid a visit to Bud Bridger.

Bud Bridger was more than America's leading newspaper columnist and radio broadcasting personality. He was a national institution. Bridger had risen from late-Prohibition-era keyhole-peeping to top-rank among the country's pseudo-journalists by aiming for the lowest common denominators in his audiences. His style of writing appealed to grade-school mentalities, he delivered his Sunday evening "news" broadcasts in staccato bursts of speech and voice-of-doom tones.

"Hello, world! This is Bud Bridger with the inside facts from the curtained corners, the skeletons dug from the closets of the high and mighty. . . !"

The public devoured his words, and Bridger's income was astronomical—but still not high enough to satisfy him. At war's end, he devised an infallible scheme for earning even more. Every month or two, he'd give his Sunday radio audience "an exclusive, red-hot Bud Bridger tip on a common stock that's bound to zoom."

The tip guaranteed its own accuracy. The masses listened and on Monday morning began frantically telephoning their brokers. The price of the stock invariably soared. Bridger chose the shares he recommended after hard bargaining with the companies that issued them. A Bud Bridger tip cost the promoters of a company a block of stock given to Bridger as a gift. When the price "zoomed," Bud Bridger sold the stock—and pocketed all the proceeds.

Jemel had met Bridger frequently in clubs and at social affairs. It was easy to reach agreement. Bridger would receive 15,000 Karamcorp shares.

"What happens to the stock is entirely up to you,

Bud," Jimmy said, feeding the man's monstrous ego. "You're the wizard."

"Sleep easy, Jimmy," Bridger boasted. "It'll go through the roof!"

Bud Bridger gave a virtuoso performance the Sunday before Karamcorp shares went on sale.

". . . Karamcorp. Remember that name, world! Karamcorp—so hot it's sizzling. Use the rent money, hock your furniture. Do anything—but don't blame yours truly, Bud Bridger, if you miss the platinum-loaded boat. . . !"

By Monday afternoon, the issue was oversubscribed in advance. By Wednesday, when the stock went on sale, those who had ordered a hundred shares considered themselves fortunate if they were allotted ten.

The underwriters' price for Karamcorp stock had been $5 a share. Within a week, over-the-counter-market broker-dealers were receiving bids at 15 and 16. A month later the stock was selling at 20½—and the end was nowhere in sight.

Six months later, the price stood at 23. Jemel fed 100,000 shares of stock into the market. The price dropped seven points. He bought the 100,000 shares back at 16. The price rebounded to 24. He sold and bought back another 100,000 shares—this time with a nine-point spread. Karamcorp then stabilized at 21. Jemel had made over $1.5 million for himself in cash—and the huge paper profits remained, a foundation on which he could build further.

He had already seen how it could be done.

13

Ironically, opportunity had been created by the same miscalculation that cost Jemel so dearly. He was not the only one who had believed the Korean conflict would lead to World War III.

Between the moment the first shots were fired in Korea and the middle of 1952, skittish depositors had drawn untold billions from their accounts in the United States and Europe—and particularly Switzerland. The withdrawals were panicky and irrational. Depositors feared that nuclear war would destroy their banks and the banks' records. They feared that their money would be physically destroyed.

Some converted their funds into gold, diamonds, rare postage stamps—a myriad forms of easily hidden, readily portable assets. But most of the money fled to new banks opening daily in places distant from what might be targets of nuclear weapons. Places like Tangier, the Bahamas—and Lebanon.

Almost all Tangier and most Bahamian "banks" were out-and-out swindles. They offered depositors secrecy, numbered accounts—and promised 8 percent, 9 percent, 10 percent, and even higher interest rates. The lures proved irresistible for the gullible— who did not know that in Tangier, anyone could open a "bank" without a penny in capital and claim $100 million or whatever he chose, as assets. These banks were opened only to take in all the money they could from depositors—and then close their doors.

With Karamcorp established and his fortunes again rosy, Jemel was again diverting large sums into his Bauer Kreditbank account. On trips to Zurich, he learned that the flight of "nervous money" was continuing. The outflow had to go somewhere. If he organized his own bank, he could attract some of it into his own vaults and use the bank as both fulcrum and leverage for further expansion of his operations.

Tangier was out of the question. Some of the banks there had already failed; many others were on the verge. Tangier would soon acquire a reputation that would scare off even the most naive depositor. The Bahamas was better—but Lebanon?

Lebanon was a natural.

Jemel was a Lebanese Arab by birth. He'd lived in the country fifteen years. He possessed knowledge and experience of the Levant. Language, customs, mentalities, methods—all were familiar to him.

"Funny," he thought, "I'll have to make a full circle and return to my beginnings." The prospects certainly looked promising.

Achieving final and complete independence in 1946, Lebanon had established a quasi-democracy dominated—and manipulated—by the merchants of Beirut, who gradually updated millennia-old Levantine devices.

A *laissez-faire* economic policy, the most permissive anywhere in the world, was imposed on the country. Merchants were free to deal as they pleased, without restriction or regulation. All currency controls were abolished, making it easy to manipulate money markets. Beirut became a center for clandestine trading of all kinds.

In 1951, the Unicameral—Lebanese Parliament —rammed through a series of laws designed to make Beirut the financial capital of the Middle East. Rules governing the establishment of banks were eased to the point where they were meaningless. Banks and bankers were offered no-limit charters and virtually exempted from any form of supervision.

The number of banks in Beirut multiplied. Where there had been less than a dozen, there were now seventy-five—and with room for more. Torrents of money—some of it "nervous" and fleeing other havens, some of it from the ever-increasing oil royalties being received by the sheikhs of oil-producing Arab states— poured into Beirut.

Jemel decided it was necessary that he see for himself.

Jemel Karami felt no sense of homecoming upon his arrival in Beirut.

He observed both those things which had changed and those which remained the same with equally detached interest as his taxi reached the outskirts of the city.

The French *poilus* and Foreign Legionnaires

were gone. The number of automobiles on the streets had multiplied a hundredfold over what he remembered. Many new buildings had gone up, more were under construction. Pigeon Rock remained a tiny islet a few hundred meters from the sheer of the cliffs along the Corniche, still a temptation to adventurous youngsters—had it been for me, Jimmy tried to recall. Yes, he'd swum out to it a few times, climbed its rocky sides.

The lighthouse thrust skyward, an oversized phallus on which the architects had botched the circumcision.

Jemel had intended to go directly to his hotel, the St. Georges. He changed his mind, told the driver to go first to the Port.

It was morning—hot and no less humid than he remembered. The streets and *soukhs* teemed, a *mélange* of humanity of every conceivable color and costume. Purple-black Negroes—servants and servitors, many the anachronistically legal slaves of Saudi or Kuwaiti masters, some spongy-bloated—eunuchs. Walnut-hued Bedouin. A sprinkling of Druses. Armenians with a greenish-yellow cast to their complexions. Men in flowing robes and burnooses. Others wearing Western-style clothing—and among them, those who clung to old customs, topped their suits off with red tarbooshes. Veiled women—and women dressed in Paris fashions. Half-naked children. Beggars. Native Lebanese policemen—arrogant and abusive to the poor, humble before those who were not.

Odors—and stenches. Harsh cries—and screamed curses. A background din of Levantine babble . . .

The old Karami *et Cie* warehouse was gone. A new concrete structure belonging to a French manufacturing company stood in its place. Jemel wondered idly—and only for a moment—if Capitaine Andrieux had ever surfaced. He instructed the driver to go on, directed him to the Ras Beirut street where the house in which he'd grown up was located. It was no longer there. It had been demolished. A new apartment-block

had been built on the site, and the neighborhood alone
evoked no memories.

"*Na'am ya sidi?*" the driver asked.

Jemel told him to drive directly to the St. Georges
now.

All Jimmy had read and heard about Lebanon
was true. If anything, understated. Beirut had become the financial and commercial capital of the oil-
rich Middle East. There was room and welcome for
new enterprise and entrepreneurs.

Government officials—some distant relatives or
old friends of Hassan Karami—assured Jemel he could
have any form of banking charter he desired, and the
baksheesh would be nominal. If he opened a bank, no
one would pry or question.

After three weeks in Beirut, Jemel was convinced.
Only one obstacle remained. He could not be in two
places at once. True, he could commute, shuttle back
and forth, and if he made Doug Ford president of
Karamcorp, Doug would run things in New York
whenever he was in Lebanon. On the other hand, the
bank would have to have its own Doug Ford—a man
completely reliable.

He thought of shifting Ford to Beirut—then forgot the idea. Doug was not equipped to operate in the
Middle East. He'd never been outside of the United
States. He remembered Russell Stanton. Russ had
been working for Whitehead MidEast Oil for some
years and had even learned Arabic. He split his time
between the States and Saudi Arabia—Kuwait. No.
Jimmy discarded that notion. Even if he made an offer that Russ could not under any circumstances refuse, Stanton wouldn't do for the job. He wasn't cut
out for the kind of operation Jemel had in mind.

He'd have to find the right man.

14

Jemel had an appointment with Trevor Aspinall, the solicitor who represented Karamcorp in Great Britain. He sat in an anteroom of Aspinall's Lincoln's Inn office. It was grim with dark wood and oil paintings of long-dead partners in the law firm.

Trevor Aspinall emerged from his office with another man and apologizing for the delay, went through a quick "Brian, Jemel Karami. Mr. Karami, Mr. Brian Lockhart" introduction.

"How d'you do, Mr. Karami."

Jimmy's mind registered impressions. Brian Lockhart. Well-dressed, medium height, ramrod posture. In his mid-thirties. Accent clipped to exact public-school tolerances. David Niven-type. English upperclass features. Eyes level, gray, shrewd—with more than a hint of hardness and ice.

". . . Mr. Lockhart."

Lockhart had served in the Middle East during the war. He recognized the successful, cosmopolite topstrata Levantine in Jemel, saw his clothes were impeccably tailored and worn. Karami's aquiline face could be bland, friendly, or that of a bird of prey ready to pounce, as occasion demanded, Lockhart thought. A man certain to be a success—and not one to have for an enemy.

They exchanged commonplaces for a few minutes.

"Well, if there's ever anything I can do for you in the States," Jimmy said, giving Lockhart his business card.

"I do most of my business in the U.K," Lockhart said, gave Jemel one of his own cards. "However, one can never tell—and please call on me if I can be of any help to you here."

190

They shook hands and Lockhart left. Trevor Aspinall showed Jemel into his private office.

"I'd guess Lockhart is a clever individual," Jemel remarked, studying the card. "Owns the Royal Home Counties and Midlands Building and Loan Society, I see."

"Yes. Brian started it when he was demobbed from the army." Something in Aspinall's manner made Jimmy grow alert. "Fine chap." Trevor Aspinall cleared his throat, changed the subject a shade too abruptly. "Some tea, perhaps, Mr. Karami?"

Jimmy knew enough about Britain's building and loan societies. Yawning loopholes in British laws made them happy hunting grounds for nimble promoters. Most were hollow shells, shaky, designed for milking by their promoters. He said yes, he'd appreciate a cup of tea, and said, "Mr. Lockhart must have put up quite a lot of money to start the society."

Even the most astute Englishman is likely to be a little absentminded when intent on pouring tea. "No. Comes from a fine but stony-broke old family. Good background altogether. Eton, Oxford, major in the Guards, DSO and all that . . ."

Jemel concluded his business with Aspinall and made discreet inquiries about Brian Lockhart through other sources. What he learned confirmed his instinctive appraisals. Instead of returning to New York, he flew to Zurich.

"I want you to buy up one hundred thousand pounds worth of Royal Home Counties and Midlands paper from English banks," he told the director of the Bauer Kreditbank. "Under no circumstances is my name to enter into it."

"And then, Herr Karami?"

"You call the paper. The RHC and M won't be able to cover it. You pass the word, and other banks holding more of its paper will demand payment. The society will be thrown into receivership or liquidated."

"You will take a heavy loss, Herr Karami!"

"Between seventy and ninety thousand dollars, according to the figures I have on Royal's total liabilities and realizable aspects. It's a bargain price for what I'm after."

Gentlemen who wear old school ties and belong to Boodles, the Guards and White's clubs do not inquire into the source of one another's incomes. But if a member of their establishment becomes involved in a public financial scandal, he is cut dead.

Thus, when the Royal Home Counties and Midlands Building and Loan Society failed with much accompanying newspaper publicity, Brian Lockhart, DSO, became an outcast among members of his own class.

Lockhart was astounded to receive a telephone call at his bachelor flat from Jemel Karami, the Lebanese-American he'd met a few months before at Trevor Aspinall's offices.

"I've just arrived in London, and Mr. Aspinall told me the bad news," Jimmy said. "I'm at the Dorchester. Could you drop around for a drink this evening? I have some things I'd like to talk over with you."

Brian Lockhart accepted the invitation with puzzlement. What could Karami want?

Later, in the drawing room of Jemel Karami's Dorchester suite, Lockhart bitterly told his side of the story.

"Seems a Swiss banker went after the Royal and Midlands," he said. "I'll be damned if I can understand why. There's a thirty thousand pound gap between what the bank paid and what it's going to get back."

Thirty-two thousand eight-fifty odd, Jemel corrected silently, fixing it in his mind that no matter what happened, Brian Lockhart must never find out that he had an account with the Bauer Kreditbank.

". . . and it's rather dicey at the moment," Lockhart was saying. "Civil actions being filed right and left, talk of criminal proceedings." It had all been trumpeted in the press, God knows.

"Not very pleasant," Jemel said. "May I ask your plans?"

"To leave England." Lockhart's gray eyes were flinty.

Jemel placed his glass on a taboret, refilled Lockhart's, then his own, lit a cigarette and said, "I'm about to open a bank."

"Not in England?"

"Lebanon. Beirut. You're aware of what's going on there?"

"Rather. And you're originally Lebanese. Excellent idea."

"I hear you're familiar with the Middle East, speak some Arabic." He didn't say he'd got the information by a careful check on Lockhart's background.

The Englishman swallowed whisky and water. "I was out there during the war. Egypt, Palestine, Iraq. Picked up a bit of the language, yes." Perhaps Karami might offer him some sort of job, for which he'd be grateful.

Jemel swirled liquor in his glass. "I've been looking around for a number-two man, Lockhart."

Brian Lockhart hastily downed the rest of his drink. Great God! A number-two spot with a new bank? It was a miraculous stroke of luck. Scuttling off somewhere with a few thousand pounds left out of what he'd milked from the Royal was one thing. But to bounce out of the muck into a good position was another. Karami was doing much more than getting him off a sticky wicket. Working together, they could rake in money. He sensed it.

"I'm bowled over, frankly," he said.

"Pour yourself another drink," Jemel urged, "and I'll give you a rundown on how I intend to organize and operate . . ."

15

The Industrial and Commercial Bank of the Levant—Incombank—was established in Beirut during September 1953.

Incombank received an across-the-board charter from the Lebanese government, authorizing it to perform all banking functions: savings, commercial, and investment.

Jemel Karami held 95 percent of the bank's stock and was its board chairman. Brian Lockhart received 5 percent and became the president of Incombank.

It was understood that Lockhart would remain permanently in Beirut, while Jemel commuted between Lebanon and New York and elsewhere, to seek out opportunities for profit, bring in the big accounts, draw the broad strokes. The Englishman was to manage Incombank's day-to-day operations, attend to the technicalities, fill in the details.

Jimmy Karami was exultant. With Karamcorp in America, Incombank in Lebanon, and his dummy companies on the Continent, he had completed the framework for an international financial pyramid of awesome proportions.

"I had a conversation with my father once, years ago," Jimmy told Brian Lockhart. "He asked me why I wanted to be richer than he was, and I quoted the old Arab wheeze about all dogs coming at a run to play their tricks when money whistles. I said then that if I was to have dogs, I wanted whole kennels of them. I'll have them yet."

"Trained and chained, eh?" Brian Lockhart smiled.

"Trained and chained," Jimmy repeated, "and willing to live on whatever scraps we care to toss them."

BOOK THREE

One Week
May 7th—13th

1

Nuqayr, Saudi Arabia. Tuesday, May 7th.

Lloyd Emmerick was almost glad to hear that Stubby Vosburgh was having trouble because it gave him an excuse to get out into the field. Where he would much rather be, under the circumstances. Russell Stanton's departure for the States the day before had left Emmerick restless, edgy, in no mood to shuffle papers in the Jeddah administrative offices. He fretted over the reasons behind R. D. Whitehead's presence in the New York home office and the orders recalling Stanton abruptly, without explanation, and the awareness that an ominous situation was gathering in Saudi Arabia depressed him even further.

Thus, when Stubby Vosburgh's message—radioed from the drilling site to Abqaiq and relayed to Jeddah—arrived, Lloyd Emmerick experienced a sense of relief. He'd have something else to occupy his mind. He told the assistant resident superintendent to take over the administrative headquarters for a couple of days and flew by company plane to An Nu'ariyah, the airstrip nearest to Nuqayr.

Stubby Vosburgh—whose short, compressed-muscular build had earned him his nickname—met Emmerick there in a sand-coated truck. The rest of the trip to the test-well drilling-site in the Nuqayr area would be across twenty-five miles of arid desert.

"What's the beef, Stubby?" Emmerick asked. Vosburgh was the drilling super on the site.

"Five native laborers quit in the last few days,"

197

Vosburgh told him. "They walked off the job, demanded we truck 'em to Abu Hadriya. Gave no reason, and I can't get anything out of the interpreter. He just shrugs."

"That's standard," Lloyd commented. Stubby Vosburgh was a twenty-year veteran of oil fields in the States and South America, but it was his first Middle Eastern tour. "Let's go. I want to get to the rig before sundown."

The drive across the desert was the usual torture. The truck cab was an annealing oven, and sand and dust swirled through it. Although the native driver followed the tracks made by company trucks during countless trips, it didn't help. The dry, hard patches of wasteland were strewn with rocks, and the men's kidneys took a merciless pounding.

They reached the drilling site at dusk. Several trucks were parked in an uneven row. A dozen or more army-style tents and a few prefab shacks. Large piles of thirty-foot-long drilling pipe. Casing, fishing tools, spare bits. Over it all towered the drilling rig. Diesel engines making their customary racket, and the normal clatter and clangor from the drilling platform, already harshly illuminated by arclights, for drilling is a twenty-four-hour operation.

"How far you down?" Emmerick inquired, getting out of the truck.

"Over a thousand feet—and the cores look good."

Emmerick nodded. They walked towards the tent that served as the mess hall for the American and Saudi technicians and members of the drilling crew. He saw the three Saudi Arabian soldiers who were assigned to the camp as guards. "All the king's men," he thought. They squatted on their haunches. Their rifles and cartridge belts were nowhere in sight. They'd probably left them in one of the trucks, Lloyd mused to himself. They usually did.

The devout Moslems had finished with the *salat il'asr*—the prayer before sundown. Emmerick and Vosburgh gulped down a dinner hastily prepared by the native cooks. Then Stubby Vosburgh rounded up the interpreter and two American members of the drilling crew and brought them into the tent.

"Mr. Vosburgh tells me some of the labor gang have quit," he said. "Any of you know why or hear anything about their being dissatisfied?"

The negative answers were unanimous. The interpreter, a self-important Saudi, emphatically denied there had been any reason. The men who'd left were doubtless chronic malcontents, he maintained.

"You'll need replacements," Emmerick told Vosburgh. "Give the Abqaiq office a howl by radio. Tell 'em to send out five new laborers in the morning. Pronto. Quote me as giving the authorization."

One of the Americans, a man in his mid-twenties but already with the weatherbeaten face of an oil-field veteran, spoke up. "No dice. The damned set went dead this afternoon while you were gone, Stubby."

"Oh, hell!" Vosburgh growled. Vehicle-mounted radios were always temperamental in desert country.

"Nothing much lost," Lloyd Emmerick said. "Have someone drive the radio truck to the An Nu'ariyah airstrip first thing tomorrow. He can raise Abqaiq from there and go on to Abu Hadriya and get the radio fixed."

Emmerick and Vosburgh were left alone.

"Any wiser than we were before?" Stubby asked.

"Nope." Emmerick yawned. "Maybe we'll learn something tomorrow." He chewed on a black cigarillo gone dead, decided against relighting it. "I'm ready to turn in. Want to be up early."

Except for the shift crew working on the drilling platform, the camp slept. Even the Saudi soldier whose turn it was to stand watch had laid his folded cartridge belt and rifle on the ground, climbed into a truck cab, curled up on the seat, and gone to sleep.

The interpreter came out of the tent he shared with some Saudi technicians. He made for the screened pit latrine in the darkness beyond the light reflected by the floodlights on the drilling rig, disappeared behind it. There was no one awake to see him continue past, angling off to his right toward a low, jagged ridge about a mile distant.

Half an hour later, several dozen men, Bedouin *kaffiyi* and *branis,* moved out from the ridge and began closing in on the camp. The drilling crew could see nothing in the darkness beyond the brightly lighted rig. The racket of the drill and the 350-hp. diesel engine powering it blanketed all other sound.

Lloyd Emmerick was asleep on a spare cot in Stubby Vosburgh's tent. Vosburgh lay on his back in his own cot, snoring.

The noise of diesel and rig ceased, cut off. Vosburgh stirred, awakened by unaccustomed silence, sat up, rubbed his face and listened. "Shit! Now what?" he growled, swung off his cot.

Emmerick was up now, too. "Got a flashlight? Maybe we can give a hand." Both men pulled on trousers and shoes, reached for heavy jackets against the night chill of the desert when Stubby switched on his flashlight.

Emmerick was shrugging himself into his jacket when everything broke loose. Rifles blasted. Men shouted and screamed.

"Raiders!" Emmerick yelled. Good Christ, there hadn't been a raid on a drilling site in years. Stubby Vosburgh stood frozen. Lloyd snatched the flashlight from his hand and plunged out of the tent.

"Asker!" he bellowed in Arabic, calling for the Saudi soldiers. *"Yalla!"* He cursed the Saudi laws and company rules that prohibited foreign oilmen from owning—much less carrying—firearms. *"Yalla!"*

Men were bursting from the tents in terror. They milled around in the darkness, yelling to each other, but their voices were faint against the crashing din of rifle fire and the shrieks of the raiders.

Tongues of orange flame stabbed from rifle muzzles. Bullets chewed into human flesh and bone, and men fell screaming or groaning in agony.

"Asker!" Lloyd Emmerick shouted again. There was no sign of the soldiers. "You bastards!" His flashlight beam swept across the faces of men running blindly, their features contorted with fear.

Emmerick started running toward the drilling rig. If he could only get the diesel started again, there would be light—light enough to scare off the raiders, light enough to stop the panic.

A running man came toward him, seemed to stop in his tracks—and then he fell, directly in Emmerick's path. Blood fountained from a ragged bullethole in his throat, and his cry of pain was a wet, dying gurgle.

Emmerick stumbled over the body, fell himself, dropped the flashlight, fumbled for it. Someone stepped on his hand. He had the flashlight, got to his feet, began running toward the rig again.

He was almost there. A hand seized his arm, spun him around.

"Kuss ummek!" A Bedouin, burnoosed, insane with bloodlust, eager to close in with the knife he held in his hand.

Lloyd Emmerick reacted by instinct. He pointed the flashlight beam squarely into the wild eyes, blinding them, and kicked with all his strength, driving his shoe into the man's groin. The Bedouin gasped, dropped the knife, doubled over.

Emmerick went for the knife, grabbed it and as he straightened up, drove the blade deep into the man's side, just under his armpit.

The rig. He turned. A sheet of flame tore the darkness. A deafening roar. The concussion slammed him flat. The bastards dynamited the rig, he thought. They've . . .

And then half a ton of steel bracing-beam fell and cut his body in half at the waist.

2

New York City. Wednesday, May 8th.

Wednesday morning had been a long time coming, Marvin Jacobs thought as he entered the Whitehead Oil Building. Now, maybe, the mystery that had gnawed at him since his telephone conversation with R. D. Whitehead would be cleared. The clock in the building lobby read 9:26. A junior executive was waiting for Marvin by the "50th floor only" elevator and escorted him up to what seemed a miniaturized boardroom.

Marvin recognized Daniel Whitehead from his photographs. The old man stood near a hybrid library-conference table on which were piled a great many thick manila folders and envelopes. He greeted Marvin cordially, thanked him for coming. Shaking hands with him was like shaking hands with an oak tree, Marvin thought.

They sat opposite each other across the narrow width of the table, in comfortable leather-upholstered armchairs.

"Please listen to what I have to say and look at what I'll have to show you, Mr. Jacobs," Whitehead began. "Afterward, you'll have a decision to make—and if you decide to call me a son of a bitch or tell me to go to hell, I'll understand."

An opening only a billionaire—or someone who wanted something very badly—could afford, Marv reflected, more baffled than ever.

The oil magnate looked squarely at Marvin and, in essence, told him what he'd said to Quentin Yeager in Oceanside, adding in whatever details he'd since learned. He studiously avoided mentioning the names of any individuals, however, referring to them only as "Mr. A" or "Mr. B." He knew the punch had to be saved for later.

Marvin listened first with fascination, then awed dismay. Why, he couldn't imagine, but R. D. Whitehead was telling him all about an international business intrigue of such magnitude that it made Marv's head swim. Fifty million tossed in here, ten billion in oil concessions at stake there . . .

"Israel is going to be caught right in the middle, Mr. Jacobs," Whitehead continued, narrowing down. "Several thousand Israelis will be made sacrificial goats. You've doubtless read that the crash of the Pan-Arab

Airways Caravelle was blamed on Israeli saboteurs—
and that the Lebanese-based terrorists 'retaliated' by
shelling the town of Ramim."

"Yes," Marvin said.

"It's only the first of what will be a series of attacks on Israel from Lebanon," the oil magnate declared. "To carry out their scheme, the people behind
it intend using it as a focal point to stir up Arab nationalist fanatics—and, at the same time, to divert attention from their real objectives." He paused, asked,
"Do you believe what I've told you so far?"

Marvin nodded unhappily. There was no doubt-
ing the old man's sincerity, and he spoke with the conviction of a man who was sure of his facts. "I believe you, Mr. Whitehead. What I can't understand is
why you're giving me the story."

Dan Whitehead took a deep breath. "Okay," he
thought. "Drop the bomb."

"Because a man you think is a good friend of
yours is involved in this thing up to his neck. Jemel
Karami is "Mr. A"—and his Incombank is the bank I
mentioned."

Marv's head snapped back as if he'd been struck.
"Bullshit, Mr. Whitehead!" he rasped. "Jimmy Karami
is . . ."

"Mr. Jacobs," Whitehead cut in. "You know that
most corporations have their spy systems." He waved
a hand at the folders and envelopes. "The Whitehead
companies have a very large and efficient one. I ad-
mire your loyalty to your friend—and I don't like
what I'm about to do. But suppose I happen to be
right about Jemel Karami. Can you risk not letting
me show you—when you might help save some lives
by listening?"

The question made no sense to Marvin, but the
manner in which it was posed held him in his chair,
silent, forcing himself to control his anger.

"You know one Jemel Karami," Whitehead said,
picking up a manila folder. "We—the people who
gather and evaluate information for me and I—know
an entirely different man. I'll start at what for you
was the beginning of your friendship. In college. Do

you know why Jemel Karami was classified 4-F during the war?"

"No. And I don't much care, Mr. Whitehead."

The oilman detached several sheets of paper from the folder and handed them across the table. "Russell Stanton won a DSC and a battlefield commission in Europe. You were at the other end, and lost an arm and got the Silver Star. Karami stayed home—because he had phony X rays slipped into his medical file."

Despite himself, Marv glanced at the papers. They were affidavits, attested to by various Selective Service officials. They declared that examination of 1943 draft-board records showed Jemel Karami had been declared 4-F because he was an incurable tubercular. X rays indicated one lung had been completely destroyed, the other almost so. The original draft-board doctor had certified Jemel Karami had less than a year to live.

"My God," Marvin thought—and for a moment, Staff Sergeant Marvin Jacobs was again leading his war-weary, understrength platoon out of the bush and into the barren clearing. The Nambus and knee-mortars opened up. "Ambush!" Marv heard his voice echoing across the years. "Haul ass!" He'd stayed, giving covering fire, hosing .45 slugs from his Thompson into the foliage where the Japs were hidden. He ran a clip dry, dumped it, was cramming another fresh one up into its place when the fragments of bursting shell axed into his arm. He'd been lucky. Luckier than the six men in his platoon who were killed . . .

Marv became aware that he was rubbing his artificial arm with his right hand. "Oh, hell!" he muttered aloud. "That was long ago. Jimmy dodged the draft. So did a few million others. If that's all, Mr. Whitehead, I'll . . ."

"I haven't even started, Mr. Jacobs. I understand that in 1948 and 1949 you served in the Israeli army as a company commander."

Marvin's full lips twisted into a wryly cynical smile. "We had all kinds of cripples. One-armed company commanders and one-eyed generals. So what's the point?"

"The point? You fought against very heavy odds. The Arabs had the Israelis outnumbered—and especially outgunned—thirty, forty to one. Did you ever wonder who supplied the guns?"

Did we ever wonder, Marv thought. *We had beat-up Enfields, junkyard Lewis and Vickers guns that would fire a burst and jam. And the Arabs? Even the irregulars and terrorists had brand-new M-1's, Brens, Schmeissers.* He remembered the kibbutz near Beersheba, overrun when the men guarding it were mowed down by the searing firepower of massed Bren guns, its inhabitants butchered. He and his company had been rushed to the scene—with ancient bolt-action rifles, fifty rounds of ammunition, and one hand grenade apiece . . .

"We all wondered," he replied bitterly—and lashed back, "Whoever supplied them, they were bought with money that came from oil royalties, Mr. Whitehead."

The old man's steel-blue eyes showed understanding, even sympathy. "The Whitehead MidEast Oil Company didn't get its first concession until the end of 1949," he said calmly. The old man's granite face changed aspect, grew coldly serious. "In any event, Mr. Jacobs, many of the weapons used by guerrillas, terrorists, and later fedayeen raiders against the Jewish people of Israel were supplied by the HJK Trading Corp. of Liechtenstein." He paused for effect. "A company owned by Jemel Karami and his late father."

Marvin's anger returned, stronger and assured. "Your great big spy system stinks, Mr. Whitehead. On two counts. First, Jimmy Karami was pro-Israel from the start. I know. Before I left the States, he gave $10,000 to an organization . . ."

"I'm sure he did," Whitehead interrupted, nodding. "What happened after that?"

"Happened? You've lost me, Mr. Whitehead. And I'm almost ready to tell you to go to hell."

"Did you tell other people of your faith what Karami had done—and if so, what was their reaction?"

"Just what I expected. My father and some of his friends gave Jimmy's company orders and . . ."

Marv's voice trailed off. No. Balls! Jimmy hadn't planned the donation to bring him business. It was too spontaneous. Besides, "I said two counts. Liechtenstein companies are supersecret. So how could you know what the HJK Trading or whatever it was bought or sold?"

"Secrets don't stay that way if one's willing to pay enough to make people talk and provide access to records, Mr. Jacobs," Whitehead said and gave Marvin some more documents. Photostats as well as affidavits.

"The stats are from the official archives in Vaduz. They're of the incorporation papers for HJK Trading. The Karamis' names are on them."

Marvin forced himself to look. They were.

"The affidavits are from people who state they sold guns to Jemel Karami as early as 1947," Whitehead went on. "Here's another document. An affidavit from a retired port official who says Karami bribed him to let the shipment listed on the attached stat of a cargo manifest as 'machinery' be loaded in Genoa even though the official knew it was really war materiel. Karami was young and a damned fool in those days. He signed his own name to the manifest. You see the shipment was consigned to Beirut."

Marvin stared, all blood draining from his face. Guns consigned to Beirut between 1947 and 1949 had gone from there only to Israel, to be used against the Jews; that much had always been common knowledge.

"Mr. Whitehead. If you knew all this, why didn't you take some action?"

"Karami didn't begin to interest me until 1953, when he organized Incombank and became active in the Middle East. That was when we started investigating and building files on him." He saw that he'd made a strong impression on Marvin Jacobs. Whitehead looked at his wristwatch. Almost an hour and a half had passed. He pressed a button on the table. Moments later, Quentin Yeager came into the room. Whitehead made the introductions.

"Mr. Jacobs, I'm going to see Russell Stanton in a few minutes. Our talk will probably take an hour," Whitehead told Marvin. "I'm going to ask you to wait. Russ may need all the moral support you can give him when he's through. In the meantime, Quent will give you some more information that is of importance." He turned to Yeager. "Take the appropriate files with you, Quent. Show Mr. Jacobs anything he wants to see; tell him whatever he wants to know."

Yeager gathered up an armload of manila folders.

"Mr. Jacobs." Whitehead's tone was serious, very serious. "After you've finished with Quent and then talked with Russ, you can decide whether to listen to me further—or come back in here and call me a son of a bitch."

Dazed and bewildered, Marvin allowed Quentin Yeager to shepherd him from the room.

Daniel Whitehead found it easy to fill Russ Stanton in on the big picture, for Stanton had seen or sensed some of the broader outlines while in Saudi Arabia. However, Whitehead again refrained from mentioning names, and this puzzled Russ.

"Any reason why the principals are an alphabet soup, R. D.?" he asked when Whitehead was finished.

"A damned good one, Russ. I wanted you to have the whole thing in mind before I spring a nasty surprise. The mastermind behind the operation is your good friend, Jemel Karami."

"What?" Russ exclaimed, half-rising from his chair. "Somebody's lying to you!"

Then he slumped back into the chair. The Old Man didn't make statements or charges he couldn't prove. Not R. D. Whitehead. Holy Christ, Russ thought. Jimmy Karami. He rubbed at his face.

"He has to be headed off, Russ," Whitehead said.

Stanton's mind raced. Sure. Jimmy was tough, shrewd, and a ruthless businessman—but then, so was R. Daniel Whitehead. Both of them would be willing to play for top stakes. But Jimmy Karami would never be directly responsible for killing a planeload of people or having some town in Israel blown apart. There were others in the thing with him—and they'd probably gone off on their own. Jimmy would be horrified if he found out.

"It—it shouldn't be very hard to stop him, R. D.," Russ declared. "Suppose I just let him know that you have all the dope, and that you'll tip off the State Department and the Arab governments. The minute he hears that, he'll lay off. Jimmy isn't stupid. He'll know the scheme will collapse."

Echoes of Quentin Yeager's fractured logic, Whitehead thought, and patiently explained, just as he had to Yeager, why any such action would be useless. Worse than useless. Karami and Miles Palmer had great influence in Washington, could block any steps by the State. The Arab governments were shot through with individuals whose real loyalties were to dissident factions.

"We'll do the stopping ourselves," Whitehead concluded. "You're one of my hole-aces, Russ. You're one of the few people who can get close enough to Karami to help bring him down."

Stanton's blue eyes widened, then narrowed. Jimmy Karami was his friend. He'd proved that over and over. He'd offered him a chance to start on a high salary when he was still in the army—and on several occasions afterward. Then there were all the other things. "Oh, no. Not me," he decided.

"I'm sorry, R. D. I owe you and the company a lot, but I'm afraid I have to disqualify myself. Whatever Jimmy's done or is doing, he's still my best friend." He nervously lit a mentholated cigarette, puffed at it, said, "I certainly won't do anything that'll help him in this thing or hinder whatever you'll do, R. D., but . . ."

"I understand," Whitehead said, with only a hint of sarcasm. He had fished a yellowing newspaper clipping out of a manila envelope. "Jemel Karami was always your close friend—and very generous to you."

He extended the clipping to Russ, who took and looked at it.

The clipping dated back to 1964. It was from Elinor Randolph's "Busybody" column. An item was circled in red grease-pencil:

"Glamor-banking-king Jimmy Karami will be best man at the wedding of oil-company executive Russell T. Stanton and beauteous Patricia Bramlett. Jimmy is loaning his *Queen Mary*-sized yacht, the fabled *Asharat,* to the couple for a two-week honeymoon cruise of the Caribbean . . ."

Russ felt icy cold and his hands trembled. Memories. Pat radiant, the reception after the wedding, and Jimmy giving them a lavish bon-voyage party aboard the *Asharat* before their departure.

He and Pat together in the master stateroom, in bed, Pat whispering happily, "Making love with you is always wonderful—but feeling like a princess makes it, well, sort of extra-sensual." They'd both laughed, and he'd kidded that he'd try it with her in one of the lifeboats and maybe that would bring her back to proper perspective for when the honeymoon cruise was over.

It had been a glorious two weeks. The 360-foot yacht and its crew were entirely theirs. They were waited on hand and foot—caviar and vintage champagne served in bed every morning for breakfast. Jimmy's orders. Wherever the yacht stopped, they were treated like royalty.

He and Pat had relived every second of it a hundred, a thousand times in the next two years. She never forgot it. She'd even kid him that if he'd taken Jimmy's offer, he might have a yacht of his own instead of having to shuttle back and forth between the New York office and the Middle East.

Pat. He could see her, hear her, almost touch her. She had been ambitious for him.

"I want you to be a success, Russ. You're better than anyone else—and I want everyone to know it."

They had been very much in love. She'd even resigned herself to being alone for the two-three weeks he'd have to spend in Saudi Arabia and Kuwait every few months. It had taken her a while, but she'd finally realized he liked his job and wanted to make good—until the last trip. Then, she had been nervous, overwrought, alternately clinging to him fiercely and snapping at him for days before he left.

"Sorry, darling," she'd apologized in bed on the last night. "I've been all out of sorts." And then she'd made love to him passionately.

Exactly ten days later he'd been told to fly home immediately from Jeddah because Pat had been in an automobile accident. He didn't learn that she had died until he got to New York, and that she'd been driving back from New Jersey after an abortion, started to hemorrhage, lost control of the car. It smashed against a tree. The collision hadn't injured her. She'd just slumped behind the wheel and bled to death as a result of the botched abortion.

It was my fault, Stanton told himself for the thousand-millionth time. *If I'd stayed home, it wouldn't have happened.* But he hadn't even known she was pregnant. She hadn't said a word—and they both wanted children. His not being there, his frequent absences—these were the only possible explanations why she had gone to a quack abortionist. Pain, the agonizing pain of guilt raked through Russ Stanton. Pat . . .

Whitehead was talking about Jimmy Karami. Yes. Jimmy was a good friend. The moment he'd heard about Pat's death, he's flown in from Beirut. Jimmy had been at his side through the worst days, during the funeral, after. He didn't know how he would have made it without cracking up completely if it hadn't been for Jimmy . . .

Whitehead's voice came to him. "A real friend in need," he was saying. "Jemel Karami. The best."

Russ paid no attention to the old man's tone. He merely heard the words and nodded dumbly.

"I was having Jemel Karami watched pretty closely during 1964 and 1965," Whitehead said softly. "Some of the things your friend was doing concern you personally—though God knows, that wasn't the reason I was having him watched."

Russ took the folder, but he was far away and didn't look at it.

"Goddamn it, son!" Whitehead grated. "Snap out of the coma you've been in for over two years! Karami was having an affair with your wife! It's all there! When you were gone and he happened to be in town, one of the women he screwed regularly was Patricia Stanton! If you don't believe the reports—for Christ's sake, we even had his apartment bugged. I can play you tapes!"

Russ stared at Whitehead for an instant. The words registered. His eyes glowed hot, then blazed with fury. His muscular, six-foot-two frame suddenly uncoiled. He leaped to his feet with such force that he sent the heavy armchair tumbling across the floor. His big hands knotted into fists, one of them crumpling the folder, for he did not even know he held it. He was ready to kill.

"You lying bastard!"

Whitehead did not move. He sat in his chair, his face impassive, his eyes calm, meeting Stanton's. Russ leaned toward him—and then stopped. The rage faded from his eyes—faded to marrow-searing hatred.

He didn't have to look at the reports. Again, R. D. Whitehead would not have made charges unless he had proof. He looked at the manila folder mashed in his hand. Now, he knew why Pat had wanted an abortion. She wasn't sure if the child was his—or knew it wasn't. His stomach churned, and he swayed. Whitehead stood up, reached across the table to steady him. "I'm sorry, son," he said softly. "I'm truly sorry."

I may have made a couple of bad mistakes today, Whitehead thought. *Real bad ones.*

Russ's fingers had relaxed. The crumpled folder dropped on the tabletop. Russ had not even glanced at it. The hatred remained in his eyes as he pulled himself free from Whitehead's hold, turned and walked out of the room.

There was an anteroom immediately outside.

"Hello, Russ."

Stanton stopped, blinked his eyes, tried to focus. Marvin Jacobs had just risen up from a chair.

"Marv. What the hell are you doing here?" Russ grated.

"Whitehead. He asked me to come down. I was with him before you were. He had a lot of talking to do. About Jimmy."

They stared silently at each other for several seconds. There was no need for words. Instinctively, both sensed how badly the other had been battered by R. Daniel Whitehead.

Russ saw the anger etched on Marvin's thin face, and it added fuel to his own outrage and hatred. He swung around on his heel. "I'm going back in!" he said, his tone harsh and grating.

Marvin understood and followed. Stanton opened the door leading to the conference room. They both entered. The door closed behind them.

3

Beirut. Thursday, May 9th.

Jemel bit nervously at his lower lip. The messages had been spewing off the clacking Telex machines all morning. They had piled up, until more than a dozen lay on his desk. One of the imponderables he'd feared had become reality, raising a dangerous trip-wire in his path.

"The stupid bastards!" he seethed. "Who were they—and where did they get their orders?"

Brian Lockhart was unruffled. "Bedous unknown," he said calmly. "Doubt if anyone gave them orders. The propaganda that's been spread around worked them into an almighty flap. They had some guns and dynamite, got an idea into their heads, saw a chance to raid and loot. An incident. Full stop."

"Full stop?" Jimmy echoed. "Brian, this will alert the Saudis . . ."

"You're letting your imagination run away. There are a hundred incidents like it every month in Saudi Arabia. You know that even better than I."

"Bandit raids and kill-fests, sure. Against Saudi villages or other tribes. Occasionally a hit-and-run looting excursion against foreign oil-company properties. But this looks to the Saudis like it's organized, preplanned. Damn it, Brian, there were six people killed, more wounded—and the Whitehead MidEast company isn't small. It can bring a lot of pressure. Our whole timetable may be knocked to pieces."

The Englishman remained calm. "No," he disagreed. "If anything, it'll send everyone rushing off after the wrong scent. Further confuse and confound. Our key people—from the ones in Riyadh down to the scruffiest of the sheikhs waiting for his gift packages to arrive will see to it."

Lockhart's analysis had a tranquilizing effect on Jimmy. You had to hand it to Brian, he thought. The man had no nerves, and his brain was a precision tool.

"We can add some insurance," Lockhart went on. "I'll have word passed to our most reliable associates in the enterprise, tell 'em to drag some herrings where they'll leave the most effective stench."

Jimmy shoved the stack of Telex messages aside. Brian's logic held. They owned more than a few second and third undersecretaries in the Saudi bureaucratic labyrinths who could—and would—drag herrings or anything else necesssary to prevent the authorities from stumbling on to the right track, for their own necks were in danger.

"I hate to shift your mind away from the main show, Jimmy," Lockhart murmured with the trace of a smile. "However, we still have a bank to run."

"Don't apologize, even as a gag," Jemel reflected. "I'm glad to have something else to divert my thinking." "That we do," he said. "I take it you have problems."

"Not really problems. I need some top-level decisions."

The function of board members in all Karami-owned or -controlled enterprises was solely to give unanimous rubber-stamp approval to the decisions of their board chairman, Jemel Karami.

"Such as?"

"HJK Trading Corp.'s three-year note for the five million we 'loaned' it falls due this week. Shall we renew?"

Jimmy meditated a moment. "No. Pay it off on paper, then buy five million dollars' worth of HJK stock." The stock had no actual value, but the bank's accountants were handcuffed puppets and the Lebanese government made no audits. "That'll add five million in securities to our assets on the books."

"Wouldn't deferred convertible bonds be better? We buy five million worth, then at some future date you can puff up HJK Trading common and when Incombank converts, we show a nice profit." On paper. Where else?

"Okay. Maybe you're right. Clear the note and stuff the hole with HJK Trading convertibles. Anything else?"

"Yes. Doug Ford was on the line yesterday. Asked me to tell you he can pick up a good industrial property in New Jersey through Karamprop." Karamprop, Inc. was the real-estate holding subsidiary of Karamcorp. "He needs a million, three hundred thousand cash to swing the deal."

Ford knew what he was doing. "Lend the money to our Caracas branch," Jimmy said. Incombank's branches were organized as independent and separate entities in many countries. "Inform Caracas to loan the money to Karamcorp. Doug can filter it down to Karamprop however he thinks best." The maneuver would enable Incombank Central in Beirut to maintain its liquidity ratio. Bank-accounting procedures equated money due from other banks with cash as immediately liquid resources.

"Right. A last item, though. You never got around to telling me what the final arrangements were with Abdul Kamal."

"Four hundred thousand," Jemel said. "You needn't worry about it now. I borrowed the gambit you used on Fred Hayworth. It's a contingency payment. He doesn't get it until after everything has been wrapped up. By then, we'll be thinking of it as petty-cash disbursement."

New York City. Thursday, May 9th.

The Saudi Arabian ambassador came with a retinue of aides to the Whitehead Oil Building. He formally expressed his government's "deepest regrets" for the "horrifying tragedy" at Nuqayr.

The raid had been the work of as-yet-unknown marauders, he declared. It was not certain that they were Saudi Arabian Bedou. They might have come from Kuwait or Iraq. However, His Majesty King Feisal had given orders that every facility be utilized and every effort made to find and summarily punish those responsible. Until that was done, the ambassador said, every Saudi would feel that he had suffered a grave loss of *sharaf*.

His Excellency had then turned to practical matters. His government would pay extremely generous *divi*—blood money—as compensation to the widow of Lloyd Emmerick and the next-of-kin of the other five Whitehead MidEast employees killed during the attack. The injured would also receive liberal compensation. The full value of all company property destroyed or damaged could be deducted from the next royalty payment.

When the ambassador and his entourage departed, a drawn-faced Quentin Yeager spoke alone with R. D. Whitehead.

"Who do we send out to replace Lloyd Emmerick?" he asked.

"No one," Whitehead replied, his voice hollow. "Send a cable to his assistant saying that he's acting resident super until further notice."

"The man's not fully qualified," Yeager reminded his employer. "We only transferred him over last year to break him in. He can't really take Lloyd Emmerick's place."

You're telling me, the old oilman thought bitterly. Emmerick worked for me almost forty years, starting as a kid roughneck on one of my drilling crews in Texas, working his way up. He'd been the best field man in the industry.

Whitehead shrugged weary shoulders. "You'll be surprised how fast he's going to learn inside that pressure cooker," he said grimly. "Have the cable sent, right away."

Yeager left.

"If I was a religious type, I'd pray," Daniel Whitehead told himself, staring into space. Instead, he cursed—silently and interminably.

4

New York City. Friday, May 10th.

Russell Stanton awoke. Partially. Something warned him not to open his eyes. He moved his head slightly, and the room pitched and heaved.

Hangover. He tried moving his head again. One of the worst ever. Consciousness and fragmented memory dragged themselves through a tunnel lined with shards of broken glass and filled with head-splitting noise.

New York. R. D. Whitehead. Whitehead? Yes. And Jimmy Karami. And Pat.

Oh, Christ. No! He jackknifed himself into a sitting position. The room rocked violently and sunlight from an open-curtained window clawed at his eyeballs. He recognized the chest of drawers against the wall directly in front of him, the bathroom door a few feet to its left. He was home. In his own bedroom. In the East Sixties apartment he'd leased after he sold the house in Scarsdale. That had been after Pat died.

Wait a second. He searched for the wisp of recollection that had snapped him fully awake. After Patricia died. Something about Whitehead. More partial memory lacerated itself surging through the tunnel. Pat—and Jimmy.

He must have groaned aloud.

There was movement in the bed. To the right. "Hi." A woman's muffled voice. "You're alive." A girl. Brunette. About twenty-two or twenty-three, and although sleep-sodden, good-looking. She turned a little. The sheet covering her slid down to her waist. Breasts from a *Playboy* gatefold. Russ searched through another set of memory banks. He saw the girl dressed—blurred, out of focus, as though behind several layers of gauze. Something about a restaurant. Hold on. Her name. Barbara?

He said it aloud. "Barbara."

"And you're Russ. Not Russell, you insisted. Russ."

The hangover crested again. The girl seemed to fade. The spasm receded, and she was back in clear view. God, a drink might help. He looked around. There was a bottle of whisky—he couldn't make out the label and it didn't make any difference—and a glass on the bedside table at his left. The bottle was open. No cork. Some liquor left inside it. He poured into the glass, downed the four fingers, gagged and spluttered until he was sure the stuff would stay down; it was rye. Or it tasted like rye. It stayed.

He looked at the girl again. Smudged recollection-images formed. They'd gone to bed and balled— or was that last just drunken-dream-fantasy?

"Afraid I drew a blank," he muttered.

Barbara propped herself up on one elbow. "You're kidding!" she exclaimed. "My God! If you're that good drunk, what are you like sober?"

"Sorry. I'm not with it."

"You got started and wouldn't stop. It was great!"

He realized for the first time that he was nude.

Hadn't given it a thought before. He rubbed his face. As he lowered his hands, he noticed that the knuckles of the right were swollen and blood-scabbed.

"Who'd I hit?" he asked, staring at the knuckles.

"I don't know. Your hand was like that when I met you."

"When you met me?"

"You don't remember that, either?" She saw from his look that he didn't. "I was having a drink with a couple of girls. You came over. You didn't seem very drunk. You looked like fun. You took me to dinner."

"Funny," Russ thought. "I must have met her early. How did I get so drunk so fast? I didn't leave the office until around three." The office. The scenes with Whitehead flashed before his eyes. He shriveled inside, reached for the bottle and glass. Three-four fingers left. He poured them into the glass. Plenty more out in the bar cabinet.

He held the glass in his hand, turned his attention back to the girl. "Must have been a late dinner," he fished. He raised the glass to his lips.

"No. Around seven."

Around seven? Russ lowered the glass. That made no sense. No matter how uptight, raging-mad miserable he felt, it was impossible to get *that* boozed in a few hours.

"You must be wrong—uh—Barbara." He realized he was still uptight, raging-mad miserable, and he wanted the drink he held in his hand. That and several more.

"I'm not. I take the same 4:05 train from Derby every Thursday, and I don't get into Grand Central until . . ."

"Every *Thursday*?" The word had snagged into Russ like a barbed hook. "Yesterday was Wednesday."

"Thursday. Today is Friday."

The hook pulled more shreds of memory from the tunnel. Jesus Christ, yes. There had been another night in bed. Alone. And he'd got up, dressed and gone out to start boozing again. Stanton's first impulse was to down the drink he still held. He got it up to his mouth once more, paused, reason returning.

I've been bombed senseless for two nights and a day, he told himself. *I don't know where I was, what I did. And now I'm all ready to start again.*

He lowered the glass slowly, and even more slowly put it back on the table. He could stretch a two-nights-and-a-day drunk out to a week, a month. *The rest of my fucking life,* he said to himself. *What I'm trying to drown can't be drowned, and trying is an asshole's play. The acid in my guts will keep on eating, until it stops, or I force it to stop.*

He became aware of his erection only because Barbara placed her hand around it, squeezing and massaging.

Piss hard-on, he thought, and now realized his bladder was filled to distended capacity. He moved the girl's hand away. He got out of bed, went unsteadily, head throbbing and legs rubbery, into the bathroom. He urinated, then fought down a wave of dizziness as he bent over the wash basin and splashed cold water over his face. It helped. He brushed his teeth.

Barbara entered as he was finishing. "I'm next," she said.

He was consciously seeing all of her for the first time. She was better than just good-looking. Much better. He felt his turgescent response.

"You must be terrific even when you're not stoned," the girl said, her eyes growing bright. She grasped his hard phallus, rubbed it against the soft flesh of her inner thigh, then released him and gave him a slight push towards the door.

"Give me about five minutes, okay?" she said.

Russ carried the empty rye bottle and the glass with whisky still in it out into the kitchen. There were two other empties lying on the stainless-steel drainboard of the sink. "And I was wondering how I got so drunk," he reflected.

There was a clock in the kitchen. It was past ten. The maid. No, it wasn't Thursday. It was Friday. She came on Mondays, Thursdays, and Saturdays when he was in New York. He returned to the bedroom. He pulled the badly tangled bedclothes straight and lay down. Barbara entered a few moments later.

She went directly to the bed, sat beside him, tantalizing him and herself by rubbing her breasts against his face and mouth. Then she changed her position, kissed his mouth, her tongue plunging deep, and rolled over, guiding him into her.

5

Beirut. Saturday, May 11th.

Jemel was dressing for the dinner that was to be held that evening by the Lebanese Bankers' Association at the Phoenicia Hotel.

His majordomo tapped on the bedroom door, entered to announce there was a transatlantic telephone call from New York. A Mr. Russell Stanton.

Jimmy was just knotting his tie. He stopped, let the ends fall dangling. Stanton? Of all the improbable . . .

"Switch the call over to the phone here."

It took a few moments. Long enough for Jemel to ponder what might have motivated Russ Stanton to telephone him. Stanton didn't ask favors. True, he worked for Whitehead MidEast, but that couldn't have any bearing. Maybe he . . .

"Mr. Karami? I have Mr. Stanton on the line," an overseas operator's voice said.

"Jimmy?"

"Yes. Hello, Russ. This is a pleasant surprise—but a surprise just the same. How are you?"

"I've been better. How about yourself?"

"Fine here. What's the trouble at your end?"

"Jimmy. Listen a couple of minutes. You've offered me jobs several times. I told you if I ever changed my mind, I'd let you know. I have. Or rather, it's been changed for me. If you still have anything open . . ."

Jemel's eyes drew themselves narrow. "What's happened? How about your vice-presidency with Whitehead MidEast?"

"I either resigned or I got fired. I'm not quite sure which. It's a long story."

Jimmy's brain worked with computer speed. The print-out looked promising, provided the time element was there.

"Effective when, Russ?"

"As of Wednesday afternoon. The Old Man has settled into the home office. He ordered me back from Jeddah. We had a talk that ended up as a battle— and I was off the payroll."

The printout was gilt-edged. Gilt-edged, hell. Solid gold. Russell Stanton's knowledge about Middle Eastern oil operations—and about the American companies conducting them—was encyclopedic. He'd fit right in, add a potent new plus-element. As long as he was kept in ignorance of what purpose he served and what was going on. That could be arranged.

Jemel pretended to cough. He needed the delay to decide the right balance. It had to be fine. Not too eager—yet give Russ no reason to suspect he was being offered a position purely for the sake of friendship.

"There are two, three different slots you're ideally suited for," Jimmy said. "None are quite as big as the last one I mentioned to you—back in '64—but all are good, plenty of opportunity and challenge. We're going to do some large-scale expanding—and you'll be able to write your own ticket in a few years." He paused. "It's impossible to discuss the details over the phone—it'd take hours." Another pause. "I'd like to talk to you personally. Face to face. Unfortunately, I don't count on being in New York for a few weeks. Is there any chance of your flying over here?"

"There isn't anything to keep me from it, Jimmy. When would you have time to sit down and talk?"

Right now wouldn't be too soon, Jemel mused. Stanton wasn't going to be window-dressing or a figurehead. Russ would provide a bonanza of information, and the faster he and Lockhart could tap it, the faster they'd take seven-league strides they'd never hoped to take so easily. But make this all sound plausible.

"Tomorrow is Sunday, and I'm badly tied up most of Monday. How about taking either the Pan-Am or the Air India flight from Kennedy Monday night? You'll arrive here Tuesday evening, local time. Can you do that?"

"Sure, Jimmy. I got used to air-hopping fast while working for Whitehead. I'll shoot you a cable soon's I know on which flight I'm booked."

Don't worry about hotel reservations. You'll stay at my place." That would simplify the brain-picking. The best pieces are always extracted during casual, after-work conversation.

"Thanks, but I'd rather stay in a hotel, Jimmy. I have a thing . . ."

Yes, damn it, Russ did have a thing about "imposing." Don't push too hard, Jemel warned himself. "I'll book you a suite at the Phoenicia."

"Great."

"And figure on staying awhile, Russ. Far as I'm concerned, you're already on the Incombank payroll— and while we're talking money, you can expect Incom to match whatever you made with Whitehead. Plus."

Jemel Karami's smile was a leer when the conversation ended. A barely credible lucky break had dropped out of the Whitehead MidEast organization chart—right into his lap. He sat for a minute, then got up and went back to the mirror and did a quick, neat job on his tie.

He turned and put on his dinner jacket. His glance fell on a Steuben glass figurine of a Weimaraner sitting on its haunches that someone had given him. He chuckled. Even the champion purebreds were coming into the Karami kennels, he observed to himself.

He went to a chest of drawers atop which the various objects he normally carried in his pockets were laid out. As always, the first thing he picked up was his *sibah*. He ran his fingers over the beads thoughtfully, and put the *sibah* into his trousers pocket.

6

Washington, D. C. Sunday, May 12th.

United States Senator Frederick Hayworth was haggard from lack of sleep and in one of his fouler moods. He and Michele had been delayed several hours en route from Europe. They'd landed in Washington just before dawn, and Mickey had announced she would not remain in the city even for a day.

"I'm going home," she declared. "I want to see Mom and Dad—and I don't care how hysterical you get."

Her plane was to leave at eight. She bought a ticket, made the necessary arrangements about her bags. That left a two-hour wait. They sat together in the VIP lounge, Fred Hayworth staying with her because he was afraid someone who counted might see her alone and wonder why he wasn't there, too. It didn't take much to start whispers in Washington.

Mickey read magazines. Fred Hayworth glared away the time, making no effort at conversation. Her flight was called at 7:40. He accompanied her to the boarding gate. There were few passengers, none who meant anything or showed that they recognized the much-publicized "Young Senator Fred." That saved them both the necessity of acting out a fond farewell kiss.

Hayworth was unable to resist a poisonous parting remark. "Don't forget to tell Iron Mike what a wonderful trip you had—masturbating your way all over Europe," he muttered, low-voiced so only Mickey could hear.

She turned, looked squarely at him. "You can't imagine what I intend to tell him, Freddie-boy," she said, eyes and tone icy. "You may get the shock of your life when you come up for reelection next year."

She swung around and went through the boarding gate. Fred Hayworth stared after her, stunned and suddenly very frightened. Without Michael Ferrenbaugh's endorsement, he was finished. Fear receded. She wouldn't say a word. She'd do anything to avoid upsetting her father—and she had too much pride to tell anyone the truth about their marriage.

He went out of the terminal. Even more than the usual number of Negroes were in evidence. The "Poor People's Marchers" were camping in Washington. Goddamn niggers, Hayworth thought. And that King Coon. He thought that was funny and grinned. Martin Luther King Coon. He'd have to shake hands with the black bastard later in the week and smear him with the usual horseshit. Thinking of him as King Coon would make it easier.

Three and a half hours later, Mickey was home. She found her mother alone. Mike Ferrenbaugh had gone to play his every-Sunday nine holes of duffer golf.

Dorothy expressed astonishment when she saw that Mickey had brought all her luggage to the house. The Hayworths' own home was only eight blocks away.

"I'll be bringing the rest of my things over, too," Mickey said. "I'm leaving Fred."

Dorothy Ferrenbaugh had reached the age and stage in life where she believed problems were best talked out in the kitchen.

"Would you like some coffee, Mickey?"

"I'd like a double shot of hundred-proof whisky —but I'll settle for the coffee, Mom."

"I suppose it had to end up like this," Dorothy thought, preparing the coffee. "I knew it was going wrong. I've felt it for years. I never did like Fred Hayworth. He always struck me as a sneak. But Mike thought—he thinks—the world of him."

She poured two cups of coffee, put them on the dinette table.

"Did you have a fight while you were gone?" Dorothy asked tentatively.

Mickey laughed. It wasn't a pleasant laugh. "We've been fighting almost from the day we were married. They've gotten more vicious and ugly. It's useless."

Dorothy stirred her coffee slowly. "You seemed to be very much in love with him."

"I thought I was. And I thought he was with me."

"He wasn't."

"No. Never. He's admitted it almost from the beginning. He married me only because of Dad."

Dorothy didn't require any further explanation of that. Mike had made Fred Hayworth his protégé, pushing him up from the state assembly to the U.S. Senate. She shook her head sadly.

"You're sure you can't patch it up, make a go . . ."

"Certain. It's impossible. I would have left Fred long ago if it hadn't been for Dad. I didn't want to hurt him—you know how he is. Now it's so bad that doesn't even count. Not with me."

Dorothy studied her daughter's face. If Mickey's expression reflected anything, it was genuine regret that she had not broken away from her husband much earlier.

"You said you thought that you loved Fred."

Mickey sighed, got up, went out to find a cigarette and came back with it lit. I might as well tell Mom everything, Mickey thought, she deserves that much.

"Mom. What I hoped for was impossible. When I was convinced that it *was* impossible, I made up my mind to forget about it. I did, too." No, that wasn't entirely honest. "I did—almost. Enough so that I was willing to settle for second best. Fred. Then he turned out to be—what? A heel? A louse? That's putting it mildly. And that's when I realized I should have settled for any small part of the impossible I could get."

Dorothy spoke softly. "You mean Jimmy Karami, don't you?"

Mickey wasn't very greatly surprised. "You knew, I guess."

"Of course I knew." She glanced nervously at her hands, then having made her decision, gazed at her daughter. "Jimmy is very much like his father in many

ways. And—well—Mike, your father, is a good husband but he's—he's a man's man. He's not . . .''

"He's not a very good lover," Mickey said, coming to her mother's aid. "I've guessed that ever since I
first found out what love and sex are all about."
She extinguished her cigarette in her saucer and the
look she gave Dorothy was tender. "What you're
trying to tell me is that you had an affair with Jimmy's
father."

"Yes. In 1941. When we went to New York and
stayed at his apartment."

"Did you fall in love with him?"

"No. I knew it was impossible from the start, and
that made it simple. But—well, I knew that I'd probably never have anyone make love to me like that
again. It was the first time I'd been unfaithful to Mike. I
tried with two other men later—but neither of them
meant anything."

Michele repressed an urge to giggle. There was
something almost incestuous about the situation. Then
she realized the urge was only nervous reaction. There
was nothing funny about her predicament. A separation
and divorce from Fred would be messy. There would
be no end of publicity, no matter how quietly they
went about it.

"I've done much more than that, Mom," she said.
"Not until I found out that Fred was going to bed with
every woman who'd lie on her back for him. Afterwards? I've lost count."

"You went back to Jimmy Karami?"

"Whenever I could."

"You're still in love with him, aren't you?"

"More than ever. He's the only man I really love,
I'll ever really love. He's the only one I want. There's
nothing I wouldn't do for him."

Automobile tires crunched gravel on the driveway
outside the house.

"Your father's home," Dorothy said. "What are
you going to tell him?"

Mickey straightened her shoulders. "Everything—
except about Jimmy."

Dorothy Ferrenbaugh dabbed at her eyes with a

Kleenex. "Yes," she murmured. "It'll be better if you don't say anything about Jimmy to him."

7

John F. Kennedy International Airport, New York City. Monday, May 13th.

Russell T. Stanton took off aboard Pan-American Airways Flight No. 2 at 9:30 P.M

Less than three hours later, Marvin Jacobs checked in at the Air India counter. He was booked on Flight No. 105. His destination: Beriut, Lebanon.

Protasis III

1

Dazzling, meteoric, sensational.

Financial writers were to spice such words freely into their stories of Incombank's growth as an international banking organization. "Boy wizard" and his "magic touch" were phrases they used frequently when they wrote of Jemel Karami.

Although hardly a "boy" (Jimmy was almost twenty-eight when he organized Incombank) Jemel Karami was certainly much younger than the vast majority of men who founded banks and became their board chairmen. As for his "magic touch," it was compounded of several factors, many so obvious they were missed by the experts and analysts who prefer to see (and create) mystiques and mysteries about whatever has to do with money in large sums.

A few, more coldly objective, observers recognized the elements in the compound of Incombank's success —and smiled to themselves, either approvingly or cynically, depending on their personal viewpoints and prejudices.

Incombank burst into the outwardly British-patterned Lebanese banking industry with all the techniques and trappings of dynamic, hard-driving (and hard-selling) American superefficiency. There was a crisp, glossily attractive veneer to draw attention; behind it, a sense of boundless energy and vitality transmitting assurance of success, even infallibility.

In the early stages of Incombank's development, Jemel Karami exploited his Lebanese origins and American business experience (and his palpable success with Karamcorp) to the full. He demonstrated that he was immensely proud to be a Lebanese, an Arab, prouder still that he could share the benefits of what he had learned and achieved with his homeland and the entire Arab world. He subtly evoked images of an emerging financial colossus that would have one great foot (Karamcorp, to start) planted firmly in the western hemisphere, the other, Incombank, anchored in the eastern hemisphere.

Needless to say, all Arabs were certain that Incombank would draw wealth away from the *amirikani* for their own gain (as an Arab himself, Jemel Karami could do no less). The American stockholders of Karamcorp, on the other hand, saw their glamorous, naturalized fellow citizen as a brilliant exponent of American enterprise, whose new bank would tap the vast reservoirs of Middle Eastern wealth and use it to increase the value of the Karamcorp shares.

Neither Arabs nor Americans had any inkling of the screens of dummy companies that had been erected on the Continent to act as two-way profit strainers. And, at the beginning, they were not used as such. Quite to the contrary.

Jemel Karami knew his first task was to attract depositors to Incombank, bring cash into its vaults. He had decided to make no special effort to attract "nervous money," on the entirely reasonable assumption that if money was so nervous that it would flee from one place, it would do the same from another at the slightest hint of trouble. While, for the moment, the Middle East was comparatively calm, upheavals large and small were inevitable. Westerners would be panicked by them. Arabs would accept them, knowing that no matter what the external appearances after any upheaval, all was bound to remain as it had been before.

Jimmy directed his main energies at Arabs, especially the oil-rich sheikhs of Saudi Arabia, Kuwait, Muscat, the Trucial States. Oil fountained from their lands, was transmuted into hard American royalty dollars—and the sheikhs sought means whereby they could make their surplus dollars earn even more wealth.

Lebanese banks paid 5 percent interest on deposits. Incombank established the same interest rate—for small depositors. To the sheikhs, who were able to deposit millions rather than thousands, Jemel Karami offered special inducements. Officially, he would pay them 5 percent interest. Unofficially—well, there would be extra dividends. Two percent, 3 percent, perhaps more in addition. Some agreed to test his proposal.

In the first year of its existence, Incombank obtained $3 million in deposits from oil sheikhs. Leaving other banking functions in Brian Lockhart's capable hands, Jimmy concentrated on generating profits that would permit payment of normal interest to everyday depositors, permit payments of premiums to the sheikhs, and still leave Incombank ahead. For this purpose, he employed his dummy companies in a profit-multiplying rather than -straining role. Karamcorp, too, played its part.

The Lebanese government exercised no regulatory authority over Incombank. United States agencies were powerless to ask even routine questions. As board chairman holding a massive controlling interest of the bank's stock, Jemel Karami was a law unto himself.

Nonetheless, Incom's initial transactions had to appear legitimate and aboveboard. Its first balance sheets had to be impervious to the closest scrutiny by the accountants of large depositors. Later, when confidence had been won, cash-proof having been supplied that money left with Incombank brought handsome returns, the self-imposed restrictions could be relaxed, forgotten entirely.

Such was the logic employed by Jimmy Karami and Brian Lockhart.

The ratio of cash on hand and loans made to highly rated banks (at interest rates at least a point below what Incombank paid its depositors) was kept high. A substantial amount was invested in supersafe (but again, low-interest-bearing) United States and British government bonds.

This left somewhat less than half of Incom's money resources available for more lucrative investments. Part of the remainder went into bankers' acceptances covering export and import shipments made by firms with impeccable credit ratings and thus qualified for prime-rate discounts—rates barely above the interest Incombank paid out.

When all the sums thus held or invested were deducted, Jimmy Karami had scarcely over $1.5 million on Incombank balance with which to turn the very large profits needed to cover interest, all bank costs, and expenses, and still leave Incom in the black after its first year of operation.

He invested the money in "securities"—the stocks and bonds of numerous fictitious companies such as HJK Trading Corp. which he owned. That the securities had no value did not matter. The maneuver freed the $1.5 million (with the securities of the investigation-proof dummies carried on the bank's books as assets) and permitted him to employ the money as he wished.

He next began to search for some venture that would enable him to at least double the $1.5 million inside eight or nine months. He examined several opportunities, discarding them all for one reason or another. Then, as is so often the case, he picked up a hint by hearing an unguarded—and, to an inattentive ear, innocuous—remark, made by a businessman at a cocktail party he attended in New York City.

". . . now Kilgallen Rubber is an example of what I mean," the businessman said, starting his fifth martini. "Better credit than the U.S. Treasury. Stock sells for 5 dollars a share—backed by at least triple net realizable assets and a big cash surplus. The Kilgallen family's always been conservative as hell and still holds the largest block. They keep their dividends down, but pay 'em regularly. It's an old folks' stock . . ."

Kilgallen Rubber. Jemel made a mental note of the name and, feigning a lack of interest verging on boredom, turned the conversation to other topics.

The next day, Jimmy had Doug Ford turn Karamcorp's best researcher loose on a deep-digging study of Kilgallen Rubber and Allied Products Co. This required a fortnight, but the results were rewarding in their promise.

Kilgallen Rubber was an Ohio corporation with

2,000,000 voting shares issued and outstanding—of which 20 percent were held by members of the Kilgallen family and their friends, and together they formed a self-perpetuating board of directors. The remaining 1,600,000 shares were in public hands—owned by some thousands of individual stockholders.

Kilgallen Rubber's net assets were over $35 million, and the company had a whopping cash surplus of accumulated earnings that exceeded $10 million. The Kilgallen board, anarchronistic and ultraconservative, clung to the practice of holding the largest slice of profits in the company.

The company was ripe—indeed, long overdue—for a raid.

Jimmy Karami knew he did not have the time for long, involved minority stockholders' suits to loot Kilgallen Rubber, nor did he want to become engaged in noisy proxy battles. For the operation to be successful, he would have to obtain a clearcut 51 percent majority of the company's voting stock. At the current market, this would require an investment of at least $5.1 million, $3.6 million more than he'd sidetracked from Incombank.

He went to Miles Palmer armed with all the facts and figures.

"We split the deal down the middle," he proposed to Palmer. "Each of us goes in for two-and-a-half million. Palmer National Trust can loan Karamcorp a million on a note to make up the difference between what Incombank has and what it needs. I'll filter the money out through subsidiaries to my dummies."

Miles Palmer did not have to ask why Jemel didn't put up the needed extra million—or take the entire five million—from his own private fortune. Palmer would not have used his own money, either. Karamcorp's stockholders and Incombank's depositors would take their load of the risk—and more. That was why public stock companies and banks existed.

"It's a juicy melon," Palmer agreed. "We'll buy slowly and quietly, through your dummies and certain of my—ah—anonymous companies and in street names, so as not to attract undue notice." He puckered bloodless lips, calculating ahead. "Even so, the buying will probably push the price up. I would estimate we'll average out at around six dollars a share." He grunted. "Palmer National will loan Karamcorp any additional amount needed." He thought some more. "After the melon is sliced, you'll have to pull us out fast, before the per-share price drops very far."

Jimmy's expression was predatory. "I don't think we'll encounter that problem, Miles. The way I see it, the Kilgallens will take every share off our hands at whatever price we average out at—just to save their company. If they don't, the front men I'll pack into the board will scream there's been gross mismanagement, threaten complaints to the SEC, civil and even criminal action. A family like the Kilgallens will pawn everything they own if necessary to avoid scandal."

"Yes," Miles Palmer said. "They probably would."

The purchase of Kilgallen Rubber stock spread over a period of six months. A 50-share odd lot was purchased here, another there. When a thousand or 1,500-share block was offered, it was bought—but only in broken lots, with 200 shares being purchased in one street name, 300 in another and so on.

The trading caused no sudden rise in price. Kilgallen stock did edge up to five and a quarter, later five and a half, and finally reached six and a quarter, leaving the average at less than what Miles Palmer had predicted. By the time the Kilgallen family and the company's board awoke to what was happening, it was too late.

Front men acting for Jemel Karami appeared at the Kilgallen Rubber and Allied Products Co.'s annual stockholders' meeting and voted in new directors and for an immediate distribution of the company's $10 million-plus as special dividends on the common stock.

The Kilgallens were overwhelmed, for their own shares and proxies they held added up to less than 40 percent of the voting stock. The cash-surplus distribution made, they bought up the Karami-Palmer shares.

When all costs and expenses—including the Palmer National Trust's loans to Karamcorp—were paid, Jemel Karami had over a million dollars left in clear profit.

"You and I should work more closely in the future, Jemel," Palmer told Jimmy, and grew confidential. "I—ah—have some rather intriguing possibilities in mind. There are many opportunities in the Middle East." He paused, cleared his throat and eyed Jemel closely. "In oil. There are still concessions to be obtained. With you on the scene and having close contact with the sheikhs . . ."

"Sorry, Miles," Jimmy shook his head. "That's not my kind of business." Nor yours, he added silently. "I'll stick to Karamcorp and Incombank and leave oil to the people who know what they're doing." The intriguing part will be watching to see what Miles cooks up. "Concessions cost fortunes—and my fellow Arabs are tough people to deal with." They'll deal with you as a banker, Miles, but peel the skin off your back if you try to bargain with them over things outside your own field. "But we can play more banking-ball together anytime."

Jemel fed the profits from the Kilgallen squeeze back into Incombank, ostensibly as dividends on HJK Trading Corp. and other dummy-company stocks previously purchased by the bank and via other plausible fictions.

The money allowed Incombank to pay its regular depositors their 5 percent interest. The sheikhs whose favor Jemel was courting received an additional 2½ percent as "extra dividends." Incombank's profits for the first year were relatively modest—but at that far greater than might have been expected for a new banking enterprise.

Word spread.

The $3 million originally deposited by the oil sheikhs was increased to $5 million, then $6—a little later to $7 million.

Before long, the growth would be even more rapid.

2

Jemel established Incombank's first Western Hemisphere branch in Sao Paulo, Brazil. The location was chosen for many excellent reasons. Brazilian law permitted organization of the branch, Banco Incom, S.A. as an independent entity, giving Incombank Central in Beirut added leverage. Trade between Lebanon and other countries in the Middle East and Brazil was brisk —and Sao Paulo had a large expatriate Lebanese colony. It was therefore no great task for Jimmy to find a competent staff and buy an indigenous board of directors, men who would follow instructions and ask no questions.

From Sao Paulo, Jimmy went to New York. Karamprop—the real-estate holding subsidiary of Karamcorp—was making its first important acquisition, taking over the luxurious, sky-scraping Wickpark Towers Apartments on Park Avenue from the receivers for the bankrupt Wickmore Realty Co. He wanted to be present for the closing and final transfer of the property —again for varied, but good, reasons.

Doug Ford, president of Karamcorp, was giving Jimmy a progress report on the Wickpark Towers deal one afternoon when Jemel's secretary called into his office.

"There's a man here to see you, Mr. Karami," she said uncertainly. "He—he says he's your brother Nuri." She'd been with Karamcorp for more than three years. She had never heard anything about Jemel Karami having a brother.

"Nuri?" Jemel asked, taken aback. He'd not seen Nuri nor spoken to him since the week after Hassan died. "All right, send him in." He turned to Ford. "I have no idea how long this will take, Doug. I'll let you know when I'm through, and we can pick up where we left off."

Jimmy braced himself. With Nuri, anything was possible. Even so, he was hardly prepared for the Nuri who entered. He had lost weight, a great deal of weight. He looked seedy, unkempt. His eyes, much too close set, always a watery brown, were sunken and shot through with red. His manner was servile, and his insipid chin twitched, giving the impression that his teeth were chattering.

"Hello, Nuri." The hand he shook was limp. "Sit down." He waited until his brother seated himself. "It's been five years, unless I'm mistaken."

"Jimmy. I want to tell you how sorry I am." Nuri tried to make it sound as though he was crawling, but somehow his voice struck the wrong note. "I said some rotten things."

You sure as hell did, Jimmy thought.

"I've been suffering because of them ever since."

Nuri recited a string of contrite lines. All lies, patent and clumsy, Jemel realized. He read the underlying message, and his patience evaporated.

"You've always been a lousy actor, Nuri. You're broke. You've gone through your trust fund. A million in five years. Now you want money from me."

Nuri pulled at his own fingers, stared at his shoe tips. "It—it wasn't my fault, Jimmy. I . . ."

"Don't tell me. Let me guess. Your 'guardians' and 'trustees' sucked you dry in more ways than one—is that it?"

"Yes. I trusted them. They seemed so nice and honest. And they were like me."

God, he's even developed a lisp, Jimmy thought. He pictured Nuri as a queen in drag and wanted to laugh.

"If you'll just help me out—set up another trust fund for me or give me an allowance. Please, Jimmy. You have so much money. So does"—here his voice took on a bitchy edge—"Felicite. She's rich, and she doesn't need money as badly as I do."

Jemel might have been more sympathetic if Nuri

hadn't made the reference to Felicite. "How much do you have in mind?" he asked icily.

"I can get by fine on a few hundred a week."

Jimmy roared with laughter. "You can, huh?" He slammed his hand hard against his desk top. "Listen, I'll see that you get fifty bucks a week—as charity. Leave your address with my secretary when you go out, and the check will be mailed to you every Friday. For as long as I don't see you or hear from you. One more visit—even a phone call—and the dough stops. For good!"

"Fifty a week? With your money?" Nuri demanded, glaring at his brother. "That won't even pay for my . . ."

"Booze. Dope? Blow-jobs? Tough shit, Nuri. You've got thirty seconds to decide whether you'll take it or leave it—on my conditions!"

Nuri fought to control the rage boiling inside him. He glanced at his older brother, read implacable determination in his expression.

"Fifteen seconds, Nuri!"

"I'll—I'll take it," Nuri said weakly.

"No see. No hear. Understand?"

"Yes," Nuri muttered. "I'll get back at you," he thought. "We'll be even one of these days."

"Good-bye, Nuri. And I mean good-bye. Permanently. Get out!"

Jemel allowed himself a few moments to cool down before he told his secretary to send Nuri Karami a weekly check for $50 to the address he'd left with her, and then asked that she tell Doug Ford to come back into his office.

"Now where were we?" Jimmy asked when Ford returned.

"I was saying that Halim has worked out a legal angle that'll let Incombank, a foreign corporation, or any overseas dummy, own the penthouse, and you'll wind up with it free." The Wickpark Towers Apartments building had thirty-eight stories—topped off by a twenty-one-room duplex penthouse that Jemel wanted as his own, as a residence for himself, Felicite, and

Mademoiselle Claire Viete. "I've gone over it with him. It's airtight. Karamcorp will set up another subsidiary to lease the penthouse and then . . ."

Ford continued. Jimmy nodded as he spoke. It was airtight.

It was Felicite Karami's sixteenth birthday. Jimmy was giving a lavish party for her in the evening, but she begged him to take her to lunch as an additional treat.

"Please, Jimmy. I'd love to go to '21' or . . ."

"We'll do better." He mentioned a restaurant then Manhattan's most chic and exclusive. Felicite was delighted.

As they entered, Errol Flynn saw them, slid off the bar stool on which he hunched drinking, and hurried over to Jemel. Felicite knew her brother had many famous friends, but she'd never dreamed . . .

What followed baffled her. Flynn kept his eyes on her while he whispered furtively to Jimmy—who suddenly tensed, clenched his hands into fists, appeared ready to hit the film star.

For a split second, Jemel intended doing just that. Then he saw the humor of the situation. Felicite *was* gorgeous, and her Arab blood had made her body ripen far beyond its sixteen years. He couldn't blame Flynn for jumping to the wrong conclusions and pleading for "seconds." Jimmy relaxed, grinning. After all, he thought, Mickey Ferrenbaugh hadn't even been sixteen the first time he'd gone to bed with her—and the thought inspired a twitch of regret that the times since had been comparatively few and far between. He'd have to arrange something again soon.

"You rumhead," he whispered good-naturedly to Flynn. "The 'edible jailbait' happens to be my kid sister!"

The actor was stunned. "Christ Almighty, Jimmy! If I'd known . . . !"

"Forget it, stud. Actually, I guess I'm flattered."

Felicite heard none of their conversation. Thrilled when Jimmy finally introduced her to the star, she was mystified when he fled after mumbling a few polite phrases. She and Jemel were led to their table.

"Did I make a *faux pas?*" she asked her brother when they were seated.

"Not you," he chuckled. "Errol. He flipped over you. Thought you were some new girl in town, as it were. Wanted your telephone number."

"Is that why you were so angry for a minute?"

"Um. It's a sort of unwritten law that you don't let guys make passes at your sister when you're around."

"What about when you're not around?" Felicite was teasing him.

"Then you don't let them. Is that an answer?"

The *sommelier* came to the table.

"May I have champagne, Jimmy?"

"Tonight. At your party. You're under the legal age . . ."

"*Pardon,* M'sieur Karami. I can put a half-bottle of ginger ale on the table for camouflage."

"All right. A bottle of the usual, Henri. I won't have a cocktail."

The *sommelier* vanished.

"About your party tonight," Jimmy said. "I've invited someone I know who'll give it a good notice in the papers. You should get to be known now that you're almost through with your finishing school. I asked Elinor Randolph . . ."

"Oh, the one you've been having an affair with for years!"

"Kid sister is growing up." Jemel thought. "I'm not sure you can really call it an 'affair.'" he said. The word implied a degree of permanence and regularity. He and Elinor went to bed together now and then. Her ardor hadn't decreased, and he still enjoyed her—but he wouldn't if it was any more frequent than that. All of which reminded him of something. "We like each other and go to bed together occasionally. Since you know so much about my sex life, I think I should know something about yours. I *am* your legal guardian until you're eighteen." He stopped—and plunged on. "Are you a virgin?"

Honey hair shimmered as Felicite shook her head. "No."

"Anyone ever tell you about precautions and all the rest?"

"Yes. Mademoiselle had our doctor give me a long talk right after I went to bed with a boy the first time two years ago. He fitted me with a diaphragm. There've only been three other boys since."

"I guess that's about par for the course, maybe a little under," Jimmy thought, giving his sister a grin that dismissed the subject.

"Let's talk about the weather, femme fatale. Here comes my champagne and your ginger ale."

"You promised!"

"Sssh." He winked conspiratorially. "The cops might be listening."

Felicite looked at him with amusement. "I don't think that would bother you at all, Jimmy."

Kid sister *had* grown up, he mused. The wine was poured, and he toasted her gravely. She sipped some of her champagne, put down her glass.

"Did you invite anyone else to the party?" she asked, a little nervously.

"No. It's your party. You made up your own guest list. Why?"

Felicite dropped her eyes, fumbled with her napkin. "I—I was afraid that you might have asked Nuri because it was my sixteenth birthday and . . ."

Jimmy stared at her in astonishment. They never mentioned Nuri's name. "Whatever gave you that idea?" he asked. "I wouldn't invite Nuri anywhere."

Felicite smiled relief. "I'm glad. I can't imagine why I thought you might, but I did. I'm still afraid of him, Jimmy."

"Stop being afraid. You'll never see Nuri again—unless it's by accident." He raised his glass. "By the way, I have a surprise for you—sort of a bonus birthday present. We're going to move in a month or so—to a penthouse on Park Avenue. Two floors—a duplex. So many rooms that you and Mademoiselle can each have your own private suites."

Jemel left the next day for Beirut, via Paris, where he would stop over for three days. Military di-

sasters in Indochina had made many Frenchmen panicky. Those who held large sums of unreported francs
wanted to exchange them for more stable currencies—
something they could not do officially because of
France's tight currency-exchange restrictions.

Boxed in with francs they feared would plummet
in value, they were selling the French money at large
discounts. Jimmy was going to buy $500,000 worth at
the panic *bourse* rates. As an officially accredited financial institution, Incombank could redeem them at
full value—for a profit of $150,000 or more.

Nuri raged hysterically when he read the item in
Elinor Randolph's "Busybody" column in the *Daily
News*.

"Terrific is the word for the party international
financier Jimmy Karami threw for his sister, Felicite,
in the Cotillion Room of the Hotel Pierre, on her sixteenth birthday. A stunning beauty, Felicite Karami
also has a million or so tucked away in her own
right . . ."

Nuri ripped the newspaper into shreds, flinging
them on the floor of his shabby cold-water-flat bedroom.

"I hate them!" he screamed aloud.

Jemel gave parties for that dirty little bitch. "And
she has all her money—while I get $50 thrown at me
once a week.

"Goddamn the two of you!" he yelled. "I hate you
both!"

He stamped and ground the scraps of newspaper
into pulp beneath the soles and heels of his shoes.

The desire for revenge seared through him.

"I'll find a way!"

He turned and threw himself down on his bed.

3

Mademoiselle Viete had gone to bed early, and it was Thursday, the servants' night off.

Just before he left for Paris and Beirut, Jimmy had told his sister she should start thinking how she wanted her suite furnished and decorated when they moved into the Wickpark Towers penthouse. Felicite had purchased every house-decorating magazine and book she could find. She had been going through her collection every evening—and she was doing it again.

The telephone rang. She answered on the extension in her bedroom.

"Felicite?"

"Yes?" Boys often called Felicite, but this was an oddly muffled voice she didn't recognize.

"Are you alone?"

Someone was playing idiotic jokes. "Yes, I'm alone."

"Don't use my name unless you are. This is Nuri." The voice had suddenly become unmuffled, familiar, even though it had been years since she'd heard it. She was dumbfounded. Nuri? Calling her?

"I—I'm alone, Nuri," she stammered, unable to think very clearly.

"Please listen. Please. It's important. I'm in some bad trouble—and it will mean trouble for you and Jimmy, too, if you don't help me. Can you leave the apartment without anybody knowing?"

Felicite hesitated. She feared Nuri, loathed him. "Oh, Nuri . . ."

"You've got to believe me. We're all going to be in trouble. I'd tell Jimmy about it, but he isn't in New York. There's no one else but you." He was pleading, begging and there was desperate urgency in his voice.

"Can't you come up here—or wait till tomorrow?"

"No. It's impossible. I'll explain when I see you."

Felicite Karami had very seldom encountered difficult situations in her life. She despised Nuri, but suddenly he was confronting her with what sounded like a grave emergency, a need to make a major decision about something that threatened her and Jimmy, too.

"You've got to make it fast, Felicite. For God's sake, you're not a baby anymore—and I've grown up. I've changed. I'd never call and ask you like this if I wasn't so scared for all of us!"

"Nuri is twenty-three now," Felicite thought —"and he *is* my brother, whether I like him or not. Besides, what harm could he do to me?"

"Where are you?"

"Take a taxi and meet me on the uptown corner of Sixth and Bleecker in the Village. I'll be waiting for you. Please hurry, Felicite. Please!" he hung up.

She straightened her long blonde hair, got a coat and her purse and quietly left the apartment. She took an elevator down to the lobby. The doorman whistled for a taxi. She got in, waited for the door to be closed before telling the driver her destination.

At ten-thirty on that Thursday night, the area near Sixth and Bleecker streets was a murky, dismal Greenwich Village backwater. The cab stopped at the uptown corner. Felicite barely recognized Nuri standing near the dark window of a poultry-in-parts store. She paid the driver, got out and walked toward her brother. He was much thinner than she remembered him—and there was something almost sinister in his manner as he slouched out from the shadows. She glanced over her shoulder, but the taxi was already pulling away from the curb.

"Nuri . . ."

"We can't talk here. Come on."

He took her arm, only held it more tightly when she recoiled at his touch and hurried her around the corner. His face, with its receding chin, was expressionless. They followed a zigzag course for several

blocks. Felicite, unfamiliar with the Village, lost all di-
rectional sense.

"Where are we?" she asked.

"Almost there. You'll find out everything in a
minute—why you had to come down here." A few
dozen paces further, a scabrous building, some of its
windows boarded, three steps leading up to a coal-black
entranceway.

"Nuri. You don't mean *here?*"

"Yes. It's a place used by some of my friends." He
urged her up the steps. She tried to hang back. Useless.
"Go on!"

The entranceway reeked of decaying garbage,
stale human urine and cat-spray. Nuri prodded his sister down a sagging hallway. He stopped in front of a
door she could barely see, said loudly, "It's Nuri." He
opened the door and nudged her inside.

A feeble light burned somewhere. There was
movement. Shapes stirring in the shadows.

"Nuri!" Felicite was terror-stricken. "Nuri—help!"
Something struck her head. She knew her knees were
buckling, and then she lost consciousness.

"She's all yours," Nuri sniggered to the four men
who had gathered around Felicite. "I told you I'd get you
something good." He moved towards a rickety chair.

"Outside!" one of the men snarled at him.

"No! I want to watch!"

"I said outside, cocksucker! You make sure nobody comes nosing around!" He swung his arm back
in a menacing gesture. Nuri scuttled out into the hallway; the door was slammed shut after him.

He was disappointed. He'd thought they'd let him
watch. Anyway, now some of the score would be settled. Felicite would pay back part of what she owed
him for causing *Maman*'s death—and part of what
Hassan and Jemel owed him, too. He couldn't watch,
but the semideserted house was silent, and its walls
were thin. He edged close to the door.

The gang-fuck would fix Felicite. She was going to have her face rubbed in shit—and rough, stiff
pricks shoved into every hole she had, and a few places
where she didn't have any. She wouldn't be the society

innocent—the too-cute-to-be-true coquette—after it was over.

He leaned close to the grimy wall, bent his head and placed his ear against a panel of the wooden door. It was still good. He could listen with pleasure to the only slightly distorted voices of the men inside the room.

"Jesus! Wotta pair o' tits. Hold 'em together for me while I stick my cock between 'em and work myself off that way . . ."

"Shut up! Pull her legs apart and lemme get into that cunt . . ."

Nuri congratulated himself. He'd figured everything down to the fine points. He was a lot smarter, a lot more clever than Hassan or Jimmy ever gave him credit for being. He'd figured how to get back at them all. He'd got her out of the apartment—alone. And he didn't have a damned thing to worry about. Not one. He would be safe. Felicite would never tell Jimmy—or anybody else—what had happened. Oh, no. Never. Everybody knew that nine out of ten girls who were raped never said a word to anyone about it. Felicite would be the last to open her mouth. She'd be scared shitless about what Jimmy would think. She'd be messing up his reputation as well as her own. If the great glamour-cock banker's sister went to the cops, the story would make the front pages of every paper in New York—and Jimmy couldn't afford to have that happen. Felicite knew it. She knew how much the horseshit reputation he'd built up meant to Jimmy.

He listened again.

"She's coming to . . ."

"Slug her again."

"Nah. We can hold her. Just shove something in her mouth."

"Get a rag."

"I got something better. Gimme room to squat down over her face."

"Jeeze! I wanna shoot off in her mouth after you're through."

"Oh, Christ! I'm going off—she's getting a mouthful!"

Nuri squirmed. He was only dimly aware that he had his penis in his hand and was massaging it, thinking of the man ejaculating. He could almost taste the semen—then he felt his own spurting, some of it sticking to his thumb and forefinger. He raised his hand to his mouth.

The men were gone. Felicite was alone with Nuri. She lay sprawled, semiconscious on a filthy mattress. She was nude, and she groaned feebly.

"Get up!" Nuri rasped. He stood beside the mattress and jabbed at her ribs with the point of his shoe. She hardly felt his kicks; they were mild, distant sensations against the background of the pain that racked her body. "Get up! You may feel sore, but you're not hurt. All you've got is a bump on your head!" He gave her a much harder kick. "Come on! Start moving—so you can go home and wash some of the come off you—and out of your snatch." He snickered. "You better gargle, too!"

Felicite struggled to sit up and it was agony, but she managed. She fought down churning nausea, but only because she knew that if she failed, if she vomited now, it would only add to Nuri's sense of triumph.

"Put on your clothes, you fucked-out whore! Then you can go home and tell Mademoiselle—and Jimmy, when you can find him—how their gorgeous heiress and pet was gang-banged!"

Intuition sharpened by fear and horror made Felicite give the right responses. "Tell them?" she whispered. "How could I tell anyone?" Her best—and possibly sole—chance to avoid further harm—even to save her life—was to convince Nuri she would remain silent.

Felicite placed a palm against the greasy wall and forced herself to her feet. "I'll never tell anyone," she repeated. "If anyone ever found out—ever." Slowly, painfully, she found her clothing, some of which was torn, and started to dress. "Nuri. Please. Please, don't ever let Jimmy or Mademoiselle know," she begged. "I'd die. Please, Nuri?"

Nuri smiled to himself. He felt content, secure. Avenged.

When his sister was dressed, Nuri said, "Just stagger around the streets until a cab or someone who wants some fucking picks you up," and left her alone.

Felicite's coat was intact. It would cover her ripped clothing and, by some miracle, she found that her purse had fallen into a dark corner. No one had touched it. She had enough money to hail a taxi and go home.

4

Nuri had miscalculated.

Jemel returned to New York a week or so after Felicite was gang-raped. Although there were no outward marks or bruises, he needed only to look at her drawn face and the expression in her eyes. He took her into the study.

"What happened while I was gone?" he asked her.

Felicite told him, watched his glacial fury gather and grow, and it was balm for her.

"Have you been to the doctor?" he asked softly when she was finished.

"Yes. The next morning. He gave me injections, made an examination. He says I have nothing to worry about. I gave him no details, Jimmy. I told him I was attacked—raped—and didn't want to go to the police. He said he'd make no report."

"One more question, Felicite." He was concerned over the psychological effect the experience had on her. "Did you enjoy sex, have orgasms, before?"

"Yes." She understood. "The doctor asked me the same. He said the shock wouldn't affect me so much then. That it probably wouldn't keep me from having a normal sex life. I don't think it will. I hope it won't." She paused, and her dark eyes flared hatred. "Nuri?"

"I'll settle with Nuri." He asked her to leave him alone in the study.

Felicite nodded and went out. His promise was enough. She would sleep soundly, peacefully that night.

Jimmy referred to his private address book, found the number. He'd had occasion to call it once or twice in the past. He dialed, made an appointment for two hours later.

The sleek middle-aged man was avowedly a "wholesale distributor," the younger, hard-faced men flanking him his "administrative assistants." Jemel's interview with them was brief. He recited facts, stated what he wanted—at one point satisfying the questions manifested by startled expressions by honestly explaining that it was what Arab tradition demanded —and agreed readily upon a price.

"We can set the first part up for tomorrow night," the middle-aged man said. "Is that too soon?"

"No," Jimmy replied. "It's not too soon."

Nuri knelt, sobbing, babbling whatever came to his spittled lips.

". . . she's lying. I never even saw her, Jimmy. I swear it. She's my sister. I wouldn't . . ."

"Hit him," Jemel said to one of the other three men in the room. A fist smashed against Nuri's nose, knocking him sideways onto the floor. He screamed and blood poured from his nostrils.

"Names, Nuri. Four names. And addresses." Jemel's tone was low, menacing.

Nuri tried to think. To remember how he'd got where he was—and where was he? He recalled the two men, two of the three strangers in the room, knocking on the door of his apartment, forcing themselves inside, shoving a gun into his belly, slapping a cloth that reeked of chloroform over his face. But this place— half private house, half doctor's office, and Jemel and the fourth man, a doctor . . .

"The names, Nuri. Now."

"Give names, and I'll be admitting everything," Nuri thought, terror-stricken. Wait. Maybe. Yes. He blurted out words.

"They forced me, Jimmy. They knew Felicite—and that she was my sister. They said they'd kill all three of us—Felicite, you, and me—if I didn't bring her down. If I tell you their names, they'll murder us. . . !"

"Hit him again."

Nuri was jerked to his feet. Fists battered at him. He screamed. The fists continued—and then he was hurled to the floor.

"Ready, Nuri? Or do you want more?"

Agonized gasps. Retching. A moaned "Yes. I'll tell you. Only don't . . ."

"Who were they?"

Nuri stammered out four names.

"Repeat them!"

Nuri did. They were the same as before. So far, the truth, Jimmy thought. "Their addresses, Nuri."

He knew only two and gave them between sobs of pain.

"That's enough for us," a harsh voice said. "We'll have all four of 'em inside a week."

Jemel's voice: "All right, doctor."

The short, spindly figure wearing a white smock came forward, Nuri, staring up from the floor, saw light glint on his eyeglasses.

"Carry him into the workroom," he said. The two men picked Nuri up. "I'll get some treatment, something to ease the pain," he thought gratefully.

The man in the smock turned to Jemel. He'd done and seen many things since losing his license to practice, but this was something new and weird, even for him. "I hear you're going to do the actual work," he said.

"Yes," Jemel said. "I have to. If my father were alive, he'd do it."

"A kind of ritual?"

"More than that. A tradition that's bred into every Arab. This is how it has to be."

"Oh." The doctor had to admit there was a savage, elemental justice to it. "Just do exactly as I tell you. Then I'll sew him up."

"It's important that he stays alive," Jemel said.

"He will. Only he'll wish he hadn't."

They went into an adjoining room. It was outfitted as a doctor's examining room and surgery. The man in the white smock gave Jemel a scalpel.

Felicite was waiting for Jemel in the study.

He entered, carrying an airline bag zipped shut, closed and locked the door, put the bag on top of the desk. He opened the zipper, took out a tightly sealed jar.

"Part of the account is paid," he muttered.

Felicite found that she could look at what floated in the clear fluid inside the jar without revulsion.

"He's not dead?" she murmured, her gaze fixed on the jar.

"Oh, no."

"What will happen to him?"

"When he's able to travel, he'll go to Beirut, aboard a Lebanese freighter. A *badawi* I know—an Abdul el Muein—will take him a bit further. To a village in the mountains. In the Chouf."

Jemel held the jar up to the light of a floor lamp, tipped it a little to one side. The amputated scrotum and testicles bobbed in the fluid.

"Nuri will be allowed to live in the village for several months, possibly a year—long enough for the knowledge that he's a castrate to gnaw deep into him."

"And then?"

Jemel placed the jar back on the desk. His mouth tightened. "I said he'll be allowed to live for several months, possibly a year." Now the meaning was unmistakable.

Felicite shifted her eyes away from the glass jar. She stepped close to Jemel. "You held the knife in your right hand?"

"Yes."

She took his right hand in both of hers, bent her head, and kissed his palm.

That, too, was part of timeless tradition.

One morning, several days later, Jemel sat at the breakfast table, reading the newspapers while he ate.

"Mm. Here's a story that demonstrates the old adage about the wages of sin," he said—very casually, for Mademoiselle Viete's benefit, but looked at Felicite, his eyebrow cocked at a sharp angle. "Listen to this." He read aloud, " 'Four men were killed last night when the car in which they were riding, previously reported as being stolen by its owner, crashed through a guard-rail and plunged into the East River.' " He put the paper aside. "Poetic justice," he grinned, reaching for a slice of toast and spreading *labeneh* over it.

"May I please have the sugar?" Felicite didn't actually want the sugar, but when he passed it to her, she had the opportunity she needed.

"Thank you, Jimmy," she said, her voice husky, intense. The rest of the account had been paid.

Jemel smiled at his sister. "My pleasure." It was. He'd once more proven to himself what could be done with money.

"You'd both better make up your minds about your suites in the penthouse," he told Felicite and Mademoiselle. "The architects and contractors will come around to see you next week. They already know what I want—and work on remodeling is scheduled to start before the end of the month. I won't be here— so it's up to the two of you."

5

A powder-train of events during 1956 assured Beirut's position as an international banking center and the financial capital of the Middle East.

Huge new oil strikes had been made in Saudi Arabia, the Trucial States, and offshore fields in the Persian Gulf. In July, Egyptian dictator Gamal Nasser seized the Suez Canal. This led to war in October—a war that shattered the Egyptian army but proved inconclusive when the Eisenhower administration exerted strong pressures on the Anglo-French-Israeli coalition opposing Egypt and forced it to end the fighting and withdraw.

The Middle East was swept by a tidal wave of hysterical Arab nationalist fervor. Immense sums of Arab money were shifted from "imperialist" Western to Lebanese Arab banks.

Then, the Tangier international free zone was handed over to Morocco. Tangier's tissue-paper "banks," fearing even cursory Moroccan audit, closed; their organizers and assets vanishing. Skittish European and American depositors who might have hidden their nervous money in Tangier now cached it in Beirut.

The influx of wealth brought another boom to Beirut. Speculation—particularly in land and building construction—mass-produced millionaires. Barren rock-plots of ground brought more per square yard than they had been worth per acre a decade before. Gaudy hotels materialized along the Avenue de Paris and the Corniche Chouran. Ostentatious apartment and office blocks sprouted by the dozen.

Beirut's banks—increased further in their numbers—stoked the speculative fires and took their share of the profits.

Jemel Karami's Incombank could boast $45 million in assets—and it had opened branches in five Middle Eastern and South American countries.

The Middle East and Lebanon were becoming focal points of attention in many high places around the globe.

Miles Palmer listened with deferential respect. His appointment as Special Adviser on Foreign Economic Affairs, made shortly after Eisenhower's reelection, was still too recent to permit familiarity towards the older man with whom he was conversing. He could not yet call him "Foster."

"Yes, Mr. Secretary," Palmer murmured at appropriate intervals while the official delivered one of his familiar self-righteous sermons.

". . . our opposition to the British, French, and Israelis was motivated by more than concern over the outcome of the election here, Mr. Palmer. Britain's moral and political decay has left us with a mission to enlist Arab support in the crusade against the spreading menace of Communism." He stopped, peered at Miles Palmer through prissy bifocals.

"Brilliant policy, Mr. Secretary."

"We are relying on you, Mr. Palmer. We believe you can help establish close, cordial relationships with the Middle Eastern banking community." He cleared his throat. "To an ever-increasing degree, that means the bankers of Lebanon."

He cleared his throat again. "Implementation of our policy will be through economic and military aid. We shall be unstinting with both. Special funds and appropriations will be provided."

"I take it you wish me to—ah—work behind the scenes?"

"I would much prefer to describe your task as one of highly discreet economic diplomacy. The Palmer National Trust Company has many good connections abroad. You should be able to perform valuable services for the adminis—for the United States and the free world."

"It will be an honor, Mr. Secretary." And a means to accomplish what I'm after, Miles Palmer added to himself.

An expanding Incombank now occupied an entire four-story building on the rue Georges Picot. It was there, in an executive suite they shared whenever Jimmy was in Beirut, that Jemel Karami and Brian Lockhart received Miles Palmer. Although the day was only mild by Beirut standards, the fleshy Palmer was perspiring freely. He mopped his face with a handkerchief, lowered himself into a chair near an air-conditioning duct.

"How do you people stand this climate?" he groaned.

"All in the mind," Jemel grinned. "Think cool and hold the thought."

Palmer did not smile. "Yes. Perhaps you're right, Jemel."

"Asshole," Jemel thought, and said, "I gather from your rather guarded words over the phone that you have some good news for us, Miles."

"Yes. At my recommendation, Incombank has been designated as an offshore lending instrumentality for the Department's Office of Special Foreign Aid Projects. With a six million dollar starting credit."

"Sounds good, Miles. Under what terms and conditions?"

"Very few. OSFAP operates under flexible regulations, and it's financed by Executive Branch discretionary funds. The credit is what's known as a paragraph 40e Private Entity Aid Credit—extended for a twenty-year period. Incombank pays no interest at all for the first ten years, 3 percent per annum thereafter. As a designated instrumentality, Incom uses the money for loans to private enterprise in any of six listed underdeveloped Middle Eastern countries—at its normal interest rates."

"The mind boggles," Brian Lockhart chuckled.

Palmer continued. "The administration wants to enable privately owned banks to encourage private enterprise," he said. "It is a most liberal program. If any loans Incom makes prove uncollectable after a three-year period, equivalent portions of the credit may be forgiven at Executive Branch discretion. All you need show is that the loans were originally granted to establish or expand industrial, commercial or agricultural enterprises and that the borrowers' default was not due to misfeasance, malfeasance, etcetera. That's accomplished easily. You simply forward properly prepared financial statements to OSFAP."

"Audits?" Lockhart asked.

"This is a crash program. The department accepts audits made by the designated lending instrumentality's own accountants."

"How much can we wipe in three years?" Jemel inquired.

"Say three million to be on the safe side."

Jimmy laughed inwardly. Six million. Three that could be loaned on paper to companies existing solely on paper—and failing to repay solely on paper. Three more, interest-free for a decade, to be loaned out at high rates to legitimate companies.

"I assume we divide the green stamps evenly, Miles?"

"No, Jemel. This credit is all and entirely for Incombank."

Karami's eyes narrowed into black slits. "How is it you want no share of the proceeds, Miles?" he asked suspiciously.

Seconds passed before Palmer answered, and when he did, his reply seemed irrelevant. "There is serious political instability in Iraq."

Jimmy and Brian Lockhart exchanged glances. "As there is almost everywhere in this part of the world," Lockhart observed noncommittally.

"Ah—but Nationalist factions are especially active in Iraq."

Jemel and his closest Incombank aide and confidant remained silent.

Palmer spoke. "Given tangible support to achieve their aspirations, the Iraq nationalists would be grateful to those who helped them."

"Very vague and iffy, Miles," Jemel remarked.

"Gentlemen, some—ah—associates of mine and I plan to offer the nationalists in Iraq private support."

Jimmy's mind flashed back to a conversation he'd had with Palmer after they'd pulled off the raiding operation on Kilgallen Rubber. Everything was clear. Miles was going after the oil concessions he wanted to get at bargain prices. If he helped the nationalists overthrow the Iraqi monarchy, they would take the immensely valuable oil concessions held in the country by British companies—and turn them over to Miles Palmer and his "associates." At least, that was Palmer's idea.

The goddamned fool, Jemel thought. *He's got the usual U.S. government misinformation about what's going on inside an Arab country. The Iraqis will soak up his money like a blotter—and win, lose, or draw, give him nothing.*

"What do you expect us—and Incombank—to do?" he asked.

"To work with us, Jemel."

Jimmy shook his head. "Actively? Not a chance, Miles. We aren't about to run any risk of antagonizing any oil sheikhs or oil companies over here."

Palmer's jowls sagged in disappointment. He really hadn't expected Karami to go along all the way. "Would you be willing to be—ah—a benevolent neutral?"

"Maybe. If you explain what it means."

"Allow my people to establish their working-fund accounts with Incombank, not leak any information about how the money comes in or goes out or where it's paid—and if you hear of anything you believe might be of importance, let me know about it?"

"That's all, Miles? Absolutely all you want?" What he asked was easy. Every conceivable shape and shade of Middle Eastern intrigue was hatched with money held and paid out from secret Lebanese bank accounts. One more or less didn't matter. Certainly, Incombank had nothing to gain from giving the shaky Iraqi regime any warnings; it would fall sooner or later, that was certain—only not in any way Miles Palmer hoped or imagined. As for tossing Palmer an occasional tip on developments—what the hell, that could be done. There were always a million and one rumors floating around—pick any dozen at random and Miles would be delighted to have them.

"That's all I want," Palmer nodded. Karami was the only Lebanese banker he could trust to any degree, and he needed a Lebanese bank through which he could handle certain financial transactions. Whatever he learned from Jemel would be an advantage. Besides, once the plans started to show progress, Karami might be induced to take a more active part. "That is all."

"And it's worth your split of the OSFAP credit deal?"

"Yes."

"Then Incombank is a benevolent neutral."

Egypt's Nasser was frantically trying to rebuild his shattered military establishment. *Baksheesh* paid to the right people in Cairo produced large orders for equipment of all kinds.

Jemel obtained a very profitable order for HJK Trading Corp. from the Egyptian government—but he didn't quite know how to fill it, and took the problem with him to New York.

He needed 500,000 uniforms for the Egyptian army. However, Egypt would buy nothing made or handled by Jewish firms or Jews. Conversely, Jewish clothing manufacturers (and most clothing manufacturers were Jewish) returned the dubious compliment. They would produce nothing intended for use by the Egyptian army.

The solution struck Jemel while flying over the Atlantic.

Marvin Jacobs.

The order called for what were only slightly modified versions of British cotton khaki battle dress. Without identifying badges or patches, and with plain buttons. With those specifications as a starter, he'd be able to talk around all the other details—as long as it was Marv to whom he talked. Jacobs wouldn't doubt his word about anything.

He telephoned Marvin soon after his arrival.

"Remember when you helped me out with shirts and trousers to fill an order after the war, Marv?" Jemel asked. Marvin did. "I've got a really big deal for you now, kid. One of my companies has an order for 500,000 modified British-type uniforms—cotton khaki . . ."

"Hey, Jimmy. Don't want to butt into your affairs —but are you sure somebody isn't conning you? The British don't buy cotton goods outside . . ."

"Oh, this is some crazy U.S. military aid program proposition," Jemel said glibly. "The soldier-suits are going to Australia or the Malay States or some damned place. My company takes the merchandise f.o.b. your factory and then packs and ships to specifications."

"That aid-program bit explains it—we've had a little business from it before, but nothing this big. Sure,

Jimmy. I'd love to fill the order for you. It's pure gravy for any cloak-and-suiter."

"Give a reasonable bid, and you're in, kid. I'll send Doug Ford out to see you. It's his account, really." Jimmy paused.

"Uh, Marv. Mind marking the uniforms with one of my company's names? We're trying to make an impression."

Marv hesitated. He preferred using his own labels, advertising Pincus Jacob & Son. "For you, Jimmy, sure," he said finally. "By the way, how's your new place?"

Jemel remembered he hadn't invited Jacobs to see the Wickpark Towers penthouse. It had been his New York home for almost a year—and the duplex had received much publicity.

"You'll have to come and take a look at it one of these days, Marv."

"Anytime."

"Maybe after the Christmas-New Year holidays. Tomorrow's December twentieth—and two days later I'm going out to the Middle West. I won't be back until the first of the year."

6

Senator Michael Ferrenbaugh's proposal seemed perfectly tailored to Jimmy Karami's desires.

Incombank had reached a stage at which Jimmy considered it entirely safe to sidetrack sizable sums of bank money and use them for long-term personal investments that would pay truly huge returns.

Mike had come up with a beauty.

The senator managed to obtain copies of the route maps for a federally subsidized superhighway that was to be built across his state. The maps were a tightly guarded secret. They would not be made public for two years—not until late 1960 or early 1961. Only then would the authorities begin condemnation proceedings against owners of properties lying along the route of the proposed highway.

Ferrenbaugh's scheme was almost as old as the legal concept of eminent domain. This grants federal, state, and local governments the right to appropriate (in return for "fair" payment) any private property required for public use.

Whenever a governmental body exercised its right of eminent domain, the asking (or, more properly, the demanding) price of private properties marked for "condemnation" soared. Anyone with advance knowledge of the exact location of a proposed public project or the route to be followed by a new highway could buy low and then sell at greatly inflated prices.

In essence, Mike proposed that a galaxy of dummy corporations be formed in his state. These would surreptitiously buy up large tracts of real estate situated astride the route of the proposed highway far in advance of its public announcement.

"When the state starts condemning, we make a fortune!" Mike enthused.

Jemel agreed the proposition was interesting. Worth a much closer look. He said he'd come out and go over the route maps with Mike personally, then inspect the properties. If he was satisfied, he'd finance the operation with a few million drained out of Incombank, he thought. The money would be tied up for two or three years—but he'd cover that somehow or other.

Jimmy suggested an additional fillip. Whatever properties were bought, they'd be sold back and forth among the corporations to raise the "last-price-paid" to high levels for evaluation purposes.

"We might even throw in some spit-and-baling-wire improvements here and there," Ferrenbaugh countered. "Balloon the bills, and I'll use my pull to make the evaluators swallow them."

Jemel was in agreement.

"When will you be out?"

Jimmy cagily stalled, arranging it so that it would

not be until Mickey was home from the state university for her Christmas vacation.

"You'll stay at our house, won't you?"

Jimmy thanked him, but said no. "I'll be swamped with other work I'll have to catch up with," he said. "I'll be bringing a suitcase full of papers I have to go over whenever I have a spare minute. I'll hire a car and driver and get myself a suite in a hotel or motel."

That would make it possible for him to be alone with Mickey. Except for the previous year, when she'd come to New York for a week during her summer vacation, they'd been together only half a dozen times since his first visit to the Ferrenbaughs. "No offense, Mike, honest. I'm just busier than hell these days."

Before leaving New York, Jemel even went to the trouble of cramming a suitcase full of meaningless documents and correspondence. He'd have them spread out all over for Mike's benefit.

Jemel discovered that Mickey had thought even further ahead. When she heard he was coming to see her father and would be staying a week, ten days, possibly a fortnight, she announced that she'd already made plans to spend from December 27th to the 30th skiing in Colorado.

"I forgot to tell you before," she said to her mother and father. "A whole bunch of students from my class are going together."

Mike and Dorothy made no objection.

When Jimmy arrived, she took the first chance she could find to tell him what she'd done.

"Four whole days with you!" she exclaimed. "I'll leave the house with luggage and skis—and come and stay with you."

She was growing more attractive every time he saw her, Jimmy mused, and felt muscle pressing against the fabric of his trousers. "Bright girl," he smiled. "Only how do I duck out for four whole days?"

"You can say you're sick."

"Your folks would only come down to nurse me —and send doctors."

"Say you're busy."

"That's what I intend saying for the nights." He thought a moment. "I've got an idea. I'll be so busy those days, I'll be able to spend only a couple of hours with Mike each morning or afternoon."

"Make it in the mornings," Mickey said. "Then I'll be able to have a little more sleep—and be recovered for when you come back."

Jimmy claimed he'd forgotten to hire a car and chauffeur and so, on the first night, Mickey drove him from the Ferrenbaugh house to the motel.

"We have an hour," Mickey said hoarsely, pulling into the garage of Jimmy's motel bungalow. "I told Mom I'd be stopping off to see one of my girlfriends."

She was already unfastening her clothes as they entered the bungalow.

Jemel was satisfied by what Ferrenbaugh showed him. The route maps were authentic, approved. Much of the property along the proposed highway route was run-down farmland, available cheap, Ferrenbaugh said.

Jimmy showed particular interest in those segments of the superhighway that were to be built where state arterial roads already existed.

"That's where we should buy," he declared. "We buy parcels of low-cost farmland along those roads. Before the route maps are made public, we run in bulldozers and excavators. We start to clear ground, dig foundations. The dummy companies owning the parcels will have all sorts of architects' plans to prove we intended building restaurants, motels, housing developments, you name it. The evaluators will have to make allowance for our potential loss of profit . . ."

"By God, you're right!" Mike boomed, rubbing his great, square-cut hands. "It's going to cost extra money, though."

"What do you estimate we can take for every dollar we put in, Mike?"

"Double. I'm going to put up a hundred thousand."

Jemel grinned. "Mike, I'm ready to put up ten million."

Ferrenbaugh stared at him, popeyed.

"Ten million, Mike. And you'll get ten percent of

my profits. That should give you all the strength you need to twist like you've never twisted before."

Jemel had it all clearly in mind. Incombank Central in Beirut and the Incom branches would loan a total of ten million back and forth to each other—reflecting good-as-cash "loans to banks" on the balance sheets. Each would make loans (which he had absolute authority to approve) to various of his European dummies—a million here, three there, two another place until the entire ten was loose and freely employable. The European dummies would then loan the money to their counterparts organized in Mike's state. There would be a two, three, three-and-a-half year wait for the payoff. It would be worth the juggling act. When the state government bought the properties, the reverse flow of cash would begin—and the profit would stick in the Karami-owned corporations in Liechtenstein and Monaco.

It was midnight, Saturday, December 28th.

Mickey Ferrenbaugh lay curled in Jemel's arms. She ran her fingers across his chest and down over his flat, tight-muscled stomach.

"We've been in bed together almost two whole days," she murmured happily.

Her voice was cut off by a loud knock on the front door of the motel bungalow.

"Hey, Jimmy! Open up! Wanna buy you a drink!" Mike Ferrenbaugh's voice—loud and drunken.

"Come on! You been working too hard!" More pounding on the door.

"Jimmy!" Mickey exclaimed. "It's Dad!" She leaped from the bed, stood bewildered in the middle of the bedroom floor.

Ferrenbaugh, the stupid bastard, Jimmy cursed to himself. Saturday night. Country-club night. He'd forgotten about that.

"Hold on a couple of minutes, Mike!" he shouted and sprang out of the bed. "Grab all your clothes that're lying around and go into the bathroom!" he whispered to Mickey. "Lock the door."

He stared at the closet doors. They were open.

Mickey's luggage and skis prevented their closing. He leaped towards the closets, jammed everything inside, made the doors close by sheer force.

What else?

He scanned the room. Cosmetics, hairbrush, comb, odds-and-ends—all Mickey's—on a bureau top. He scooped them off, flung them hastily under the bed.

Oh, Jesus! Her overcoat and purse were out in the living room. He dashed out, gathered them up. By then, Mickey was inside the bathroom, and the door was closed. Coat and purse went under the bed, too.

"Jimmy! Open this damn door 'fore I freeze to death!" Mike was bellowing from outside.

"I'm coming!"

A last look around. Shit! A shoe. Mike just might recognize it. He snatched it up, thrust it into a bureau drawer. His dressing gown hung over the back of a chair. He yanked it over him.

He went out, closing the bedroom door behind him. He went to the outer door, unlocked and opened it. Mike Ferrenbaugh, a bottle of whisky in one hand, stood in the doorway.

"Kee-kee-kee-krist, it's cold!" he said, bulling his way inside, tracking snow all over the carpet.

"Thought you needed a drink." He put the bottle on a table, took off his overcoat before Jemel could stop him. "You've been workin' too much!"

"Where's Dorothy?" Jimmy asked nervously.

"Took her home. Came over by m'self to have a drink with you."

Jemel put a hand on Ferrenbaugh's shoulder. "Look, Mike. I'm dead tired. I was just going to sleep. How about a raincheck?"

"Nope." The stubbornness of a drunk. "If you're tired, nothing like a nightcap." He looked around him blearily, searching for glasses. "Paper, paper all around —and not a damn glass anywheres. He started toward the bedroom.

Jemel headed him off. "I'll get them," he said hurriedly.

"Nah. I have to use your can anyway. Got to take a piss bad."

Jimmy blocked the door. "Uh-uh, Mike." He gave Ferrenbaugh a bawdy wink and a man-to-man dig of fist into ribs. He lowered his voice to a confidential whisper. "I'm not alone, Mike."

Ferrenbaugh's jaw dropped and comprehension dawned. He leered. "Waal now, damn it, Jimmy, why didn't you tell me that in the first place. If I'da known you had some chippie you were banging, I'd have gone off quiet—just like I'm going now." It was his turn to do the rib-digging. "Have fun—only don't catch nothing."

Jemel helped him on with his overcoat. Mike started for the door, forgetting his bottle. Jimmy grabbed it and handed it to him. He was afraid Ferrenbaugh might remember and come back for it.

"I'll hafta piss outside," Mike chuckled.

Jemel waited until Ferrenbaugh had splashed his urine against the front wall of the bungalow, got into his car and driven off. Then Jimmy returned to the bedroom. He was surprised to find Mickey lying on the bed, even more surprised to observe that instead of being shaken and frightened, she was glowing, excited, sexual. Puzzled, he began to take out the things he'd hidden under the bed.

"Leave it all there," Mickey said. She'd discovered that fear had made her want him even more. The instinct to protect and be protected, she thought. That and the sudden fright underscoring what she knew. Her hold on Jimmy was tenuous, fragile. He could—and would—break it whenever he pleased. Her arousal was emotional as well as sexual.

"Leave it all," she repeated. "Please. Come here to me. I want to feel you inside me. To feel you and hold you there."

7

Jemel soon discovered that Miles Palmer was backing the wrong faction in Iraq. The elements led by General Abdul Karim Kassem—which Palmer and his associates were covertly supplying with funds—were more Communist than Arab nationalist. Jemel predicted they'd take whatever they were given and give nothing in return.

"Kassem will spit in your face," Jimmy warned Palmer. "He's been making secret deals with the Russians." He urged Miles to switch sides. "Support the Ba'athists instead. They're much more likely to pay off on their promises."

Palmer scoffed at the advice. By then, he was on a first-name basis with "Foster"—who had also been beguiled by General Abdul Kassem.

"The administration is convinced of Kassem's sincerity," Miles declared, superior and omniscient. "When Kassem overthrows the present regime, Foster will quickly recognize his new government. Abdul Kassem will be grateful to the administration. He won't dare go back on his word to me."

"Both you and the administration are going to be badly burned," Jemel thought, "but why argue with the deaf and blind?" In any event, he and other leading men of affairs in Lebanon were aware that the impending coup in Iraq would have repercussions affecting Lebanon. These were of greater importance to him—and they would have to be used to advantage.

Iraq's General Abdul Karim Kassem chose July 14, 1958, to stage his *coup d'état*. It was an instant and complete success. King Faisal II, close members of his family and his key advisers were slaughtered. Kassem assumed power, establishing himself as the country's dictator.

Suddenly emboldened, dissident factions inside Lebanon started riots in Beirut and a halfhearted rebellion in outlying areas of the country. This eventuality had been foreseen by Beirut's ruling merchant elite. The Lebanese government reacted according to plan. Beirut was sealed off and calm restored with swift, ruthless violence. The rebellion was confined to the hinterlands, where it degenerated into sporadic skirmishes.

Lebanon acted. America overreacted. U.S. warships were rushed to Lebanon and U.S. Marines poured ashore—without a shot being fired—"to protect Lebanon from Communist aggression," Foster told Miles Palmer (who believed) and the entire world (most of which laughed).

American intervention raised a storm of protest from innumerable quarters—inside Lebanon and out—but not from Lebanese bankers, who saw it as a unique boon. Dramatic notice had been served that Lebanon was shielded by the armed might of the United States. What greater guarantee could the rich in the Arab world have of Lebanese safety and financial stability?

Whatever nervous money was hastily withdrawn from Beirut banks was more than matched by new flows of Arab deposits. Oil-rich Arab states and sheikhs saw that the money they placed in Beirut bankers' vaults was guarded against social or political upheaval by the military power of the United States.

Less than a month later, the Eisenhower administration was forced to admit it had made a major diplomatic blunder by landing its troops in Lebanon. The Marines were withdrawn and the warships departed—but Beirut bankers and the wealthy sheikhs who had accounts with them were satisfied.

The Americans had made another grave error. On August 2nd, the United States formally recognized General Abdul Karim Kassem's new regime. Kassem wasted no time shattering all the illusions of the Eisen-

hower administration, its Secretary of State—and Miles
Langford Palmer.

Kassem tore up all treaties with the United
States, denounced America as "an imperialist aggres-
sor," abrogated all military pacts with the West—and
openly allied his government with the Communist bloc.
While his representatives stopped short of actually spitting into Miles Palmer's face, they did sneer with contempt when he tried to collect the oil concessions that
had been promised him in return for the several million
dollars he'd supplied to Abdul Kassem.

"There were no written agreements," a third secretary at the Iraqi embassy in Washington sniggered.
"It is your word against that of General Kassem and his
ministers. Besides, Mr. Palmer, if you make any open
claim, you will be confessing that you committed several crimes—using your official position of trust for
private gain among them."

Miles Palmer, head of the Palmer National Trust
Company and Special Adviser on Foreign Economic
Affairs to the Eisenhower administration, had to accept
the bitter fact that he had been beaten.

When Jemel next saw Palmer—in New York, during late November—he refrained from rubbing in the
defeat. Miles, in a self-flagellating masochistic mood,
did it for himself.

"Your advice was better than what I received from
Foster," he admitted to Jimmy. "Nothing went as it
should have. Everything went wrong. My associates
and I lost upwards of seven million."

"We all lose once in a while," Jimmy said.

Palmer's mood changed. "What do you think
might happen if I did what you suggested in the first
place and gave support to the Ba'athists?"

"Nothing. Kassem will keep them totally impotent
for a few years. Anyhow, the Ba'athists would realize
you were second-guessing, take your money and treat
you the same as Kassem did. Write Iraq off, Miles.
Forget it."

"There are other countries with oil in the Middle

East," Palmer mused aloud. "Other countries—and other possibilities."

"Which you'll doubtless fuck up just as badly," Jimmy thought silently. Miles Palmer hadn't learned any lessons, and he'd never grasp the basics of Arab politics or psychology. However, precious few Westerners could.

"Yes, there are, Miles," he said.

"Can I count on you, Jemel?"

"No further than before. 'Benevolent neutrality' is still my limit."

Incombank's financial statement for the year indicated its assets had increased by another $25 million, and three more foreign branches had been opened. Altogether, Incom had made a remarkable showing for a bank that had been in existence only five years.

"Another five years, and Incom will be the biggest bank in the Middle East," Jemel predicted confidently to Brian Lockhart.

Quite a goal, Lockhart reflected. One requiring even more rapid multiplication of resources each and every year. It was possible. Jimmy did have a flair —a near-genius—for pulling in money. The sole drawback was that he often moved so fast, he outran himself, leaving a mass of loose ends and details to be tidied up in his wake. *But what the devil am I complaining about?* Lockhart asked himself. *Jimmy brought me into this when no one else would have touched me with a barge-pole—and that was why, to do the tidying up. I haven't lost anything by it, either. I've got my share.*

Just the same, he'd long ago learned it helped to sound a cautionary note occasionally, to make Jimmy slow down the pace of the pyramiding.

"I s'pose it can be done," he said. "Only we're still a fair way from being out of the danger zone, Jimmy."

The bank's financial statements looked good—the accountants who'd prepared them were the best—and they'd stand up under any ordinary scrutiny. The weakness lay well below any visible surface. If any large depositors suddenly decided they wanted to withdraw large amounts of cash, there would be a hellish pinch. Much of the bank's cash resources had been "loaned" to or "invested in" Jimmy's (and, to a much lesser extent, Brian Lockhart's) dummy companies.

The companies had used the money to invest in an assortment of long-term projects and propositions like the land deal Jimmy had gone into in America with Michael Ferrenbaugh. The returns on these enterprises would be large. Eventually. There was the catch. The money was tied up, here and there. For two, even four—in some cases, more—years. Frozen solid. Very little of it could be made liquid in a hurry. Not without heavy losses.

"Damn few banks, are ever really out of the 'danger-zone,' Brian. Christ, I certainly don't need to tell *you* that. You know more about banking than I do. What's the whole principle of banking? Nothing but a gamble against time—and against the possibility that all its depositors will wake up with the same impulse one bright morning and line up in front of the tellers' windows demanding their money."

True enough, Lockhart conceded silently. Banks had to use a greater or lesser portion of the money entrusted to them and invest in ventures that produced profit, but involved greater or lesser degrees of risk.

"Brian. Did you ever hear of a bank anywhere that didn't make 'special' or 'preferential'—or choose your own label—loans to enterprises in which its own directors had a personal financial interest?"

"As a generalization, no, I haven't."

"Okay. So look at it from another angle. Ours. You and I run Incombank. To all intents, we own it. Our directors and officers say yes when we nod, no when we shake our heads. Sure, we use bank money to finance our private deals." He smiled. "I'd even argue the bank's money is safer that way. We're going to make damned sure there's profit—and after we've taken ours off the top, Incom gets its end. Eventually, all the cash that's out will be fed back into the house."

There were yawning holes in Jimmy's logic, and they both knew it. Just the same, it contained sufficient grains of truth to make it valid—provided Incombank stayed ahead in the race against time and there were no mass withdrawals by depositors.

Jimmy was the boss, Lockhart shrugged mentally —and almost all Lebanese banks were following the same policies. That was why they were established in Lebanon, so their owners and directors could freewheel.

"Just do me a favor," Lockhart said. "Let's take a brief intermission—say sixty days—on the pyramiding. I need the breathing spell to catch up on the embroidery. It'll take me that long to give us some documentation-in-depth." He had to do the complicated paperwork of actually shuffling stocks and other securities, transferring them back and forth, to give some substance to transactions that had been made.

"Sixty days? Okay," Jimmy agreed amiably.

Lockhart produced a legal-sized sheet of paper. The most pressing current headache. Words and phrases were written at the left side of the sheet, figures opposite them on the right. At the bottom, an underlined total.

"The bad news," Jimmy muttered.

"Wouldn't go so far as to say bad. Merely urgent."

Jimmy studied the paper. An accurate and unadorned statement of how Incombank Central and its branches stood at the moment, with projected predictable profits and expenditures for the next six months.

The underlined total represented the gap between the two that would have to be bridged.

$1,020,000.

Money that had to be generated without disturbing the already delicately stretched accounting fabric.

"We still have a million four-hundred-thousand outstanding in phony loans made from the free-gift half of the OSFAP credit Miles swung for us," Jemel said.

"Correct."

"Rig up defaults totalling eight hundred thousand. I'll prod Miles to get us superquick action and have OSFAP forgive that much of the credit." He nipped his lower lip between his teeth. "HJK Trading and a couple of other dummies have a hundred thousand loose. We'll ladle that back into the bank as special dividends on the companies' stocks owned by Incom. I'll sell some other paper we're holding to Karamcorp at a hundred thousand profit." He leered. "There's the million, Brian. You can probably find the odd twenty thousand tucked away in the back of some cashier's drawer." He lit a cigarette. "So we've got the cash-flow deficit covered—and I'll give you a sixty-day breather."

"What are you going to do in the meantime?" Lockhart asked.

"I, Brian, am going to live the high life. The spas and *boîtes*—all the elegant fleshpots."

Lockhart nodded approvingly. One of Jemel Karami's prolonged, outwardly purely-for-pleasure sprees never failed to bring in a few millions more in deposits.

Jemel was hardly the first to discover the fallacy of the time-honored convention that held bankers could inspire trust and confidence only by being ultraconservative and staying out of the limelight. But he certainly did as much as any to prove the tradition a hollow myth.

The flamboyant superrich were much more inclined to have confidence in those they believed to be their own kind. Once their confidence had been gained —and this fact made widely known—the snob-appeal factor became operative. The status-seeking ordinary rich were eager to follow the example of their more famous financial betters.

Jimmy had begun building his image even before his father's death—with Elinor Randolph's help. It hadn't taken him long to be considered "good copy" by café-society columnists and financial writers. He'd continued to glamorize himself at every opportunity after he established Incombank, for whatever added to his glamor gave more luster to his bank.

Neither international press nor public saw any paradox in the growing reputation of Jemel Karami, the playboy-financier. The circles in which he moved, the people with whom he was obviously on intimate terms were his references—and the highest recommendations for Incombank.

Jimmy spent the sixty-day "breathing spell" he'd

given Brian Lockhart in the same manner that he'd spent similar intermissions in the past. His personal progress could be traced readily by anyone who read European or American newspapers, and behind each item there lay some other story that did not appear in print.

"International Croesus Jemel Karami and Maria-Pia Gritti, Italy's sex goddess who out-lollos Gina by several centimeters, spent their weekend melting the ski slopes at Gstaad without ever leaving their hotel."

Maria-Pia introduced Jimmy to Italy's richest film producer—who had a million dollars' worth of Italian lire on which he'd paid no *tasse* cached in safety-deposit boxes. Jemel guaranteed him absolute secrecy —and 5 percent interest. The money went to Incombank.

"Louis Gallaudet, the French wine king, and playboy-banker Jemel Karami dined last night at the Tour d'Argent, each with a female companion whose beauty would require every superlative in the language and even then lack adequate description."

Gallaudet Freres, the company Louis headed, floated a $50 million stock issue shortly afterward. The issue was underwritten by a banking syndicate headed by Jemel Karami's Incombank—and Gallaudet later used his considerable influence to enable Incom to open a branch in Paris.

"Why no one watched last night's opening performance of *Entrez sans Frapper*. Left to right in the photograph above: Aly Khan, Nina Dyer, Moia (Miss Great Britain) Burke, Jemel Karami, Juliet Grecque, and Porfirio Rubirosa. Every eye in the capacity audience was fixed on the box they shared rather than on the stage."

By then, of course, Aly Khan was living on what for him was practically a dole—but through him, Jemel picked up a $2 million time deposit from a Pakistani who had become a London slumlord and had no desire to pay Her Majesty's Inland Revenue Service a ha'penny in taxes if he could avoid it. For his part, Rubi channeled an equivalent amount of Trujillo family money into Incombank—but insisted on being paid his usual 2½ percent commission for the services he rendered.

Jemel went on to New York.

8

Jimmy's legal guardianship of Felicite ended when she had reached eighteen. Under the terms of the trust established by Hassan Karami, Jemel was to act as its administrator until she reached thirty or married.

Jimmy had already doubled the value of his sister's legacy, and she enjoyed a huge income. While continuing to live in the Wickpark Towers penthouse when she was in New York, Felicite had purchased a summer home for herself in Cape Cod and was about to buy a villa on the French Riviera. She spent much of her time traveling—and she, too, was becoming an international café-society personality.

Her many—and short-lived—romances were often reported by gossip columnists. So much so, that few found it any longer necessary to identify her as Jemel Karami's sister.

Jimmy believed Felicite had the right to live her own life. Nonetheless, finding that she was at home when he returned to New York City, he felt a chat with Felicite about her future might be in order.

They talked in the library of the penthouse—a large, yet somehow intimate, room that Jimmy particularly liked, for it doubled as office and place of relaxation and, from its 38th-floor vantage point, afforded a breathtaking view of Central Park and the soaring buildings that bounded it to both south and west.

"You've got a long and serious look, Jimmy," Felicite said.

"Just a little uncomfortable," he confessed. "I always am when I start playing the big brother—which, thank God I don't do often."

"Go ahead. I probably won't pay any attention to what you say, anyway." Her lovely face was smiling, but she was only half-joking.

Felicite was changing—whether for better or worse, Jimmy couldn't decide. He settled for "maturing," and said, "Hell, I'm not going to lecture you! I just want to ask you a couple of questions. Like do you have everything you want and need."

"More than enough. Some of the checks I get. . . !"

"I play your money along with my own," Jimmy said. "When I run the stock down on Karamcorp and its subsidiaries, I buy for you as well as myself. When Doug and I shove it up a few points, we sell. You see . . ."

"Oh, please, don't try to explain," Felicite declared. "I haven't the slightest idea how it all works, and I don't care as long as the money keeps coming in."

"Okay. Then there's the big question. What do you plan to do—I mean, any ideas of getting married or . . ."

"God, no! Not for years—if ever. I'm not at all like you when it comes to money. I mean I'm not interested in making more—or even how it's made for me. But when we're talking about marriage, you and I are practically twins."

"How's that?"

"Oh, Jimmy! You're being coy!" she laughed. "We're both highly sexed—maybe oversexed. You want all the women you can get—but you'd never want to be tied down to anyone. Am I right?"

Jemel hesitated, thinking. Of all the women he'd known, had affairs with—and he couldn't begin to count them, he mused—only two had ever really got under his skin. Elinor Randolph—but he no longer had any feelings towards her save for an increasingly infrequent desire for a romp, and that was how he thought of it, as a romp. And Mickey Ferrenbaugh. Mickey. As a wife? Tied down to her. Uh-uh. That would kill everything off.

"You're right," he agreed.

"I'm the same with men," Felicite said with a

shrug. "They're fun—for a while; then they become bores." She wrinkled her brow. "There's another difference between us, I think. I'm spoiled—but not so much that I can't admit it to myself. That's why I want a man, and then get tired of him and want the next attractive one I meet. It's different with you, Jimmy."

"How? I'm curious to hear."

"You—well, for you, women are like making money, and I'm not trying to be cute with puns. It's the conquest thing with you. You see a big deal, you want to close it fast, take your profit and go on to the next. It's a victory, but after you've won, you're just that much more eager to win again. The same with women." She paused, her liquescent eyes knowing. "Jimmy, I'll bet that doing business excites you sexually. It does, doesn't it? Tell me the truth."

It did. To deny it would be senseless. "Yes," he said. "Is it all that obvious?"

"It is to me," Felicite chuckled. "Remember, I'm your sister—and I've been observing you for a long time." She gave him an impish look. "Besides, I've met a few men who are the same way. Very good lovers, too, most of them. Are you, Jimmy?" The last three words slipped out by themselves and Felicite was startled to hear herself speak them. She wondered if they had been an unconscious invitation. She studied Jemel warily. Evidently, he was lost in other thoughts and hadn't heard her.

"How about my giving a party for your big birthday, *soeurette?*" Felicite would be twenty-one in a few months.

"Oh, I'm sorry, Jimmy. I hope you won't be disappointed. Carlos has one all planned—I was going to tell you and ask you to come."

"Carlos?"

"Carlos Perino. You know, the tin and copper mine . . ."

"I'll be damned!" Jemel exclaimed, smiling. "Carlos and I traded girlfriends back and forth last summer on the Riviera. We're friends. Didn't he tell you?"

"No. Maybe he thought he'd better not." Felicite

giggled. Jimmy and Carlos had "traded girlfriends back
and forth." And she'd been to bed with Carlos. That
was incest once removed right there. Sort of incest by
proxy.

At the end of 1959, Incombank's statement of
financial condition reflected total gross resources of
$103 million.

Karamcorp (at least on paper) was a corporate
complex with $80 million in assets.

Jemel Karami totalled up his own private fortune.
He had over $12 million in his secret Swiss bank ac-
counts. That figure would double, then triple and qua-
druple when his long-term deals started paying off.

9

"They sprung it on me!" Mike Ferrenbaugh
stormed, pacing the floor of Jemel Karami's penthouse
library. "The rotten bastards! They must've got
wind . . ."

"For Christ's sake, stop ranting and stamping up
and down!" Jimmy Karami barked at him. "Sit down
and talk sense!"

"I've told you!" Ferrenbaugh said. "The highway
route maps have been changed. Redrawn. The right-
of-way won't come within two miles of any property
we've bought!" His hands trembled. "Altogether, I've
tossed over two hundred thousand dollars down the
drain!"

Jemel glared at him icily. "You've tossed two
hundred thousand!" he snarled. "I'm in for twenty
million, big shot!" They'd both doubled their original
investments in the highway-condemnation speculation
because it had appeared more and more attractive with
each passing month. The twenty million was Incombank money, siphoned off and covered by worthless

notes from dummy companies. Jesus! The money had to go back into the bank—and soon—or not even Brian Lockhart and all the accountants in the world could keep the balances convincing. The whole structure would crumble if the money was lost. Jimmy could never bring himself to part with his personal wealth —but even if he did, the twelve million wouldn't make up for twenty.

"Who are the rotten bastards you're bellowing about?" Jemel demanded.

"The governor and the state highway commissioner. They're going to pull the same deal we had figured."

"God damn it, have a talk with the governor. Tell him we'll give him a split of the profits!"

"That won't do any good," Mike mumbled. "He and I are on opposite sides of the political fence. He hates my guts. If I came out against shitting in the streets, he'd have the state legislature pass a law making it a felony to crap anywhere else."

"You've got pull in Washington. Threaten to cut off federal appropriations."

"All I'd cut off would be my own head with the voters."

"Don't let Mike's panic infect you," Jimmy warned himself. "Be scared—there's every reason to be scared. Twenty million—no, a hundred and three million—reasons to be terrified. But don't *run* scared. Get a grip—and think. There has to be an angle."

"This highway commissioner?"

"No. He and the governor are like this." Mike held up two fingers, one crossed over the other.

"What if we give them all the profit—and just pull out what we put in."

Ferrenbaugh shook his head. "They know if they bust me, produce proof that I had a deal on the fire, they'll not only finish me, but bust my whole party in the state for years. That's something else they're after."

"I couldn't give a damn about you or your party," Jimmy thought.

"When will the new route maps be made public?" Jimmy asked.

"Next month. The governor and his boys have bought up the land . . ."

"God damn it, just answer my questions!" Jemel's eyes were coal-black and burning with anger. "When next month?"

"Right after the fifteenth."

Four weeks. Not much of an edge, but an edge.

"Mike. What do you know about the governor and this other bird? Do they fuck around?"

"Huh? Fuck around how?"

"With their pricks, you dumb bastard!" he was furious again. "Do they ball women? Are they fags? Do they have any sex life?"

"Yeh. The governor does, anyway. He's married, but he plays around, with whores mostly. I hear he likes —uh—parties, too."

"You mean orgies?"

"Yeah, so I've been told."

Gears snapped into mesh. Dangerous? Of course. But no less dangerous than losing $20 million and seeing a $103 million bank collapse.

"The junior senator from your state—Whalen— he's in the same party as the governor, isn't he?" Ferrenbaugh nodded. "That's my answer. I'm going to dump you, Mike—dump you so hard, you'll bounce . . ."

"What?"

"I'm tossing you overboard. Now, listen to me . . ."

Senator Rodney Whalen's eyes shifted back and forth between the $50,000 in currency that lay on his desk and Jemel Karami, who sat across from him.

"It's simple," Jemel said evenly. "Mike Ferrenbaugh lost a fortune for me during the Korean war. He fed me inside information that was all wet. He's lost me twenty million more on this superhighway. I don't like to be suckered. I want to get even with Ferrenbaugh. Shut him off. The fifty thousand is yours if you'll help. There's another hundred thousand for you and a hundred and fifty thousand for the governor if we make it, finish him off politically."

"I'll have to talk to Governor Miller."

"Let me do my own talking. Introduce me to him —and I'll bring his fifty thousand down payment with me."

"I can't leave before tomorrow."

"That's fine with me."

Senator Rodney Whalen and Governor Alvin Miller knew that Jemel Karami, international financier, was a multimillionaire. Still, they couldn't quite understand.

"You're offering a lot of money just to get even," Miller said to Jemel.

"I'm an Arab. We Arabs are willing to pay high for what we call *akhad taro*—to take our revenge." Jimmy paused. "Besides, after Mike is finished, I'll need a friend in the Senate. If I show you people I'm willing to pay, maybe Senator Whalen will be that friend."

The two politicians exchanged glances.

"We can get at Mike from several directions," Jimmy continued. "I have a great deal on him personally. We might even play real dirty. I happen to know his daughter spent a weekend with a man in a motel—which in this God-fearing state, gentlemen, is worth . . ."

"A hundred thousand votes—if you can prove it," Alvin Miller said.

"I can prove it. When it's necessary."

They talked another hour—and their deal was made.

"This is Wednesday, gentlemen," Jimmy said. "I'd like to toss a little party to celebrate our understanding. Will Friday night do for you both—oh, a stag party, by the way."

A man who tossed around a hundred thousand dollars as easily as Jemel Karami must give some party, Whalen and Miller thought.

"Can we bring a few other guys?" Miller asked. He could gain mileage with close political cronies through this.

"Just let me know how many by tomorrow—so I can provide enough entertainment."

After arranging for the rental of an **entire floor**

in the Chesham, the best hotel in the state capital, Jimmy telephoned Doug Ford in New York.

"Charter two planes. One for today, another for Friday morning." He gave Ford a list of the people and the equipment he wanted flown out immediately. As for the second aircraft: "Round up two dozen. Hundred-dollar-a-night class. They'll get two-fifty apiece and all their expenses."

"The Mann Act, Jimmy," Doug warned.

"I'll worry about that." His tone was sour. "When you're hanging from a cliff, it doesn't matter if you drop one mile or two."

There were eight male guests besides Whalen and Miller. The party began as a party at nine, transformed itself into an orgy by eleven—and remained that way until the next morning.

"I had a great time," a bleary-eyed Alvin Miller croaked, weakly shaking Jemel's hand. "Great. Anything you want from here on in, you'll have it."

"I know I will," Jimmy thought. He said, "Thanks. We'll do fine together."

Jemel wasn't ready for Mike Ferrenbaugh until late Saturday afternoon.

"Get yourself up here to the Chesham, quick!" he ordered Mike over the telephone. Ferrenbaugh arrived in half an hour. By then, the technicians who'd arrived aboard the first chartered plane had departed, their work done.

"The rest is up to you," Jimmy informed Mike. He spread out scores of photographs enlarged to ten-by-sixteen size. "Look at this one," he said, holding up a glossy print. "The Honorable Alvin Miller—his face in perfect focus—screwing one dame, having his balls licked from behind by another. A nigra-gal, as you people out here would call her." He selected a second sample. "Or this. Miller, Whalen, and ensemble in a fabulous tangle. You have to look close to see who's doing what to whom—but when you do, it's all pretty obvious."

He waved his hand toward some reels of 16-millimeter motion-picture film and beside them, spools of recording tape. "We have it in movies and sound, too."

Governor Alvin Miller had a smug, self-satisfied look. Senator Michael Ferrenbaugh's request for the Monday-morning audience could mean only that the old fart was coming around to crawl and beg. A pleasing prospect.

"Good morning, governor."

"Senator. Pleasure to see you. Sit down. Make yourself comfortable."

"I won't be staying very long, Alvin." Mike stood close to the governor's desk, placed his briefcase on its top. He opened the case. "I have some things here that'll interest you." He took out some photographs. "They'll also be of interest to every minister, schoolteacher, newspaper, women's, and service club and Chamber of Commerce in the state—if you don't make a sudden executive decision and decide you want to have the new highway follow the original route." Mike started flipping the photographs one by one across the desk to Governor Alvin Miller.

Jemel accepted the prices set by evaluators on the condemned properties without haggling. He wanted no more risky delays.

"We take what's offered and be glad we saved our skins and came out ahead," he told Mike Ferrenbaugh, who was quick to agree.

Jimmy stayed in the state capital for three weeks. He had reason to reflect that Felicite had him measured down to zero tolerance. Doing business did excite him sexually—especially after nerve-shattering tensions had been eased by winning.

Jimmy was insatiable after he knew Alvin Miller was beaten. He kept on two of the call girls he'd hired for the orgy at the Chesham. He used them both—often—in between the several afternoons and evenings he managed to spend with Mickey Ferrenbaugh.

Mickey at first believed the intensity of his hunger —even greater than any he'd ever demonstrated before —was inspired solely by his desire for her. Then her father gave her a much expurgated version of the narrow escape from financial catastrophe on the land speculation. Dimly, she began to realize the same truths that had led Felicite Karami to her own conclusions about her brother. It didn't matter, Mickey admitted to herself. She loved him.

Jemel made two other decisions during his stay. He gave the photographic negatives, the motion-picture films, and the tape recordings to Mike. They'd enable Ferrenbaugh to wreck Miller, Whalen, and their party in his state during the next election just as they had intended to wreck Ferrenbaugh. Then, he determined to add a few more national legislators to his bribe rolls. A couple of tamed and trained senators and an assortment of congressman would be just that much extra insurance.

When the properties Jemel owned through false-front companies in the state were all sold, he received a gross total of $31 million. Of this, slightly more than $6 million was his own clear profit, considerably less than he'd anticipated, yet satisfactory, all things (the close shave with disaster foremost among them) considered.

Incom's $20 million was fed back into the bank by a tightly controlled reverse-flow process. "Loans" that had been granted to certain Karami companies in Liechtenstein and Monaco were paid off, while certain others redeemed their "bonds" that had been "purchased" by Incombank.

New deposits and the $20 million in the vaults provided a sound base for what Jemel visualized as explosive expansion.

10

"Ever read the advice Major Browning gives in *Hoyle's?*" Jemel asked Brian Lockhart.

"About playing roulette? Of course. Why?"

"He points out that most people make the big mistake of doubling their bets when they're losing—when they should do the doubling during a winning streak."

Jimmy had his *sibah* out of his pocket and was twirling it around his finger. Brian recognized all the signs. Jimmy had some spectacular new scheme in mind.

"We need a new building for Incombank. An Incom Central Tower. The biggest, flashiest office building in Beirut. A Lebanese-scale skyscraper that'll dwarf everything around it."

The concept was sound, solid, Lockhart thought. People were impressed by shows of wealth and success anywhere—and doubly so in the Middle East. The trend was all towards making ostentatious displays of corporate splendor.

"I'm with you," he said.

"Wait. I'm not finished. Incom should also build its board chairman a house. A mansion about the size of Victoria Station—and so loud it'll be a tourist attraction. Not that I intend staying in Beirut any more often or longer than I have been—but there's nothing like the gaudy and vulgar to impress my fellow Arabs. I want a house that'll make you and me cringe whenever we look at it. The richer sheikhs are bound to flip over it then."

"True," Brian agreed. "It sounds as though you intend to concentrate more on Middle Eastern customers."

"To a degree. The new Kennedy administration in the States worries me. I'm afraid the happy Foster era days may be over. The French and British aren't in the best of shape. But that oil keeps pouring up—and the royalties grow bigger each year. The more of that money we can attract, the faster Incom will grow."

Lockhart couldn't argue with that, either.

"Then, Brian, I am going to build myself a yacht."

This was something the Englishman hadn't expected. "A yacht?" he echoed. "You move around too fast, Jimmy. A yacht would . . ."

"The kind of yacht I'm going to build won't be used for traveling from one place to another, *khawaja* Lockhart. It's going to be a floating pleasure dome. One of our bigger business assets."

"It's a pretty obvious effort, Jimmy," he said. "People will say you're imitating Onassis."

"Not for long. He bought a war-surplus frigate and had it converted. I'll have mine designed from the keel up—and with a twist. The tub will be bigger, faster and its interior will be something out of everyone's Arabian Nights fantasies. Exotic. The most glamorous vessel afloat. I'll even sign on a permanent troupe of belly dancers if necessary—and, come to think of it, I'm only half-kidding. Listen. Persian carpets. Damascus swords with gold handles and scabbards for particularly important guests to take home as souvenirs. The best chefs money can buy to turn out cordon bleu dinners—or *mezzeh* and whole-roasted sheep, followed by *halawa, ghoraibeh* and all the rest. The press will make the yacht famous overnight—and after I get a few famous people aboard, everyone else will beg . . ."

"Mm," Brian Lockhart murmured. Jimmy's instincts for showmanship were unerring. "I think you have me convinced." He laughed. "No magic lamps or flying carpets?"

"Lamps, no. But I'll top Ari with the flying carpets. The *Christina* carries a bimotored amphib. I'll have one bigger—plus a helicopter that can take off right from the deck."

"The Greek will choke on his own bile," Brian thought.

"Get started on plans for the Incom Tower and the house," Jimmy said. "I'll look after my shipbuilding project myself."

Michele Ferrenbaugh contrived a plausible excuse for a trip to New York, planning carefully so she would arrive at a time when Jemel was there.

Jimmy sensed that she had come to talk to him rather than to make love, and this disturbed him. He didn't like his relationships with women to become overly complicated. Not even his relationship with Mickey.

They had dinner together in the dining room of his penthouse. Dowling, Jimmy's butler, and the footman moved noiselessly, serving them. Mickey ate very little, did not touch her wine. When she spoke, her conversation was forced. Evidently, whatever she had to say would have to wait until later. When the strained dinner was over, Jimmy took her into the library. He felt relaxed there and believed the surroundings would be conducive towards making Mickey finally reveal what was on her mind—or, preferably, divert her from it to thoughts of bed.

He kissed her. There was none of the usual hot, instantaneous response. It would be conversation, after all. When Mickey said she wouldn't care for a highball, he mixed himself a tall Crawford's scotch and water and sat down, facing her.

"Something's bothering you, darling," he said— and realized the banality of the remark. "You want to tell me something." That didn't sound like much of an improvement. God, how he disliked situations like this. He hid his annoyance by holding up his glass politely and drinking.

"Jimmy. I wanted to see you. I had to see you." There, that was a start. Now to go on. "I had to tell you personally." She paused to control her tone. Each word that followed had to be torn out by main force. "I may be getting engaged."

The glass in Jemel's hand tipped dangerously. He grasped it more firmly. *Why should I feel like I've been kicked in the balls?* he asked himself. He'd always known it couldn't last forever, that it would have to taper off and end sometime. Maybe it was because the affair had lasted so long—but they'd only seen each other at widely spaced intervals, he theorized. He'd never been with Mickey over any protracted period, never long enough for her to fray at the edges in his mind and feelings—whatever the hell those feelings were.

He finished his drink before saying, "Mickey,

'may be getting engaged' is about the most inconclusive line I've heard." He'd hardened his tone—in self-defense.

"Jimmy. I'm almost twenty-six. And I've been in love with you since I was five. More so every year, every time I see you or think of you. Only I'm old enough to realize that you'll never comprehend my definition of love, and barring a miracle happening in the next few minutes, I'll have to settle for second best. Someone I know has proposed to me. I told him I'd think it over for a month."

She saw Jemel get up, followed him with her eyes as he walked to the bar in a corner of the library, made himself another drink. She tried to guess his thoughts from the manner in which he moved and held himself. It was useless. He was casual. Far too casual —but Mickey's emotions, thrusting themselves through their own wringer, prevented her from seeing that.

"Am I allowed to ask who did the proposing?" Jemel asked, returning to his chair. She still had freckles and her nose was delightfully tilted, he mused. Her face was pale now, but no less lovely for it. She shifted position in her chair, her incredibly firm breasts alive beneath her dress.

She told him. He was Frederick Hayworth. A state assemblyman she'd met a year before at a political rally she'd attended with her father. He was thirty-one. They'd gone out together often.

It abruptly dawned on Jimmy that he'd never given much thought to what Mickey did, whether she went out with anyone else or not. Since the morning at the Ferrenbaughs' lakehouse, he'd—well, he had to admit it—he'd taken Mickey for granted. Considered her as—almost as property that he didn't necessarily own outright, but against which he held an ironclad lien.

"Are you in love with this—with Hayworth?" *Another banality,* Jimmy thought. *What the devil is wrong with me?*

"I like him very much. I'm in love with you, but if I wasn't, I'd probably be in love with Frederick Hayworth. He's like you and yet he isn't. The things about him that remind me of you most are the things I like in him least. Those that are entirely different are the ones I like in Fred the most. And I can't understand any of it—except that if I can't have you, I'll take Fred and do my best to make both of us happy."

"Have you been to bed with him?"

"Yes."

"And?" A small-time politician from the American Middle West as a lover?

"There's nothing lacking in our sexual relationship. And there is an added factor—something we've never had, Jimmy. He tells me he loves me and that he's in love with me. He tells me he wants to be with me—and to marry me."

She felt her eyes mist, made a supreme effort to prevent mist from turning into tears. She waited. "So much, so very much is up to you, Jimmy," she thought.

Jemel stared into his glass. For an instant—but only an instant—he caught his lower lip between his teeth. Then the corners of his mouth tightened. The message was plain enough. Michele Ferrenbaugh was ready for a husband. He didn't doubt the sincerity of her motives in coming to see him. She was a woman —and she was giving him a choice. Only he didn't want to be a husband, and he didn't want a wife. Not even Mickey. Maybe especially not Mickey. Her kind of love was exhilarating—when the dosage was intermittent. Day after day and month after month, it would be shackling, depressing. Asphyxiating.

"I'm very fond of you, Mickey. More fond than I've ever been of any woman," he said. "But I can't give you any advice. These things are for people to decide for themselves."

He put his half-finished drink on a table by his chair, got up and went to her. She stood up before he reached her. He put his arms around her and kissed her lips, gently at first, then employing the *fahas* technique. It failed to arouse her. She returned his kiss tenderly, held him tightly for a moment, then pulled herself away.

"Please have Dowling bring my coat and purse," she said.

"Mickey, darling . . ."

"No, Jimmy. I'm not spending the night with you. I can't. I've made my decision. You made it for me, my love."

"I'll have the chauffeur bring the car around downstairs and take you wherever you want to go."

"No, Jimmy. Just have Dowling get my things and put me in the elevator. I'm at the Pierre. It's only two or three blocks—and I'd really like to walk. Alone."

She managed to hold back the tears until she was in the elevator and it had started down.

Jemel stood in front of the closed elevator doors, staring at them for many long seconds. Then he made two telephone calls. They were of brief duration, and when they were over, he rang for his butler.

He almost barked out his words when he told Dowling to get the chauffeur. "Have him pick up these two girls at their apartments," he said, handing the butler a slip of paper with two names and addresses scrawled on it. "Tell him to bring them both back here. Fast."

Dowling hurried off, glancing at the slip of paper. He recognized the first of the two names. It was the dark-haired actress who enjoyed being whipped and beaten. So, the butler mused, his employer was in one of those moods.

11

Jimmy's mansion on the rue d'Australie (he was already thinking of it as a viceregal palace) was not quite finished, and his yacht (he'd decided to name it the *Asharat*, after the Phoenician sea goddess) was undergoing final fittings in a Clydeside shipyard.

However, the Incombank Tower—construction of which had been given first priority and rushed through

—was ready for its formal opening during the last week of September 1962.

Jemel invited bank clients, notables, and his friends from all over the world to be his guests for the opening. Incombank took over three of the newest and most luxurious among the hotels that had proliferated along the Beirut beachfront: one reserved for Westerners who came with wives and families, another for men who wanted both women and liquor, with the third reserved for religious Moslems (no pork or alcohol, but hashish and boys in addition to a wide selection of girls).

The event was marked by much *sharaf*-enhancing pomp and ceremony. The Lebanese parliament passed a resolution praising Incombank (now the largest in the Middle East) and both the Christian president and the Moslem premier delivered laudatory orations.

The celebrations lasted throughout a Friday-to-Monday weekend. Although it seemed to Jemel Karami that he had to be everywhere at once, he did manage to spend a little time alone with various of his friends among the guests.

Miles Palmer was generous—even florid—with his congratulations.

"A magnificent building, Jemel," he declared. "You've done an astounding job all around, my boy. The entire international banking community marvels at your fabulous success."

"You do some pretty remarkable things yourself, Miles," Jimmy responded. Palmer had survived yet another change of administration in Washington, remaining in a prestigious economic advisory capacity, and his Palmer National Trust Co. was an increasingly important factor on the American financial scene.

"I'm afraid I move much more slowly than you, Jemel," Palmer said. "However, I have hopes of making a most significant advance before long."

Jimmy knew what he was implying. Incombank had continued to act as the "benevolent neutral" banking outlet for money Miles Palmer and his "associates" were sending into the Middle East. And Jimmy was aware that Palmer had changed his tactics somewhat.

He still had the same aims—to obtain oil concessions —but he was making a two-pronged effort. On the one hand, he continued to give financial support to dissident factions—in Saudi Arabia and the Trucial States. On the other, he was openly bidding for concessions against established oil companies in such countries as Libya and Iran.

But he was running true to predictable form, Jimmy knew, for he had much more reliable sources of information than Palmer and was usually told of what Palmer was doing almost before he did it. Miles's appraisals of internal situations within Arab countries were invariably mistaken. He backed the wrong sides. He fumbled even on his legitimate bidding for concessions. He bid low, expected bribes (which might have helped, had they been given to the right persons, which they were not) would bring him bargains. In the previous six months alone, Palmer had lost out on three different concessions when Enrico Mattei, the whirlwind head of Italy's $2 billion ENI petroleum empire, topped his bids by more than 50 percent.

It would be interesting to learn how Palmer expected to make a "most significant advance before long," Jemel reflected—and tried a long probe. "I was sorry to hear that Mattei beat you out on those bids," he said.

Palmer's flab-jowled face darkened. "Enrico Mattei!" he rasped. "He's not going to outbid me again, I promise you that!" Having blurted out the words, he seemed to lose his composure for a moment.

"Damned if he doesn't act like he's said something he shouldn't have said," Jimmy thought.

Miles returned to stodgy, pompous normal and changed the subject.

Felicite had come to Beirut from Italy, where she'd attended the Venice Film Festival and then spent two weeks motoring through the country with a brawnily handsome Yugoslav actor she'd met in Venice. She brought the actor to Beirut with her.

"You and Bogdan should become wonderful friends," Felicite told Jimmy. "And I want you to like my brother, Bogdan." Her voice had a dreamy, disembodied quality.

Jemel gazed at her steadily. She was still lovely, and her eyes were still large and very dark. But there was something wrong with the pupils. He took a closer look at Bogdan. Same thing. He gritted his teeth, cursing inwardly. Sure. He used hashish occasionally—and, very rarely, opium, Arab style, mixed with date paste and a bit flicked off with a fingernail then held under the tongue while sipping hot tea. But Felicite and the actor had been playing around with heavier stuff. How big was the monkey and how long had Felicite been carrying it?

"Oh, Jimmy. Can you advance me some money here in Beirut?"

"Yes. How much do you need?" And what for, but he didn't ask her that.

"Ten thousand?"

"Dearest heart, it would be better to have more." Bogdan spoke with an accent so heavy and so real that it sounded phony.

"Twenty, Jimmy?"

Christ, Felicite was keeping the bastard! "If you're sure you want it." She nodded, the movement of her head slow. He wrote a note on a sheet torn from a memorandum pad. "Take it around to the bank. See any officer out on the platform."

Mike Ferrenbaugh crushed Jemel's hand and pounded his back.

"You're the only man I know that could get me to come out to this part of the world!" he boomed. "When I get around folks who don't speak American, I just don't function right. I get all shook up."

"Did you come alone, Mike?" On the slim chance that Mickey might have accompanied him.

"Sure did. Dot wanted to stay home—because of all the things to do with the wedding and all."

"Oh, that's right. Mickey is marrying that assemblyman, Fred Hayworth. I got a wedding invitation last week."

"He won't be an assemblyman after November,

Jimmy." Ferrenbaugh's chest swelled with pride. "Whalen's term is up, and he's running for reelection. I've got Freddie Hayworth on our party ticket to oppose him."

"You seem awfully sure Hayworth's going to win."

"He will. The wedding's set for two weeks before election. You know how voters are. That's enough to give him a plurality—but when I pass around those photographs of Whalen and Miller at that blowout you framed at the Chesham, Fred Hayworth's going to win by a landslide!"

Jemel's smile was bogus. "Give Mickey my"— he was going to say "love" but paused, wondering whether to say "best" instead. He discarded the idea. "Give her my love. And my best to Hayworth," he added hastily. "I hope to meet him one of these days."

"Can't you make it for the wedding, Jimmy?"

"Not a chance. You can see what I'm up against here. It'll take me months to get the new central offices running right."

Abdul el Muein's English had long since become almost perfect, and much of his fawning servility had disappeared. He had advanced far—by his or almost any Bedou's—standards. He served as confidential factotum and intermediary for several important Kuwaiti sheikhs.

"Do you have a moment to discuss business?" he asked Jemel.

"I always have all the moments necessary to discuss business," Jimmy said.

"The Sabah family's financial adviser, Sheikh Nasib al-Harith, has recommended that the Sabahs open an account with Incombank."

Jemel felt an inward surge of wild elation. The Sabahs were the ruling family of Kuwait. Their income from oil royalties totaled over a billion dollars a year. Any part of that money channeled into Incombank . . .

"I would consider myself honored to serve the Sabahs," he said.

"We can talk further in a few days."

Jimmy got the hint, and he was familiar with Abdul el Muein's weakness.

"You are staying at the Semiramis?" That was the hotel reserved for devout Moslems, and, representing conservative sheikhs, el Muein could stay at no other as a guest of Incombank.

"No, I am at the Phoenicia. Sheikh Nasib insisted that I come officially, rather than as a guest. I have Room 412."

"When will you return there?"

"In an hour."

"Let me make you a present. It'll be there a half hour after you return."

When Abdul el Muein had gone, Jimmy telephoned Beirut's leading—and most expensive—procurer.

"A different boy each day for the next week," Jemel said in Arabic. "Each must be young—under twelve—and plump. And if you send but one who is not tight-sphinctered, I will personally cut out your heart by refusing to pay you."

That would keep Abdul el Muein amused and happy.

By Tuesday morning, all the celebrations had ended, and the last of the guests had flown back to whatever countries were their homes.

Jemel Karami and Brian Lockhart were holding their first regular conference in the luxury of the board chairman's suite on the top floor of the new Incom central building.

"A memorable bash," Lockhart commented, "and a profitable one. Not counting whatever will come in from the Sabahs, we picked up around twelve million dollars in new or added deposits—with promises of more."

Jemel nodded, looked around him once again. Elegance and opulence. High, airy ceiling. The walls panelled in choice, magnificently grained woods. Costly fabrics, fine leathers. A panel of tiny Patek Philippe clocks—one for every time zone around the globe—

set flush in the warmly glowing, free-form vastness of the palissandro desk. An enormous sheet of tinted glass covered half the wall that faced toward the sea in the direction of the port area.

Jimmy walked to the window, looked out. "Come here a moment, Brian," he said. "Down there." He pointed a finger. "To the right of the Mosque Omari." The mosque, a sorry hash of Byzantine, Moorish, and Auvergnian architecture, is the sole monument of ancient history surviving within Beirut's city limits. Near it runs the murky cleft of a narrow *soukh*. "Just beyond where the *soukh* ends. An ugly dung-colored building with a flat roof."

"I see it."

"My father's office was there. On the second floor. Chafic Sabbagh, then Beirut's leading—and, as I recall only—native Lebanese electrical engineer, had the office directly above. On the third—and last—floor. Now, further to the right. Across the Avenue Weygand and beyond, to the port itself."

"Yes." Brian Lockhart was attentive, and not a little surprised. In all the years, Jimmy had said almost nothing about his Lebanese boyhood to him. These were all things Lockhart was hearing for the first time.

"Opposite the yacht-club jetty on the breakwater. There's a pier jutting out into the basin. Has a double row of warehouses on it."

"Umm." Brian nodded.

"The second warehouse in the left-hand row."

"Yes. White concrete like the others, but a green roof."

"There, Brian, once stood a scruffy shed with an unpainted corrugated metal roof. The Karami *et Cie* warehouse. A bitch of a place. A good 130 degrees Fahrenheit inside on a summer day." *And I wonder what Capitaine Raoul Andrieux's last thoughts of it were on a spring night in 1941.* "My father made me practice my arithmetic lessons by counting sacks and bales."

"A long way, eh, Jimmy?" Lockhart murmured.

Jemel gave a short laugh. "Funny. When I stop to think of it, it's not at all long." He paused, cocked his head to one side and looked at Brian. "Did I ever tell you how my father used to do business?"

"You've never gone into details."

Jimmy sat, leaned far back in his chair. "Hassan Karami had an array of French army officers and civilian bureaucrats he paid off regularly—and he gave them all the free liquor and sex they wanted." His eyes shifted and stared up at the ceiling. *"Plus ça change, plus c'est la même chose—or tel pere, tel fils,"* he mused aloud. "Both apply, I begin to realize, although I haven't a clue what particular importance either have." He gazed at Lockhart again. "Would your computer brain care to estimate how many hangovers or orgasms we bought for our guests over the last few days?"

"The brain not only boggles, it short-circuits," the Englishman chuckled. "You evoke images of oceans of drink and rivers of semen. All the same, *rien ne réussit comme le succès.*"

When the ruling family of Kuwait made a "token" —a "trial"—deposit of $5 million, Incombank gained enormous added prestige and *sharaf* throughout the Arab world.

It was the ultimate seal of approval; for wherever Sabah money went, there was certain to be profit and safety.

Streams of fresh deposits poured into Incombank. Far ahead of Jemel's hopes, Incom moved into the lead. Almost overnight, it leapfrogged, became the Middle East's largest and strongest banking institution.

On the surface.

12

Momentum: product of mass by its velocity.
Incombank soon topped all other banks in the

Middle East—but still, it only ranked 436th among all the banks of the world. There were giants that dwarfed Incom.

Incombank, Karamcorp, and the multitudinous subsidiaries had a total gross worth of $215 million.

But banks like the Bank of America, Chase, Barclay's, Royal of Canada, Credit Lyonnaise and scores of others counted their deposits in multiples of *billions,* paid out larger sums in interest to depositors each year than Incombank could show as its total resources.

Momentum was the answer. Build up both mass and velocity, and I'll push Incom and Karamcorp past the billion mark by 1967, Jemel vowed to himself.

The story made headlines in every newspaper in Europe, the Middle East and North Africa.

Milan, Italy. Oct. 27th. (ANSA): Enrico Mattei, 56, near-legendary "czar" of the Italian petroleum industry, was killed in the mysterious crash of his private executive jet aircraft near here today. Two other persons aboard, William F. McHale, an American correspondent for *Time* Magazine, and the pilot of the plane were also killed in the accident, which officials say has no apparent explanation. Mattei, whose recent wholesale acquisition of drilling concessions in many parts of North Africa and the mid-Orient have been the envy of oilmen everywhere . . .

Jemel Karami's left eyebrow climbed to its apogee as he read the story in Beirut. He recalled his last conversation with Miles Palmer—and the cryptic, inadvertent remark he'd made about Enrico Mattei.

He'd have to check this one through, Jimmy thought. Closely.

The wedding had been lavish, a major event.

There could be no honeymoon. Mickey Ferrenbaugh Hayworth understood this from the start. Radiant bride and handsome bridegroom had to spend the next two weeks campaigning. It was exhausting. After making a half dozen speeches and shaking several thousand hands during a day, Mr. and Mrs. Frederick Hayworth would fall into bed and sleep the few hours before they had to get up again and start the same routine with a woman's club breakfast or an early-morning appearance at a rural community hall.

Under the circumstances, Mickey had no reason to wonder why Fred Hayworth's desire to make love to her had diminished to the vanishing point. Neither of them had a moment or an ounce of energy to spare at the end of the day.

Then, less than seventy-two hours before the elections, some anonymous source inundated the state's religious groups, professional, fraternal, and service clubs with highly compromising and obscene—and unquestionably genuine—photographs of Senator Rodney Whalen and Governor Alvin Miller engaging in sexual acts with various women, including black women.

There was hardly any need for Frederick Hayworth to campaign after that. He and his bride were even able to spend an entire morning sleeping in their hotel room. When they awoke, they still had two hours to spare before their first scheduled meeting with local party officials.

Mickey experienced a twinge of disappointment when Fred got out of his twin bed, mumbled good morning and went into the bathroom, shaved and showered and started to dress.

He's still worn out, tense, she told herself.

Frederick Hayworth was elected senator over Rodney Whalen by the largest majority in the history of the state. The victory celebration was held in the ballroom of the Chesham Hotel in the state capital.

"You go on up to the suite," Hayworth told Mickey shortly after 4:00 A.M. His face was flushed. He'd had too much to drink—which was natural, Mickey readily conceded. "I've got to have a confab with some of the party big shots."

Michele Ferrenbaugh had been to other election-night victory celebrations with her father. She knew that the "big shots" had departed, gone home to bed, as soon as they knew the results. The ballroom was almost empty. Only the last of the freeloading small fry remained.

"Fred, can't you put it off? You need some rest."

"I'll get rest later. Now I have to see these guys." He left her and she went up to their suite.

It was almost ten in the morning when he stumbled into the bedroom, waking her. He was staggering drunk. "That's politics and smoke-filled rooms," Mickey thought, more sympathetic than amused. She got out of bed and went to help him.

"I'm awright," he mumbled. He managed to take off his overcoat and dinner jacket. Mickey disregarded the lipstick smears on his shirt. They were customary souvenirs given successful candidates by enthusiastic women voters who'd downed a highball or two.

"Congratulations, senator—my love," she said, kissing his neck and helping him slide his white suspenders straps off his shoulders. "We'll start to make up for the last two weeks after you're over the hangover you'll have." She laughed tenderly, kissed his neck again. "I love you, Fred—and I'm terribly proud of you."

He lurched away from her, steadied himself against a chest of drawers, and clumsily took off his trousers.

Mickey's hazel eyes stared, wide, unbelieving.

The front of his shorts was dark with dried blood.

Menstrual blood.

"Fred." Her voice was a hollow echo from the ice-chamber of her being. She was no prude and had no maudlin illusions about the fidelity of husbands. But today of all days—and wallowing like a drunken pig, not even bothering to look, not even noticing. "Fred. Didn't you want me?"

Hayworth came out of his fog and realized she was gaping at him. He glanced down, almost toppling forward, made sounds that might have been a laugh and stripped off his shorts. He staggered to his own bed, deflated himself onto it.

"Didn't you want me?" Mickey repeated.

"Talkaboutitlater." I got everything I really wanted out of marrying you last night, when Rod

Whalen conceded the election, he thought—and then he was asleep.

Emile Bustani was one of the wealthiest and most influential Lebanese businessmen. His Contracting and Trading Company—CAT—had long surpassed the $2 billion mark in worth and had branch offices in practically every major city throughout the Middle East and Black Africa. Emile Bustani received virtually all construction contracts granted by the Kuwaiti government and was on intimate terms with the emir. He moved in exalted circles. Britain's George Brown, Egypt's Nasser and America's Dean Rusk were only a few among the top-level political leaders and diplomats with whom he maintained friendly relations.

An ardent Pan-Arabist, Bustani expended vast amounts of effort and money in an attempt to reconcile the frictions between various Arab countries and form one united "Arab nation."

On March 15, 1963, Emile Bustani, two friends and his pilot boarded one of Bustani's private airplanes, an Aero-Commander, for a flight from Beirut to Damascus.

The plane was airborne at 0753 hours.

At 0810, the pilot radioed Beirut that the plane was in trouble. He was turning back. All communication with the Aero-Commander cut off three minutes later. The plane was seen plunging into the sea—"objects falling from it." All aboard were killed. Only two bodies were recovered. Emile Bustani's was not among them.

Jemel Karami's initial reaction to news that Bustani had been killed was indifferent. He knew Emile Bustani only slightly. There was no CAT or Bustani money in Incombank. In fact the multimillionaire contractor sat on the board of directors of the Arab Bank of Ammam, Jordan.

Then things clicked together. First Enrico Mattei. Now Emile Bustani. Bustani's dynamic Pan-Arabism had been one of the strongest forces keeping dissident factions in Kuwait and other oil-rich countries in check.

Working through front men, Palmer had aligned himself with the straight Nasserite factions in the Middle East—those which hoped Egypt would swallow the oil-producing Arab countries. Bustani, though personally friendly with Nasser, recognized that an Egyptian-led "Arab nation" would be a disaster.

Thus, while Miles Palmer's intermediaries fed money to pro-Nasser dissidents in an effort to stir them into open rebellion, Bustani countered dollar for dollar, buying off revolt-minded sheikhs and tribes.

Jimmy had previously confirmed his suspicions about a link between Palmer's machinations and the death of Enrico Mattei. It didn't take him long to establish a similar connection in the case of Emile Bustani.

None of this worried him, but it started him thinking along broader lines and convinced him he should take some elementary precautions.

Jemel's "viceregal lodge" was completed and furnished in all its raucous grandeur. It was there, on a terrace overlooking the Corniche, that he conferred one morning with Brian Lockhart.

Jimmy first dismissed Miles Palmer's continuing efforts to sidle into Middle Eastern oil, and he did it with contempt.

"Miles will screw up," he told Brian. "As usual, he's backing the wrong horse—that swaybacked nag, Gamal Abdul Nasser. The Nasser factions in oil-producing countries are small and weak. They're also tabbed and watched because they make so much noise. Let Palmer piss away all the millions he wants—they pass through Incom, so we're that much ahead."

Jemel turned to more important topics.

"We haven't made the most of the Arab nationalist sentiment, Brian," he declared. "I know how we can —and to maximum advantage."

He dangled his *sibah,* allowing the bright eastern Mediterranean sun to reflect from the colored beads.

"Offhand, what would you say is the one and only thing that all Arabs consider a common cause, about which all are in agreement?" he asked.

The answer came instantly. "Israel. The Jews."

"That's it. Anyone doing business in the Middle East has all his political sins—or lack of them—immediately forgiven if he can prove he supports the sacred anti-Israeli cause. Right?"

"Yes."

"Incom has to start showing its fervor. We have to select a likely assortment of anti-Israeli organizations—terrorist groups and whatnot—and give them generous, regular donations. That will show that Incombank has its heart in the right place—and is willing to put money where its heart is."

"What about the American and European Jews we have as depositors or with whom we do business of one sort or another?"

"There aren't that many—and, in any event, we don't have to make the donations with a lot of fanfare. Let the organizations know, of course—and then the word will spread quietly. It'll never get back to the Jews in the States or Europe."

It could be done easily enough, Lockhart thought.

Jemel put the Moslem rosary into his pocket. The beads, warmed by the sun, felt slick.

"Then I have a new project. Incombank is going to buy itself an airline—or rather, two, make them into one—and call it Pan-Arab Airways."

Lockhart scowled. In the eastern hemisphere, the airlines that weren't consistent money losers could be counted on the fingers of one hand. "Which lines do you propose buying?" Jemel named them. The Englishman's scowl deepened. Both were Lebanese-owned and among the worst money losers of all. They were inefficiently managed; their equipment was obsolete, their maintenance bad.

Jimmy read his thoughts. *"Sharaf,* Brian. Prestige. With a vengeance. The most ambitious and persuasive appeal to Arab pride anyone ever dreamed up. The name itself tells the story. Pan-Arab Airlines. Linking all the Arab countries with each other." He smiled. "Emile Bustani must be spinning around on the ocean bottom for not having thought of it."

Brian Lockhart began to see. By God, Jimmy

might well have come up with another of his inspired
flashes. He listened attentively.

"We dump all the old planes for whatever they'll
bring. We buy new equipment. The British and French
governments are subsidizing their aircraft industries by
arranging low-interest, until-the-hereafter loans to finance purchases. We can buy a nucleus fleet of Comets.
Tridents, and Caravelles, back it up with a lot more
piston jobs the American airlines are selling off at
bargain prices—DC-6-B's, Constellations . . ."

"What about personnel? Flying, ground—and particularly management?"

"We'll hire what we need. I'll bring in American
executives to run the operation—at least at the beginning." He was thinking of Russell Stanton as president.
He'd offer Stanton up to $100,000 a year—plus stock.
Guarantee to make him a millionaire in ten years.
Give him whatever he wanted. Russ could go after
—and get—the air-freighting business from American
oil companies operating in the Middle East. They air-
freighted almost everything. The business would
amount to millions each year.

"Pan-Arab will be a symbol," he went on. "A
symbol to every Arab—the way Aer Lingus is to every
Irishman and El Al is to every Jew. The Arabs will
bless Pan-Arab Airlines and heap praises—and chauvi-
nistically motivated deposits—on Incombank for making it possible."

Almost a certainty, Lockhart reflected. Only there
was the drawback. No matter how financed, the project
would require twenty-five, thirty million in cash to buy
up the existing lines' stock, purchase new planes and
parts, renovate facilities, hire people. Incom would see
no returns for years from the airline. The cash would
be tied up.

Jemel gazed out over the Mediterranean. The airline would give Incombank and all the subsidiaries and
the hollow-shell Karami companies quick access to every city of any size in every country in the Middle
East, North Africa, and much of Europe—perhaps
even in North and South America. Why, even currency
and gold could be shipped and shuffled back and forth

when there was need to make quick and secret trans-
fers.

Then there were U.S. foreign-aid and military-aid
programs under which many kinds of goods and items
were air-freighted. Mike Ferrenbaugh could probably
swing some of that business to Pan-Arab—so could the
extra senator and two congressmen on whom he's already made a down payment with gifts of Karamcorp
stock. Even Mike's protégé, the freshman Senator Frederick Hayworth, should be able to add a little push
when Mike cracked the whip.

Jemel's mind detoured for a moment. He still
hadn't met Hayworth, and he wanted to, because he
was curious to meet the man Mickey had married.

Mrs. Frederick Hayworth. He'd heard nothing
from her since she sent him a friendly thank-you note
for the wedding present he had some fashionable New
York gift-selection agency choose and forward in his
name. Mickey must have been transformed into the
happy housewife, he thought, trying to ignore the caustic bite of something approaching jealousy. *Approaching, my ass,* he confessed to himself. *I am jealous.
She's still under my skin . . .*

"How much time do I have to assemble this project?" Brian Lockhart's voice cut short his meander-
ings.

"This is March. The two lines should be all bought
up by the end of June. You can jam through a consolidation in another month, six weeks, and we can
start buying and hiring right after. Pan-Arab should
be a going concern, fully operational, within eighteen
months from today."

"That's damned fast, Jimmy. We'll be spreading
very thin again."

"Sit down with your pencils and adding machine
and figure out how we can bleed the necessary cash
out of Incom and plaster the gaps with paper," Jimmy
shrugged. "You'll find it's a cinch. With an airline,
Incombank will have a big edge—run the race against
time at jet speeds."

He stared out to sea once more. *I wonder if Mickey
kept the scrapbooks in which she kept clippings about*

me, he thought—and how much did she tell Hayworth about us?

13

Jemel's yacht, the *Asharat,* created a sensation. He saw to that.

Its first cruise was short—from England to Monte Carlo and return—solely for members of the press, who repaid their host's hospitality with glowing superlatives.

". . . breathtaking Oriental splendor that reflects the most discriminating taste and stops short of the vulgarity to be found aboard the yachts of other famous men . . ."

Paris-Match ran eight pages of color photographs of the *Asharat,* its salons, staterooms, swimming pools (there were two), Turkish baths.

Few reports failed to mention the Dassault twin-turbine-engined amphibious airplane and the eight-passenger Bell helicopter or the 48-foot Chriscraft cruiser the yacht carried.

The American magazine *Look* devoted most of its four color pages of photographs to the *Asharat*'s kitchens—one for owner and his guests, another for the yacht's officers, a third for ordinary members of the crew. *Look*'s food editor went into raptures about the varieties and quality of the yachtboard cuisine.

British newspapers and magazines emphasized technical aspects as well as luxury. "It's 360-foot length makes the *Asharat* the largest private yacht afloat. Its powerful engines, also made in Britain, give her a maximum speed in excess of 21 knots (although, according to Mr. Karami, no such speeds are contemplated during normal cruises) and the latest compensating stabilizers, improvements on those installed by Cunard on its liners, reduce pitch and roll even in the heaviest seas . . ."

Only the faggy gossip columnist for the British *Daily Express* sounded a small, discordant note. "The darker-than-olive-skinned Jemel (he seems to revel in being called by the nickname Jimmy) glibly answers all questions save those asked (with intentional waspishness) by your correspondent. The Levantine Midas avoided telling how much he spent to build the yacht or would spend annually operating it by plagiarizing a hackneyed line attributed to the elder J. P. Morgan. 'Nobody who has to ask what a yacht costs has any business owning one.' Looking for all the world like a young Rameses about to order a subject beheaded for *lése majesté,* he utterly refused to reveal whether the cost would be borne by him personally, or shared (in major part, as your correspondent suggested) by the shareholders in his companies."

Jimmy could have overloaded a dozen *Asharats* with rich or famous (or both) personalities who would have eagerly gone on the yacht's second cruise—from England to New York.

He chose his guest list with infinite care—and with purpose.

Sir Andrew and Lady Penelope Coddington. Sir Andrew was Britain's wealthiest industrialist and held a key cabinet ministry in Prime Minister Harold Macmillan's government.

Adolphe Nivernais. The enigmatic French financier Paris newspapers frequently referred to as "the Zaharoff of the *Bourse.*"

These three were of prime importance. He selected six other names from among his friends. Two men— one noted for his erudition, the second for his wit— and four women. Three of the women were lovely and successful young actresses. They were for Nivernais and the two unattached extra males. The fourth was Elinor Randolph—by now a foremost chronicler of international society, whose favorable reports on the cruise would be of great added glamorizing value.

At almost the last moment, he learned that Felicite had arrived in Cannes with Claus von Doeppler, the playboy heir to a German auto-manufacturing fortune. He invited them and they accepted. Jimmy believed he could make a closer reading of his sister along with the other things he intended to accomplish during the sea voyage.

The first two days out were perfect, the sea a flat, shimmering sheet under a sky empty of clouds. Soundproofing had reduced the throb of the *Asharat's* engines to a point where one had to strain to hear or be aware of them.

There was swimming, deck games, sunbathing, bright conversation over cooling drinks and under awnings or in bars or salons during the day. Caviar and champagne were always available for snacks. Lunches were sumptuous. Dinners more so, followed by dancing to the better-than-fair five-piece orchestra.

Jemel had his first opening to insert the thin edge of a lever with Sir Andrew Coddington on the second night, after dinner. Sir Andrew—paunchy and in his early sixties—had taken a postprandial "turn around the deck," and came into the Shaharazad salon bar. Jimmy happened to be passing through at the moment, and except for the barman, the salon was deserted.

"Thought I'd have a whisky," the British cabinet minister remarked, hoisting himself up on a bar stool upholstered in rich morocco leather.

"Mind if I join you?"

"Delighted!"

"What brand do you prefer? I always have Crawford's, myself."

"Damn it, I thought only we British knew the brand. Not much of it gets out. It's about the best, y'know."

"My father was introduced to it in Lebanon—by General Allenby's officers after the First War. He never drank anything else."

"Bless my soul!" Jimmy Karami was one of the most civilized Lebanese or Americans he'd ever met. In every respect. The barman was pouring their whisky.

"I like it," Jimmy went on. "In fact, I must remember to have one of my people get in touch with the distillers. Have them make up miniatures for Pan-Arab Airways."

"Cheers!" Sir Andrew raised his glass, swallowed happily, said, "Afraid I'm not with you, Jimmy. Pan-Arab Airways? Never heard of them."

"Incom's new airline. Barely conceived as an idea, and a bit of a gestation period ahead—but it'll be a reality."

Coddington wanted to hear more. Much more. Jemel told him, in a casual, offhand manner, over a total of three whiskies-and-water.

"I plan on establishing routes to several points not touched by the lines we're buying," he finished. "Of course, I'll have to obtain authorization from the countries concerned, but that shouldn't be insuperable."

"Perhaps I can help you, my boy," Sir Andrew smiled. He had the Chancellor of the Exchequer, the Transport and Aviation ministers in his vest pocket. "I'm certain we can arrange something for the purchase of Comets—and give you route-rights to England and what's left of our colonies." He slid off his bar stool. "Shall we find where the ladies are hiding and join them?"

Jemel and Coddington found the others in the main—the "Palmyra"—salon, where Adolphe Nivernais sat on a cushioned divan with one of the actresses, his bony hand fondling her thigh. Sir Andrew joined his wife and the other actress, squeezing his corpulent body between them. Jimmy sat down next to Elinor Randolph on a divan forming an angle with another occupied by Felicite and Claus von Doeppler. Felicite was laughing. She seemed to be in excellent condition and spirits, Jimmy thought, but he'd have to talk to her anyway.

He looked at Elinor. She was almost forty. You couldn't tell—until you got close up, Jimmy mused. Funny thing about red-haired women. They're inclined to sag more than others. He reached into a pocket for his cigarette case. Using the pretext of offering it to her, he whispered, "Nightcap in my stateroom tonight?" He couldn't have her feel herself the woman scorned.

She turned her head and gazed at him. Strange, he thought, the breasts and facial muscles soften, the eyes get harder. She nodded, and the eyes weren't quite so hard. She took a cigarette. He lit it for her.

He'd had her at fever pitch a moment before and now, suddenly, she went cold beneath his body.

"Elinor . . ."

"Let me get up, Jimmy. Please." Her face was seamed with sadness; there were tears in eyes that had gone empty.

"Please, Jimmy."

He obeyed, baffled. "Aren't you feeling well?"

Elinor had already got up. The walls of the stateroom were mirrored. She saw herself reflected unto infinity on all sides. "No," she said. "I'm not feeling very well." *Because I love you too much and I know you too well. I know your every thought and feeling.*

"Want me to call the ship's doctor—or is there something I can do?"

"There's nothing you can do, Jimmy," Elinor murmured. Her manner changed. The hardness returned to her eyes. "How old is the ship's doctor?" She forced a smile on that.

"He's . . ." Jimmy stopped. It had hit him. He hadn't fooled her. She'd sensed that he'd been forcing it, almost as though performing a duty.

Elinor's eyes read the Braille message that had etched itself over his features. *And I helped make him what he is,"* she told herself.

"Don't worry, Jimmy," she said aloud. She stared into the nearest mirror, turned away. Looking into a single mirror made the hang of her breasts appear more pronounced. She found her bra, put it on first, hurriedly. "I won't cut your throat." *I'll go right on, building you up, playing my dirty inside joke on myself—and hold my breath to see how it all ends.* She laughed heartily at herself. "For God's sake, don't move off that bed, Jimmy. You don't have to prove your masculinity to me—and you *can't* prove that you're still burning for me, no matter how you try."

She put on the rest of her clothes, went to the bed

and gave him a long, tender kiss. "That's a good-bye—but just to the sex part. Let's see each other every once in a while after the cruise is over."

"Yes." He was almost grateful to her. "Elinor . . ."

"Stay right where you are," she said, and went toward the door. "I'll send something in to you. It won't take more than five minutes. You'll like it."

She was gone.

Jemel stared after her. He got up from the bed, lit a cigarette. It was closer to ten minutes than five, but there was a knock on the door. He opened it. The actress who had been sitting with Lady Coddington came into the stateroom. She wore a nightgown and thin negligee.

"Elinor said you wanted to see me." She vacuumed Jemel's still naked body with her eyes, smiled and began taking off her negligee. "I guess you want more than just to see."

She knelt down in front of him, then pulled her lips away and stared up at him. "Redheads have a taste all of their own, don't they?" she laughed.

He seized her head with both hands and pulled it back between his thighs.

Adolphe Nivernais was an entirely different type than Sir Andrew Coddington. Anyone hoping to talk business with him had to make a direct approach, state facts succinctly—and declare what there was in the proposal for Adolphe Nivernais.

The next morning, shortly before lunch, Jemel invited Nivernais into the office that formed part of the owner's suite aboard the *Asharat*.

"I have a new project underway, Adolphe," Jimmy said. He rapidly outlined his plans to form Pan-Arab Airways. "We shall want to buy three Caravelles very soon—and we shall also want to sell 40 percent of the shares in Pan-Arab Airways."

"The first is simple, *mon cher ami*. I have influence. The second? Why doesn't Incombank do this through normal channels?" He waited for an answer, his gaunt, predatory face immobile.

The reply had to be honest. Completely honest,

or Nivernais would terminate the discussion immediately. "Because the shares will be worth almost nothing. Only if someone who has no connection with Incom creates a huge artificial demand and pumps up the price . . ."

"*Bien.*" Nivernais had guessed it from the start. "And for me?"

"Ten percent of the selling price."

"Twenty-five."

"The difference between ten and twenty-five is fifteen. I'll cut it in half, split it with you. Seventeen-and-a-half—and a free pass to climb aboard Pan-Arab's stewardesses whenever you want."

"*D'accord.*" Jimmy knew how to present a proposition, how to bargain without wasting time—and how to inject a light note into the bargaining. And he was a most generous host. All qualities Adolphe Nivernais liked.

"Your bed looks like something Raymond Loewy would design for Hugh Hefner—based on an original theme by Haroun-al-Raschid," Felicite laughed. Jimmy had brought her to his owner's suite after dinner. "How many women have you had in it?"

"So far, only four. Two during the press cruise, two this trip." Not counting Elinor. He sat on the bed, she on an oversized ottoman nearby. "As long as we're talking about my sex life, how is yours?"

"Claus is fun—or will be until we reach New York. He'll start to wear if I stay with him much longer."

"What happened to Bogdan?"

"Bogdan?" For an instant, Felicite hesitated. "Oh, the Yugoslav I brought to Beirut! God knows. We went to Istanbul from there. I left him in the hotel and flew to Paris the next day."

There was nothing wrong with his sister's eyes now—but Jimmy decided to ask. "What were you and he using—and don't tell me nothing . . ."

"I'd never dream of it! Cocaine."

"It didn't get to be a problem?"

"Oh, Jimmy! It was fun—for a little while. Then

t got to be a bore. Everything gets to be a bore sooner
or later."

She's no longer able to admit to herself that she's
spoiled, Jemel reflected.

"I like to try new things. That's all there is to
do, really." She stared at herself with apparent nar-
cissistic pleasure in the mirrors that sheathed the walls.
"I like myself, too. It's nice to be beautiful."

She is beautiful, Jimmy mused.

"M'mselle once told me there were only two things
I really loved. Myself and you, because I was like you
in so many ways." Her mood changed; she looked
away from the mirror and gazed at her hands. "She
was wrong. I loved her, too. I miss her."

Odd, Jimmy thought, Mademoiselle Claire Viete,
so long a part of whatever could be described as the
Karami family, had been dead over three years, and
neither her existence nor her passing had left any imprint on his mind.

Felicite leaped up from the ottoman in another
flash-change of mood.

"Let's go back to where everybody is," she said.
Jimmy stood up. His sister looked at him slyly. "Who
were the women this trip?" she asked.

"Two of our cinema princesses."

"Not Elinor Randolph?"

"Yes and no."

"That's a story, I'm sure. Tell me what happened
between you."

"Someday. Not now." They went through the office. Felicite stopped. There was a battery of telephones arrayed on the massive antique desk. "I wanted
to ask you the other day. I know there's a phone in
every stateroom—but why do you have so many?"

"This one's for shipboard communication. That's
a direct radiotelephone line to Incom. The next one's
the same to Karamcorp. The last is for making ordinary
ship-to-shore calls. You can do it from your stateroom
extension, too. This is just a spare."

"Can I make a call to New York from here?"

"Sure. Only, as I said, the extension in your stateroom . . ."

"Claus might walk in and hear me. I want to call a man in New York—so he'll be ready for me after we arrive and I get rid of Claus."

"Help yourself. Just give the man who answers the number, and he'll get through for you inside fifteen minutes."

When Jemel had gone, Felicite locked the doors, placed her call. Then she hurried into Jimmy's stateroom, turning on all the lights. She lay down on his bed, propping herself into a half-sitting position and pulled her skirts high above her thighs. The fingers of her left hand tugged aside the filmy crotch of her panties. The fingers of her right searched through a silken tangle of pubic hairs to moist swollen tissue and moved in slow, sensual circles. She could see a myriad replicas of herself in mirrors. All of them experienced orgasm together, at the same instant as she did, and seeing made her feel that she had experienced them all herself.

14

Jemel's guests all understood that the cruise ended in New York. They would return to England and the Continent by air—at Jimmy's expense.

The *Asharat* was anchored in the Hudson River. A series of parties were given aboard her—for the New York press, then customers of Karamcorp, next executives and key employees of the company and its subsidiaries and, finally (and for this party, the caviar and vintage Krug's once more abounded) for important members of the Manhattan banking fraternity and officials of the New York State Banking Commission.

It was at this party that Jemel announced his intentions to open a New York City branch of Incombank. Normally, Manhattan bankers would have taken such an announcement sourly. They knew that, because of a quirk in American banking laws, foreign branches established in the United States were exempted from any form of federal regulation or control. However, the fact that Jemel Karami had thought to invite New York State Banking Commission officials altered the picture. The state did have authority over foreign bank branches within its borders. While this still left the foreign banks with a great competitive advantage over their American counterparts, Karami's invitation to the officials appeared as in earnest that he planned to operate as fairly and ethically as any other bank.

Then, of course, the bankers realized, Incombank had branches in many countries around the world, and Karamcorp and its subsidiaries did a global business. The rapidly growing Karami financial empire would bring in wealth rather than take it out. Lastly, the presence of an Incom branch in New York would provide many American banks with a new, convenient —and profitable—channel of financial communication with the Middle East.

After the party was over, Jemel had a good night's sleep. The following morning, he informed Halim Chalhoub and his and Karamcorp's other attorneys and accountants to start the machinery rolling to establish the branch. He would capitalize the bank at $1 million to start.

He used his own money, drawing it from a secret Swiss account. The exception to prove the rule, he told himself. When Incombank of New York City was a success—and he'd arrange that it would be in record time—he'd sell a minority bloc for more than the million he invested.

Russell Stanton was away on one of his periodic field inspections in Saudi Arabia and would not return to New York for a week.

Jimmy had better luck with Mike Ferrenbaugh. The Senate was in summer recess. Mike was home. And so, Ferrenbaugh told Jemel, were Mickey and Fred.

"Can you and Hayworth spare a day for me if I fly out tomorrow?" Jimmy asked. Part of the rush was because he had to work fast, start pulling strings—part because he wanted to meet Fred Hayworth. And to see Mickey. "I have a few things I'd like to talk over."

" 'Course we can!" Iron Mike's voice assured him. "You come on. In case Fred's got anything else on tap, I'll tell him to cancel it." He laughed heartily. "Have something to tell you myself." Much pride.

Mickey is going to have a baby, and Mike is going to be a grandfather, Jemel thought. *She's going to have Frederick Hayworth's baby.* It shouldn't bother him, but it did.

"Mickey's pregnant, is that it?"

"Nah! Nothing like that . . ."

How does a "whew!" feel and why does it feel at all? Jimmy wondered.

". . . I'll tell you when we see you. Will you stay with us this trip?"

"I will, Mike, if it's no inconvenience. Just for one night, though."

Ferrenbaugh met Jemel at the airport—in an official Cadillac limousine complete with state trooper chauffeur.

"How come a state car, Mike?"

"It's what I have to tell you, Jimmy. The way we clobbered Whalen and Miller and their bunch at the last election, my party's going to have a stranglehold on this state till God knows when. The top boys in Washington decided to thank me."

"With a limousine and chauffeur?"

"They're just a snippet. I'm quitting the Senate when my term's up next year—let some younger buck have a chance. I'm going to be the party boss, the elder statesman and kingmaker right here in my home state!"

"I didn't think senators ever retired voluntarily," Jimmy commented. He wasn't happy about the news. Mike in the United States Senate was one thing—Mike as a Border States local party boss another. The other legislators he had on the string didn't have anywhere near Ferrenbaugh's influence and seniority—and he wasn't yet sure how far he could rely on them.

"This one's going to, Jimmy. I'm getting to the age where I want to take life easy. No quorum calls or committee meetings or visiting constituents to take on sightseeing tours. Just sit back, give the orders, get my cut—have a few at the country club on Saturday nights . . ."

He droned on. Jimmy didn't listen.

The state trooper pulled the Cadillac up in front of the Ferrenbaughs' house, opened the car door, saluted smartly, and carried Jimmy's bag into the house for him.

"Mickey and Fred won't be over for another hour or so," Dorothy Ferrenbaugh said after giving Jimmy a warm hug and a kiss on the cheek. "Mike wanted to have a chat with you alone before they got here."

"Aw, hell, I told Jimmy just about everything driving in from the airport, Dot. So you might as well call the kids and tell 'em to come on now." He turned to Jemel. "You'll be surprised by Mickey. She's changed. Grown up. Best thing she ever did was to get married."

Mickey. Lovely as ever in a yellow silk dress, but not meeting his eyes, her greeting timid, almost reticent, pulling her hand free a beat too quickly.

Frederick Hayworth. Tall. The matinee-idol photographs of the young Senator Hayworth hadn't exaggerated. Shock of brown hair, artfully contrived to look boyishly unruly. The cleft in the chin that male voters considered an indication of friendly integrity, aroused maternal or erotic instincts in females. The handshake practiced, professional.

And the eyes canny, clever behind their camouflage screen of cordial sincerity, his manner a shade overaffectionate toward Dot, overfamiliar with Mike, overfriendly towards Jemel—and not quite what it should be with his wife, Mickey.

Jemel allowed the general conversation to flow around him, adding a remark here, answering a question there, finding something to ask himself when it seemed he should, simulating interest in the replies.

". . . sure sorry you couldn't have been here for the wedding . . ."

". . . papers and magazines have been full of stories about your yacht . . ."

". . . how's your sister, been reading about her a lot, too . . ."

"Oh, she's fine. Came across with me. Told me to give you all her best regards. One of these days, I hope we can all take a cruise together."

". . . Dot gets seasick . . ."

". . . now, Mike, that's not true. I even went sailing with Fred on the lakes, didn't I, Fred?"

"You did beautifully, Mom. That's really why I married Mickey—because I wanted a good sailor for a mother-in-law."

Mickey said the least of anyone present, Jemel noted. Once or twice, he caught her looking at him. Her expression bore an uncanny, inexplicable similarity to the sadness he'd observed in Elinor Randolph the night of the fiasco aboard the yacht. He was warmed by an inner sense of triumph. The marriage had flaws, deep flaws, somewhere. Hayworth was something less than the perfect husband, Mickey anything but the idyllically happy housewife. A crack in the Togetherness show-window.

". . . while the girls see about getting us some lunch," Mike was saying.

The three men went to Ferrenbaugh's den.

"Fred knows just about everything I do," Mike declared. "I haven't kept any secrets from him, so you can talk free, Jimmy." He offered cigars. Hayworth took one. Jemel didn't.

"I know my way around," Fred Hayworth said, and added, "Thanks to Mike." Maybe the devoted son-in-law had big ideas of his own.

Jimmy's comment was said mildly. "I guess we all owe Mike a lot. He's been helping me out for many years." He flashed Hayworth a smile. "We've pulled off more deals than I could count." Pause. "We've had our share of close scrapes, too, eh, Mike?" A hint to remind them both that it had been Jemel Karami who'd provided the ammunition with which to destroy the Whalen-Miller political machine.

"Damn right. Those snapshots Jimmy got snapped put you in the Senate, Fred," Mike agreed hastily.

"Don't I know it!" Even hastier and more emphatic concurrence from Hayworth. Out loud. To himself: *Karami saved his own neck, then tossed Mike the leftovers. I don't owe Karami anything—yet. The question is what's he trying to buy now, and what's he offering to pay?*

There were several items on Jimmy's mental shopping list. Route-rights to New York for Pan-Arab Airlines. Military and foreign-aid and air-freighting contracts for Pan-Arab. Mike to sit on the board of the Manhattan branch of Incombank. Some words spoken to the Internal Revenue Service to call off a forthcoming audit of the books of a Karamcorp subsidiary. More words to the SEC concerning another corporation he was forming. Odds and ends.

An hour passed, Mike nodding acquiescence to almost everything. He'd do his utmost. Hayworth for the most part silent, simply listening.

"Can I count on you, too, Fred?" Jimmy asked.

The reply was a fishhook baited with modesty. "I'm a first-termer, Jimmy. No seniority. Not much pull." He ran fingers through his hair—a much-rehearsed gesture, Jimmy saw, for the hair stayed as it had been before when Hayworth had finished. *Maybe the bastard has it permanent-waved and set,* Jemel laughed to himself.

"I have only one vote, and don't control any others," Hayworth continued. *Which is going to change and soon. Soon's I bust loose and start grandstanding.* "I can't promise very much."

I may not like this guy, but he's going to go far, Jimmy decided. He was keeping it hidden, but there was ambition and drive in the man—and down-deep hardness. *Takes one to know one,* Jemel mused. *Lay it on the line—it'll save trouble later.*

"I think Mike mentioned you're a lawyer, have a law firm, Fred." Hayworth had gone to the state assembly from a one-room law office he shared with an ambulance-chasing partner. "As a start, one of my subsidiary companies will retain your firm. We'll see where we go from there."

It was satisfactory. For a start, Hayworth thought. Whatever he took in from Karami as a retainer would be useful. The girl he'd been keeping had developed expensive tastes since his election to the Senate. He owed money.

Jemel contrived an excuse to encounter Mickey alone in a corridor after lunch.

He faced her. "Hello, Mickey," he murmured.

"Jimmy." She seemed to sway forward toward him. Her hazel eyes were haunted, yearning. He was certain he could have had her—then and there.

"It's good to see you again," he said, then raised his voice to normal level. "Guess I'd better go and talk some more with your father—and Fred." His smile was open, friendly. Keep her guessing awhile, he thought, standing aside to let her pass. Eventually, whatever was bugging her marriage would reach the point where she'd come to him—running or crawling. It would be worth playing the little game, worth the wait.

15

A week of furious activity in New York—then the call to Russ Stanton. A Friday evening invitation to dinner at Jemel's penthouse.

"Wouldn't miss the chance to see you, Jimmy. It's been over a year since the last time. Only I'd like to bring my fiancée."

"Your *what?*"

"Fiancée. Pat. Patricia Bramlett. No formal announcements or any of that crap, but we're getting married soon. I was meaning to ask you if you'd be best man when we'd settled on a date for the wedding. Which will leave you the last of us, A-rab."

The last? Oh, yes. Marvin Jacobs had got married some years before, had a couple of kids. "Congratulations—and my sympathies to Miss Bramlett." Jimmy wanted to get Russ alone, on a man-to-man basis. He'd have to switch tactics. All to the good. Having Stanton's fiancée present would be a help. Women wanted their husbands to be rich, successful. Dazzle her with the prospects, and she'd do the selling job. "I'd be delighted to have you both over for dinner."

Jemel had expected that any woman Russell Stanton finally decided to marry would be attractive, out of the ordinary. But this?

Patricia Bramlett was startling. Stunning. All the more so because there was nothing conventional or typecast about her beauty. A tall, slender ash-blonde with violet eyes and a figure any sculptor could consider a masterpiece if he'd created it. A magnificent package of contrasts and paradoxes that would make any man with an ounce of brains and balls climb walls and walk upside-down across ceilings.

Alabaster and ice and a regal bearing wrapped in a peacock-blue dress that would have been a vulgar shriek on any other woman. On Patricia Bramlett: perfect. In impeccable taste. Underneath the ice, superheated passion and love for Russ, evident whenever she looked at him and her violet eyes caught fire. Jesus—what a woman!

Jimmy finally got around to taking a good look at Stanton—sunbronzed to the color of mahogany, still a hard-muscled, flat-bellied six-two. Completely at his ease. Obviously reciprocating all he received from Pat, a two-way relationship that clicked, meshed, balanced —in bed and out.

"We'll have a drink or so in the library before dinner. Okay?"

Martinis. Pat and Russ admiring the view from the windows. Pat noticing the Corot and the Matisse on the walls, impressed by them, the three-carat emerald-cut solitaire on her left hand reflecting light as she gestured when she spoke. Later, her face warming with pleasure at Russ's evident enjoyment over being with his old friend—yet remaining protective, loving.

She said the right things naturally. The flash of her long, slender legs and the movements of her body were provocative without conscious effort on her part. Stanton was a lucky son-of-a-bitch, Jemel mused. He'd plumbed layers of snow and ice and tapped the molten core of a volcano.

Russ was surprised there were only three of them for dinner. It wasn't like Jimmy to be without a girl, not even for dinner with an old friend and his fiancée. Explanation came while they were on their second round.

"Since you've asked me to be best man, Russ, I wanted to see you and Pat alone. Have some questions to ask. One. When are you getting married?"

"Depends how things stack with the company," Russ replied. "Soon's I can shake free for a whole month."

"Two. Made any plans for your honeymoon?"

"Not really. Pat's been doing the travel-folder bit."

"It only confuses me," she laughed. "I was never good at geography. We'll probably wind up with a weekend at Niagara Falls."

"That answers question three. What to give you two for a wedding present. I personally recommend a Caribbean cruise. Sunny days, romantic nights. The *Asharat* will take you and bring you back."

"Your yacht?" Russ spluttered. "My God, Jimmy, we couldn't accept . . ."

"Yes, you can. It'll keep the captain and crew busy. They loaf too much." He flicked a glance at Patricia Bramlett. She was gazing at Russ, leaving the decision to him, but Jimmy knew she was hoping he'd accept. Women are women—even when they're Snow Queens with volcanoes inside them—Jemel thought with satisfaction, and said, "Anyone hungry yet?"

Jemel's chef had prepared a memorable dinner. Food and wines were served by Dowling and the footman as though it were a state banquet. Patricia thawed further as Jimmy adroitly encouraged her to talk about herself. He learned she was a fashion designer (which explained the near-miracle of the peacock-blue dress), not quite twenty-six, and that while Russ was having a house built for them in Scarsdale, she fully intended to continue working after their marriage.

"Russ makes four trips a year to Saudi Arabia —anywhere from two weeks to a month each time," she said cheerfully. "I'm not going to sit home, moping and feeling sorry for myself whenever he's away."

Jemel shifted his attention to Russ. "Aren't you in a sort of rut with Whitehead MidEast? Still shuttling back and forth . . ."

"It's not really a rut, Jimmy. R. D. Whitehead owns the company. Quentin Yeager's the president. There are four vice-presidents. I'm one of them." He was neither boasting nor complaining. "I'm in the forty-thousand-a-year bracket and can look forward to ten-fifteen more in time."

"And you have a one-in-four chance of having the lucky number if this man—Yeager, is it?—leaves or retires."

He made it sound like he considered it a sad waste of potential. "You're a personal challenge to me, Russ," he said silently. "I've tried to figure your price before, offered you jobs straight out—and missed. I'm not making the same mistakes again. I'm dropping king-sized hints that'll have their biggest impact on the future Mrs. Stanton. She'll work on you. I'll bet on it."

"Not all that cut-and-dried," Russ said. "There are stock options and fringe benefits—not to mention the security you've heard me hold forth on more than once."

Ah, yes. The security. But Incombank and Karamcorp were a far cry from Karami & Co. There wasn't a financial analyst anywhere that didn't consider them rock-solid. "You're a lucky guy, Russell T. You got"—he beamed a smile toward Patricia—"or are getting everything you wanted."

He noticed she was listening to every word said, her violet eyes shades darker. Sharp mind. Her antennae were attuned for every nuance.

"Let's go out to the *Asharat*," Jimmy suggested.

"We can have coffee and drinks aboard—and I'll show you around the coal barge you'll be riding in on your honeymoon."

Patricia's compliments on the furnishings and decor of the yacht were sincere. Russ was particularly impressed by the Dassault amphibian and the Bell helicopter.

"I set out to out-Onassis Onassis," Jimmy said candidly. "But they're only a starter set for an airplane collection Incom's going to make. We'll have our own airline before long." He related his plans for Pan-Arab Airways.

"Most of the knots are unsnarling," he summed up. "Biggest remaining obstacle is finding someone to run the operation after it's all set up."

"That shouldn't be too difficult," Russ said.

"Oh, no? You know what Arabs can do to botch up any management job. Pan-Arab will need top American talent at its head. A crack overall executive who understands how to establish efficient systems and keep 'em efficient. What's more, he has to be someone who knows the Middle East—an old Middle East hand accustomed to dealing with Arab bureaucrats. Brian Lockhart—who runs Incombank for me, Pat—and I've agreed that when we find the right man, we'll be glad to offer seventy-five a year plus stock to start.

"You know, the three of us have a problem," he said. "If you're going to have a reception after your wedding, how can I arrange a bon-voyage party aboard —or would you like to have the reception here? It would be a twist. Fun, no?"

"I'm sorry, Jimmy," Pat spoke up. "My parents insist on having the reception . . ."

"Then we'll have a party aboard afterward—just before you sail."

The wedding took place during the first week in January. It was a small, quiet affair. Aside from Jemel and Marvin Jacobs and his wife, Russ had invited only a few friends and distant relatives (his mother had died in 1961). Jemel was surprised he asked no one from Whitehead MidEast.

"I keep my company and private lives in separate compartments," Russ explained. "That's something else I like about Whitehead MidEast. We're all friendly—but there isn't any of this play-company-politics-while-playing-golf-together crap. The executives' wives don't have to take turns giving dinner parties. Not at all the way the management manuals would have it."

Patricia had invited a considerably larger number of guests, but even so, there were not over a hundred people in the church or at the reception. Slightly more than half of these came aboard the *Asharat* for the bon-voyage party.

Jimmy left the newlyweds and their guests in the Palmyra salon and personally showed Marvin Jacobs and his wife Sybil, a dark-haired, pretty woman over the ship. Both were awed.

"Russ and I always knew you'd make it, Jimmy," Marv commented. "I've been betting on you. When our kids were born, I bought each of them 500 shares of Karamcorp—and the stock's in the safe-deposit box. At the rate you're going, the kids'll have a nice bundle by the time they grow up."

They made their way back to the main salon, had a final glass of champagne with Russ and Pat, and then the bon-voyage party broke up so the *Asharat* could set sail at exactly midnight.

The cruise had been meticulously planned so that even while they felt they had seen and done everything, Russ and Pat could still have ample time to themselves, luxuriate in each other even while they luxuriated in the splendor around them.

They had Jemel's master suite. At nine each morning, an apparently ghostly steward—he made no sound audible through the door to the sleeping stateroom—delivered iced vintage champagne and a half-pound tin of beluga to the adjoining lounge. When the yacht touched anywhere, all the formalities were taken care of by the ship's officers. The Stantons—it took them a few days to think of themselves as such—were met, escorted, shown the sights. If they wished to take longer trips overland, the licensed airplane pilot who was part of the ship's complement took them in the helicopter. If they wished to fish, or cruise close inland, the Chriscraft was lowered, manned by a second officer and a steward—and they went where they pleased.

They reveled in the splendor of it all.

It was on the ninth morning out and they were sunning themselves at the edge of the outdoor swimming pool when Pat suddenly sat up and gazed at her husband, her violet eyes very dark and very serious.

"Russ, are you going to take the job Jimmy offered you?"

Stanton was no fool. He'd been aware that hints Jemel dropped about his projected airline and its need for an American executive were more than idle conversation. He hadn't thought that Pat had picked up the message.

He sat up, kissed her on the mouth, and traced his fingers over the satin tops of her hard, exquisitely shaped—and now bikini-haltered—breasts.

"No, darling," he shook his head. "I'm not. I'm going to pretend I never read the signals, and if he asks me openly, I'll refuse."

"Why?"

"Oh, for a lot of reasons. I started with Whitehead MidEast when it was first organized. I—and don't laugh at me—have a proprietary, almost a parental, feeling toward it. I helped build up that Middle Eastern operation."

He paused and reached for a cigarette. "Then there's an element of personal loyalty. Most people probably wouldn't believe it, but R. D. Whitehead does that to you—he inspires loyalty. You may get sore as hell at the old coot, yet you'll bust your back for him. It's a quality some rare few combat commanders had during the war. It's tough to explain. Patton had it—and God, how he was hated. So did General Maurice Rose—only he was liked . . ."

"But Jimmy Karami is your friend—probably the best friend you have."

"There's another reason. The main reason. Knowing Jimmy the way I do, I'd never be sure in my own mind that he wasn't hiring me just because of that, because we were friends."

"You're being silly, Russ! Do you honestly believe anyone would make an offer of seventy-five thousand dollars a year—and an interest in a company—just to do a friend a favor?"

Russ grinned, kissed her cheek. "Look around you," he whispered in her ear. She did, not comprehending. "What do you see?"

"The yacht. The ocean. A sailor going toward the bridge . . ."

"Pat. Can you imagine what this ship cost? How much it costs to run it?"

"A fortune."

"Several fortunes. Seventy-five thousand a year means nothing to Jimmy. He could spend it on a generous gesture and never miss it."

Pat Stanton's feminine intuition told her Jemel Karami might make generous gestures—but with sound motives behind them. "I think he really wants you to work for him because you'll do a good job," she said.

"Maybe. Only, like I said, I could never be sure—and it'd bug the hell out of me. Would you want me to take the job under those conditions?"

"Oh, Russ. It's just that I want you to be a success. You're better than anyone else. I know it. I want everyone to know it."

"I'm not exactly a failure," he said, taking her in his arms. "I have you for a wife, a job that'll do a little more than maintain us at subsistence level—plus a friend like Jimmy Karami. And as long as I keep you as a wife and the job I have now, I'll keep Jimmy as a friend."

He kissed her passionately. She returned his kiss. "Let's go in to the stateroom," she murmured against his lips.

"Um-huh." He lifted her up easily and carried her bodily along the gleaming deck.

16

Jemel stared down at the crazy-quilt panorama of Beirut rooftops baking in the May heat, seeming to sag under the weight of the oppressive humidity. Even the Mediterranean appeared to have been beaten into sluggish submission by the heat. He was grateful the sounds and smells of the streets far below could not reach to the topmost floor of the Incombank Tower—and that even if they could, he was insulated from them as he was from the heat by thick, treated glass. The mosque caught his eye. He laughed to himself. He always did when he saw the powerful loudspeakers mounted near the tops of the minarets. Not even the muezzins climbed stairs anymore. They stayed in the mosque, flicked the switch on the public-address system, and wailed their calls to prayer into a microphone made by A. G. Siemens in Germany.

A tap on the door. "Come in, Brian."

Lockhart looked slightly frayed—not by the heat outside, but by the sleepless night he'd spent preparing all the documents Jimmy wanted.

"Get to bed at all?"

Lockhart shook his head, put a pile of papers on Jemel's desk, slumped wearily into a chair. "Not a wink."

"Sorry. I wouldn't have asked . . ."

"Good Lord. I know that, Jimmy."

Jemel seated himself behind the desk. "How do we stand?"

"Not at our best." He divided the stack of papers exactly in half, handed the top half—the originals—to Jemel, took the other, carbon copies, himself. "Cash and other real liquid assets are low again."

"When aren't they? I'll have eleven million in from Adolphe Nivernais next week."

"That'll help. Not for long, though."

The purchase of the two run-down Lebanese airlines, their consolidation into Pan-Arab Airways, and the costs incident to pumping the first breath of life into the line had spiraled. West German and Japanese bankers were sweeping across the Middle East, offering the oil sheikhs 8½ percent interest on deposits. To holds its accounts, Incombank had been forced to meet the competition, raise its "extra dividends" to total 8½ percent—an interest rate demanded even by medium-bracket depositors.

In a few years, Incombank would be in the clear. The tens of millions siphoned off into Karami front companies for long-term speculative ventures would start coming back. The ventures would begin to pay off—at double and triple, enabling the fronts to pay off their "borrowings" from Incom and make up all concealed shortages—with plenty to spare for profit.

"Actually, we look good," Jimmy said. "A few more years of maneuvering. Starting in 1971 we'll have more spare cash than any six banks in Beirut."

"I've been on the conservative side in my projections—and, yes, the big upsurge will start in four years. However, right now, we have two squeezes. There's Pan-Arab . . ."

"Pan-Arab is not going to be as big a load as you think, Brian." Sir Andrew Coddington had done his bit, and three Comet IV jets and five Vickers Viscounts had been delivered—with the British Government providing long-term financing of 82 percent of the purchase price. One jet and one Viscount were to be leased back to a British-owned airline at a rental that would equal their purchase price in three years. Thus, Pan-Arab would be acquiring those two aircraft virtually free—paying only the nominal 2 percent annual interest on that portion of the loan that financed their purchase. Coddington had even obtained approval for Pan-Arab to fly the Beirut-London run. That might not produce much revenue, but it would provide Pan-Arab with immense prestige.

Adolphe Nivernais had not only unloaded the first batch of Pan-Arab stock, but he had obtained approval for Pan-Arab to fly in and out of Paris. More revenue there, and no less prestige than the London route.

Mike Ferrenbaugh was lining up U.S. government air-freighting contracts, and two other senators were working on approval for Pan-Arab to fly Beirut-New York City.

The problems still facing Pan-Arab were the down payments to the British government, and cash needed to buy other aircraft—the French were being coy about selling their Caravelles on long-term credit, and American airlines with obsolete piston aircraft were also requiring payment in cash. Renovation of ground facilities was costly—and while almost all Arab countries were enthusiastic and cooperative, final agreement and approvals required heavy outlays of *baksheesh*.

Lastly, there was the presidency of the airline. Russ Stanton and his bride had returned from the honeymoon cruise more than four months before. They had overwhelmed Jimmy with their gratitude, but Stanton had made no reference to the hints that had been dropped. Jimmy dropped more, and he was convinced that Patricia wanted Russ to take the job—but so far, there had been no word.

"I'll wait a little longer—and if there's still nothing when I go back to the States, I'll pull every salesman's trick I know," he told Lockhart. "Not on Stanton. On his wife."

"Suppose you fail. Do you have anyone else in mind?"

"I won't fail. Now, what's the other squeeze?"

The Englishman shrugged wearily. "Cash."

Jemel's sensual mouth twisted into a leer very familiar to Lockhart—and Lockhart felt better already.

"Eleven next week from Nivernais," Jemel said. "And around twenty today. Adequate?"

"Twenty today? That's incredible! It'll give us all the elbow room we'll need for the next year! But how. . . ?"

"The Arab League's Arab Petroleum Congress is meeting in Beirut."

"I know. I attended one of their dinners the night before you arrived."

"The chief delegate from each Arab oil-producing country is coming to a party I'm giving aboard the *Asharat*. It'll be some party, take my word for it. While we're still eating—and before the *bints* and *bhang* come on, I'm announcing Pan-Arab Airways' hitherto-secret pan-Islamic policy."

"Which will be?"

"Practically free fares for all devout Moslems desiring to make the *hajj* to Mecca from any oil-producing Arab country. Even the poorest will now have a chance to make the pilgrimage."

"Jimmy. Have you run off your trolley? We'll lose . . ."

"Brian, you must have been born under the sign of Cancer. You're a nagging sort," Jemel laughed. "I'm informing the delegates that their respective governments can tell the populace that *they* are subsidizing the fares for the greater glory of Allah and the welfare of their subjects' souls. They'll cheer—and they'll agree as meekly as lambs when I suggest that each government should show its gratitude to Incombank by pulling a few million out of competing banks and putting them into Incom." He stood up, stretched. "A typical Incombank bonus service to depositors, I'll even promise to get Ferrenbaugh and my other housebroken U.S. lawmakers to use their influence on American oil companies and make them raise oil royalties a point or two in the interest of bettering relations with the Arab States." He went back to the window, gazed now at the *Asharat* lying at anchor a thousand yards off the port. It would be warped into a berth in another hour or so. "Did I say twenty million? It might even go as high as twenty-five."

"Do you want these papers any longer?" Brian asked, feeling much better.

"Leave my set. I'll go over the lot carefully. Now get yourself home and catch up on your sleep." Lockhart was halfway out the door when Jemel stopped him. "So you'll sleep more soundly, Pan-Arab will have only two used piston-job planes available for the pilgrims. And those only two months out of the year."

17

Whenever R. Daniel Whitehead's private industrial intelligence organization obtained any information that seemed of special importance and significance, it was forwarded to him without delay.

Reports that Jemel Karami, head of Incombank, had entertained selected delegates to the Arab Petroleum Congress aboard his yacht and that certain promises had been made and agreements reached, more than met the criteria.

Whitehead read the reports in his Oceanside, California, home. He gave his orders to the man who headed his "research service."

"Get all the additional dope you can. Have Karami watched as closely as possible in Lebanon. Whenever he's in the States, have him tailed, and bug his office and apartment. I don't care what it costs. I want to know whom he sees, what he says, when he shits, spits, or sneezes." The Arab League was pressing for increased oil royalties. It could be Karami had agreed to throw his considerable influence on both sides of the ocean behind the League's demands —and that would lead to tough complications.

"Right, R. D. Only he's bound to catch on that he's being watched, and as for bugs, he probably has everything swept periodically."

"I doubt it," Whitehead said dryly. "Karami's megalomania has grown to a stage where he's sure he's smarter than anyone else. He'd never dream that anyone would dare use tactics against him that are as simple as the obvious."

Jemel played it carefully, telephoning the Whitehead MidEast Oil offices to be told what he already knew. Mr. Stanton was in Saudi Arabia.

"Thanks. This is Jimmy Karami, a personal friend. I'll call Mrs. Stanton."

All open and aboveboard. It wasn't quite eleven. He placed a call through his secretary to the fashion-design house where Patricia Stanton worked.

"Mrs. Stanton is on the line, Mr. Karami."

"Hello, Pat. Russ's office tells me he's where I was yesterday. I wanted to talk to him. I wonder if you could have lunch with me?"

"Yes—I think so. Where shall I meet you?"

"I'll send my chauffeur and a car"—yes, the Rolls —"for you. What time would suit you?"

"I usually have lunch at twelve-thirty."

"He'll be in front of your building and bring you around to '21.' I'd call for you myself, but I'm knotted up. A last-minute flurry over the opening of the Incom Manhattan branch next week."

He drove up in his white Ferrari just as the Rolls was pulling to the curb. He left the Ferrari double-parked, met Pat as the doorman helped her from the limousine, and he led her toward the entrance.

"Your car?" Pat asked.

"It'll be taken care of," Jemel replied.

"Of course, Mr. Karami," the doorman said.

They were hardly seated at one of the best tables when a telephone was brought to the table. "A call for you, Mr. Karami."

"Thank you" to the waiter, "Sorry, please excuse me" to Patricia, "Karami" into the telephone. Pat watched him. He seemed able to concentrate on the telephone, and at the same time, make her feel he remained fully attentive to her. He spoke quietly, mainly in decisive monosyllables after brief pauses to listen. "Yes . . . No . . . Three now . . . No . . ."

Finally: "Then wipe them." He hung up the telephone.

The Rolls-Royce, his arrival in the Ferrari at the same moment, the call. Close timing, Pat thought and coolly asked, "Was that done for my benefit?"

"Why would I bother?" He stared at her almost disdainfully, and she felt blood rise to her face. "I hardly need impress you with the fact that I'm in business." His eyes never wavered from hers. "That's why I asked you to have lunch with me. I want to talk business to you. About Russ. Or did you have some other idea?"

Pat's face burned. She tore her eyes from his. "Why in the name of God am I reacting like this?" she asked herself, found no answer.

A figure materialized beside the table. "Would you care for a cocktail, Pat?" Jemel's tone was now warm, amiable.

"Yes. Please. A bloody mary."

"Bloody mary. Martini."

He looked at Patricia again. "About Russ," he said. Who had precisely the qualifications Pan-Arab Airways required and whose evasiveness had begun to eat deeply into him. "I told you both I'm organizing an airline. I want Russ to be its head. The president. I'm sure . . ."

Their drinks were served.

". . . that Russ knew I was offering him the position even before your wedding. At seventy-five thousand a year. I'm now ready to raise the figure to a hundred thousand. Basic salary—plus additional benefits. Stock, pick up his retirement plans." He saw her hand flex involuntarily, her violet eyes widen. "Furthermore, he'll receive three hundred thousand dollars in tax-free cash if we terminate his contract before the end of three years. If he remains longer, the same amount will be paid him as a bonus—and we'll talk upward revision of the salary."

Jemel smiled, raised his glass. "Your husband is my friend. I like him. But if he doesn't take the offer, he's a damned fool. Cheers."

She lifted her own glass. Her hand shook slightly. Russ could more than double his present income, become a millionaire. He *would* be a damned fool to refuse the offer, she thought—and rebelled against herself for thinking it. She drank rapidly, trying to drown her twinge of disloyalty. Russ was Russ, and she loved him. She'd fallen in love with him just as he was. Is.

Her mind raced. *I didn't fall in love with him as*

*a success symbol, but I want him to be a success. No,
I wouldn't have fallen in love with him if he'd been a
$60-a-week clerk—because that type of man lacks some-
thing basic. Personality. Vitality. Whatever. Something.
But I went out with much richer men than Russ, slept
with some of them, got proposals of marriage from them.
None were half, a tenth—a thousandth—of the man
that Russ is. That's why I want so much for him to be
successful, because he is so much better than anyone.*

"Jimmy." She spoke very softly. "You don't really
understand Russ. Yes, he knew you were offering him
the job." She put down her glass. "We talked about it
on our honey—when we were on our honeymoon
aboard your yacht." She failed to realize that breaking
the continuity of her sentence, rephrasing it, was already subconscious acknowledgment of obligation.
"would you like to know why Russ doesn't accept?"

"Naturally." That's how it starts, Jemel grinned
inwardly. First the wife cheats on her husband with
words—passing what he'd said on to another man.
For his own good, she rationalizes. Later, she doesn't
need to rationalize. He listened while Patricia recounted what Russ said about his feelings toward
Whitehead MidEast and its owner—and how he feared
that Jemel's offer might have been made as a favor to
a friend.

"Idiotic!" he snorted when she was finished. "Russ
is worse than a damned fool. He's naïve. Does he
imagine I'd pay anyone a top salary to run a multimillion-dollar corporation just because he's my friend?"
Karami's eyes, hard, smoldering with what appeared
to verge on anger, held Patricia. "If he's that poor a
judge of character, maybe I don't want him at all!"

Her back stiffened. "Now you're being blind!
Russ likes and respects you," she said, shielding and
protecting the man she loved. "He . . ." She caught
herself. Russell Stanton didn't need to be defended.
Her eyes blazed. "I should have told him what I
sensed about you . . ."

"That I'm a ruthless accumulator?" Jimmy interrupted, smiling pleasantly. "That I use any means to
get what I want?"

Her silence was an affirmative reply. She gazed at him, mesmerized, suddenly feeling the force of the man opposite her. He suddenly stood out sharply, as sharply as his compelling, falconlike features. He wasn't Russ's friend now. He'd come into focus as Jemel Karami, a year younger than Russ and a multimillionaire, of international fame and stature, a man who could build—or destroy. "Three," he'd said calmly into the telephone, and "now" and finally, "then wipe them." Three million, and if the money wasn't there immediately, act without mercy—crush. Is that what it had all meant? Probably. What else could it mean?

He had power. Immense power. Banks and companies, yachts and penthouses were simply trappings. It was the power of wealth. Raw, savage . . .

"Would you like to order lunch?"

She tried to keep her voice steady. "I'm really not very hungry. Order something light for me, please." *Russ, I love you.* She formed the words in her mind, clung to them desperately. *I love you, Russ.* It was almost a litany.

The signs were subliminal, but Jemel recognized them. She'd do everything she could to get Russ for him. If she succeeded, she'd be a bonus. If she failed —a consolation prize.

"Perhaps some clear consommé and eggs benedict to follow?" he suggested.

Jemel gave a lavish cocktail party to mark the opening of Incombank's first American branch on Fifth Avenue near 51st Street. More than three hundred guests were invited; almost four hundred attended. They included the Lebanese ambassador, bankers, businessmen, newspaper reporters, financial writers, the usual complement of free loading gatecrashers—and Mike and Dorothy Ferrenbaugh and Fred and Mickey Hayworth.

Jemel kept an eye on Mickey as he circulated through the crowd. He noticed that when she took a fresh drink, it was emptied much faster than it should have been. He waited until she was moving alone from one knot of people to another and intercepted her.

"Looks like you're doing my celebrating for me," he said, taking her once-more-empty glass and signaling to a waiter for another.

"Have one with me—just with me, Jimmy?"

"Sure." He took two drinks from the laden tray the waiter was passing. He handed one to Mickey, touched its rim with that of his own. "Here's to what? I'm drinking to you, and you can drink to . . ."

"Jimmy," she broke in, ignoring what he said. "I'm going to be shopping all afternoon tomorrow. Alone." Her eyes, a little blurred, were pleading.

"Strange coincidence. I intended staying home at my apartment all afternoon. About one, one-thirty?"

She nodded.

She can walk back in exactly where she walked out, Jimmy decided, selecting the library as the place to receive Mickey. When Dowling ushered her in, he kissed her cheek, gave her a fond hug, then released her, leaving her off balance, for she had been poised to embrace and kiss him passionately.

"Care for a drink?" Difficult to be casual, but he managed.

"I had two before I came up. Courage-builders. Pride-salvers. Do you think I need another?"

The pressure in his loins was intense. Not yet. There were a few things he wanted to learn first. "No," he said. "Sit down here, Mickey." Same chairs placed into the same relative positions as on the last occasion she'd been to the apartment.

"What went wrong, Mickey?"

The abrupt question was all she needed. She'd been unable to tell anyone else. It was all bottled up inside her—and now it poured out. Frederick Hayworth had married her to further his political ambitions. As Mickey's husband, he would have Mike Ferrenbaugh as his patron.

"He didn't really love me. He doesn't love anyone but himself—and his ambitions." Mickey paused. "I think I'll take that drink now." When she had it, she went on. "I don't know much about psychology, but once he was elected, he hated me—because I'd helped him. He hates Dad, too, I think, for the same reason."

"It's not an unusual reaction under the circumstances," Jimmy said mildly. "The biting-the-hand bit. How does he act in bed?"

"He doesn't come near me." She drank. "There's nothing wrong with him. He's normal sexually. Except that he prefers to buy women. For money. Mistresses, call girls, whores." Her voice dropped. "So I've been sleeping around, too."

"Why don't you leave him?"

"He can prove I've been to bed with other men." She spoke in a whisper. "He'll show the proof to Mom and Dad. It would break their hearts. Besides, what difference does it make? If it wasn't Fred, it would be someone else—and not the person I really love. It wouldn't be you, Jimmy." She looked at him, her eyes moist. "You wouldn't marry me—or anyone else. I know that." She fell silent for a long moment. "But— but will you make love to me? I want you. I . . ."

"Let's go upstairs," he said. He'd learned all he needed to know. He took her hand, pressed it against the muscle rigid beneath the fabric of his trousers. "That should answer your question."

Russ Stanton returned from Saudi Arabia.

Jemel invited him and Patricia to dinner at his apartment. Russ countered with an invitation for Jimmy to visit them at their home in Scarsdale.

"My place first, then yours," Jemel insisted. Let Russ and Pat have another taste of luxury, and then the contrast of their surroundings will be even greater when I go there.

Jimmy made it a dinner party of sixteen in his penthouse. He invited people of fame and importance. Russ and Pat took it in their stride, mingling easily, but Jimmy was conscious that Pat gave him several long, enigmatic looks throughout the evening. Had she guessed his motives—or was there another reason? No matter, the net result would be the same.

He went to the Stantons' the following week.

Their house, although new, spacious and well furnished and decorated, was still upper-middle-class suburban. As were the five guests—two couples and an extra girl because Jemel said he'd be coming alone.

The two men—in the same income bracket as Russ—were ill-at-ease, awed by the presence of Jemel Karami, the international banker and playboy. The three women fawned and twittered. He was every bit as glamorous as the newspapers and magazines said he was. The "extra" girl—a latter-day and somewhat older version of the vacuous teen-agers Jimmy had bedded when he first arrived in America—spent the evening raping him with her eyes, touching with her hands and pressing her breasts against him at every opportunity. The contrasts glared. They'd have to impress Russ, Jimmy thought.

Jemel lunched with Russ in New York a few days later—and openly offered him the presidency of Pan-Arab Airways, on the same terms that he'd previously recited to Patricia.

Russ refused. Jemel held his thwarted rage in check and tried to argue. It was useless. Stanton's sense of values prevented him from accepting. He related the story to his wife that evening.

"Aren't you being a little foolish?" she asked. "You might be throwing away a chance of a lifetime."

"I explained how I felt. As long as I had any doubts at all in my mind, I couldn't do a decent job, no matter how I tried."

"But Russ, the money—and the responsibility. The job would be a challenge for you. And you and I could be together. You wouldn't be spending a third of your time away from home."

"Would you want to pack up and move to Beirut, live there?"

"I'd want to live anywhere—as long as we could be together."

Russ might have weakened, changed his mind—but several things happened that same week. One of the four Whitehead MidEast vice-presidents was shifted to another Whitehead company. The man pro-

moted to take his place was much junior to the other
three—and that lowered the odds against any one of
the trio's chances for promotion to the presidency.
Then Quentin Yeager called Russ into his office and
informed him he was getting a $7,000-a-year raise and
a $20,000 tax-paid bonus.

"R. D. thinks you're doing a fair job, Russ,"
Yeager says. "Coming from him, that's like an acco-
lade from anyone else." Actually, he was almost as
surprised as Russell Stanton. All he knew was that
he'd received a rush-call from R. D. that Stanton was
to be given the raise and the bonus.

Russ didn't give Jemel's offer any further serious
thought.

No.
It was definite. Final.

"Stanton is out!" Jimmy rasped to Doug Ford.
"We have to start scouring around here in the States
and abroad for a top airlines executive. The optimum
is an American, German, or Swiss with heavy Middle
East experience and oil company contacts. We won't
find it, and we'll have to settle for less—of that I'm
sure." He cursed, thrust his hand into his trousers
pocket, grinding several of the beads of his *sibah* together. "Phone Lockhart. Have him start working on
it from that end, too."

He waited until three days after Russ Stanton's
next departure for Jeddah. He called Patricia.

"Care to let me cry on your shoulder over a drink
and dinner?"

"Russ," she thought, "Russ, you kind, wonderful
damned fool." "Yes," she said. "It's not your fault.
It's not anyone's fault. And I love you, Russ, I adore
you, but it's something only a woman would understand—even though she loathed herself." "Will you
send the car—or shall I take a cab to the Wickpark
Towers?"

She wore a white dress, and she was alabaster
and ice, just as she had been the first time Jemel saw
her. Only the violet eyes refracted inner fire. She sat in

the armchair, holding her martini glass, the eyes fixed and steady on Jemel, who leaned against one of the library shelves and raised his own glass.

"To all our disappointments." He drank the contents of the glass without taking his eyes from her.

Patricia's hand trembled. She drank. Two large swallows.

"You bastard," she said coldly. He'd got her there. How? By willpower? What they call "animal magnetism"? Just the draw of what he was and symbolized? Cerebrally, she was ice. Sexually, she was aflame. "You bastard," she repeated. "I feel like a whore."

Jemel eased himself away from the shelf, put down his empty glass. "Only because that's how you want to feel. It soothes your conscience." He walked across the room, stood in front of her. He took the glass from her hand, tossed it aside. It fell on the carpet without breaking.

He leaned down, seized her arms, pulled her to her feet. She stood, motionless.

His hands, slender and strong, grasped the neckline of her dress and with one long and powerful, sweeping motion, ripped the cloth from her body. Still, she did not move, and their eyes remained locked, blazing.

He reached behind her back, tore apart the catch holding her bra. Her breasts were upswept cones, perfect, with coral nipples stretched into needlepoints. He seized her breasts, crushed them in his hands. She gasped, flung her head forward, her mouth open. He met it with his own, his tongue probing. She closed her teeth on it savagely. He pulled it free, cursing, dug his fingers deep into the flesh of her breasts. She groaned, sucked his lower lip in between her own, biting blood from it.

Jemel whirled her around. Pat let her knees go slack, falling onto the thick-carpeted floor, pulling him after her. The fingernails of one hand raked the back of his neck. The other clawed feverishly at his trousers fly, tearing the zipper open, gripping his swollen sex.

He stripped away her panties. Her legs drew up,

the muscles tightening, thighs parting and hips raising
to receive him. He groaned with pleasure. It was as
though he was thrusting himself into a caldron of
molten lava. She was moaning, and her hips pounded
against his as if in furious vengeance for the orgasm
already engulfing her.

The fashion-design house for which Patricia
Stanton worked was small. A controlling interest could
be bought for $70,000.

Jimmy spoke to Marvin Jacobs.

"Russ's wife is talented," he said. "I'll put up the
money if you find someone you can trust to use as a
figurehead. We can have her made head designer. I'll
pull strings and get her publicity. Only no one—especially not Russ or Pat—is to know we have anything
to do with it."

Marvin smiled with benign enthusiasm. "Natch.
I'd like to do something for Russ and Pat myself. I'll
even split the investment with you."

"Done. But for God's sake, not a word to the
Stantons."

"Of course not." He chuckled. "We may even
make a profit on the deal."

"It'll be profitable for me," Jemel thought. "Let
Pat Stanton get a taste of success herself, and her ambitions for her husband will turn inward. Neither of
them will dream what—or who—hit them, but the
higher she climbs, the smaller Russ and his lofty principles will look to her."

18

Patricia Stanton despised herself. She'd fallen for
Jemel Karami's omnipotent Croesus image like some
moronic movie-fan magazine reader. She prayed he

would not call her again, was immensely relieved when he didn't.

She was determined never to see him again alone. If she had to with Russ, she'd somehow manage to carry it off. She would have to, for if Russ ever suspected that she and his best friend . . .

Russ was her husband, and she loved him. She didn't need or want anyone else. Least of all Jemel Karami. Sexually great, yes. A master technician. Like a machine that could generate tremendous heat, but no warmth—and still remained a machine. Russ didn't have to employ exotic techniques—and God knows, some Karami had used that night had been wild, way-out. Russ was every bit as much a man without them—and he was warm, loving, human. To have cheated on Russ with Jemel Karami was worse than any ordinary infidelity. It was sick. Insane.

Pat forced her guilt-sense under reasonable control before Russ came home from Saudi Arabia. Under reasonable control. Spells of moody, introspective silence occasionally intruded on the love and affection she lavished on her husband. He'd notice them, ask what was troubling her.

"I'm just thinking how much I love you—and how good it is to be with you," she'd reply. It was the truth, but the moods were brought on by conscience. "I just sometimes feel a little sad because I know you'll have to leave again—even if it is only for a few weeks."

One evening, he asked her, "Sorry I didn't take Jimmy's offer?" It was the first time Jemel's name had come up in their conversation since Russ had returned.

"I'm glad!" she replied—too quickly and forcefully. "I'm very glad!"

Odd, Russ thought, she had encouraged him to accept. However, it was a woman's prerogative . . .

The Comet IV's jet engines thundered, and the plane started down the runway, gathering speed—and was airborne, its landing gear retracting gracefully as it steep-angled out over the Mediterranean.

Now the higher-pitched whine of a Viscount's turbo-engines, as it taxied into takeoff position. A hundred yards from the Beirut Airport terminal building —a low, supermodern structure of brick, chrome and glass—the motors of a DC-6-B coughed, belched blue-white smoke from their exhausts, caught one by one, props spinning, engine noise growing into a deep-throated roar.

All three aircraft—Paris-London-bound Comet, Medina-Jeddah-Dhahran-run Viscount, and Damascus-Amman-Cairo-shuttle DC-6-B—were emblazoned with the green-on-gold "Pan-Arab Airways" identification painted the length of their fuselages in both English and Arabic.

That these and the dozen other assorted aircraft comprising the Pan-Arab fleet carried less than break-even-point passenger and freight payloads on their various scheduled flights was not important. What counted was that the airline had become an operating reality within the time limit originally set by Jemel Karami.

Establishing Pan-Arab Airways had raised Incombank's status to a peak in all Arab countries. The payloads would be increased. Somehow. In the meanwhile, the heavy operating losses would be absorbed. Again somehow.

The main remaining problem was that of finding a qualified top-level executive for the line, which was being sketchily managed by a handful of vice-presidents and supervisors under the direction of Jemel Karami and Brian Lockhart.

Jemel had "goddamned" Russell Stanton whenever the subject of Pan-Arab came up, and it came up often. Stanton would have been ideal. A seasoned overall executive with a strong drive. Long Middle Eastern experience. Contacts with oil companies. A talent for organizing and the intangible but priceless quality of "command presence," that got orders and instructions carried out.

Neither Jemel nor Lockhart could devote the time needed to manage the airline properly and concentrate on increasing its revenue. As it was, the added load of overseeing Pan-Arab had been holding Jimmy too long in Beirut, preventing him from going on the globe-hopping tours that pumped cash-plasma into Incombank. Men with the qualifications—and of the caliber—that Pan-Arab required were simply unavailable.

There were top executives, yes—but they had no Middle Eastern experience or lacked any oil-company contacts. The few who met the last two requirements on closer investigation proved to be mediocre-to-poor executive material.

Brian Lockhart finally found an at least temporary solution to the problem.

"Seems we've run across a chap who might fit the Pan-Arab bill," he announced to Jimmy one morning in October. "An American. He's headed two nonscheduled airlines and has a little Middle East experience. One of the nonsked lines he directed had some—not many, but *some*—oil-company air-freighting contracts. He's not top-notch, but by far the best we've encountered so far."

"Goddamn Russ Stanton again," Jimmy thought. "If you think he'll do, hire him," Jimmy said. "Work out some sort of agreement where he's working a short-term renewable contract with a salary in the thirty-to-thirty-five-thousand-a-year range—plus a percentage of gross revenue over a certain minimum. That might make him shag his ass."

"The word, Jimmy, is 'arse,' and it's an excellent idea."

Patricia Stanton was ecstatic, bubbling. A Mr. Louis Epstein—he was in the garment trade—had bought the controlling interest in the company for which she worked. He'd gone over her fashion designs, liked them, and she was being made the head designer.

"He says he'll start a promotion campaign—and I'm being raised to twelve thousand a year!" she told Russ breathlessly. "It's my use of color he likes most. He wants the house to push a 'Pat Stanton Rainbow-Swirl' line!" She kissed him fiercely. "Isn't it wonderful!"

"Only what you deserve," Russ grinned, hugging her tightly, sharing her joy, feeling very proud and happy. "Just the same, it calls for a celebration. How about a champagne-soaked night on the town?"

She kissed him again, long and hard. "Let's celebrate upstairs in the bedroom," she murmured. "Then we can have a midnight snack in the kitchen—and do some more celebrating afterward." She touched his face, her eyes both passionate and tender. "I love you, Russ. I love you very much."

"It's mutual, Mrs. Stanton."

It was the week before Christmas, and the message caught up with Jemel at the Crillon in Paris. Felicite was in a private clinic near Zurich.

Deft shuffling had cut one Comet IV out of the Pan-Arab fleet, and it had been converted into a luxurious executive aircraft for use by Incombank's Board chairman. The plane was at Orly, and Jimmy flew immediately to Zurich.

"Just nerves, and a couple of bad trips," Felicite told her brother.

"LSD?" Is it that she's had a bad spell or is her beauty really starting to fade, he wondered.

"Yes. I was at Zermatt, skiing, and the whole crowd . . ."

Jimmy didn't listen. Her honey hair was dulled. Could dark, luminescent eyes fade in color?

". . . like a nervous breakdown. I'll be fine in a week."

"Ever stop to consider it might be smart to slow down a little?"

Felicite's eyes glowed into life, and her lips twitched into a mischievous smile. "Did you?"

"*Touché.*" There was nothing else for him to say.

The clinic's head doctor prattled on about "emotional disorganization" and "pathological boredom" and indications of "the possibility of profound personality disturbance." A Freudian, he recommended psychoanalysis and larded his arguments with the jargon words and phrases of his profession.

"The decision is up to my sister," Jemel told him. "Have you talked to her about it?"

"Yes. She refuses."

"Then that's the answer."

He returned to Paris the next day. Two years before, one of his Liechtenstein companies had invested $11 million (borrowed on notes from Incombank) in a project to build luxury apartments on the outskirts of the French capital. Difficulties in assembling the land parcel, the De Gaulle government's delays in giving approval for demolishing existing structures in order to build new, labor strife and other snags had thrown the entire project a year or more behind schedule. The completion date had been originally set for 1968—and now there was no hope of recouping investment or realizing profit until well into 1969. It was imperative that he speak to the right people, head off any further delays.

Jimmy chain-smoked during the flight from Zurich to Paris. "Damn it, I should have gone to Ankara first from Beirut. There was six million dollars in sidetracked Incombank money tied up in a Turkish potash plant that was still a long way from returning a dollar —that needed some sharp prodding, too.

"I'll let that slide for a while," he decided. "I'd better go on to New York when I'm through in Paris. Pan-Arab Airways still wasn't cleared to fly scheduled runs into New York." He'd have to give Ferrenbaugh and Hayworth and the other Washington rainmakers a jolt.

Pan-Arab and Ferrenbaugh and Hayworth made him think of Mickey and Pat. He'd arrange to see Mickey as soon as he got to the States. He'd hold off on Pat, though. She wasn't ready yet.

The pilot of the Comet had begun his descent from cruising altitude. They'd be landing in a few minutes. He pushed the call button. It brought the sleek sloe-eyed stewardess assigned to the craft hurrying forward to where he sat on a divan located directly over the wing.

"You'll come to the Crillon with me for the night after we land," he told the girl. Both her smile and her nod were eager.

Christmas—and several double ryes—had made Mike Ferrenbaugh mellow and expansive. He was home, and he had his family around him.

". . . have to take my hat off to you, Fred," he was addressing his son-in-law. "You sure done picked the right horse to ride, like we used to say when I was a kid on the farm. You have an instinct."

Immediately after President John F. Kennedy's assassination in 1963, Senator Frederick Hayworth had sensed there would be an upsurge of militantly "liberal" feeling throughout the country. Despite the objections of party bosses—including Mike Ferrenbaugh—he'd bloomed as the outspoken, courageous champion of liberal causes and "young people." It made him nationally popular. Some people said that he even resembled President Kennedy. Lyndon Johnson's landslide victory against Barry Goldwater had underscored the accuracy of Hayworth's estimate of public feeling.

"I'm barely in gear, Mike," Hayworth said smugly. "I'll be the most liberal Liberal you ever saw. I've got my eye on the 1972 elections. No reason why I can't do what Kennedy and Johnson did."

Mike belched quietly. "Keep going the way you are, and there isn't," he agreed, and suddenly grew sentimental. "Mickey," he said to his daughter, who sat on the opposite side of the living room. "When are you 'n' Fred going to get down to serious marriage business and make me a granddad?"

"We have time," Fred said hurriedly. "For a while, we want to keep that blissfully happy young married couple image. Kids would detract."

"You may be right," Ferrenbaugh nodded solemnly.

Mickey mumbled some excuse to leave the room and go into the kitchen. She was thinking of a Christmas long past, when she'd first seen Jimmy Karami.

Patricia wished she didn't have to go to the cocktail party alone. There wasn't anything else she could do. Russ had left for Jeddah soon after New Year's Day. He wouldn't be back for another week.

And she had to attend. The "Pat Stanton Rainbow-Swirl" line was catching on, attracting growing attention and favorable comment. Items about it had already appeared in several trade papers—and even in a few general circulation newspapers' fashion pages. Louis Epstein's promotion campaign was having its effect. Some of her friends were even predicting the slick fashion mags would be coming around to do stories soon.

But the cocktail party. It would run true to form. Bitchy, limp-wristed queers and bitchy, battle-ax-faced women. Fat little bald men trying to rub up against a breast or buttock, and younger, leaner men hunting for a lay for the night. Then there would be a sprinkling of truly interesting people, successful men and women who knew how to act and talk, were familiar with all that went on, trading stories and gossip which, even if embellished a little for effect, still had their basis in facts not generally known. People only a cut or two below the level of those in Jimmy Karami's circle . . .

What on earth ever made me think of him?" Pat asked herself. *Anyway,* that's *a fading memory. At least, I can think about him in a detached, objective manner—as a sort of gilded success symbol, and that leaves him a one-dimensional figure.*

19

Fred Hayworth was hesitant.

"None of us in the Senate can afford to push too hard for anything called *Pan-Arab* Airways," he hedged. "We have the Jewish vote to worry about."

"Bull. Shit." Jemel Karami made it two words. The fact that Hayworth sat in the same chair in the library that Mickey had occupied the night she made her decision to marry him tickled his sense of the sardonic. "I wonder how he'd react if he knew how often she's been back since," he asked himself and said, "The Jews have other things to worry about." He peered closely at Hayworth. "I'm guessing your colleagues have made you the spokesman. Speak up. How much?"

Hayworth said something about expenses and difficulties.

"Ten thousand apiece for you and the other two senators," Jimmy said. "The congressmen get five apiece. And you, Fred, will have a hundred shares of Pan-Arab as a bonus. All payable when Pan-Arab gets route clearance."

He got Fred Hayworth out of the apartment a safe hour before Mickey arrived.

Jemel was breakfasting on the dining terrace of the house on the rue d'Australie.

"Tea, Brian?" he inquired when Lockhart appeared.

"Yes, thanks." He grimaced. "Don't you ever tire of that cheese?"

"The *labeneh?* Nope. One of the few childhood tastes I've never lost." He poked at a slab of the creamy white cheese with a knife. "Did you know that the Lebanese believe it's a cancer preventative? Made from ewe's milk—and sheep are the only animals that don't have cancer. Or so the story goes."

Brian recognized Jemel's mood as excellent-to-superior. He seated himself, and a servant brought tea.

"I gather you and the leading statesman of Lebanon were in harmonious accord last night," Lockhart remarked, starting his tea-pouring ritual.

"Cousin Rashid was like a brother," Jimmy laughed, grew serious. "Can you scrape together ten million cash immediately?"

Lockhart paused, abandoned the tea-things. "Jimmy, the fluidity situation is damned precarious again."

"We don't have to pull the money out of Incom for long, Brian. We'll only need it until the fall of next year—when we get it back double."

Brian went back to his tea-formulation. "So much in so short a period?"

"Yes. Less ten percent of the net for Abdul Kamal, of course. We buy up two thousand acres of Khaldeh Beach property. Cost, around a million-and-a half. When we've assembled the parcel, the Ministry of Tourism buys it from us for three. To develop into a big new tourist-resort area." He lit a cigarette, inhaled deeply. "See? No fear of cancer. The *labeneh,*" he grinned.

"The other seven-and-a-half million we need will go into a housing development," Jemel went on. "A complex of a thousand units. The Lebanese government buys them all when they're finished—for fifteen million. It'll be used as a housing-center for army officers and civil servants and their families. Abdul Kamal guarantees both deals. We'll be paid a year from this coming November. Rashid's pitch will be that both projects are his idea for marking the twenty-fourth anniversary of Lebanese liberation."

November 22nd is the day Lebanon somewhat arbitrarily sets as its day of national celebration.

Brian Lockhart frowned. "Ten. For let's see. Eighteen—nineteen months," he mused aloud, thinking, reviewing figures in his mind, devising stratagems. "It'll be tight, but we can do it." He glanced at Jemel. "Let's hope Kamal delivers."

Jimmy shrugged nonchalantly. "He will. He runs Lebanon the way we run Incombank. There's no one above him to argue. What he says, goes." He corkscrewed his cigarette into a hammered-silver ashtray. "Speaking of goes, how goes Pan-Arab?"

"Still in the red, naturally. Slow, steady improvement though."

"Good. Get started on Khaldeh Beach and the housing project."

"Definitely. I like projects that ripen fast."

Jemel's attention wandered. He was thinking of something entirely different he was certain would ripen within the next few months.

Patricia Stanton's face glowed with delight.

"Look, Russ!" she exclaimed, holding open copies of the September issues of *Vogue* and *Glamour*.

"Stories on 'Rainbow-Swirl' fashions in both—in the same month!"

Russ beamed. The piece in *Vogue* was short, but accompanied by a photograph of Pat. *Glamour* featured two pages of pictures showing models wearing dresses she had designed.

"Terrific, honey!" he said. "I'll order a hundred copies of each for you."

"I already did," Pat said sheepishly. "I can't get used to any of it!"

"You will, when you've run Balmain out of business," he laughed.

Pat looked at him and said, quite seriously, "There's no reason why we can't become as famous and successful as the French houses."

"There are no more French houses," Russ declared, straight-faced. "They were closed down not long after the war. Played hell with my leaves to Paris when I was with AMGOT in Krautland."

"What?" She stared at him for a moment—and then laughed. "You idiot!" She stuck a playful finger in his ear. "Did you ever go to any of those French whorehouses before they were closed?"

"Only twice. Far too much amateur talent around." He started to run his fingers through her hair, stopped. It had been carefully sprayed. He tickled her neck instead. "Hey, no response?"

Pat was staring at the open copy of *Glamour*. "That shot," she said, pointing. "The lighting is all wrong for the dress. Sometimes, photographers and fashion editors can be so utterly stupid . . ."

During the periods when Russ was in New York, he and Pat drove down from Scarsdale together each morning. He dropped her off at her office, continued downtown to his own, and in the evening, picked her up at work and they drove home together.

A few days after the *Vogue* and *Glamour* issues appeared, Russ met his wife and, after she was settled into the right-hand bucket seat of the Mustang, said, "Jimmy called me today . . ."

No shock or stomach clutch, Pat thought with satisfaction.

". . . invited us to a party at his place Saturday night . . ."

I don't even feel as though I need manufacture an excuse to beg off.

". . . very posh. Seems he's heard about you and the designing. Thought you might like to meet the duke and duchess of Hartwich . . ."

Suspicion rose inside Pat. Jemel had a motive—she sensed it. What could he do, she asked herself. She'd be going with Russ. She'd be perfectly safe. Nothing could touch her as long as Russ was there. Besides, if the duchess of Hartwich, a regular on the Best-Dressed Women list, would say a complimentary word about "Rainbow-Swirl" . . .

"I'd like to go if you would, Russ." She had designed a gown for herself that she was saving for a special occasion, where it would have significant impact. A bold creation of gold, black, white, and cyclamen in diagonal slashes masterfully employed to enhance her perfect figure and accent both her ash-blonde hair and violet eyes. This would be *the* occasion to wear it.

Tense anxiety over meeting Jemel again gave way to other emotions. He was suave, gracious, and he made her feel, how Pat could not imagine, as though nothing had taken place between them.

"Come on, Pat, Russ. I'll introduce you around."

The faces and names were famous. Hughes Carlton, the mining magnate. Nicky Hilton. Claudia Montclair. Tallulah Bankhead.

"You remember Elinor Randolph. She was aboard the *Asharat* for your bon-voyage party. Get together with Pat later, Elinor. A plug for her in your column will be a personal favor to me."

Has he or hasn't he? Elinor looked closely at Pat. He has. She studied Russ. All male. Intelligent. Fine personality. Only he lacks the bastard streak. That explains it. Oh, well. Some of us women are masochists. "It'll be a pleasure, Pat. Spare me ten minutes later."

Pat's heart leaped. Elinor Randolph's "Busybody" column. Before she could say anything, Jemel was leading them away for more introductions.

"The duke and duchess of Hartwich . . ."

"Oh, balls, Jimmy!" the duchess sniffed. "Ian and Nancy." She bathed Pat with a magnificent smile. "So you're Pat Stanton, the 'Rainbow-Swirl' girl. Jimmy's been telling me about you. Where did you get that sensational gown?"

Patricia smiled. "It's trite, but I ran it up myself."

The duchess gave her husband, Jemel, and Russ a scathing look. "Buzz off and bash the bishop or whatever you men do without women." She took Pat's arm. "We're going to have a chat. I want you to design some things for me . . ."

Euphoria, Pat thought. The bucket seat seemed to hug her.

"Russ," she murmured.

"Uh-huh." Dawn is eye-deceiving. He concentrated on his driving.

"How much money was represented at that party?"

"I'd need a computer," he grinned. "Billions, I suppose."

Success and wealth, Pat mused. Success and wealth. Plugs in Elinor Randolph's column, orders for designs from the duchess of Hartwich. Success . . .

Russ Stanton left for Saudi Arabia a month later.

When Jemel called and invited her to a cocktail party, she went—alone and without hesitation.

She stayed the night at Jemel's apartment.

During the ensuing months, she discovered it was easy to compartmentalize her mind and emotions. Her occasional ventures into pure sensuality with Jimmy, and her love for her husband didn't really contradict and clash, she told herself. Like contrasting colors chosen with artistic taste, one brought out the values of the other—and the pressures created by mounting success demanded violent outlet, even while she required Russ's love and the warm stability of marriage.

By the end of 1965, Patricia Stanton's salary had been raised to $25,000 a year, and she was thinking of quitting to open her own fashion house.

Incombank's financial statement for the year showed the bank had passed the billion-dollar mark in total resources. Still largely on paper, covering a multitude of diversions, Jemel Karami knew. However, not for much longer. Soon the great ingathering would begin.

The Khaldeh Beach and government housing deals in Lebanon would pay off in November. After that, everything would snowball as his long-term investments and speculations started to mature, bear cash fruit that would fill all the holes, make Incom as genuinely solid as any bank in the world.

20

Pat counted back days. Once, twice—a dozen times—with the same result.

Her menstrual periods had always been regular. Proverbial clockwork. On the dot, a twenty-eight-day cycle.

She had been due on March 10th.

It was now the 15th.

Give it a few more days, she thought, *I've been working too hard. Maybe that's it.*

By the 20th, Pat felt certain. Felt. She'd still have to wait before any test results would be reliable.

"Are you sure you're feeling all right, honey?" Russ asked her. She had become increasingly nervous and irritable. "Maybe you ought to take a little time off—or even see a doctor for a checkup."

"Don't nag at me!" she snapped at him. "I'm fine!"

Half an hour later, she came to him, tears in her

eyes, kissing him, clinging to him. "Russ, darling. I'm sorry," she apologized. "It's my work and knowing that you're leaving again next week." She buried her head in his neck and shoulder.

There were several repetitions in the next few days. A burst of temper, then apology, intense love and affection.

"Russ, I wish you didn't have to go," Pat murmured the night before his departure. "I'm going to miss you. Terribly." He kissed her face, tasted tears. He'd be gone three weeks, Russ thought. If her nerves hadn't settled down when he returned, he'd force her to have a checkup. "I love you, Russ. You know that don't you?"

The first test was positive. She had another. The same. Pat was pregnant.

Christ, what do I do now? she asked herself over and over, muttering aloud as she paced through the rooms of the house, her panic building.

She wanted a baby. She wanted Russ Stanton's baby. Only she couldn't be sure. Russ had gone on a week-long trip to Jeddah in February—some emergency or other, and who cared what it was?—and she had seen Jemel twice while Russ was away. Her mind went over it all for the millionth time.

The chances that the baby was Jimmy's were slight. But they were still there. She didn't want Jemel Karami's child. Never. And she didn't dare risk having a baby that inherited any of his distinct physical characteristics. Jimmy had shown her photographs of his father. They were almost replicas of each other. Jemel's sperm would transmit some of his traits—the aquiline features or the dark eyes or the dark skin—and Russ would know immediately . . .

The half bottle of brandy Pat drank didn't help.

Guilt, fear, dread—and panic—remained. Russ would know, and their marriage would be over. She couldn't lose Russ.

Pat didn't sleep that night. The next day, she made inquiries. Someone recommended a doctor near Trenton, New Jersey. He charged a thousand dollars, but was worth it. He was good, could be trusted. Money was no problem and the fact she would be having the abortion away from familiar surroundings satisfied her psychological need for secrecy. Pat decided on the doctor in Trenton.

"I don't advise your driving back to New York this afternoon," the doctor said when it was all over. "I recommend you stay in a hotel or motel nearby."

"All right," Pat said. Anything to end the talk. *I couldn't stand spending the night anywhere near here. I'll drive home. Straight home.*

"You'll probably have some pain." He handed her a box of pills. "Two with water every three hours." He cleared his throat. "Stay away from liquor and any form of sexual activity for about ten days to be safe."

It's done, Pat thought. *I can breathe again. Please God, that it wasn't Russ's baby. I'll have to believe that it wasn't. I'll have to make myself believe that it was Jimmy Karami's bastard.*

She felt a little weak and drove the Mustang toward New York along secondary roads, where the traffic was less. She couldn't trust herself on the high-speed superhighways.

Thoughts and emotions kaleidoscoped. She wanted to get home. And no sex for ten days? She had never wanted Russ so much. Only Russ. Jimmy? Not again. Not ever again, she knew that. And she wanted to become pregnant again. Quickly. As soon as possible after Russ came home. She realized that she had a desperate need to have her husband's child.

A twinge of pain. Maybe she could make it home to Scarsdale before the pain got too bad. She pressed a little harder on the accelerator. There. A steady sixty-five—no, make it seventy. The road was clear and the car handled beautifully. Seventy. Hold it there.

"Oh!" Another twinge, much stronger. Pat closed her eyes against it for only a fraction of an instant, but when she opened them, the car was already turning out of the side road.

She slammed her foot on the brake pedal with all her strength. The powerful brakes grabbed, held, brought the Mustang to a lighting-fast stop that avoided a collision by a good fifty-foot margin—but threw Pat forward against the steering wheel. Hard.

Now the pain was excruciating. She worked the stick going from low into second, stayed there while she fumbled in her purse with one hand. She found the box of pills the doctor had given her, worked two from the box, put them in her mouth and gagged a bit as she dry-swallowed them. She shifted into high.

I'll go right to bed the minute I get home, she said to herself, gritting her teeth. She glanced at the speedometer: forty-five climbing to fifty . . .

Something warm, wet spilling on to the seat between her thighs. Spilling, then pouring.

"Oh, my God, no!"

Blood. Hemorrhage. The shock of hitting the steering wheel must have . . .

The blood was a torrent. It formed a pool in the depression of the seat. She could feel it spreading rapidly, working around to the back of her buttocks, running off the seat onto her legs and the floor.

Terror. *I've got to stop, get help.*

She stepped on the brake pedal. The mere movement of her foot from the accelerator caused a fresh gout of blood to pour from her. She pressed the brake gently. Don't bang up against the steering wheel again, she warned herself—dreamily, from a distance where there was no pain. Don't . . .

The windshield turned black, opaque. Her hands slid from the wheel. The Mustang was doing less than fifteen miles an hour, but it angled off the road, bumped once or twice, struck a tree and stopped.

Light as the impact was, it made Pat slump forward against the steering wheel. I must've stepped on the brake too hard after all, she thought—and then she realized what was happening to her.

"Russ," she said aloud. "Russ, I . . ."

Elinor Randolph's voice had a ripsaw edge discernible even over thousands of miles of telephone cable.

"I suppose you know that Pat Stanton died last night?"

"Yes," Jimmy said. "There's an item in the *Daily American* here today. Killed in a car wreck in New Jersey. I'm sorry as hell to hear . . ."

"She wasn't killed in a car wreck. She bled to death after having an abortion. Her husband's already been notified and is flying in from Jeddah. I suggest you come over too, Jimmy."

"I'd be glad to, if it would do any good, but it won't . . ."

"Listen to me, Jimmy, you poor, sad son-of-a-bitch. You were balling Patricia Stanton. I knew it if no one else did. My guess is that she had the abortion because the baby was yours."

Jemel's spine iced. I only wanted to rub Russ Stanton's face in it. I never intended anything like this.

"What can I do?"

"Jimmy! You actually sound helpless and frightened! Something I've never heard before. It's music, and I feel like Christopher Columbus. I've discovered that you do have a conscience—microscopic though it may be."

"Suppose Pat kept a diary or some damned thing like that," Jemel thought. "God knows what Russ would do if he ever found out."

"What can I do?" his voice was stronger.

"Put on the biggest hypocritical prick act of your career, my friend. Be here to give Russell Stanton comfort and support."

"Elinor . . ."

The line was dead. "God, I am sorry about Pat," Jimmy thought—and Russ does still think I'm his best friend. Besides, if I'm there, it'll divert any possible suspicion—and if anything does come up, I'll know it and be there to control the situation."

Russell Stanton didn't know how he could have got through the days before the funeral, the funeral itself and the days immediately following if it hadn't been for Jimmy Karami.

Marv Jacobs was right there, too. But Jimmy? *He*

hardly left my side for so much as an hour, Russ would frequently recall to himself. *He stayed right with me, doing more than any other human being would— or could—have done.*

21

Jemel was asked to address the September 1966, entering freshman class at the American University in Beirut on the subject of "Banks and Banking in Lebanon." Remembering that both his father and grandfather attended the university (in reality, by Western standards, on a par with an easygoing junior college), Jemel agreed.

He stood on a lectern before some two hundred students and, after going through the routine curtain-raising remarks about feeling honored and then telling a brace of funny anecdotes, began his address:

"Non-government-owned banks are the heart of the free enterprise system they epitomize. Their foundation stones are trust, honesty, integrity and an understanding of other people's problems. However, they are business establishments pure and simple. They are in business to make profits—not only for themselves, but for all their clients, the community, the nation as a whole."

He wondered how many of the teen-age Levantine faces staring up at him were struggling to keep themselves straight. Not many, he thought. These youngsters were of a different breed. Very Westernized.

"How, you may ask, do banks make their profits? The answer is that they deal in money. They make money from—or, if you prefer, with—money."

Your grandfathers—and some of your fathers— started as moneylenders in two-by-four stalls in some stinking *soukh*.

"Where does a bank get its money to start? Mainly

in loans from people or groups or business firms that trust it and its management. These loans are called 'deposits.' "

And you use every trick imaginable to get them into the bank.

"Interest paid on deposits is therefore really interest paid on loans made to the bank, a fee paid for being allowed to use other people's money."

As bait. The bigger the account, the bigger the bait has to be out here.

"For the most part, depositors can demand to withdraw their money from a bank whenever they please."

But you keep your fingers crossed that few do.

"To cover its operating expenses, pay interest due to depositors and still make a profit so it can remain strong and expand, a bank finds work for the money others entrust to it. The bank makes loans of various kinds. It invests in government bonds, other securities such as stocks and bonds issued by companies that are in need of working capital or capital for expansion."

Good God, many of the youngsters were furiously scribbling notes!

"Naturally, it is up to the directors and officers of a bank to make certain all loans and investments are made wisely and well. Borrowers must show they have adequate collateral to protect the bank—and its depositors from loss—if they are unable to repay. Any securities purchased are carefully analysed to determine if the issuers are dependable."

We Lebanese bankers find that the companies to which we loan and whose securities we so often buy are just as dependable as ourselves. After all, we own them—and there must be one or two in your bunch who will catch on someday and make his own fortune.

"Lebanon has a completely free economy. The only one of its kind anywhere in the world today. That is why we Lebanese have prospered."

Well, 10 percent of us, anyway—and that includes your parents, or you wouldn't be going to the American University.

"One-third—full one-third, mind you—of Lebanon's national income is derived from the operations of Lebanese banks. Without those banks, there would be none of the Lebanese commerce for which this country has been famous since the time of the Phoenicians."

A burst of applause. The only pride-in-roots a Levantine has lies in identification with a civilization of which there has been no trace for over two thousand years.

"A few words on slightly more technical aspects of banking. There are certain rules-of-thumb for measuring the strength and reliability of a bank. One of the best . . ."

As long as there are no outside or government audits and no large and influential depositors have an urge to pry and manage to do so.

'. . . is how much of its resources is in the form of liquid assets. These liquid assets are actual cash, loans to other banks, government obligations, top-grade securities. Assets that are—or can be immediately turned into—cash. A high proportion of liquid assets—a high liquidity ratio, as it's called—insures that a bank can instantly pay out what, by the law of averages, is any foreseeable demand by depositors who wish to withdraw their funds."

He paused, went on.

"How high should such a ratio be? Around 30 percent is considered sound in banking circles. It is the ratio which Incombank maintains."

Who's to say that loans to Incom branches aren't as good as if they'd been made to the Bank of America or Chase—or that the stocks and bonds issued by my Liechtenstein companies aren't top-grade securities?

"This is protection for the depositor. Lebanese banking laws give him an added and different form of protection. He enjoys secrecy. No one can find out how much he has deposited in the bank, when he deposited it—or what use he makes of it. I'm sure most of you wish you enjoyed the same legal protection when your parents ask you what you've been doing with your money."

That was good for a laugh.

"Unlike some—in fact, most—other countries,

Lebanese banks are also granted certain advantages by the law. We bankers can make both short- and long-term loans and investments. We can, under Lebanese charters, buy and sell securities, originate new issues, underwrite additional issues and distribute securities. We can therefore make the Lebanese economy grow faster and larger."

To say nothing of keeping the printing presses going, spewing out handsome new stock and bond certificates.

"Then, Lebanese banks do not labor under the restrictions that retard banking in many other countries. A Lebanese bank can own and operate industries and business that have nothing at all to do with banking." He paused to give maximum effect to his punch-line. "That is why all Arabs can say that there is a Pan-Arab Airways linking all our countries and the Western world, and why we Lebanese can proudly say that Pan-Arab Airways is Lebanese-owned!"

An ovation. Still no profit, and the three new Boeing 707s for the transatlantic runs to New York and South America and six new Caravelles had cost a staggering amount. Just the same, Pan-Arab Airways was Incombank's greatest prestige asset throughout the Arab world. It demonstrated that Incom was the bank for all Arabs everywhere.

When the applause died down, Jimmy threw in the clincher. "If anyone asks you about banking in Lebanon, tell him this: One Lebanese bank, operating under Lebanon's free-enterprise system, owns an airline twice the size of that built by our Jewish neighbors to the south. Built and operated by their government—with money poured in by millions of rich Zionist Jews!"

The two hundred students in the audience leaped to their feet and bellowed approval at the tops of their lungs.

22

It happened suddenly, without warning, a month later.

Intra Bank, an important Lebanese bank that showed $250 million in assets, closed its doors. It had run out of liquid assets.

The panic began.

Thousands of small depositors stormed the bank's main office and branches in Beirut. Sirens shrieked and there were occasional rifle and pistol shots as helmeted police and troops fought back the mobs.

The panic spread.

Other banks were besieged by everyday people —workers, small businessmen, shopkeepers—who demanded their deposits. In cash.

Another bank collapsed. Then another and another.

Jemel had not underestimated the value of *sharaf* and prestige. The Incom Central Tower, Incombank's position as the largest Middle Eastern bank—and most of all, its ownership of Pan-Arab Airways had made a strong impression. Enough to delay massive withdrawals a few days. The biggest would be the last to be suspect.

"But it'll hit us, too," Jemel nervously predicted to Brian Lockhart. He stood at the huge window nearest his office desk, looking down into the streets. Traffic had all but ceased. Police and military vehicles and ambulances raced along the boulevards, tore recklessly through the narrow streets.

"Actually, it's started—although only on a small scale," Lockhart said grimly. "We had two-hundred thousand dollars' worth of withdrawals yesterday above our normal average."

Jimmy swung away from the window, chewing

362

his lip. "I'd say three days, four at the outside before our depositors hit their stride." His telephone rang. He grabbed it, listened, grunted, slammed down the receiver. Two more Beirut banks had shut down.

The telephone rang again. He took it. "What? No. I'm sorry. We can't. Not a *piastre.*" He was silent for a moment. "How do I know it won't go down a rathole? Your promise? Don't make bad jokes." He depressed the receiver lever, then jiggled it. "No more calls!" he snapped, slammed down the receiver. "East-West Credit Bank," he growled to Lockhart. "Micholz, the board chairman. Wanted a 'million-dollar cash loan for a month.' " He began pacing the floor.

"How much actual cash do we have, Brian?"

"Around thirty-one million."

Let any two important sheikhs get worried and want their money—and that would be erased.

"How about legitimate other liquid assets?"

"Legitimate? Eighty-nine."

Eighty-nine and thirty-one. $120 million. Not enough to withstand a run like those on other banks.

"We have nine million or so cash being held by Leichtenstein dummies. Some of the money's been committed by them, but not paid out yet. Pull it all in. We'll worry about the commitments later." That made $129 million. Still short.

The telephone jangled. Jimmy stalked angrily to the desk, snatched it up. "I thought I told you—oh. Yes, of course. Pay it out." His hand shook when he'd replaced the receiver. "There goes nine million of the thirty-one cash. A Telexed order from Sheikh Suleiman Haikan in Medina to transfer his entire account to Barclay's." He lit a cigarette, took two puffs, stabbed it out. "We had to pay out."

"Of course. Any sign of hesitation—and they'll swoop."

Jemel resumed his pacing, gnawing at his lip. There wasn't time to negotiate large loans from the giants like Barclay's and Chase. They wouldn't loan a copper penny to any Lebanese bank with a panic on unless they fluoroscoped the books—and that would amount to the same as a run. Finish.

"Get a coded urgent cable—no Telex it through —to Doug Ford. Have him transfer eighteen million of Karamcorp cash to Incom. That'll balance off Sheikh Suleiman's nine, give us one-thirty-eight total."

It sounded like a lot of money, even to Jimmy, but he knew it wasn't sufficient. More than $750 million of Incom's assets were balanced off as liabilities in the form of deposits owed and payable to depositors. The $138 million gave coverage for little more than a fifth of that amount.

"Go on, Brian. Get the money in from the Leichtenstein companies and send the orders off to Doug Ford."

Lockhart started towards the door, stopped. "We'll still . . ."

"I'm bringing some of my own money in. Fifty or more."

"Oh." Brian stared at him. "I have four. Do you want that?"

"*I* don't want it. *We* need it. Every million is worth ten now!"

"I'll have it transferred right in." He left.

Jemel hadn't asked Lockhart from where he'd have the money transferred. By tacit agreement, they kept the locations of their own secret bank accounts to themselves. Neither knew where the other kept his personal profits. The arrangement was an outgrowth of Jemel's original fears that Lockhart might guess why his building and loan society had failed if he learned that Jimmy had an account with the Bauer Kreditbank, the Swiss bank that had wrecked the Royal Home Counties and Midlands.

Jimmy flung himself down in his chair. His total personal fortune consisted of $50 million in secret Swiss accounts, another $10 million in cash that was hidden in safety-deposit boxes around Europe and America. That, and his stockholdings. He made notes on a pad. It would be another month before Abdul Kamal could deliver on the Khaldeh Beach and the housing projects to bring $20 million cash for the ten Incom had invested. Forget that, he told himself. Concentrate on the personal money.

Forty-five from the Swiss banks—leaving five, to show the Zurich gnomes he wasn't scraping bottom. If they thought he was, they'd move in for the kill themselves.

Then I'll unload ten million worth of stock in Karamcorp and its subsidiaries. Jimmy scribbled figures. Any more, and I'll not only shove down their price, I'll be tipping off the world that the Karami empire is in trouble.

The ten in the safety-deposit boxes? There wasn't time. It would take him a week, even jet-hopping from one city to the next, to collect that. And he couldn't send anyone else. Only he knew their locations. Only he had right of access to them. Hell, each box was even in a different name. He had banks, box numbers, and the names memorized.

He went back to figuring on the pad.

Forty-five from the Swiss accounts. Ten from quick stock sales. Brian's four. That made $59 million—added to the $138 million, it gave Incombank $197 million with which to work.

Jemel wanted a round-sum $200 million. Three million more.

The $200 million would be an adequate safety-margin for a little while. It would give Incom and its branches a chance to pay out—and him elbow room for other maneuvers to raise more cash if the run really got bad.

Three. Fast. He racked his brain. *Shit, I have it. Felicite's money.* The principal of her trust fund was up to a shade over three million. Jimmy was still the administrator of the fund. He could have the entire amount transferred immediately. It would give him the round figure.

He called in his secretary. For the next two hours he alternated between making overseas telephone calls and dictating cables and Telexes.

Panic mounted. Two more Lebanese banks failed to open the next morning.

The pinch was getting closer to Incom. Cables. Teletype and Telex messages. Orders to transfer a total of $22 million in the accounts of various oil sheikhs to European and British banks.

"Pay out!" Jemel rasped when each was brought to him.

Money was coming in. His forty-five from the Swiss accounts. The three from Felicite's trust fund. Brian's four. Incom Central was in turmoil. Bank officers, bookkeepers, and clerks were inundated with paperwork. Funds to be credited, funds to be debited, sums that had to be transferred. Large sums that had to be broken down into lesser amounts, allocated, notifications to be made, confirmations sent out, received, checked, and double-checked.

Before the day was out, another Beirut bank had crashed.

The Lebanese government urged calm. No one listened. Beirut, Tripoli, Tyre, and the inland cities were close to chaos. Mobs rioted. Now more shots were being fired as police and troops clashed with fear-stricken mobs.

Incombank's staff remained at their desks throughout the night, struggling to catch up with the backlogged paperwork. Jemel Karami and Brian Lockhart used up secretaries in relays, rapping out orders and memoranda, both acutely conscious of the inner fear that clutched at their guts, each fighting his own battle to retain outward appearances of calm and confidence.

Jimmy's intuition warned him the small depositors would descend on Incom Central and Incombank's Lebanese branches the following morning. But the small responded to flamboyant dramatic gestures.

"I want bundles of cash piled waist-high behind every teller's window here and in every branch we have in Arab countries," Jemel instructed Brian shortly after midnight.

They were safe elsewhere. Telexed and cabled messages from European, Black African, and South American branches indicated no signs of trouble. The New York branch even reported a somewhat-higher-than-average net increase in deposits.

"When the mobs come in the morning, have the tellers toss out the money," Jemel continued. "Get the officers behind the counters to help pay out. We'll beat this thing yet." With much luck and even more gall. I hope.

More than a thousand people were lined up in front of Incom Central's doors in the morning. Riot police wearing American-style steel helmets over their berets and holding bayoneted rifles held them back until the doors opened. Then not even bayonets could hold the mob. It surged into the bank, howling, jabbering. Men and women. Young and old. Each waving a passbook, each demanding cash.

"Isma' minni!" each yelled. "Attend to me!" They fought and clawed to be first at the tellers' windows. *"Bihyatak*—I implore you!"

"Ihda—keep quiet!" the tellers snarled, futilely, for the most part. They snatched passbooks, checked figures, grabbed banknotes, counted out whatever the account showed, zeroing the passbook, thrusting it back at the yammering clients. *"Yalla*—get out!"

On the top floor of the Incom Central Building, Jemel Karami was at his desk—tense, belly in knots, overnight beard-stubble electric-razored off, fresh-dressed in clothes brought from his house by his valet.

Bank officers, Brian Lockhart, clerks, and secretaries streamed in and out. Dropping reports or messages on his desk. Asking for instructions. Rushing off to obey orders. The telephone rang constantly. He would snatch it up, growl, listen, issue terse instructions, bang down the handset.

"Shu haida? What is that? *Nakdiyi*—cash. *Bi-ak'rab wakt*—as soon as possible . . ."

Receiver back on hook. Rapid-fire dictation to a haggard secretary.

Telephone again. "How much?" In English. "Sure. Transfer it wherever he wants." Slammed down handset. Eyes scanning a Telex message. Another insistent ring. *"Qui! A l'instant!"*

A notification brought in personally by Lockhart. The money was in from Liechtenstein and Karamcorp. Good. The telephone once more.

"He telephoned from Damascus for his three hundred thousand dollars. Get it to him. And listen. Send a separate account for the cost of the call—with a nasty letter saying if he's so worried Incom will pay the expense. Of course, it's an insult. That's the idea. Make copies of the letter, pass them to Lebanese newspapermen." Bang.

A cable from his New York stockbrokers. The Karamcorp and subsidiary shares had been fed into the market. Ten million was on its way.

The phone. "American press? Send them in."

A typed memorandum thrust under his nose. He scanned, signed. The memo was whisked away. Jimmy looked up. "Come in, gentlemen." The American wire-service correspondents in Beirut. "Sorry I don't have much time. You can see why."

"What's your forecast for the situation, Mr. Karami?"

Jimmy shrugged. "The weak will be shaken out. The strong will emerge stronger." The telephone rang. "Excuse me." He snatched up the instrument. *"Mais certainement. Faire ses frais*—pay away." He hung up.

"Have you any theory about what caused this panic?"

"Some bankers ran out of money." That with a grin. An appreciative chuckle or two in response. Seriously, "Incombank hasn't. And it won't."

Yet again the telephone. "Sure. Transfer his million to Bank of America. Transfer it wherever he wants." End conversation. A secretary with a slip of paper. Jemel glanced at it, scrawled his initials.

"Mr. Karami. Do you believe this panic reflects any fundamental fault in Lebanese banking practices or the laws governing them?"

"The only practices I can pass judgment on are Incom's. We're paying, we're solid. When this insanity has passed, we'll still be in business. As for Lebanese laws—guys, have a heart. I'm just a guest in this country—even though I was born here. I'm an American citizen. I can't make public comments about Lebanese laws." The phone jangled. Jemel lifted the handset, put his palm over the mouthpiece. "Look. I'm swamped. Why don't you both come around to my house this evening. Eight-thirty. I'm giving a party. Black tie. You're invited."

"A party in the middle of what's going on?"

"Why not?" A laugh made to sound easy by sheer willpower. "I've got nothing to worry about." Nothing except for goddamned near everything. "See you this evening." Hand off the mouthpiece. "Karami . . ."

Nearly a score of Lebanese banks collapsed during the October 1966 financial crisis.

Incombank survived.

Its deposits were depleted by more than $100 million—and there were other blows.

Lebanon had come very close to revolution. The Lebanese government, terrified of open and bloody rebellion by its citizens who had lost their savings in the bank failures, drained its treasury. Money was "loaned" to the receivers and liquidators of the bankrupt banks to pay off the small depositors, the working and middle-class people who, having no money left, felt they had nothing further to lose (and perhaps something to gain) if they rebelled, overthrew the government.

These citizens had to be bought off. The first Lebanese government "loan" was made to the small depositors of Intra Bank. It totaled over $17 million and was made with the proviso that depositors whose accounts had been less than 15,000 Lebanese pounds ($5,000) only were to be paid off.

More millions were hosed out to the small depositors of the other banks that had failed. Revolt and political collapse were thereby averted. However, nothing remained in the treasury to aid those banks that had managed to pull through—and numerous commitments (official and unofficial) made by the Lebanese government had to be canceled or "indefinitely postponed." Among them were the Khaldeh Beach tourist-resort and the army officers' and civil servants' housing projects.

The $20 million Jemel Karami had expected Incombank to receive in November would not be paid. It could not be paid. The $10 million Incombank had paid for Khaldeh Beach land and to construct the housing units was gone.

"Or as good as gone," Jemel admitted to Brian Lockhart. "With conditions as they are, no one in his right mind would buy Khaldeh Beach land—unless we sold at pennies on the dollar—and advertised to the world we're shaky and in desperate straits for money."

There was no need for either of them to mention the housing project. The units had been slapped together. Workmanship was shoddy. The structures had a dreary, cheap-mass-production look. Only a corrupt government would ever dream of buying so miserable a housing complex. Certainly, no private individual would voluntarily rent one of the units—much less buy it. The sole possible escape hatch—the sale of the project to the United Nations for use to house some of the 100,000 or so Armenians and Palestinians in Lebanon—had been slammed shut on first tentative inquiry. The UNESCO officials permanently posted in Lebanon said they had neither funds nor authority. The refugees would continue to live in the leprous, eyesore *bidonvilles*.

"Some of our depositors are coming back with their money," Lockhart said.

"In dribbles," Jemel countered bleakly. "It's a month and more since everything calmed down. Out of the hundred-plus we lost, we've got back about thirty-five."

"The rate should snowball."

"Not fast enough. Not without special inducements."

"Our biggest clients stayed with us," Lockhart said. "The Sabahs didn't shift a *piastre*." Thank God. If the Sabahs had pulled out their money, Incom would have crumbled. "We might exploit that fact as proof we're solid."

"Lacks punch. Larger extra dividends would carry more force."

"We can't afford them." We can't even afford the extra 3½ percent we have been paying. The "extra dividends" had eaten deeply into Incom's resources over the years.

"We have to afford it. We must keep pulling in more cash until 1969. Then we can stop juggling. After '69, everything squares away automatically. The jackpots will start to drop. Until then, we have to keep up the front—and keep the balls in the air."

Both men lapsed into a long, meditative silence, their thoughts running parallel.

The same elements that had made Incombank's spectacular rise possible were its greatest weaknesses.

In order to attract large depositors—and have huge amounts of cash with which to work—Jemel had offered premium interest rates. These equalled (and in some instances exceeded) the bank's profits on legitimate transactions. The gap was closed by using depositors' funds and camouflaging the tactic through accounting fictions. Like foreclosing a mortgage on a property worth, say, $100,000—then inflating its value to $300,000 on the books, where it was carried at that value as a frozen asset of the bank.

Then, the money Jemel sidetracked into dummy companies—against their stocks, bonds or notes—had been sunk into long-term ventures. Projects that would pay large—even enormous—profits, but only after several years. The first of these would begin to "drop" as "jackpots" in 1969 and eventually solve all Incombank's financial problems. However, during the interim, the money was locked in. Tight. Cash could not be realized on the ventures beforehand without taking losses as large as the profits would be if they waited.

Prestige and *sharaf* were another immense drain. Pan-Arab Airways was a tangible as well as an intangible asset, true. But it was not yet bringing in a profit —and to sell it? Who would buy an entire Lebanese airline unless, again, at only a tiny fraction of its value. The "fronts"—of corporate and personal splendor— also took a heavy toll of the bank's cash. Incom Central Tower was impressive—and costly. So, to lesser degree, were the flashy, elaborate branch offices. Jemel's house on the rue d'Australie swallowed more than $100,000 a year in maintenance, staff salaries, property taxes, and other costs and charges. His yacht, the *Asharat,* built for several millions with Incombank funds, annually blotted up sums many times the multiple of what the house cost.

"A final sprint," Jemel mused aloud, breaking the silence. A last, all-out, two-year-long effort—and the race against time would be won. "We'll use every ploy and angle to get through '67 and '68. No matter how we spread, what chances we take, they'll be worth it."

23

Incombank had been making regular and generous contributions to anti-Israeli terrorist groups based in Lebanon, Syria and Jordan, and HJK Trading Corp. sold them weapons, ammunition, and exposives.

The money and services were well spent in that they bought Incom widespread support from almost all Arab countries. Egypt was the exception. Jemel had no faith in Egypt's President Nasser, whom he considered a political *hirbayi*—chameleon—with no real strength behind the menacing words he spouted. Even more important, Nasser was despised by the rulers of oil-rich Arab countries. They recognized his ambition to topple them, establish puppet governments, and seize all oil wealth for Egyptian interests.

Jimmy was aware that Miles Palmer still cherished dreams of snatching up oil concessions—and even established facilities and producing fields in the Middle East. He'd got nowhere, though. Not even the ably created coincidences of Enrico Mattei's and Emile Bustani's deaths in aircraft crashes had helped. Arab countries rejected any bids made by Palmer and his associates out of hand. They preferred to grant concessions to long-established, experienced foreign oil companies.

Palmer clung to the notion that a Nasserite Middle East would drop what he sought into his lap. He supported Egyptian fedayeen terrorist groups with money and arms. The Palmer National Trust extended liberal loans to the Egyptian government. Miles Palmer firmly believed in Gamal Abdul Nasser.

Incombank was almost back to where it had been before the panic.

Jemel had to leave the money he'd taken from his personal fortune, from stock sales, out of his dummy companies, and Felicite's trust fund in the bank. Every cent had to stay to close the gaps, give some substance to Incombank's boasts.

The task of bringing in new deposits and directing the activities of Incombank, Karamcorp and his other enterprises kept Jimmy fully occupied, diverting his attention from a new crisis developing in the Middle East. The tempo of raids and attacks into Israel by guerrillas and terrorists based in Syria and Lebanon had been increasing since January. Reading or hearing about the raids, Jemel dismissed them as routine—the usual pinpricks.

He was entertaining a group of wealthy Incombank clients aboard the *Asharat*, cruising through placid Mediterranean waters off Tripoli on April 7th, when the news came over the radio.

"Israeli forces have launched a massive reprisal raid against Syria. Six Russian-made MIGs of the Syrian Air Force have been destroyed, and the Syrian ground forces have taken heavy casualties."

Jemel's guests agreed it might be a good idea that they return to Beirut immediately. The incident could come to nothing—yet, on the other hand . . .

Middle Eastern tensions mounted rapidly after that.

Jemel arrived in New York during the first week in May.

The Incombank branch in New York was the healthiest of all the bank's branches. He encountered no difficulty negotiating $5 million in loans for the branch from large New York banks. A million-and-a-half came from the Palmer National Trust.

Newspaper headlines were telling of Syrian troops massing along Israel's borders when Jimmy had his final conference with Miles Palmer regarding the loan.

"Things don't appear very promising in the Middle East, do they, Jemel?" Palmer remarked at one point, completely out of the context of their discussion. "Think there will be a war out there?"

"Possible. I hope not. The Israelis are too strong."

"Nonsense!" Palmer snorted. "If the Syrians attack from above and the Egyptians from below, they'll smash Israel like this." He brought his puffy hands together in a clap. "With Jordan and Saudi Arabia . . ."

"Miles. Take my word for it. You're a little off-base. There's internal dissension in Syria. The Syrians may fight, but they've got no lasting power. You'll hardly find the Saudi Arabian government rushing to help—not with troops and equipment, at any rate, Jordan . . ."

"The Egyptian army will be in Tel Aviv within a week after it starts moving," Miles predicted with certainty.

"You've been thoroughly bamboozled and buffaloed, Miles. The Egyptian army couldn't defeat a Boy Scout troop. It's rotten to the core. The officers are cowards and bullies. The ordinary soldiers hardly know which end of a rifle the bullet comes out of."

Palmer was deeply disturbed. Jemel Karami spoke with authority. Could it be that he had been misled? He made a mental note to fire off a cable to a CIA agent in Cairo—who supplied him with much information about Egypt in return for under-the-table payments.

A week later, Palmer was to receive a lengthy report—a copy of which Jemel would see (as he managed to see most of Miles Palmer's "confidential" correspondence with the Middle East). Jimmy relished the lines that read: "Your informant, whoever he may be, obviously has little knowledge of the true situation out here. Furthermore, it is evident that he lacks the requisite training and experience to assess military potentials.

The Egyptian forces are highly trained in the use of their Russian-made equipment, the quality of which is vastly superior to any materiel possessed by the Israelis . . ."

Jemel was in Paris on June 1st, when the Israeli government announced the appointment of General Moshe Dayan as Israel's Defense Minister. He knew that any bluff made by Syria and Egypt would now be called. He left aboard his Comet IV for Beirut immediately. The last thing he or any other Lebanese banker could afford to have happen in the Middle East was a war. A war could wreak havoc with the entire Middle Eastern banking industry—especially with the banks of Lebanon, none yet fully recovered from the October financial crisis.

Lebanese bankers met with the country's political leaders—and laid down the law.

"No matter what develops, Lebanon can't get involved!" they told the prime minister.

"But the public . . ."

It was Jemel Karami who cut him short. "If you let one Lebanese soldier cross into Israel, we'll throw you out of office five minutes later. I think I speak for every banker present—Moslem or Christian." There was a murmur of unanimous assent. "We'd rather see you sweeping streets for a living than to have the entire economy wrecked."

Kamal might have been willing to fight Israelis. He did not dare fight the bankers of Beirut.

The war began on June 5th, ended six days later.

The Egyptian, Syrian and Jordanian armies were pulped into submission even faster than Miles Palmer had believed Egypt and Syria alone would "smash" Israel.

Lebanon stayed out of the war, avoided military disaster.

Nonetheless, Beirut's bankers suffered heavily.

All tourism—a major source of foreign exchange in the Middle East—stopped dead. Individuals and companies in Egypt, Syria and Jordan who owed money to foreign banks—including Lebanese banks, to which they owed a total of numerous tens of millions —used "war losses" as a convenient excuse to halt all payments. Then, as Nasser had ordered the Suez Canal blocked, trade and commerce volume plummeted.

There was worse to come.

By mid-July, Jemel Karami and Brian Lockhart realized they were faced with a crisis of even more formidable proportions than those of the October panic.

"We're below the most optimistic safety level— and the drop isn't slowing," Lockhart said, the latest day's balance sheets in his hand.

"The only consolation is that no other Lebanese bank is any better off," Jemel muttered. "It has to slow down. It can't continue!"

Nervous money had taken flight from Lebanese banks the same day that the Middle Eastern war began. None of it had come back after the war ended. The confidence of foreign depositors in Lebanese banks, badly shaken by the October crisis, was completely destroyed by the war. The Middle East was too unstable, they began to realize. Another war, and Russia and the United States would both be drawn into it. They would leave the Middle East devastated—and not even the vaults of Beirut's largest banks were proof against nuclear weapons.

"We could stand the loss of the nervous money," Jimmy went on, glum and worried—more worried than he'd ever been. "But the sheikhs . . ."

Large Arab depositors were closing their accounts, switching their money to Switzerland, Great Britain, Italy, the United States. They feared not only war, but also internal upheavals which might follow in the wake of the Arab defeat. Six among Incombank's more important clients had withdrawn a total of more than $32 million since the first days of June. There were signs that others would follow.

Two more did within the next week. Another $12 million.

Jemel flew to Kuwait, obtained an audience with

Sheikh Nasib al-Harith, financial adviser to the Sabah family.

"We are Arabs," he argued. "Incombank has the cause of all Arabs at heart. It is why the bank established Pan-Arab Airways, why it has paid high interest to such clients as those whom Your Excellency serves. We must have some help in restoring confidence—not only in Incom, but in all other Lebanese banks. Arab banks."

Sheikh Nasib nodded. It was true. "I shall recommend that 20 million dollars more of the Sabah money be deposited with Incombank. You may make this known in every Arab country."

The $20 million did help. And, for a time, the confidence demonstrated by the Sabahs stemmed the outgoing flow. Then, in October, Jemel could sense it begin again. On October 21st, the Egyptians sank an Israeli destroyer. Three days later, the Israelis retaliated by shelling the city of Suez and demolishing Egypt's main oil refinery.

Within forty-eight hours, almost $30 million in Incombank deposits were withdrawn, transferred to banks far from the Middle East.

"Can you hold things together for a couple of weeks?" Jemel asked Lockhart.

"Do my best."

"I'll be moving around—transferring money in to you."

There were only two months left in 1967, Jemel reassured himself. Soon after that—all would be fine. Cash to carry Incom through was the imperative.

He cleaned out the safety-deposit boxes. Ten million. The five in the Swiss accounts had to remain—for the same reasons as before. He flew to New York. Another $6 million worth of his stock in Karamcorp and its subsidiaries went out.

"You're cutting your majority down pretty far, Jimmy," Doug Ford observed.

"I still hold fifty-one percent of Karamcorp—and I'm not selling another share of that."

"What about the subsidiaries? You're down to as

little as forty percent on a couple. A sharpster could start buying up, get a majority, break into the structure from the bottom up."

"It's a risk I have to take."

Felicite telephoned Jemel at his apartment. She was in Bermuda—and she sounded impatient, annoyed.

And drunk.

"Jimmy! Some stupid shits in one of your offices have got me all fucked up with my bank. I'm told there's nothing—*nothing* in my accounts. No checks have come in for almost a year!"

Felicite had her personal accounts with the First National City Bank. Income from her trust fund was paid into her accounts quarterly. *Or had been,* Jemel thought. *I dumped all her money into Incombank last year and forgot to give any instructions about sending money into her personal accounts.*

"A slip-up someplace along the line," he soothed his sister. "I'll take care of it right away."

He could hear a man's voice, muffled, in the background. Then Felicite's voice again. "Cable me twenty thousand here." Another Bogdan, Jimmy wondered. "And fire whoever's responsible. I've been terribly humiliated!"

"I'll . . ." He stopped. There was a click. The connection was broken.

He placed a call to Brian Lockhart. In Beirut, it was still mid-afternoon.

"I was about to phone you, Jimmy. We lost seven today—but what you've been shifting over is holding the line for the moment, anyway."

"You'll be getting more." Somehow. He told Lockhart to send "around $150,000" to Felicite's account. "Make it jagged-end dollars and cents," he added. "So it looks like regular interest payments." He didn't want any probing questions from anyone, not even Felicite.

Luck, Jimmy thought. Pure damned luck. Almost like an omen. The two items on the same page of the same newspaper. The first that Senator and Mrs. Frederick Hayworth would be spending three days in

New York City. The senator would be making several speeches. To Jewish organizations on the need for giving more military aid to Israel. To Negro groups explaining his newly proposed program for "the rapid achievement of complete desegregation throughout the country and full opportunity for all Negroes" and, finally, before a Central Park "militant youth rally."

The second story, four columns to the right and further down the page, announced "stepped-up Commodity Credit Corporation credits for export sales of wheat, corn, cotton . . ."

He telephoned Hayworth's office in Washington. Who was calling? A moment. The moment passed. Yes, Senator Hayworth would speak with Mr. Karami. First try, another bit of luck, Jemel thought.

"Just read you're coming up here, Fred. Care to stay at my place? I'd love to have you."

He had a deal in mind, Hayworth reflected. I'm game for the deal—if there's enough in it. He said, "Can't accept the hospitality, Jimmy. Wouldn't look right. Mickey and I would like to see you, though."

I *have* to see you—and I'd like to see Mickey. Very much. "Great. When and where?"

They came to Jemel's apartment on their first afternoon in New York.

"Can't stay for more than an hour," Hayworth declared. "We have to hold a press conference at our hotel."

It was an elaborately nothing hour. General chatter. Jimmy and Mickey managed to exchange looks that said they would meet alone at the first chance. Hayworth said if Jemel had anything of importance to discuss, they could "get together" the following morning.

"Meet me at my hotel, Jimmy," he said. They got up to leave. "At ten."

"I may not see you before we go back to Washington," Mickey said, holding out her hand. "Tomorrow's my free day—until six. I'm going to catch up on my shopping."

Jemel spoke to his butler as he was going out in the morning.

"Mrs. Hayworth will be here sometime before noon, Dowling. If I'm not back by then, tell her to wait. I'll arrive as soon as I can."

"Yes, sir."

The knowledge that he would be meeting Mickey a little later made Jemel dispense with formalities.

"Incombank has a Lebanese affiliate company that imports food and food products wholesale, Fred," he said. "It can buy an awful lot of surplus American wheat, corn, and soybeans. Incombank will issue the necessary letters of credit for the affiliate, guarantee its paying for the shipments." He smiled. "As I understand the regulations, that's all the Commodity Credit Corporation needs to issue a foreign bank a credit so it can turn around and finance the purchase of surplus food commodities."

Hayworth's eyes grew cunning. CCC credits were a great racket. Foreign banks got huge sums of cash for long periods from the agency—at costs that were a laugh. The bank and its affiliate could diddle around for a year or more, using the CCC money before the orders were actually placed and shipped and payment required.

"No clash with your Liberal image either, Fred. Brave, good little Lebanon that didn't get itself involved in the shooting war against the Israelis. You'd be helping keep an Arab country neutralized by urging the CCC to make the deal."

Hayworth's eyes demanded to know what else there would be in it for him. Aloud, he asked. "How much surplus food would your bank's affiliate want to buy?"

"Ten—twelve million worth." Much more, and the CCC would have to take its time about granting the credit. This way, it could be done in a matter of weeks—if Fred Hayworth pushed hard enough.

"Say eleven, Jimmy. It's a good figure."

"Lucky—if it's made on the first roll." Jemel raised his left eyebrow. "Y'know, Fred, you should have a nest-egg tucked away in a numbered bank account.

In Lebanon, say. Even Incombank. Let's pick a number. I'll do it. One five oh-oh-oh-oh. Number and balance to match."

Account number 150,000—with $150,000 deposited in it, Hayworth thought. *Nice*. A little more than he would have asked, considerably more than what he would have settled for if Karami had been in the mood for hard bargaining. "I'll do my level best."

"I haven't a doubt. Fact is, Fred, I'm counting on having Incombank open that particular account number in thirty days. Right after the CCC credit is granted."

"I'll try to keep the schedule. Care for a drink?"

"Thanks, no. It's not even eleven—and I have an important appointment."

"Has Mrs. Hayworth arrived, Dowling?" Jimmy asked as he stepped from his private elevator.

"Yes, sir. She said she'd wait for you upstairs, in your bedroom suite."

24

Came.

And went.

It was about all that could be said for the $11 million received from the American Commodity Credit Corporation. Or for the other sums—fortunes by any normal standards—that Jemel Karami extracted here, scraped together there, seemed to conjure out of nothing in another place.

The money came in to Incombank—and it went out.

Incombank, a giant among Middle Eastern banks, was a weak pygmy caught in a multidimensional press of Arab and international politics and power plays. It was plain that the six-day war the previous June had settled nothing. Middle Eastern tensions were spiraling to new, lethally explosive peaks.

Terrorist raids against Israel resumed on a larger scale than before. They were countered by Israeli reprisals. Russia was feverishly rearming Egypt. The Red Fleet had made an appearance in force in the Mediterranean, turning what had long been an Anglo-American lake into a potential focal point for nuclear confrontation.

The victory of Israel over the Arabs in June (and the very existence of Israel itself) were the pretexts. Erosion of the Middle Eastern situation and subversion of existing regimes in oil-rich Arab countries were the real intent. Oil—more than half the entire world's oil reserves—was the ultimate prize.

Inside Saudi Arabia, Kuwait, the Trucial States —wherever there was oil—renegade elements and dissident factions hoped to exploit the situation. Each group was determined to depose the rulers and their favorites and take their places, reap the oil-royalty wealth.

A semblance of internal order was maintained, partly through use of iron force, partly by bribes both governments and certain oil companies lavished on the dissidents. Beneath the surface, the ferment continued—and no one was more aware, or unnerved, by the danger than the oil sheikhs. Their own countries —or the entire Middle East—could erupt at any moment. And if there was an eruption, they would get out ahead of the howling, blood-hungry mobs. Their refuges would be Cote d'Azur villas, palatial Swiss chalets, South American estancias. It was a wise precaution to send their money on ahead, get it out of the threatened Middle East and its highly vulnerable banks.

Thus, the drain on Incombank's resources continued. Each new spasm of internal unrest in an Arab country, every serious clash between Israel and terrorists raiding inside her borders, each new threat voiced by West or by East motivated new withdrawals of funds from Arab banks. Lebanese banks. Incombank.

Whatever money was brought in on the one hand, Brian Lockhart was forced to pay out on the other. Millions and more millions in deposits were ordered transferred to European, North and South American banks.

Incom's cash dwindled. Even if sold, the majority of the bank's frozen assets would never realize anywhere near the ballooned values at which they were carried on the books. Jemel's long-term investments financed by money siphoned off from Incombank could not be liquidated without crushing losses . . .

And I can't sell any more Karamcorp stock unless I'm willing to give up control of the company and its subsidiaries, Jimmy reminded himself repeatedly. Outside control would mean that all the intricate, interwoven stratagems and artifices would be exposed. The entire structure would collapse.

A year or two is all I need, Jemel thought over and over again. Three at the outside. Then the fluid cash would flow in a steadily increasing stream into Incombank. The money would give all the depth and strength needed to the outer shell, filling in the crevices and fissures. The facade figures would be transformed into solid realities, placing the Karami financial empire on a sound, on an impregnable, footing.

Yet, with only a year or so more waiting to go, he was losing the race against time, bit by bit, gradually falling behind. The volume of money that had to be paid out, the withdrawals . . .

Brian Lockhart knew it, too.

"Our cash resources are shrinking faster than I care to think," he declared. His normally impassive, British aristocrat's face was beginning to show strain. "A few more large withdrawals and the normal attrition of costs and expenses, and we'll be in the worst sort of trouble. Within months. We won't make it through to the middle of the year."

He glared into empty air. "The first time I went under, it was because a Swiss bank pulled the rug from under me. Damn it, that I can swallow. Whatever the reasons, they were business, and there's no mercy in business when money's involved. I'm not a bloody fool. I understand that. But this time, we both stand to be cleaned, left stony, Jimmy—and why? Bloody politics scaring cowardly buggers, is why!"

Jemel ignored Brian Lockhart's reference to his earlier financial misfortune.

"We're not licked, Brian." Not yet. Not for the moment. I'd hate to make any forecasts about six months from now, though. "The political situation is extremely fluid." I wish I could say the same for Incombank "A great many things can happen." None of them good. "There could easily be an overnight change?" To what? Utter chaos?

"The last-minute arrival of the Bengal Lancers to save the garrison on the Khyber went out with the last J. Arthur Rank thriller," Brian observed acidly. "Thanks for trying to bolster my spirits, Jimmy. Unfortunately, they're becoming more bolster-proof daily."

Jemel's teeth sawed at his lower lip. "Any means of puffing more air into the balance sheets?"

"None. None that would alter the picture for more than seventy-two hours even at our present rate of shrinkage." His tone became glacial. "I'm saving those for last, Jimmy. We might need them. Desperately." He didn't need to add the rest. To get that much of a head start if the collapse began. He changed his tone, warming it. "Any inspirations for making any more cash materialize?"

"No. I can't go to the Sabahs again. We don't dare raise the 'special dividend' rate any higher to attract new deposits; it would be a dead giveaway that we're pinched." *There is still the $5 million balance in Switzerland—but I'm leaving it there until the last possible split-second.* "Our credit with other banks is so close to the limit that we couldn't borrow enough to cover the week's payroll."

He drummed on his desk top, studied the panel of timepieces set into it. One for every time zone. There had to be some answer. Some out. There always had been. There always was.

In Paris, two o'clock in the afternoon. No. Nothing in Paris. Adolphe Nivernais had shoveled out every last share of Pan-Arab Airways stock and every last bond the market would take without gagging—and possibly vomiting it all back up. Not a franc out of France.

Britain? The pound had been devalued a few months earlier—*and thank God we sold $20 million worth short,* Jimmy mused, *we made a badly needed $3 million on that deal*—but Britain was useless to consider. Incom owed money on the Comets and Viscounts, and it had borrowed to the limit from British banks.

New York. Eight A.M. there. The offices still empty. A few million people just getting up, dressing, gulping down breakfast, on their way to catch commuter trains and subways. Futile to think of New York, too, regardless of what hour it was there.

Free association led Jimmy's mind from hours to years. Back over the years. The tight bind he'd got himself into during the Korean war. Even before that, when his father was still alive. When he'd made Hassan the proposition about not going back to college if he managed to show Karami & Co. $50,000 in gross profits before the fall school term started. Jesus! I remember how I was up against the wall then. Plastered flat against it. I took the order for 400 tons of 72-inch paper from the publisher in Pittsburgh, added consent to a $10,000 penalty clause and forged my father's signature to the letter. And I couldn't find the paper.

Jimmy took pleasure from recalling how his youthful fear had mounted. The memory seemed to ease the ulcerating anxieties that gripped him now. My guts don't snarl themselves into pretzels anymore—but that doesn't mean that I'm not . . .

Jemel turned to Lockhart.

"We've exhausted every conventional—and more than a few unconventional—angles and sources. All we need is a new approach." And a willingness to take risks commensurate with what we stand to gain or lose. Risks—and the "no mercy in business where money is involved" bit that Brian had mentioned.

Lockhart was still completely mystified, but he snapped alert. The set of Jemel Karami's falcon-face, the rising glow in his eyes, the sardonic twist of his full lips. They were familiar. Hallmarks of a Jemel Karami mental process getting underway. Gathering momentum.

When—and in what form—the end product would appear was a good question, Lockhart knew from past experience. It could be in moments—or in weeks. However, it would come. Loose, untidy, all unraveled at the edges. Bold, imaginative—even brilliant—at the core. Where it mattered most. With a much better than fair chance of success, Brian conceded to himself.

Jimmy had the instinct, the intuition. He'd find the needle, even if he had to burn the haystack. But if it was the needle they were after and didn't care about the hay—what matter?

I don't care how messy the edges will be, he thought. *I'll play repairman, seam-tucker, scrubber-upper, charwoman—any bloody thing. And with pleasure. As long as whatever Levantine sleight-of-hand trick he devises will pull us through. Save our hides. Let me recoup the four million I threw into the pot—pot? more like a rathole as it looks now—during the October '66 panic and get my share of what will begin pouring in beginning with 1969, and I'll polish his boots.*

Jimmy had apparently become oblivious to Brian's presence. He was thinking, sensing that he was on to something, not able to identify what.

Analyze Palmer, he told himself. *Maybe that'll help nail the nebulous hunch chasing itself around the back of the brain. Quick. Miles Palmer. Worth a hundred million personally. At least. Wealthy, with position, prestige, Social Register listing—and a full column in Who's Who.*

Miles drooling avarice? Not that, either.

Vulnerable?

Now, we're getting somewhere. Miles Palmer is vulnerable. His kind of avarice-plus-hypocrisy, multiplied by a sense of importance, squared by obstinacy, raised to the third power by his fury at ever being shown to be wrong—these were qualities that would make any man vulnerable.

Go to Palmer for a huge loan, coerce him into

granting it? No. There were no means whereby he could be coerced. Miles invariably covered his tracks and, to top it all off, he had an uncanny ability to remain close to the seat of power in the United States. He'd slid easily from Eisenhower to Kennedy and finally Johnson administrations—a highly respected, "nonpartisan" fixture as unpaid "Special Economic Advisor."

Lay it on the line with Palmer and ask for a loan? God, no. The New York branch of Incom—and one or two others—already owed the Palmer National Trust several millions. Miles wasn't in a very amenable mood about lending money, anyway. He'd taken an agonizing drubbing at the hands of the Egyptians. Nasser had reneged on all payments to the Palmer National Trust after losing the June war. The loss there was $20–$30 million, minimum—plus all the other millions Palmer had sluiced out to the fedayeen terrorists over the years.

Still, the intuitive hunch nagged and teased at him. Like a phrase or name or thought that shows itself for a flash-fraction of an instant around some murky corner of the brain, then ducks out of sight and reach before it can be grabbed to permit identification.

I'll never get it like this, Jemel decided; *in fact, I'll never get anywhere like this. I'm not thinking straight, logically, the way I have to think—or else.* He surfaced from his meditations, looked at Brian Lockhardt.

"Ever hear the quote attributed to the elder J. P. Morgan?"

"Only the one about people who own yachts."

"There's another. He always had gorgeous women around him. Some moron reporter once asked him why. He's supposed to have said: 'My boy, every man has two heads. When one of them is stuffed with hard, dry business problems, he always thinks more clearly after stuffing the other into a soft, wet vagina.'" He got up from his chair. "I believe it," he said seriously. "I'm going home and fuck those two girls I've got visiting at the house."

Lockhart smiled—with hope, not amusement. If

Jemel Karami had an idea forming, sexual release
would speed the process, by some bizarre means sharp-
en his wits. He'd seen it work far too often with Jemel
Karami and men like him. He'd even given it a name
in his mind. The Entrepreneur Syndrome.

25

The mental chase to pin down the Miles Palmer
hunch led Jemel nowhere. Not as such. He had abandoned it entirely after several days, began to spool up
again inside as he contemplated Incombank's—and his
own—worsening dilemma.

On January 16th, Britain's Prime Minister Wilson
announced that all British military forces would soon
be entirely withdrawn from the Persian Gulf and the
Far East. The news was predictably interpreted, and
caused equally predictable reactions. What little influence Britain was still able to bring to bear in maintain-
ing stability in the Middle East was about to vanish
completely. The British were abandoning states and
rulers they had established and supported. Another
straw, and it dismayed and unnerved several Arab oil
princes who had good reason to fear the future after
Her Majesty's troops, military aircraft and war vessels
were gone.

More money deposited in Lebanese banks was
hastily withdrawn and shifted to banks in the countries
where the jittery princes planned to exile themselves
if—more like when—the British props were taken
away from under their archaic feudal systems. Incombank felt its share of the repercussions.

"How much?" Jemel demanded at the end of the
bank-day on the seventeenth. He didn't need to make
the question any more elaborate.

Brian Lockhart understood. "We lost two million

in deposits from Oman, a shade under a million from Qatar. Most of the Oman money went to Brazil."

"Didn't you try to have it transferred to our branch in Sao Paulo?"

"Yes. Even explained in infinite detail it was an independent entity. A *Brazilian* bank. The retort was that it was still affiliated with a Lebanese bank—and if there was a war or revolt in the Middle East or Oman . . ."

"Okay, Brian. I've heard their arguments myself." He offered Brian a cigarette. They sat, silently asking themselves and each other the same questions. How long can we hold? Six more months? Five? Less?

And it all had seemed so near, so sure, such a very short while before. Now? Daily, 1969 grew farther and farther away. It might have been the year 1980, for all the good it would do. By then, receivers would be running Incombank. They'd seize whatever funds started to come back into Jemel's Potemkin-village companies—for the money Incombank had supplied those companies was "covered" by their stocks, bonds and notes, held in the bank's vaults and carried on its books and records.

There would be nothing coming to Jemel Karami and Brian Lockhart.

I still have the $5 million in Switzerland, Jimmy thought. That'll get me a long way. Even if Lebanon does what it did with Beidas, issues a warrant for arrest, gets an Interpol warrant to boot, I can beat it —because I'd be smarter than Beidas. The $5 million is sufficient to buy just about everything. Including plastic surgery, if that's necessary.

Five million. Immense wealth to 99.9 percent of the people anywhere in the world. But a nosedive for me, he mused. *Back to where I started,* he added, remembering Felicite's three million. She'd have to have that back. Or would she? Hassan had left her a million. I built it to three. If I lose, she'll have to take her bruises. She'll have to be satisfied with the one million. That'll keep her in studs . . .

He caught himself. *Let her be satisfied with a mil-*

lion—but drop the rest. After all, she is my sister. Now where was I?

It would be four, then. Four million. That was all. If there was a break, he'd never be able to get a cent out of his Karamcorp stock. That would all be seized, impounded, thrown into the receivers' hoppers ...

Bullshit! Jimmy lashed himself out of his despairing mood. *In 1966 I could have cashed in for almost $100 million. Myself. Personally. If we can somehow —by some miracle—hold until '69, my share of the total proceeds over the ensuing six years will come close to the $300 million mark. I'll be worth almost a third of a billion—with Incombank as sound as Chase and Karamcorp as good as General Motors to boot.*

And I'm sitting here, thinking about cashing in my last five, running with four of it.

Bullshit!

Give up—give up, hell, dump—everything I've worked for? Dump and scuttle off, wetting my pants as I go?

There. Has. To. Be. A. Miracle. He formed each word separately, held a mental image of it before going on to the next, as though he could work the miracle there, instantly, at his desk.

"Maddening!" Brian Lockhart spoke up suddenly. "The whole bloody thing is—oh, hell, there aren't words. We're going to be shredded by events and situations over which we have absolutely no control! None!" He leaped out of his chair and stalked the floor like an enraged animal, slamming his fist into his palm. He halted, whirled around, faced Jimmy. "We're as powerless as the ten-shilling-a-day latrine sweeper!" He grew calmer, but he looked tired. His always military-squared shoulders slumped. His steely eyes, sunken in their sockets, lost their customary assurance. They were baffled, unbelieving.

"Yeah, Brian," Jemel muttered. "I know. It's what makes me want to beat my head against the wall." He glowered at the desk blotter before him. "I've always been up against situations where I could exert some influence—by using salesmanship, gimmicks, payoffs, whatever." He, too, felt weak, puny—a nothing. "You can't control this one, though. No one can! A bunch of Arab countries. Millions of Arabs. God knows how many factions and groups. The big nations and their powerplays. Israel. Shit! Why go on?"

He started to place a cigarette between his lips, changed his mind, angrily threw the cigarette aside.

"Brian, if . . ."

He stopped. His telephone was ringing. He'd given orders not to be disturbed unless the caller was someone of importance. His secretaries knew whom he considered of importance.

"Karami," he answered and listened. *"Inrammait' ktir*—I regret it very much," he said. "An oversight. Tomorrow. *Ashukurak we-bkhatrak."* He replaced the instrument in its cradle. "Damascus & Cairo Export," he said to Brian. "Wondering when the monthly $10,-000 would arrive." The Damascus & Cairo Export Co. served as camouflage for collecting funds for the PLF, one of the several anti-Israel terrorist and guerrilla groups Incombank supported with regular contributions.

"My fault, Jimmy," Lockhart said. "There've been so many other things, I've let that end slide for a couple of weeks, I'm afraid."

"To hell with 'em. They're the least of our worries."

Suddenly Jemel's eyes narrowed until the eyeballs were all but invisible. He appeared to freeze in his chair. Damascus & Cairo Export. A brain valve was activated, shunting him directly from Damascus & Cairo Export Co. to Miles Langford Palmer. Other circuits were closed, went into operation. Now, at last, his thought processes had come full circle and the idea that had haunted—but eluded him—was there. And not just the idea. The broad outlines were forming faster than he could follow them.

Slow down. Let the segments register before you let them join together. Look at the pieces. Piece here, joins with piece there. Perfect fit. Try putting pressure on the assembly. Harder. No. It's okay. Next. Not like that. Reverse it. There. Clicks right in . . .

Jemel had no concept of how long he sat there, immobile, seeing nothing but what flashed across his mental viewing-screen. He later thought it must have been upwards of an hour. Brian Lockhart swore it wasn't over fifteen minutes.

Whatever the time, he finally began to relax, the sardonic smile etched across his face as if by acid. His eyes returned to their normal size and shape, but they were bright, intense. "Brian," he said, his muscles uncording. He was a little surprised to find that Lockhart was back in the chair opposite and watching him intently. "Brian." He repeated the name and spoke with almost gentle softness. "I think we may have a way out. More than a way out." He gazed at Lockhart, his eyes glacial now. "Tell me something. What would you do for one hundred million dollars—all your own?"

"Anything." He meant just that—and he would have given the same reply if the same question had been asked but the sum was only a small fraction of the amount Jemel mentioned. "Anything at all." He was certain that Jemel Karami had finally come up with an inspired stroke—and something told him the loose ends would be infinitely worse than merely messy. Yet he hadn't the slightest doubt that Jemel was thinking in terms of billions—and if he got his billions, Brian Lockhart would have his hundred million.

"The biggest coup in the world," Jimmy was saying, his tone and look unchanged. "It's been staring us both in the face and we've missed it." He reached blindly for a cigarette, put it into his mouth. Lockhart flicked a lighter. Jemel exhaled smoke through his nostrils, a bird of prey poised to tear living flesh blowing cigarette smoke through its nose—or breathing fire—Brian reflected, remaining silent, waiting.

"So big, it staggers even my imagination," Jemel went on. "So simple, it's unbelievable. And we're the only people anywhere who have all the basic tools. All we need is to do some very fast work, do a bit of plagiarizing from the man who's going to finance us —and be completely willing to do just as you said. Anything. We're not helpless at all, Brian. We can control the situation—turn it into any shape or form we want. By creating the events that make the situation."

The Englishman had to ask. "What are we going after, Jimmy—and how?"

"What? Roughly half the oil in the Middle East," was the reply, cold and flat as the ice covering an Arctic pond. "The how is something you and I will start talking about after we leave here and get over to my house." He laughed, snuffed out his cigarette, his left eyebrow climbing. "What's the largest unit you commanded during the war?"

"A company—except for a few months toward the end, when I had a battalion."

Jemel got to his feet. "I think you're about to be put in command of an entire army." He held off a few beats. Not for effect on Lockhart, but to savor his words before speaking them. "We'll not only make it into 1969 with Incom. We're going to jump it up to rank with Barclay's and Chase. Almost overnight." Another pause. "You see, Brian, we're going to solve the Middle East problem. Not the U.N. Not Nasser. Not the Americans or the Reds. We. You and I."

26

On its face, Jemel Karami's scheme was totally implausible, a lunatic fantasy.

And that was precisely what made it feasible.

Magnitude of scope. Outrageous audacity. Impact that would paralyze all reaction until it was too late.

Yes, there were historical precedents.

Basil Zaharoff had done the same in the Balkans. U.S. fruit companies once used similar strategy in Latin America. Lacaze in French North Africa, De Beers in the southern part of the African Continent . . .

The list could have been extended almost indefinitely to prove it had been done before, bolster the contention that it could be done again.

But Jemel required no rambling discourses on historical precedents to convince Brian Lockhart. An explanation of his initial, rough draft blueprint was sufficient to demonstrate the validity of his logic and the structural strength inherent in the outlines. Whatever reservations either of the men might have had, whatever objections they might have raised under normal circumstances were smothered by the desperate situation they faced and the chilling fact they were without other alternatives.

Jemel spoke tersely, rapidly.

The Middle East was a splintered jumble of countries whose mutual distrust more often than not reached the level of violent hatred.

Syria and Jordan blamed Egypt for their defeat in the June war.

Egypt was still beset with economic problems.

Iraq was again threatening to invade and seize Kuwait.

Relationships between Kuwait and Saudi Arabia were less than cordial.

Oman, the Trucial States and the small, independent sheikhdoms lived in constant fear of their larger neighbors—and both Western and Eastern powers.

What few Arab alliances existed were meaningless, frangible.

The sole point on which all Arab nations agreed: Israel was a cancer that had to be cut out of the Middle East. Yet even here, there were bitter differences. Each Arab country blamed the next for not having done—or not doing—enough to hasten Israel's annihilation.

Internally, the Arab states were in even worse condition.

Yet another bloody *coup d'état* was expected in Iraq at any moment.

Saudi Arabia was corroded from within by Ba'athists, local chiefs and tribal leaders hungry for larger shares of oil royalties, diehard Nasserites and other disgruntled factions.

Kuwait was infested by envious minor sheikhs who wanted to depose the Sabahs, usurp their power and their enormous wealth.

The Trucial States, Oman and the independent oil-rich sheikhdoms were all equally shot through with dissident elements, hell-bent on revolt.

But the rebellious factions within each country lacked central direction and common purpose, and they feuded and squabbled among themselves.

Such were the background and basis for Jemel Karami's idea for a master coup.

"We'll enable Arab nationalists to realize their aspirations and destroy obsolete feudal tyrannies," Jemel declared, his tone sarcastic. He had taken his *sibah* from his pocket, slowly rolled the beads between his fingers. "We'll finance, engineer, and direct 'popular revolts.' "

A relatively few upheavals taking place simultaneously, following a down-to-the-hour schedule, would suffice. They would give the impression and carry the force of an all-out, spontaneous revolution across the face of the entire Arab world. Existing governments, precariously situated at best, would disintegrate instantly, their heads and officials, already poised for flight at an instant's notice, rushing pellmell to prepared places of safety abroad.

"The rebels will take over, each indigenous group assuming control within its own country—but all with the same stated aims. *Jihad* against Israel. Immediate nationalization of foreign-owned oil concessions and properties. Plus the ancient dream of Pan-Arabism come true—in a form palatable to all. Each new regime retains its independence, each country its own identity. They simply join in a loose association of new Arab states, with a benign coordinator-mediator as the association's figurehead."

"Who will be?" Lockhart inquired.

"Abdul Kamal, who else? He should be acceptable to everyone, and he'll leap at the high honor. Pulling him into the picture will also give us absolute freedom to act in Lebanon and use every agency, facility and person at the Lebanese government's disposal."

"God, yes!" Unquestionably. Lockhart felt energized, vitalized. The inner confidence and excitement building inside Jemel Karami had been transmitted to Brian Lockhart.

"Incom, you, and I possess the basic equipment to make this thing work. We have the confidence of Lebanese-based terrorist organizations. We can use their more reliable men to contact dissident leaders everywhere and maintain close liaison with them. Incom has branch offices in every major Middle Eastern city. Pan-Arab Airways has direct in-and-out access to those and many lesser cities."

Jimmy stopped, shifted position in the commodious armchair in which he was sitting, spoke again. "Let's focus down to some specifics for the moment. Pan-Arab Airways has a total of thirty-seven aircraft of varying types. From the most modern down to old DC-6's and DC-4's. All can be quickly converted to carrying freight." As they often were and did. "Naturally, we can't use them all. Certain scheduled flights can't be canceled without arousing suspicion." He leaned forward.

"Suppose, Brian, that on a given night twenty or so of those planes are lined up here at the Beirut airport. Each is loaded to capacity with crates of 'machinery.' Ostensibly, they're freight charter flights destined for as many different cities or outlying airstrips in Saudi Arabia, Kuwait, Oman, the Trucial States. They take off at intervals, their cruising speeds and destinations matched, computed so they'll all land wherever they're going at the same time. Within minutes of each other."

"Can be done. Easily." Lockhart nodded, very much alert.

"As each plane lands, it's met. Not by local Pan-Arab reps or freight handlers. By hard-core dissidents, all primed, plans made, objectives clearly established. They take the 'machinery'—that turns out to be rifles, machine guns, ammunition, explosives. Within an hour or two, they're on the rampage." Jimmy snapped his fingers. "That's how it happens. Dozens of simultaneous attacks. The shock waves will be magnified a thousandfold. Kings and emirs, prime ministers and generals, soldiers and police will panic, stampede for the nearest exits."

Easy to visualize the terror spreading. Take Saudi Arabia. Fear-stricken officials at Yenbo telephoning or radioing Medina to report an attack by rebels, pleading for reinforcements—only to hear that a battle rages in Medina as well. And that Medina's calls to Riyadh were going unheeded—because the capital itself was under attack.

Meanwhile, radios would blare and teletypes would clatter out frantic bulletins concerning identical incidents taking place in Kuwait, Oman, Bahrein. The panic would be self-generating, build on itself, expand into a force no existing Arab government could possibly resist.

"I said we'd be plagiarizing—from Miles Palmer," Jemel continued calmly. "Adding improvements, needless to say. Our deal with the rebels is this. In return for our aid, the new regimes will give the task of managing and operating nationalized oil properties to a consortium organized and headed by Incombank. On cost-plus-fees-plus-royalties contracts. The same deals the present governments get from the oil companies—only reversed."

"There's the chance of American government intervention."

"We head that off, too. Abdul Kamal will urge the new regimes to pay compensation for sequestered properties. Incom will form a syndicate made up of *all* Arab banks to underwrite the bonds the new governments will give foreign oil companies as compensation."

"But that . . ."

"Wait. Payment will be made on the basis of the asset-values of the properties as shown on the oil companies' books."

A magnificent touch, Lockhart thought. Oil companies had their own peculiar system of accounting —and this would be used against them, leave them without a leg to stand on.

An oil company that purchased a concession for, say, $10 million, carried the concession on its books at that value—even if the proven reserves of oil in place on the property ran into the billions. Then, most oil companies depreciated the book value of their installations and facilities at top speed. A plant that cost $20 million to build and was good for twenty years was written down to a fraction of that value within three to five years. In short, "compensation" for sequestered properties would be at the rate of a few—a very few—cents on the dollar.

All legal and aboveboard, however. The American government could raise no more than mild objection. Any attempt to intervene militarily would risk U.S.–Russian showdown, for the Reds were certain to hail the "popular uprisings," gain all the political capital they could from them.

There wasn't a flaw anywhere in Jemel's overall scheme. Yet there were innumerable questions. "It'll take money, Jimmy," was foremost among them. "Much money. In cash."

"Miles Palmer," Jemel said. "He'll supply the money. In return for a half share of what we make. It's a promise I'll make at the beginning—with no intentions of keeping it for long. We'll ease Palmer out when we have no further need of him."

There would be much need of him at the start, though. On several counts. *Palmer is the only logical source for the cash, because what we're going to accomplish on a grand scale is what he's been trying to do for years, and half a giant loaf is better than the whole of a single slice,* Jimmy mused. *His past experience with abortive oil grabs is another useful contribution—a surefire guide to what and whom we have to avoid. Then, he can throw his weight around in American financial circles—and in Washington—appearing to help while actually hindering, slowing down machinery, influencing sentiment and decisions to the detriment of the oil companies and to our advantage.*

"Time," Brian Lockhart murmured. His brain was already reeling off the myriad things that would have to be done, the preliminary preparations, the tentative approaches to individuals, the coordination, the timetabling, the details—and the imperative for secrecy, for meticulous care . . .

"Time is something we don't have," Jemel said. "We have to move faster than we've ever moved before. We'll spend the next week—ten days at most—refining the blueprint. Then we get moving. I'll handle the strategy. You take care of the tactics." *And we stay wound tight until it's all finished. Or until we are.*

27

It seemed as though everything had to be done at once.

Some preliminary goals were achieved more easily than others.

"Naturally, you will remain invisible until the coup has proven successful, and the new regimes are firmly established," Jemel assured Lebanon's political leader. "Only then do you step forward, offer your good offices, and propose a loose association of New Arab States. It shall also be you who will urge that compensation be paid for confiscated foreign properties. You will thus be the great hero of all Arab nationalists everywhere—and the symbol of moderation and reason to the Western countries. Your place in history will be secure."

Few men can resist such temptations. "You can count on my cooperation. I shall give you all the aid I can behind the scenes beforehand."

"You honor me, Cousin Rashid," Jemel said, "and I am grateful to you."

Drawing up tentative schedules was child's play for Brian Lockhart.

"The money you'll obtain from Palmer should give us a bit more leeway," he told Jemel. "I'm planning for a date at the end of July." That was the height of summer, when key civilian officials and high-ranking police and army officers traditionally left their posts and offices for vacations in cooler climes.

Culling out the most trustworthy members of terrorist groups proved more difficult. They had to be selected with the greatest care, and it was essential that each one chosen be imbued with fanatical belief in the cause and plan, and both convinced and bribed to a degree that would insure he would work efficiently and secretly.

"The complete and final destruction of Israel and the Israelis can only be accomplished by concerted action," was the strongest selling point. "Once the old and corrupt feudal governments have fallen, those that take their place can act together under unified guidance and leadership without any sacrifice of their own independence."

A hard-core cadre of fifty men drawn from PLF, PLO, and other groups was finally formed.

The task of picking the most reliable dissident faction inside each Arab country was even harder. Every scruffy leader of a nomad tribe would have sworn by Allah and his hopes of living in the two gardens of Paradise to do whatever was asked of him in return for a few thousand dollars and a dozen modern rifles. Every group that opposed a government—whether openly (which few did) or covertly (the number of these was beyond count)—could be trusted to make promises, and trusted even further not to keep any of them.

Ba'athists, Nasserites, and pro-Communists were automatically eliminated from consideration. Although each group already possessed some semblance of organization and was quite willing to engage in acts of violence, its members had deep, basic loyalties to political philosophies that could not permit Jemel Karami to realize his real aims.

It was necessary to form nuclei of otherwise uncommitted and unaligned renegades and malcontents. Men whose hatred of those who governed them ran deep and was based largely on envy of the wealth enjoyed by their rulers. Wealth they desired for themselves. In the long run, Jemel realized, these were the most dependable types. They could be bought at the start, and their loyalty held by the assurance that whatever money they received now was merely a token of the immense fortunes they would have when they were in power.

At painful last, in mid-March, the various factions that would be used as tools inside each Arab country were picked. Members of the cadre drawn from the anti-Israel terrorist organizations were sent to them—with money and instructions. Getting the "liaison men" to their destinations was simple. They went from Lebanon on various outwardly legitimate pretexts aboard Pan-Arab Airways flights.

Jemel Karami had postponed his approach to Miles Palmer, saving it for the last, when he was sure that the entire mechanism was assembled. He planned to see Miles sometime in late May or early June.

Brian Lockhart saw his minutely calculated schedules falling apart. The "bit more leeway" he'd given himself and Jemel in his projections was evaporating.

The first three weeks of March had seen a heavy increase in terrorist raids into Israel from Jordan. On March 21st, more than 15,000 Israeli troops—supported by tanks and aircraft—conducted a reprisal operation that swept ten miles into Jordan before the Israelis, satisfied, withdrew.

Howling mobs demanding retaliation took to the streets in Arab cities. Shouts demanding that King Faisal of Saudi Arabia and Emir Sabah of Kuwait be dethroned and killed or banished were heard louder than before. They had never sent their armies into action against the Jews—and what money they contributed toward the "Liberation of Palestine" was niggardly, a miserly dole from their limitless fortunes. Or so the mobs shouted and the placards some of their members carried declared.

"The sheikhs and the rich merchants have their wind up again," Brian informed Jemel a few days later. "We've suddenly dropped another four million. If we tighten the belt much more, it'll cut us in half."

Could Incombank keep on until the end of July?

It was going to be close. Very close, Jimmy thought—and had another inspiration.

"Incidentally, when the fuse goes off, we'll do something I think is pretty clever. We'll freeze all accounts of over half a million. Refuse to pay until 'the situation clarifies.' It'll only hurt those who're on their way out—and make us look good to the masses and people on their way in."

"True and a damned good idea," Lockhart said. "But what about July?"

"Wait a few days."

On March 29th, Jordanian artillery blasted Israeli positions. Israeli air strikes put the Jordanian batteries out of action. Some days later, the 141st Egyptian Commando Battalion struck deep into Israel. The United Nations urged that its observers and truce teams be admitted to Jordan and Egypt. Both countries refused.

"We've dropped three-point-seven million, Jimmy." Brian Lockhart had never seemed so grim. "July is impossible. We can't even make it until June—and even May is questionable unless our cash is replenished. We can't muck around any longer. Not even a day. We must have cash immediately—and revise our scheduling. Move things up a month, probably more."

Any further delay would be fatal, Jemel admitted. He still had the five million in Swiss banks. The money would have to be transferred into Incombank, regardless of what the gnomes thought.

"I'll have five by tomorrow," he said. My last. But what was five million against billions?

"It's not going to . . ."

"I'm flying to New York. I'll raise fifty from Palmer."

Brian looked dubious. When Jimmy first mentioned Miles Palmer, he'd figured the amount to be pried from Palmer was somewhere in the twenty-million range. Fifty seemed much more than could be reasonably expected.

"Fifty will cover every possible contingency," Brian said. "Can you get Palmer to lend us that much?"

"With the right bait, yes." He had to have a large sum in one chunk to ease the constant cash pressure so that he could concentrate on the big project. The biggest of all projects. "I'll talk him into floating a Karamcorp stock issue, advance the money against that."

"You'll be diluting your equity in Karamcorp."

"Brian, when we've got the management contracts to run most of the oil fields in the Middle East, I can buy all my stock back out of my pocket money. If we don't have those contracts, my equity in Karamcorp won't be worth a dime anyway." *And neither will I. I'll be broke.* He pushed the thought from his mind. It chilled his blood.

Jemel had anticipated that his negotiations with Miles Palmer would be lengthy, involve verbal fencing, bargaining, innumerable meetings and conferences. Miles held the upper hand. He could always plead the necessity for "consulting with associates" to stall, drag out the proceedings. Jemel could not appear too eager, or Palmer would nail him to the wall.

The only way to speed matters was to bait Palmer into making the first aproach.

"How are things in the Middle East?" Palmer asked sourly soon after Jemel arrived in New York, and they were lunching together.

"Depends on how you mean, Miles. In general, screwed up. When viewed from the proper perspective, certain facets are brighter than ever."

"Not banking, certainly?"

"No. Most banks are going through a wringer."

"Then what, Jemel? The trade in olives and dates?"

"Oil, Miles."

Palmer almost choked on his food.

"You've read about the new strikes, I'm sure," Jimmy went on blithely. "Terrific activity in Persian Gulf offshore fields—and shippers have discovered it costs about the same to use supertankers and send them all the way around Africa as it did to ship with smaller vessels through the Suez." He held knife and fork in midair, managed a sympathetic expression and tone. "I'm really sorry you had such rotten luck . . ."

Palmer's first thought was that Jemel was rubbing it in.

". . . because if ever the time was right for—shall we say 'easing into' oil operations out there, it's now."

No, Miles decided, *he wasn't rubbing it in, and he'd always been right in the past. I should have listened to him.*

"I've abandoned those ideas," he said in a rare burst of candor. "I threw away enough money."

Jemel had taken a mouthful of food, chewed and swallowed it. "It's a pity," he said, casual yet sincere, reaching for his wineglass. "Nothing makes a man feel worse than to write off an investment." His manner indicated he meant "write off an investment and see somebody else take it over and rake in the profits."

Palmer's nose sharpened. Cautiously now, he warned himself. If Karami had any inside information, any shreds of it would have to be drawn from him subtly.

"I imagine the general ferment over there has altered everything, even the oil situation," he remarked.

You're as subtle as a cop with a club, Miles, Jimmy said to himself, and aloud, to Palmer: "Mm. Drastically." He let it go at that, went back to his food.

Miles Palmer's interest was aroused. He'd be damned if he wanted to throw any more good money after bad, but if Karami actually knew anything . . .

Incom was opening its second New York City branch later that month. Palmer used this as an excuse to see Jemel at his Karamcorp offices the following Monday.

"I happened to be in the neighborhood . . ."

I'll bet you did. Jimmy smiled inwardly.

". . . and remembered about the new branch. I thought I'd drop by and perhaps we might find some mutually beneficial . . ."

He droned on. Jimmy pretended to listen, smiling, nodding occasionally.

". . . and when my associates and I were bidding on oil concessions, we should have let Incom take care of it for us. On a fee or commission basis, of course." Palmer puffed his flabby cheeks. "Hindsight. However . . ."

"Might have helped then," Jemel said cryptically. "Wouldn't do you or anyone else any good anymore."

"I don't understand."

"Long, involved story, Miles. There are drastic changes in the offing in the Middle East." He lit a cigarette. "Here, too," he shunted the conversation. "Now that Johnson's announced he won't run for reelection, the Democrats should have a wild free-for-all deciding on a candidate. You have any guesses?"

It was on Monday, April 13th, that Miles Palmer made his direct approach. He visited Jemel's office again —by appointment this time.

"We've been friends and business associates for many years, Jemel," he began. "I think we know each other well—and we know a great deal about each other."

"We do, Miles." Jimmy looked a little puzzled.

"I'm going to be very frank—and I'll ask you to be the same. Some men I work with closely and I have been seeking to—ah—to branch out into the oil business for some time. Of this you are aware. We made a number of errors. After the war between Israel and the Arab countries—and the, ah, disappointments we experienced, we decided to cease our efforts."

He cleared his throat. "Now, Jemel, I sense that you have knowledge of new and different patterns forming in the Middle East. I've discussed the matter with my associates. If, in your opinion, there are fresh opportunities to obtain concessions at attractive prices, we would like you to work with us."

Jemel finally allowed himself to be talked into agreeing that he would give the matter thought.

28

Jimmy intended to play Miles Palmer along for two weeks or so, tempting and titillating him so he'd grant the most liberal terms.

But the teletype message from Brian Lockhart on April 16th changed everything. Innocuous phrasing translated into a message that said, in essence, there was serious trouble. It could not be discussed over the telephone or entrusted to cables or teletypes in any code—and Jemel's presence was necessary in Beirut.

Jimmy flew to Lebanon the same day.

"The Sabahs have heard rumors that Incom is in difficulties," Brian Lockhart reported. "Sheikh Nasib is sending Abdul el Muein from Kuwait to go over everything with me. He'll arrive in Beirut on Friday."

Jemel cursed. He was certain he knew where the rumors had started. In Zurich, after he'd cleaned out the five million from the accounts there. He'd been afraid that would happen.

"El Muein is shrewd," he muttered.

"He'll see through everything if he looks closely —and he will," Lockhart said in a tight voice. "Then the game's up, Jimmy. When he reports what he's found, the Sabahs will demand their money—over sixty million. We won't be able to pay—and that's the end."

"Give me ten minutes to think." *God, I feel sick. I'm sweating like a pig, and my hands are shaking.*

The ten minutes stretched to twenty, then thirty.

"Brian."

"Yes."

"You said you'd do anything for one hundred million dollars."

"Yes."

"Then stall el Muein as long as you can when he gets here. Use every excuse and pretext you can. Give him lectures on banking. Quibble over pennies, hold off letting him dig too deep—until Wednesday morning. By then, I should have the fifty from Palmer—even if I have to hold a gun to his head. I'll notify you the moment it's set. Then, you suddenly admit to el Muein that Incom is in a very tight spot."

He stopped, gnawing at his lip. "I know Abdul. He'll be out for praise and bonuses from the Sabahs. He'll want to bring everything home in a surprise package, all gift-wrapped. He'll want papers committing Incombank to transfer all Sabah money elsewhere."

"Umm. That's how he'll operate," Brian agreed. "Still, the money will be transferred after he reaches Kuwait—and Palmer's fifty million plus ten from our next-to-nothing available cash will go. We'll be done, anyhow."

"Brian. You'll see to it that Abdul el Muein flies back to Kuwait as our guest aboard a Pan-Arab Airways flight. You'll also see that one of the crew takes a rather heavy parcel aboard the plane—as a favor. For delivery to Kuwait. You can get what goes into the parcel from the Damascus and Cairo Export Co. I'm sure you can also arrange to have a very convincing set of documents on hand, signed by Adbul el Muein, showing that he discovered everything in order ..."

Another hour of talk, a twenty-minute drive to the Beirut airport—and a half hour after that, Jemel's own plane was airborne, returning him to New York.

Jemel tried to blot out the mental vision of clock-pendulums swinging back and forth and hour hands racing around clock faces at blurring speeds. Will born of desperation enabled him to maintain a calm, casual exterior.

". . . and that's the situation, Miles," he summed up. "You and your associates asked me to 'work' with you. I'm going you several better. I'm cutting you in for half. In return for all the pull you can exert on Wall Street and in Washington with the administra-

tion—*and* for fifty million dollars cash. In advance
against a new Karamcorp stock issue."

"You appear to be in a very great hurry, Jemel."

"Take it or leave it, Miles. The preliminary paperwork and financial statements for the Karamcorp
issue were prepared a couple of weeks ago. Here they
are. You can go over them."

"This is Friday," Miles Palmer said. "I can't get
together with my associates until Monday—and it's impossible for me to have any answer for you until the
day after that."

"Suits me. I'll be expecting you at my apartment
at ten o'clock sharp on Tuesday morning."

The pendulums barely moved and the hour hands
seemed stationary over the weekend. On Monday afternoon, a guardedly worded cable from Brian Lockhart indicated he was stalling Abdul el Muein without
any apparent difficulty.

Monday evening, Jemel was invited to a dinner
party. He attended, met an attractive blonde girl—
whose name failed to register and which he could never
remember—and she accompanied him home to his
penthouse. The suspense that had built up inside him
made it a night for sex, not sleep. He was still awake
at nine-thirty—and downstairs to meet Miles Palmer at
ten.

When Palmer finally agreed to advance the $50
million on Jemel's terms, Jimmy sent Brian Lockhart
a cable.

BALL IN YOUR COURT PARTNER

The cable set the machinery in motion, creating a
train of events that kept Jemel Karami in New York
until Wednesday, May 1st, when he flew to Beirut for a
meeting with Sheikh Nasib-al-Harith, financial adviser
to the Sabah family.

Once he was certain the Sabahs would leave their
money with Incombank, Jemel Karami knew that there
would be no more problems, that nothing could now
stop him, prevent his scheme from working.

The telephone call from Russ Stanton in New York on May 11th was like an added omen of good fortune. It had taken more than twenty years, but Russell T. Stanton was finally coming into the kennel to play his tricks.

"He's dropping into our laps at exactly the right moment," Jemel told Brian Lockhart. "Stanton is a crackerjack prize I hadn't counted on."

At first, they'd concentrate on picking Stanton's brains. They'd have around ten days for that. Ample, if handled properly. Russ knew whatever was worth knowing about foreign oil companies and their operations in the Middle East. Their internal organizations. The locations of their key installations. Their security arrangements and emergency plans. Their relationships with existing governments and various officials. A host of other facts that would fill in the few remaining important information gaps. The information gained would be priceless, greatly facilitating the work of both the liaison men and those who'd actually stage the revolts, do the shooting and burning.

Later, after the Incombank consortium had the contracts for managing and operating the newly nationalized oil peoperties . . .

". . . by then, Stanton will be so closely identified with us, he'll be on the blacklist of every oil company in the world," Jemel said. "He'll have to stay on, take our orders. We'll have a top, experienced man to run the operation—for whatever bones we care to throw him."

"Is he good enough?" Lockhart asked. "After all, if he was sacked . . ."

"I'm more inclined to think he quit—over some issue that bruised his sense of principles," Jimmy grinned. "Stanton was R. D. Whitehead's fair-haired boy for years, built up the whole Whitehead MidEast Oil operation in Saudi Arabia and Kuwait for the old goat." The grin shaded into the cynical. "Stanton could have gone on to any of several other oil companies as president in the last few years. Only he's the loyal type."

"Wonder why he approached you instead of an oil company for a job?" Lockhart mused aloud.

"For the reason that means most to Russell T. Stanton. I'm his best friend, Brian. The friend who always stood by him whenever he needed help. Isn't that reason enough?"

"Most certainly," Lockhart said, the ring of bemused irony in his tone exactly matching that in Jemel's. "And any friend of yours is a friend of mine."

Jemel doodled on a memo pad. "He'll be here Tuesday night. Have an office made ready for him. Something in the executive-vice-president class to make him feel wanted. I need him buttered, in a mood to talk freely—and rapidly. We have to feed what we learn from him out to our people before the May twenty-fifth deadline."

"Shall I look after arranging female entertainment to enhance the mood—or will you take care of it?"

"That's something we don't have to bother about."

"Oh? Is Stanton homosexual?"

"No. Just still mourning over a dead wife. I told you, Brian, Russ Stanton is the loyal type."

BOOK FOUR

Twelve Days
May 14th—25th

1

Beirut. Tuesday, May 14th.

The big Boeing 707 made its landing approach from seaward, angling down over azure-blue water, the strip of white beach and then the scarlet sands that broad-frame the Beirut airport runways. Smooth touchdown. Swelling thunder of reverse-thrusting engines. Pilot snubbing brakes. Plane slowing to taxiing speed.

". . . personal effects. Passengers continuing on to Karachi . . ."

Russell Stanton unfastened his seat belt. His face was a blank. The acid that had been pumping through his veins had eaten all expression from his features.

". . . we hope you have enjoyed your flight. Thank you."

The stewardess's voice cut off with a scratchy click, and the usual Muzak-grade Mickey Mouse music spewed from the loudspeakers. Turning off the runway, the plane taxied on to an apron near the main terminal building. Engines, switched off, whined down into silence. The forward first-class compartment hatch was cracked open. Russ Stanton remained in his seat. His raw nerves couldn't take the abrasive jostlings of the first-off sprinters already milling in the aisle.

A uniformed Lebanese official of some sort entered the cabin through the open hatch. "Mr. Russell T. Stanton, please."

Russ got up, excused himself past the baleful stares of the now-blocked other passengers. "I'm Stanton," he told the uniformed man.

"Good afternoon, sir." Fingers touching cap visor. "Mr. Karami has arranged freedom of the port for you. Please come with me."

Russ gave a curt nod, followed the man. Straight through. No stop at Customs-*Douane-Kumruk*. Mr. Stanton's luggage would be taken directly to Mr. Karami's limousine. Superfast, supercourteous rubber-stamping of indefinite-stay entry visa into passport. "This way, please, Mr. Stanton."

Gut-clutch, violent, corrosive as Russ spotted Jemel's tall, slender figure in the terminal. *Swallow your poison*, Russ ordered himself. *Swallow and save it, hard as it's going to be. For how long? For as long as necessary. Hold it all inside. Force the facial expression to blend into the right mix.*

"Russ! Great seeing you again. Welcome to Beirut!"

Bite hard on the bullet—or my own liver. But hold the smile, make the handshake firm, sincere—so goddamned sincere I want to puke. Suck him in. "Mar'haba. Min zaman ma shufftak." *Grin. Hide clawing hatred, keep it hidden. Mask it with the All-American-jerk touch he expects, that'll feed his Levantine bastard ego.* "How the hell are you, A-rab? Damned nice of you to be here to meet me." *Break the handshake. An old-buddy clap on the shoulder. Beam—but for Christ's sake, don't show teeth.*

People were staring at them. Jemel Karami's face was famous. He was the Arab world's leading *sirraf* and *ragil a'mal*—banker and businessman. The slightly taller sunbaked *amirikani* with the pale yellow-reddish hair who spoke Arabic must himself be important to be met personally and so warmly greeted by Jemel Karami.

"My car's right outside."

A gleaming Rolls-Royce. Tint the tone with envy. "Do you buy these things wholesale, Jimmy, or rent them from Hertz?"

Jemel caught the note. New and novel, coming from Stanton. An indicator he's become malleable. That would simplify matters.

The interior of the Rolls was cool, air-conditioned, dehumidified.

"We're going to my house," Jemel announced. "I couldn't get you reservations at the Phoenicia. Convention in town or something."

"You're a goddamned liar." Said good-naturedly and with a smile, but merely saying the words helped somewhere inside.

"Be my guest a few days. You can always go to a hotel later."

"Man, I'm always taking from you!" Now brace, get this rough one out. "Done it for years." Go on—and don't blow it. "Even—even my honeymoon with —Pat." *Jesus, I made it, except for the voice breaks, and he'll read those wrong. It won't be his last mistake. Knowing that is what makes all of this possible, worthwhile—the universal antidote.*

He still can't shake his memories of Pat, Jemel mused, and he's still grateful, feeling indebted. Useful and reassuring to know. "I'd really be disappointed if you didn't stay at my place. Make me feel lousy."

"I give up. How can I refuse?" *I could, so easily that it'd astound you, only that isn't what the script calls for. I've got to stick close to you. Regardless. Hammer in a coy touch.* "Only not for too long. Agreed?"

"Agreed." *Instinct tells me he's ripe for almost any proposition. He'll take the job, stay in Beirut, do what I want.*

The Rolls did the three miles from the airport to Boulevard de Mazraa in two-and-a-half minutes, slowed, turned left, continued on to where the boulevard becomes known as the rue Corniche Chouran. On their right, glittering new hotels, apartment blocks, office buildings. To the left, a somnolent Mediterranean surf washing against sandy beaches and white rocks. Here and there on the right, dismal gaps. Skeletons of unfinished hotels and office blocks. Obviously, work on them had ceased many months before.

"Looks like the big Lebanese boom had a few teeth knocked out," Russ commented.

"The October, '66 bust," Jemel said.

Ahmed, Jemel's chauffeur, braked, turned right for two blocks, then left into the rue d'Australie, nosing the limousine into a driveway. Towering, electrically controlled wrought-iron gates swung open. Russ stared at the house that lay beyond the gates. Enormous. Vaguely Moorish-flavored Raucous Modern. A horror that might have been perpetrated by the combined efforts of Kings Ludwig of Bavaria, Farouk, and Saud.

"A monstrosity," Jemel laughed. "The inside is worse. Just remember the kind of mentalities we have to impress out here." He made the "we" imply that he already considered Russell Stanton a business associate.

Russ was given the main guest suite. Jemel's valet unpacked for him while he showered, changed into slacks and sports shirt, then went downstairs to the bar lounge, where Jimmy was waiting for him.

"I'm just starting on a Crawford's and water. What would you like?"

"Gin and tonic, I think." The barman mixed the drink in a flash.

Jemel suggested they sit outside, on one of the terraces. It looked out over the Corniche Chouran, now ablaze with multicolored lights, with the dark masses of the Raouche cliffs and Pigeon Rock beyond. A few miles out to sea, a brilliantly lighted cruise ship moved slowly towards the port.

Daytime sounds had quieted, but the evening was not still. Automobile traffic was heavy along the Corniche road and other thoroughfares. Horns blew and tires squealed against the background shrill of cicadas.

Jemel's talk prowled briefly, then went to the nub. "How come you left Whitehead MidEast? I thought you were set there for life."

"So did I," Russ remarked bitterly, took a long swallow of gin and tonic. *Control the facial muscles. Karami's sitting in deep shadow—I'm catching the light that comes through the glass doors from inside the house.* "So did I until a few weeks ago. I was in Jeddah when your—Pan-Arab's Caravelle blew up." Pause. "I imagine you've heard of Abdul el Muein?"

"Knew him very well." Stupid to lie, folly to say any more.

"Among other things, he was the bag-man for the tinhorn Bedou who raid in the north of Saudi Arabia. Whitehead MidEast paid him, he paid them. With el Muein dead in the crash, we had problems. Who'd take his place? My first impulse was to come up here, ask you to use your contacts and maybe find out. Only you were in the States. I sent Lloyd Emmerick, our resident superintendent instead to smell around." Another large swallow of liquor to dilute acid that grew more corrosive with every distortion he mouthed. "Emmerick heard 'sabotage,' got rattled and called Yeager, the president of Whitehead MidEast. Yeager went into a flap, tore off to see R. D. Whitehead himself. R. D. got a touch of the hysteria and went roaring to New York—and I received a 'return immediately period'-type cable."

He finished his drink. "I'd like another of these things."

Jemel pressed a button. The barman appeared on the terrace, took the empties, returned with refills and left, closing the stainless-steel-framed, tinted-glass-paneled doors behind him.

"R. D. called me on the carpet," Russ continued. "One, we'd been having some arguments with the Saudis—all my fault. Two, I had no right sending Emmerick to Beirut. Three, I'd bungled by not forcing el Muein to tell me whom I should contact if anything happened to him. Having got all that off his chest, Whitehead told me to see him again the next day."

Russ opened his gullet, poured down his fresh drink, did a slow self-controlling count as he put the empty glass on a small table, lit one of his menthol cigarettes.

"He started in where he'd left off." Stanton inhaled cigarette smoke deeply. The lines to follow would be rough. "He said my work had been slipping ever since Pat and I got married. Pat 'thought she was better than other people.' Her 'high-hat' ideas 'evidently infected' me. Then R. D. said that while he was 'sorry' about Pat's death, he was 'disappointed' because I hadn't 'gotten back to my old efficiency level afterward.'" Russ stamped out his cigarette in an ashtray on the little table. "I blew up. Told him he had no right bringing Pat's name into it, and I was resigning."

"Can't blame you. I know how you've always felt about Pat."

"If anyone does, it's you, Jimmy." Russ almost choked on the words. "It didn't end there, though. Whitehead became abject with apology. Pleaded he was seventy-three, inclined to be short-tempered and say things he didn't mean. He asked me not to resign. I fell for it, agreed to stay on."

Stanton fine-tuned his senses to gauge the responses his following remarks would elicit. "A few hours later, we got word that a test-well site we had near Nuqayr was raided. You probably read about it . . ."

"Read about it?" Jemel exclaimed. "The raid cost Incom plenty in deposits!" He regretted what he'd said the instant he spoke. Incom's cash drain was none of Stanton's affair. *I can't just let it dangle there, though.* He toned down his voice. "Couple of sheikhs got rattled. It might have been a curtain-raiser for something worse. Each pulled out around a million, sent the money to Switzerland or someplace." At that, cheap compared to what the loss would've been if the incident had provoked investigations in certain directions.

To you, it's just a question of money, you motherfucker. "We had six men killed," Russ went on, telling his story, betraying none of his churning emotions. "Lloyd Emmerick among them." Lloyd and his stinking black cigarillos, tough as steel, murdered. "Also a drilling super named Stubby Vosburgh. Both had worked for Whitehead a long time. When R. D. heard the news, he yelled that it was my fault for having handled el Muein 'wrong'—that I was responsible for getting the men killed, the rig blown to pieces."

Russ lit another cigarette. "Like I told you over the phone. I'm not sure whether I quit or got fired. I just turned around, walked out—and didn't go back." It held together. Any point Jemel could possibly check on was true, accurate. The rest? Logical and convincing.

All worked out to provide a means for beating the son-of-a-bitch at his own game and balancing accounts.

Jemel was more than satisfied. *I've already got a choice morsel of information free,* he thought. Stanton's story shows that Whitehead MidEast will be one less factor to worry about. The company's management was coming apart at its main seam. All right. Now to probe deeper into Stanton himself.

"So you're through with Whitehead MidEast—and congratulations. What would you like to do next?"

Russ kneaded sincerity with lingering rancor: "I could give you a lot of horseshit answers, Jimmy, but I won't." He held off for a few beats. "Let's just say I've finally wised up. I want to make money. Big money."

He's on the leash. "You can. Listen to me. Incombank's grown mainly on Arab money. We have no oil-company accounts. I want to go after their banking business. Deposits. Short-term financing. Underwriting issues for their overseas subsidiaries. The works."

"Plenty of business available if you can get it."

"If *you* can get it. Brian Lockhart—the president of Incom—and I know nothing about the oil business or how oil companies operate. Your first job will be to clue us in, organize the bank's new oil-industry operation and go after the business. You're on the payroll for a hundred thousand a year as of yesterday—and we'll haggle about the fringe stuff later. Your office is ready, by the way, and I'd like you to start tomorrow."

All ties right in with R. D.'s theories, Russ mused. *From here on in, it's my job to keep up the act no matter how much it repulses me, no matter how much I'd like to do otherwise. Play good old Russ Stanton, faithful friend and organization-chart square.*

"Tomorrow?" he echoed. "You move fast."

Jemel got up, stepped from the shadows into the light. His grin spanned time, came straight from their Dunhill College days. "I expect this new project to bring in healthy profits, Russ. *Not quite how you may think and infinitely more than you can imagine.* "The sooner we start, the sooner we'll begin earning them

—and the faster you'll pile up that million I've often said you'd make if you and I worked together." He opened the doors leading inside from the terrace. "What do you say to dinner?"

"I say fine, boss."

He's doing everything but wagging a tail, Jemel thought.

Lebanon's attitude towards Jews is ambivalent.

The number of Jews living in the country is small. Less than 6,000. They can hold no public office or government jobs. Socially, they are ostracized by both Moslem and Christian Lebanese Arabs. At best, it can be said their presence is tolerated, and they are for the most part artisans, small shopkeepers and the like.

On the other hand, it is not the custom of the Levant to discourage anyone—regardless of race, creed or color—who wishes to spend money. Thus, while political expediency bars entry to anyone holding an Israeli passport, Lebanon eagerly welcomes European and American Jews who go there each year—by the several thousands—as tourists or to do business.

Although by far the oldest of Beirut's four-star-A —luxury—category hotels, the Saint Georges on the rue Minet Hosn and situated directly on the beachfront is the one in which wealthy foreign Jews are most likely to stay. They are least likely to attract unwanted attention by their presence there or suffer any snubs because of their religion by either the totally prejudice-free management or the hotel's Swiss-trained staff.

Marvin Jacobs had cabled the Saint Georges from New York, requesting an indeterminate-stay reservation of a two-room suite. Marvin's Air India flight landed a few hours after Russ Stanton's arrival in Beirut. Marv went through the usual immigration and customs formalities and took a taxi directly to the Saint Georges.

His reservations were in order.

"Excuse me, Mr. Jacobs," the room clerk inquired politely. "Do you have any idea how long you'll be with us?"

"Oh, a week or two," Marvin replied, keeping his

voice casual. "Possibly longer. My trip here is a package tour in a sense. Business and pleasure. I have several textile manufacturers to see. I want to soak up some sun and do a little gambling at the casino. I'm not in any rush—want to do everything slow and easy." *Until the siren goes off.*

"We'll do whatever we can to make your visit pleasant, Mr. Jacobs," the clerk assured him. "If the hotel can be of any help, please ask."

"I will, thanks." *One thing I can be certain of is that when I'll be needing help, it won't be from any hotel.*

Marvin went up to his suite. Having only one good arm slowed the process of unpacking his bags and putting his clothes away in closet and drawers. Finished at last, he sat down with a copy of the Beirut trade directory with which every luxury-class hotel room in the city is supplied. He thumbed through it, noting down the names, addresses of all textile manufacturers and manufacturers' agents in the city.

I might have to see them all, he thought ruefully. *No telling how long I'll have to fart around, pretending that I'm doing something, before I hear from Russ and find out just exactly what the hell we are supposed to do.*

He completed his list, closed the trade directory, started to put it aside. The back cover caught his eye. It was a full-page advertisement.

"Incombank—The Industrial and Commercial Bank of the Levant, S.A.L.—welcomes you to Lebanon," Marvin Jacobs read. "Whether you are here on business or to relax and enjoy yourself, Incombank is always ready to serve you and all your banking needs. Our head offices are in the Incom Central Tower—one of modern Beirut's outstanding landmarks—and we have five other branches, in various parts of the city. Speaking of our branches, you will find them throughout Lebanon, the Middle East and in Africa, Europe, North and South America. Incom is a world bank. Why not stop by *any* of our branches and learn why it should be *your* bank, too."

Fat fucking chance. Marv mused, read on.

"Our pleasure is the swift, reliable global service we offer all our clients—large or small. Our pride is their complete satisfaction."

God, what drek!

"Assets total over $1,250,000,000 . . ."

And I used to believe it!

". . . we perform all banking functions. For those who desire utmost discretion in their banking transactions, Incom offers numbered bank accounts and other guarantees of complete secrecy . . ."

How hard can a hard-sell get on a single page?

". . . and countless other services, including many not normally within the scope or capability of other banks . . ."

Like blasting apart jet airliners and having the Israeli town of Ramim shelled, Marv thought, and he was seized by sudden fury.

". . . Jemel Karami, Chairman of the Board . . ."

Cocksucker!

Marvin hurled the trade directory across the room.

I only hope—God, how I hope!—that R. D. Whitehead was right. That Russ and I can nail him.

Some way.

Any fucking way!

2

Beirut. Wednesday, May 15th.

Jemel and Russ arrived at the Incom Central Tower at nine in the morning. The first order of business, it seemed, was an introduction to Brian Lockhart.

"Heard a great deal about you from Jimmy over the years," Lockhart said, shaking Russ Stanton's hand. "I'm looking forward to working with you."

A hard character, zero Centigrade temperature, Russ thought, showed only the appropriate smile and made all the appropriate top-executive-level reciprocal comments.

"You two have some things in common," Jimmy interjected. "Both majors—in the same war, only different armies." He laughed. "You can swap war stories—but not on company time, huh?"

I'm glad I didn't have to soldier under—or with —Major Lockhart, Russ mused. *We had his kind of officer in our army, too. Chickenshit. Pure prick. They all have the same weak spots. I might as well make the most of them and get off on a right foot with him.*

"I got to know quite a few of your people after the war, when I was with AMGOT," he said. "Great bunch of guys. Some of the finest officers I ever met anywhere."

"AMGOT? You were in Europe, then?"

"Yes, ETO. Infantry. Then AMGOT in the U.S. Occupation Zone in Germany."

"I mucked out the war here. Middle East and North Africa."

"Compared to you, I had it easy. Europe was a breeze in comparison to what you must've had in these parts." The Lockharts of all armies invariably preened and gloated when told they'd had it tougher than other soldiers. And this particular Lockhart was no exception.

"Wasn't a garden party precisely," Brian allowed, touching his moustache. "No more than got the Eyties and Jerries mopped up then we had to establish some sort of order and discipline among the bloody natives."

I'll bet they were bloody by the time you got finished with them, Russ thought. *Count off every tenth man and order Private Atkins to cut loose with his Bren gun. No wonder you British lost your empire.*

"Hope you had more leeway to deal with the bastards than we did in Germany," Russ said gravely. "The politicians in Washington tied our hands." Lockharts invariably blamed everything on politicians. British Lockharts specialized in despising American politicians.

"I certainly took no nonsense from the natives," Lockhart declared, and there was a glint of nostalgic pleasure in his gray eyes. "Nothing to equal a show of force. A few executions in the public square—and things quieted down." He thawed sufficiently to give Stanton a half-ration smile. "Good to meet a Yank who's willing to admit the bloody bunch of ponces you had in Washington made a botch."

"Old soldiers never die," Jemel cut in. "They just talk everyone else to death. I suggest you two campaigners follow me in single file so we can show Russell Stanton, hundred-thousand-a-year civilian, his office and let him get down to work."

Russ was willing. What points could be made with Brian Lockhart had been scored.

Stanton was assigned a three-room suite of offices on the twelfth floor. He made the awed comments he felt were expected of him.

"You two must be nuts to think I'll get any work done here. I'll have delusions of grandeur, start to believe I'm the president of Standard Oil or Morgan Guaranty—or both." He stared around at what was to be his private office. Immense. On a sliding scale of a 100, only 25 points or so smaller and less luxurious than Jemel's. They were giving him the full treatment. Plus. One executive secretary, two assistants—all female, all fluently trilingual: English, French, Arabic. Everything from rooms to languages triplicated.

Jemel and Lockhart exchanged glances. Russell T. Stanton was suitably overwhelmed. Now to milk him of what was needed as rapidly as possible.

"I told Russ about what we intended doing," Jemel said, apparently for Brian Lockhart's benefit. "I admitted that since neither of us knew anything about the oil business, he'd have to educate us first so we could determine how the new operation will best mesh with Incom's general setup and other activities." He waved a hand to indicate they should all sit down, dropped himself into a black wood and white leather armchair.

"Unfortunately, Russ, Brian and I have a problem," he went on, speaking now to Stanton. "This project will become an important part of Incombank's operations—but it'll still be only a part. Brian has the entire banking organization to look after, and I've got to keep an eye on Brian and on Karamcorp in the States as well."

He offered cigarettes from his case. Lockhart took one. Russ shook his head, holding up a green-and-white menthol pack.

"Neither Brian nor I can devote the time we'd like —and should—to boning up on oil-company facts and figures. Otherwise," the Dunhill College grin again, "we could go at it the way you, Marv and I did in Cell 38, North Dorm. Sit around a table and kick the details back and forth until we all had them clear and straight. That would be a marathon, take weeks." He drew on his cigarette, forced smoke from his nostrils.

Russ had assumed the relaxed-alert-executive pose. Although he could have guessed within plus-minus-five-degree accuracy what Jemel was about to "suggest," he concentrated on what was being said. It made it that much easier to keep his mind off the other thoughts that boiled through it.

"Now, I'm not about to tell a man with your experience how to handle his job. But I remember from college that you had a knack for analyzing broad concepts and knocking them down into their components. My idea, Russ, is that it's the ideal system for accomplishing what we're after here. Suppose you spend today dictating—to one of the girls or into almost any make machine you prefer, we have just about all that're made. Start off with the big, general picture. I'll have whatever you dictate typed up during the night. Brian and I will each have a copy of the transcript on our desks in the morning. We'll go over them, indicate what portions or aspects we'd like to have you elaborate on."

Brian Lockhart leaned forward to snuff his cigarette out in an ashtray on a low table set in front of the chair in which he'd seated himself. He looked at Russ, then Jemel from under his brows.

"I can have my annotated copy sent back here by ten in the morning," he said.

"So can I," Jemel nodded. "Then you can read over the notes and dictate the expanded comments and answer whatever questions we've raised. The typing-reading-annotating process will be repeated. Each day, Brian and I will be learning more, yet narrowing down to the finer points so we can outline a program that'll click right into place, ready to function without disrupting the rest of the bank's machinery. With luck, it shouldn't take us more than a week. What's your view, Russ?"

"I think it's good, Jimmy," Stanton said. "Quick, efficient." He seemed to think reflectively for a moment. "I start—for the sake of argument—by listing the various oil companies that operate in the Middle East and North Africa. I take each one, give you a general rundown on what concessions it holds and where. A light once-over on ownership, financial structure, production, transportation, refining, marketing, and so on. Then, again for the sake of argument, you or Brian feel you want to know more about how company A finances short-term capital requirements and if and where company B is drilling additional wells. I add more details. For example, I tell you that A has a working arrangement to get money on notes from so-and-so bank. Then you might come back to me and ask if I know the interest rate and whether there's any overlap in directorates or other special relationships . . ."

"Exactly!" Brian Lockhart affirmed.

Russ stood up, walked around to the large desk that was to be his.

"There's a beauty of a Phillips tape recorder right here," he said. He picked up the handsomely designed hand-microphone with thumb-flick controls for start, stop, record, rewind, playback. "I've used this model before. Like it. Should do fine, unless the typists have any other preferences."

"That *is* their preference," Lockhart said, not knowing whether it was or not.

Russ looked at his wristwatch. Ten-forty-something. "In that case, much as I hate to toss my superiors out of my office, I'll ask you both to leave. You're keeping me from my work."

When they'd gone, Russell Stanton settled himself into the Workomfort chair behind the desk. He stared at the hand-mike for several minutes, thinking back to another three-way conversation. The one he and Marvin Jacobs had with R. D. Whitehead after he'd met Marv in the reception room—and then they'd gone in to see Whitehead together.

"We'll have to stop Karami," Whitehead told them. "No one else will—or can. Not in time, because it would take too long to find out what he's really planning. You can get close to him, Russ—because he thinks he can keep right on playing you for a sucker. He'll use you—and while he is, you can birddog."

"He knows I work for you," Russ objected. "How. . . ?"

"Son, when this confab is over, you and I are going to stage the loudest, nastiest "I-quit-you're-fired" episode since the days when Ed Doheny used to throw vice-presidents out of his office bodily. The news will be all over the industry within hours—and when you ask your old friend, Jemel Karami, for a job, he'll bite."

"Where do I come in on this?" Marv Jacobs demanded.

"In your own way, you've got every bit as much motive to block Karami as Russ has—and you and Russ can trust each other, while I can trust both of you. You're the backup man—free to move around while Russ will have to stick close to Karami. Soon as Russ learns anything, he contacts you—and you fly back here, because there isn't a telephone line, cablecode or letter out of Lebanon that's safe. When I know what's shaping, I'll throw everything I have into the scrap. So, while you're mainly a courier, Marv"—they'd been "R. D." and "Marv" for almost an hour by then—"it's pure Elbert Hubbard, but in this case, the message to Garcia won't be Hubbard horseshit. It'll be real, honest-to-God real—and urgent."

Whitehead had turned to Russ. "You'll discover part—maybe more, maybe less, but part—of what we need to know just from learning what it is Karami wants out of you. Whatever it is, give it to him—everything. Without reservations. Remember, he'll think he's sucking you in, but you'll *know* it's the other way around."

Russell Stanton grunted, reentered the present. He thumbed the hand-mike switches to "On" and "Record" and checked the machine. The spools were revolving smoothly. The indicator lamp glowed. The fine-tune line was right on the head. He leaned back in his chair, began speaking into the mike.

"Original and two. Memo colon. To colon Jemel Karami and Brian Lockhart. Subject colon all caps special project period. From colon Russell T. Stanton. Unnumbered graf. The following is a general report on American oil companies operating in the Middle East and North Africa period. Information is provided by company comma in alphabetical order according to company name period.

"Numbered graf one. Aminoil—spelled cap A, lower m-i-n-o-i-l colon. A consortium of several independent oil companies period. Largest shares are held by colon Phillips Petroleum paren one-third paren semicolon Hancock Oil and Signal Oil paren fifteen percent each paren period. In figures nineteen forty-eight Aminoil obtained the exploration and drilling concession on the undivided half share of the Neutral Zone owned by the Sheikh of Kuwait period. Original terms of the contract were colon subparagraph a, down payment colon figures dollars seven million two-hundred-and-fifty thousand period. Subparagraph b, minimum per barrel royalty to the sheikh colon figures thirty-five decimal five U.S. cents per barrel . . ."

Lockhart accompanied Jemel back to his executive suite after they'd left Russell Stanton's office.

"Well, Brian," Jemel asked. "What's your reaction?"

"On the whole, favorable. Stanton strikes me as the sort of otherwise intelligent chap who grows up having ideals and illusions that're bound to be shattered sooner or later. When they break—or are broken for him—he wakes up to reality. A bit tardy, but awakes nonetheless."

"In other words, you trust him?"

"You're leaping to conclusions. I trust him insofar as I'm certain he'll provide all the information he's promised. End of sentence. Beyond that, I'm not so sure. Obviously, one of his remaining ideals is his loyalty to you. This, in turn, is based on the still-intact illusion that you are his best and most genuine friend. Shatter that illusion, Jimmy, and there's no predicting what Stanton might do. Let him realize that you're using him, and he'll turn on you."

Jemel nipped his lower lip between his teeth. "Um. I've thought of that. Got any suggestions?"

"I can only tick off the alternatives. One, tell him the truth—take him in on the whole scheme. Two, resign yourself to the distinct probability that after everything comes off ten days from now, Russell Stanton will add the fractions in his head and reach the correct sum. In which event, kiss your hopes of having him manage Incom's oil enterprises a fond *adieu*. Three, strain the faith he has in you—and his credulity, which may or may not be without limit to its elasticity —further and invent some tale that will make Incom's role in the forthcoming upsets appear heroic. Four, place him in a position where fear will force him to stay on and, at the same time, prevent him from making any move that can harm you—or us—regardless of how badly his Karami illusions are shattered and how much he wants revenge."

Jemel stared silently at Lockhart. He was forced to agree with Brian, but he wasn't happy with any of the alternatives. It was too late—and dangerous—for the first. The second meant he'd win only a tiny portion of what he wanted out of Russ Stanton. The third? Any fiction would only postpone an undesirable result. The fourth. Russ wasn't likely—wait. Not unless the threat lay apart and away from Jemel Karami and Incombank, came from the "outside," and I could "save" him, Jimmy thought. He'd have to feel he owed me a debt so great that he had to overlook my having used him.

"I'll mull it over, Brian," he said. "Do the same yourself. Maybe we can stumble across an answer."

3

Beirut. Thursday, May 16th.

"Fantastic piece of work," Brian Lockhart said. "I spot-checked some items available from other sources. He's completely accurate."

It was a few minutes before ten, and Lockhart and Jemel were discussing the thick reports the typists had prepared during the night from Russ Stanton's taped dictation.

"Have you annotated your copy?" Jemel asked.

"Yes. Narrowed him down to facets our liaison men will want to know about—but included enough red herrings so the pattern won't leap out at him."

"I've done the same. Here. Take my copy down to Russ along with your own."

Lockhart took the copy, started to leave, halted, "Stanton's staying with you. Did he say anything last night?"

"Not much. We had a drink together. I went out to dinner. He had his at the house. I brought a girl home. He was asleep when I came in. Why?"

"Merely wondering if the first alternative wouldn't be the smartest gambit. The man's every bit as valuable as you claimed. Were he to show any signs of—realistic avarice, shall we say?—the actual project and a share in the actual profits *might* interest him."

"Risky," Jemel shook his head. "Suppose I told him all and then he decided to play hero, put out the fire before it starts?"

The Englishman's slight shrug was eloquent. "We know people who can cause accidents to happen in case of emergency."

"That we do," Jimmy murmured. "I'll think it over for a few days and try to feel him out."

Russ Stanton's elbows were on the desk, and he rested his head in his big hands. He'd read over both copies. The annotations made no sense. The points Jemel and Lockhart wanted him to expand on seemed to have been chosen at random. At two randoms, for one set varied greatly from the other.

There was no discernible pattern. That it was all deliberately misleading, he didn't doubt for an instant —but misleading him away from what?

I give up trying to find the pattern this round, he decided. Maybe it'll begin to emerge in a few days. It would have to emerge eventually. I'll just go down the line each morning and fill them in on whatever they've queried until the real outlines begin to show through.

He picked up Jemel's copy, stared at the top page, reached for the hand-mike. Why in hell would Jemel Karami be curious about the *stateside* refining operations of Hancock Oil Company, which held a 15 percent share of Aminoil? A good question. He worked the microphone controls.

"Original and two. Memo colon. To colon Jemel Karami and Brian Lockhart. Subject colon all caps special project paren Roman numeral two paren . . ."

4

New York City. Friday, May 17th.

R. Daniel Whitehead had slept badly. The fissures in his weathered-granite face were deeper, more closely pinched and there was tired nervousness in his eyes and the quality of his voice.

"No word from Beirut?" he asked Quentin Yeager. A needless inquiry. There could be no "word," and if there had been any Yeager would have told him right off.

"I think I'm beginning to get cold feet, Quent. Not for myself, but for those two boys I sent over there." Yeager was silent, he could think of no comment to make. "This waiting, not being able to do another damned thing until the coin drops, gets to me."

I'm just too old for this sort of stuff, Whitehead reflected. *Win, lose or draw, it's going to be my last big fight. When it's over, R. Daniel Whitehead is going to retire. Sit back and allow the younger generation to take over. He shot Quentin Yeager a glance. Yep, he affirmed a decision that had been making itself in his mind for some while. Quent was the best of the various Whitehead companies' presidents. I'll step aside, move him into my place when this is wrapped up.*

Russ Stanton will go into Quent's slot as president of Whitehead MidEast. That is, if Stanton comes out of the mess alive. My feet aren't cold, Whitehead thought. *They're frozen.*

"I've a number of marketing proposals I'd like to talk over with you, R. D.," Quentin Yeager said. "When will you . . . ?"

"Christ! Let's get started right now." *Anything to keep me occupied, to make the waiting time pass a little faster.*

Miles Palmer's attitude towards the bland, moonfaced little man went far beyond the borders of contempt. He was nothing but a hand puppet that had no voice or will of its own and nodded or shook its head only when the drawling windbag from Texas flexed his fingers.

". . . and he requested me to come to New York and obtain your opinion, Mr. Palmer," the little man said meekly.

I can just picture the Lone Ranger "requesting" you or any of his other stooges to do anything, Miles thought. *He snapped at you—and you cannonballed out of Washington right into my office.*

"I believe someone is blowing things out of proportion," Miles declared. "I have had many contacts with the financial leaders of the Middle Eastern countries over the years." He paused, and with the hint of a sneering cutting edge to his tone, added, "As a banker and as a special adviser to previous administrations. The situation in the Mideast is no different than it has ever been. A powder keg, yes. In constant turmoil, yes again. However, for you to become nervous over some unsubstantiated rumors passed on by 'agents' of dubious reliability—that approaches the preposterous!" He grimaced. "I hardly imagine you people want another Vietnam on your hands."

The moon-faced man turned ashen-pale. *Any mention of Vietnam will do it to all of them,* Palmer chortled inwardly.

Moon-face recovered sufficiently to croak out a last question. "Then I may report that you observed nothing in the Middle Eastern economic sector to cause you any alarm?"

"Definitely!" Miles declared. "Nothing at all."

I'm doing my part to cover Jemel Karami's trail over here, he reflected. *I only wish I had some inkling of how things were progressing with him over there.*

Whenever she was in New York, Felicite Karami used her brother's Wickpark Towers penthouse as though it were her own. The domestic staff was glad her visits were infrequent, for she gave all-night parties that left the apartment a shambles.

There had been such a party that started on Thursday night. The last guest had not departed until dawn. The last but one. The Italian Count Federico Bellini, Felicite's latest lover. He was with her in Jemel's bedroom—and bed.

Felicite lay on her back, her thighs wide and eyes closed, moving her hips slowly against the play of Federico Bellini's mouth and tongue. When she felt herself building to orgasm, she opened her eyes, propped herself up and added visual enjoyment to the other sensations. She liked to see Bellini's coal-black hair buried between her legs, his hands kneading at her breasts, his slender body, the skin rather dark—deep suntan laminated on to natural olive.

Federico was good. One of the best, Felicite mused. He could last for hours. She moaned, reaching orgasm, lay back, moving gently again as he continued, wanting another. Although she'd known Federico for what—almost four months now?—he still hadn't begun to bore her.

"Mmm." The sensations were pleasurable. Probably heightened by whatever was in the capsules they'd taken. He'd said they were something new. They were. They made her feel giddy-good and heightened the sensitivity of her erotogenic zones. "You know, Federico, I like you."

He let his lips and tongue linger a few seconds before raising his head and looking at her. "I adore you, I worship you, *bellezza*," he said—and quickly balanced off the sentimental with a broad smile that displayed his white teeth, saying, "Shall we drink to us together?"

Felicite giggled at the word play. In Italian, "drink" carries the same sexual connotation as "eat" in English. She swung herself around in the bed and took him in her mouth. God, he was big!

Suddenly, Federico rolled away from her, sat up, legs crossed and mimed a lean, sharp-featured Buddha pouting as he contemplated rigid phallus instead of navel. "How often have I begged you to marry me?" he asked.

"I've lost count." Felicite laughed hilariously. Whatever had been in the capsules was still working. "I've lost count, count—and my cunt seems to have lost a count, too." It sounded so funny. Count, count, cunt, count. She tried other combinations, then ran down.

"I'm begging you again."

"Begging me to do what?"

"Marry me. Become the Countess Federico Bellini." *And make me the husband and brother-in-law of countless millions, countess.*

"Federico. I like you. Why should I marry you?"

"Because it's something you've never tried before."

I'll be damned, Felicite thought. *I haven't, have I?*

They flew to Nevada on an early afternoon plane and were married there that evening. They picked up a taxi driver and a waitress to act as witnesses and then took them back to their hotel. It was Felicite's idea to have a foursome on the wedding night. The taxi driver and waitress were willing, but they wanted to be paid. Felicite gave them each a hundred dollars.

She was astounded at the intensity of the pleasure she derived from watching Federico with the waitress. Foursomes were nothing new—but it was the first time she'd joined in one with Federico. Still, that didn't explain—and then the realization struck her.

"Federico," she called to him, oblivious to the cab driver's clumsy thrustings inside her. "You really do look a lot like my brother Jimmy."

5

Beirut. Saturday, May 18th.

Jemel was relieved to hear that Russ Stanton intended to spend the day sightseeing. It would save the need for going to Incom Central to meet with Brian Lockhart. He could have Lockhart come to the house, and they'd be able to talk freely, without fear that Russ might blunder in on them.

"I've always wanted to see Baalbek," Russ announced at breakfast. "Never had the chance before."

"Take the Rolls and Ahmed—or one of the other cars."

"No, thanks, Jimmy. I've already arranged to hire a car and guide." *The reason I'm going to Baalbek is none of your chauffeur's business.*

The dissident groups were ready, poised, their plans made, their timetables refined, the "liaison men" had reported, and their reports stood up under search-

ing scrutiny. Within hours after the aircraft carrying
their loads of weapons and explosives landed at the
various designated airports and strips, the revolt would
erupt.

There was only one discordant note—and it was
serious.

"Always some fucking last-minute snag!" Jemel
rasped angrily. "Goddamn all Arabs! They'll never
learn to leave well enough alone!"

Several of the leaders of rebellious factions had
suddenly declared they did not believe Abdul Kamal
was the right man to head the association of post-
revolutionary Arab states. Their objections were that
the Lebanese politician had not pursued a sufficiently
aggressive policy against Israel. While he did permit
anti-Israeli guerrillas to operate from Lebanese bases,
no Lebanese troops had been committed to battle during 1948–49, in 1956, or in 1967. Kamal did not
satisfy the extremists.

"We're only a week from the deadline!" Jemel
ranted. "It's impossible to find anyone else between
now and then . . ."

"Calm down, Jimmy," Brian Lockhart urged.
"We don't have to find anyone else. A dramatic dem-
onstration that Kamal is among the Arab leaders whom
the Israelis hate most and all objections will vanish.
He'll be hailed as the new Mohammed!"

"We only have seven days remaining, Brian!"

"Ample." Lockhart's laugh was short, spearing.
"One quickly improvised stunt will do it. Canned
goods, my friend. Canned goods."

"What the hell are you talking about?"

"We've taken pages from Miles Palmer's book.
Let's take one from *Mein Kampf.* Just before Hitler
marched into Poland, Heinrich Himmler dragged some
prisoners out of a concentration camp and had them
dressed in Polish Army uniforms. A fake attack on
a radio station inside German territory was staged. The
'Polish soldiers' were machine-gunned 'by heroic frontier guards.' Their dead bodies were 'proof' that the
Poles attacked first."

"I remember something about that. I can't see it as . . ."

"Jimmy. Our friends at the Damascus and Cairo Export Co. will be happy to oblige by rounding up a few stray Jews, dressing them in Israeli commando uniforms—and arranging to have them killed as they're attempting to attack King Hussein's palace in Jordan —and Kamal's residence here."

Jemel's left eyebrow had climbed to its limit.

"Foolproof," Brian continued. "The Jordanians will love the idea, and I can manage all the tactical planning with Damascus and Cairo. It's up to you to convince Kamal."

Not only foolproof, but it would immensely strengthen the entire "popular revolt" scheme. World opinion would swing heavily against the Israelis for attempting to assassinate two Arab leaders—and Israeli denials would be sneered at in light of the "positive proof" that gunshots, a few exploding grenades, and the dead "Israeli commandos" would provide.

"How many men would be involved?" Jemel asked, swallowing, then wetting his lips despite himself.

"Seven total. Three for the palace in Amman. Four here. Of course, when you talk to Kamal, remind him to give orders to the police. They mustn't launch any investigations into the sudden disappearances of a few Beirut Jews." He saw that Jemel had got up and was walking away. "Where are you going?"

"Here. To the telephone. I'll make an appointment to see Kamal today."

The ruins of Baalbek lie a little more than fifty miles inland from Beirut, at the foot of the western slopes of Anti-Lebanon, the mountain range that walls Lebanon to the east. Built originally in the time of the Phoenicians, Baalbek was renamed Heliopolis after its conquest by Alexander the Great. Under Roman rule, it was built into a vast complex of enormous temples —below them labyrinths of subterranean passages.

Time, earthquakes, invasions all helped reduce

Baalbek to among the world's more impressive ruins. But Russ Stanton did not go to Baalbek to view the temples of Jupiter, Bacchus, and Venus, nor the immense Sacrificial Courtyard that has remained in a remarkable state of preservation. He was there to meet Marvin Jacobs, as they had arranged to meet while still in New York. On Saturday. At 11:00 A.M. Near the raunchy ticket-booth at the mouth of the covered passage leading to the Acropolis.

Stanton arrived first. He wandered around the area near the ticket booth, his Hasselblad dangling against his chest from its leather neckstrap. Marvin arrived fifteen minutes later. They bought tickets, fell in with a group of tourists, then edged away, out of earshot.

"I've been seeing textile manufacturers," Marvin said. "That covers my activities. What about you?"

Russ rapidly related all that had happened since he landed in Beirut.

"Whitehead was right about the who, what, and why—I'm sure of that," Stanton concluded. "The exactly where and how are still mysteries. Karami and this Lockhart are masters at the art of keeping things to themselves. I'm not even close to finding out the direction in which they're heading." The pattern continued to elude him. "The *when* is what bugs me most. I have a hunch it's going to be soon."

"Three to six weeks was Whitehead's estimate," Marv reminded him.

"There's an uptight undercurrent in everything Karami and Lockhart are doing that makes me think they'll pull their switch before that. Two to four weeks, maybe." He scowled. "It's rugged, Marv, hanging around that bastard, playing buddy-buddy, when all I want to do is beat him into a pulp and then spit into what's left!" Hatred, rage, loathing—they were all in his expression, in the unconscious cording of his muscles.

"Easy, Russ," Jacobs said quietly. "Try to sweat it out a little longer. Maybe you'll run across what we're after in the next week or so."

One week was all that was left.

Only seven days and nine hours.

Jemel Karami stifled an exasperated groan.

"I've told you!" he exclaimed. "You'll be in no actual physical danger. None at all. You won't even be *in* your house. The PLF will deliver the bodies dressed in the uniforms, drop them around the grounds together with weapons that have apparently been fired. Then the PLF men will spray the walls of the house with sub-machine-gun bullets. Other PLF men in Squad 16 uniforms will shoot several bursts into the air. When the police and troops arrive, it will all be long over. You, Abdul, will have been saved from an Israeli commando attack. Can't you understand it?"

"I won't have to be inside the house?"

"No. For the thousandth time. Not while there's any shooting." Jemel curbed his rising anger. "Listen. I'll be with you. We'll get you inside the house in the moments between the time when the shooting stops and before the police and soldiers get there. You don't believe for a moment that I would risk my life?"

"You will remain with me?"

"Yes. An hour later, Abdul, you'll be the greatest figure in the Arab world. An Arab nationalist hero who was saved from martyrdom by a mircale. By the grace of Allah. You'll be living proof that God protects the Arab cause against Jewish treachery."

"Yes." Only partial agreement, as evidenced by a plaintive whine: "Hussein will be saved, too. It will detract from my . . ."

"Audul. An attempt on your life alone would raise doubts. A simultaneous effort against Hussein prevents suspicion. It will detract nothing. For God's sake, can you conceive 'newly liberated Arab states' wanting to be associated under the leadership of a Hashemite king?"

Total agreement at last.

Jemel returned to his house, where Brian Lockhart was waiting.

"All right, Brian. Order your 'canned goods' from Damascus and Cairo Export."

"When do we want delivery? Wednesday, perhaps?"

"Wednesday night would be good."

Lockhart gave Jemel a long, penetrating look. "One thing more, Jimmy. I imagine the local PLF chap will want us to be present when the merchandise is— um—prepared for shipment."

Jemel was startled. "Why?"

"As assurance that they won't be left high and dry if anything goes wrong. They won't chance having all the responsibility thrown on them, with no assurance that we'll be forced to back them, save them from trouble."

That was reasonable. "Wouldn't it be enough if just you were there?"

"Of course it would be—for the PLF," Lockhart replied with cool candor. "Not for me. I want assurance that I won't be left high and dry, either."

"I see." *I'd want the same, were our position reversed.* "All right, Brian, we'll both go." He suppressed a shudder, hastily veered off on to another subject. "Tomorrow is my day for Tom Hruska."

Thomas Hruska was the most recent in a series of five Pan-Arab Airways presidents. The previous four had come and gone.

"I've invited him to stop by for a drink in the early afternoon," Jemel went on. "I'll give him the big pep talk."

Lockhart chuckled. "Shouldn't be difficult. Hruska is hardly the brightest man in the world."

"That's why we hired him, wasn't it?"

6

Beirut. Sunday, May 19th.

Thomas Hruska's predecessor as president of Pan-Arab Airways had been an intelligent, able executive. Jemel and Brian decided to fire him in March, when their plans for the oil coup had taken its first shape. They needed a dull, unimaginative clod at the head of Pan-Arab until after the scheme had been realized. Thomas Hruska filled the bill. In his mid-forties, he'd tumbled himself out of middle-management positions with an assortment of small airlines. He could only take orders and follow routine. Ideal.

It was only Hruska's second visit to the Karami mansion on the rue d'Australie, and he was no less awed than before. He wished he could have brought his wife, but Jemel Karami had told him to come alone.

Jemel led Hruska out on to a terrace. After they were served drinks, Jimmy made certain the doors were securely closed.

"What I'm going to tell you is confidential, Tom," Jemel began. "If everything works out right, you'll have a ten thousand dollar bonus. If it doesn't—or you get a single leak—Pan-Arab will have a new president."

Hruska nodded.

"Incom has worked out a number of deals that can really give Pan-Arab tremendous public-relations mileage. Worldwide publicity. The bank has a batch of air-freighting contracts. Machinery and equipment consigned to sixteen different destinations throughout the Middle East."

Jemel swallowed some of his scotch, offered Tom Hruska a cigarette, took one himself and leaned forward into Hruska's lighter flame.

441

"Brian and I believe it'll be a record-breaking performance if every one of those shipments arrives at its destination at the same hour—and close to the same minute."

"Say, that does have possibilities!" Hruska exclaimed—not quite sure what the possibilities were, but certain this was the right comment.

"Saturday evenings are Pan-Arab's lightest traffic periods, I believe."

"Yes. Like for most airlines."

"Get together with Brian in the morning. We want sixteen aircraft—you might have to drop a scheduled flight or two—and their flight crews, less cabin personnel, ready to receive heavy freight next Saturday afternoon. You and Lockhart will work out the load-distance-speed combinations. To save a lot of red tape all shipments will be officially consigned to Pan-Arab at destination. So you'll be able to get all the necessary flight-clearances from the countries concerned easily. They'll be classified as house-charter flights. We'll let the local Pan-Arab managers worry about customs and all that sort of crap."

Tom Hruska said, "We can do it."

"Sure we can," Jimmy agreed. "A cinch, if you'll do your part. Now, *after* all the shipments have been unloaded, the planes returned to Beirut and the consignments broken down and delivered locally, then we announce publicly what we've done." *Like hell we will, but by then, you'll have done your job and will be scared shitless to open your mouth.* "Tom Hruska president of Pan-Arab Airways will call a press conference—and reveal the story of the biggest coordinated commercial mass air-freight flight operation ever conducted in this part of the world. Get it?"

"And how!" Now he did. It was a terrific gimmick—and a $10,000 bonus for Tom Hruska. "I'll see Brian first thing tomorrow and get working."

"I know I can depend on you, Tom." *Depend on you to keep your mouth shut, grind out all the detail work—and keep quiet until nothing you could possibly say would alter anything.* "Care for another drink?"

Chevy Chase, Maryland. Sunday, May 19th.

Mickey Hayworth paid the cab driver and walked up the concrete path that led to the door of the white-brick two-story house that served—had served, she corrected herself—as her and Fred's Washington home for two years.

She took the front door key from her purse, unlocked the door. The air was close, foul. Littered ashtrays, empty glasses. Almost one in the afternoon. Freddie must be sleeping off a bad one.

She ignored the disorder around her. I couldn't care less any more, she thought, and went directly upstairs to Fred Hayworth's bedroom. The door was open. He was in bed, asleep. At least he'd managed to get his clothes off for a change.

"Fred!" she called out loudly. "Wake up, damn you!" She couldn't bring herself to go to the bed and couch and shake him. "Fred!"

He came alive slowly, opened his eyes, groaned, sat up, groaned again, saw her and glared.

"Get washed, have a drink to steady yourself, and then come to my room," she said, giving orders. "Like I told you over the phone yesterday, I have some news for you, Freddie-boy."

She turned around and left. She went to her own room.

There were two empty suitcases in the closet. They were all she needed. Most of her clothes were home—in her parents' house—already, and there wasn't much she wanted to take with her. Almost everything could remain behind with Fred, along with the almost six years they'd wasted of each other's lives.

She found there was even less she wanted to take than she'd thought. Only one suitcase was full. The other less than half-way.

Fred Hayworth finally made his appearance. He wore slacks, T-shirt, and a bathrobe. He'd had considerably more than one drink to steady himself. He'd taken on enough to tip the scale in the opposite direction.

"What the fuck is this all about?" he demanded.

"I'm leaving you, Fred. I'm getting a divorce. I don't feel that I owe you a thing, but I thought I'd tell you to your face, rather than over a telephone." She was completely calm. She'd spent the last week going through the emotional wringer with her parents. *Not a drop left,* she thought.

Hayworth's face—"he should be a movie star," women voters gushed—was nasty-ugly. "In a pig's ass!" he sneered. "When Mommy and Daddy Ferrenbaugh hear that their precious daughter's cunt has been a public free-parking zone for years, they'll have heart failure—and you wouldn't want that, would you, dahling?"

"They already know everything." Mickey's features were sad. "There's nothing you can tell them." *Except about Jimmy, and I have to take a chance that you won't think that's any more important than any of the others.*

Senator Fred Hayworth's sneer vanished. His jaw dropped slightly. She was telling the truth. She wasn't lying. She *had* gone home and told her parents.

"You rotten. . . !"

"Yes, Fred. It was rotten. Dad took it hard. Very hard." She turned away, opened a last drawer. Nothing there she wanted. She closed it.

"What did you tell them about me?"

"Only the minimum of the truth." Mickey began closing the second suitcase.

"You cheap whore! Found yourself a steady fuck, I suppose!"

She ignored him.

"Too bad you can't wrap your snatch around your old boyfriend Jimmy Karami's wog-cock."

Don't move a muscle, Mickey warned herself. *Don't let him guess that Jimmy means anything more than a lay to me.*

"Wouldn't surprise me if you've had more than one nigger prick stuck into you, too."

Hayworth stood about a foot inside the doorway. He swayed a little, placed a hand against the wall to steady himself. The movement switched his mind away

rom trying to get a reaction out of Mickey. He had
other problems. If Mike Ferrenbaugh pulled out party
upport, Fred Hayworth's charisma would be worth-
ess.

"Mickey . . ."

"Stop it, Freddie-boy." She had the suitcase
closed. "I can read your mind like the top 'E' on an
eye chart. Dad told me he'd make you a deal. Let the
divorce go through without any noise, and while he
won't personally do anything to help you, he won't
turn the machine against you, either. That'll leave
you with a little better than even chance to be re-
elected. Let out a squeal—and the machine finds itself
a new candidate."

Mickey lifted the suitcases off the bed, put them
on the floor. They were surprisingly light.

"I'm taking the car to the airport," she announced. "I'll call you from there and let you know
where I've parked it."

I'll make another Senate term, Hayworth thought
*—but quiet or not, the divorce will finish any hope of
ever going further, getting the presidency. Even if the
voters swallowed it—and they probably wouldn't—I'd
need Mike Ferrenbaugh and the other party bosses
pushing.*

"Get away from the door, Freddie."

A fury exploded inside him. "You fucking bitch!"

He lunged for her, fist clenched. He didn't see the
suitcases, tripped, fell headlong. His head cracked
against the wooden bedstead, stunning him. He tried
to sit up. Hangover, the drinks he'd downed, and the
blow on his head made it impossible. He retched, rolled
over on his back.

It had all happened with such speed that Mickey's
brain didn't really register until she saw him sprawled
on his back. He was cursing and gagging on liquor
that he couldn't vomit up or swallow down again. To
hell with him. She picked up one suitcase, had to move
a step to reach the one that had caused Hayworth to
trip.

He saw her move closer. He cursed again, struggled, made a gurgling sound and spewed over himself.

He thrust out a hand, seized Mickey's ankle. She cried out, afraid now, tore her ankle from his grasp.

"I'm going to break your face open, you come-licking, no-good . . ."

He'd hooked his elbows on to the top of the bed, had his feet and bent legs braced to haul and lever himself into a standing position.

Mickey never knew whether it was physical fear, a violent expression of accumulated hatred or pure impulse that caused her to do it. But instead of running or even shrinking from him, she stepped closer, almost between his knees. She lifted her foot and brought it stamping down, with every ounce of her strength and weight, smashing the heel of her shoe into his genitals.

He slumped, screaming in agony.

Mickey picked up both suitcases and walked from the room. He was still screaming, but she paid no attention. She felt nothing. She didn't even look back.

7

Beirut. Monday, May 20th.

Jemel and Brian compared notes on the memorandum Russ Stanton had dictated the previous Friday.

"I'm shifting the show planned for Abqaiq to Al Mubarraz," Lockhart declared. "From what Stanton indicates here, it's much better for our purposes. Our people merely blow a branch feeder line to the main Trans-Arabian Pipeline, which means less serious damage we'll have to repair later. However, since the feeder line runs through the Ghawar oil field, the effect will be even greater on the Saudis. They'll rush every available man to the scene to protect the field." He pointed to the map of Saudi Arabia spread on Jemel's desk. "The men will be drawn from Abqaiq, leaving it defenseless. Our friends can take the whole TAPline

complex there without firing a shot or wrecking any
of the main installations."

"That is better," Karami agreed. The object was
to create the most panic with the least damage to the
properties that the Incombank consortium would have
to operate afterward. "Is there time to change the instructions?"

"Yes. Our PLF 'liaison men' have set things up to
allow flexibility."

"Any other changes?"

"A few. I'll see they're made. Another day, and
we'll have all we need from Stanton regarding facilities
and installations. We'd be smart to veer him off on to
costs and secret contract provisions after that." He
cleared his throat. "We're still running the chance
that he'll walk out on us after Saturday. Or have you
got any ideas on how to hold him?"

"None yet." Jemel gave Lockhart his copy of
Russ's memorandum. "Send this and your copy down
to Stanton." He folded the map of Saudi Arabia, thrust
it into a desk drawer. "Incidentally, I imagine Tom
Hruska is already waiting in your office. Paint a bright
picture for him."

"Of course."

Jemel tapped fingers on his desktop. "Oh, yes.
Transfer one hundred thousand dollars to the National
City in New York for my sister. Debit it against her
capital account here." He grimaced sourly. "Make a
mental note to change her name on our records. She's
now Countess Felicite Bellini."

"You're . . ."

"No, I'm not joking. I got a cable from her. She
married the worst of the Bellini brothers—and they're
both champion pimps and penny-ante fancy men. She
married Federico. In Nevada. Last week. The hundred
thousand is only the beginning. He'll squeeze her dry."

"Isn't there something you can do?"

"Later, maybe. After we're out of the woods. Until then, she's on her own." *I think Felicite has screwed
up her life. She thinks she's enjoying herself. Who's
right? Who knows? What was it she once said? That
we were very much alike in some ways. Then, there*

*had been the time she was in a Swiss clinic. "Ever stop
to consider it might be smart to slow down a little,"
I asked her, and she answered with: "Did you?" She
does her thing, I do mine.*

"Come back and see me after you've talked with
Hruska, Brian," Jemel said.

Lockhart departed. Jemel reached for his morning mail, preculled by secretaries who knew which letters he cared to see—and, of these, which were to be
delivered to him unopened, on top of the pile. He
didn't have to look at the return address on the upper-
most envelope. He immediately recognized Mickey
Hayworth's distinctive feminine handwriting.

Letters from Mickey were rare, and Jemel tore
open the envelope, his curiosity aroused. A single
sheet of notepaper. Dated May 16th.

> Dear Jimmy,
>   Very briefly and only to prevent any embar-
> rassments in case you have any contact with Fred
> during the next few weeks. I am leaving him and
> will soon file suit for divorce. I've worked it all
> out with Dad. While there's bound to be publicity
> about the divorce itself, we've found a way to
> avoid unpleasantness.
>
>   As Always,

Signed "Mickey." Short, innocuous. It could be
read by anyone. To Jimmy, the between-the-lines messages were clear. A warning to be on his guard if he
had any dealings with Fred Hayworth in the near future. An assurance that Mickey and her father, Mike
Ferrenbaugh, would somehow force Hayworth into allowing the divorce to go through without contesting it
and raking up old scandals. Mickey was telling him
that he didn't have to fear that his name would be
brought into the suit.

Crazy coincidence, Jemel mused. *Felicite marries
a worthless bum and Mickey decides to get rid of
another equally worthless bum—both in the same
week. Plus one, minus one. The sum remains the same.
    Or does it?
    It doesn't. How can it? I'm dealing with two en-*

tirely different sets of books. Felicite is my sister. We're the last of the Karamis—and she's not even a Karami anymore. She's a Bellini—and I hate to speculate how that mess will turn out.

Mickey. Mickey is Mickey—and she's going to get a divorce. She'll be single again—in what?— months, perhaps a year. Still in her early thirties. Still under my skin. Not so that it's a constant irritation— but more than any other woman has ever been. And for a hell of a lot longer.

Say the divorce takes a year. During that year that all my long-term deals start to pay off—not that they loom so important now. They're big, sure, but the biggest jackpot of all will have dropped first. It'll drop by midnight next Saturday.

He reread Mickey's note.

As always. Since she was five. A long time. Ever since she was a child—mental electricity arced across a huge gap—and what's going to happen with Incombank and Karamcorp and all the rest? When I've finished the pyramid. The pyramid I've been building on what Hassan Karami thought was his own pyramid —and then who's going to take over?

"It has been frequently postulated that the psychological dynamics of the drive to procreate are rooted in the desire to achieve immortality, to continue the life of the self . . ."

I read that somewhere just the other day. I . . .

The ring of a telephone. Automatic response of picking up the instrument, saying, "Karami."

"Monsieur Adolphe Nivernais is calling you from Paris, Mr. Karami."

"Put him through."

. . . no, forget it, for the time being. Whatever further thought I give to Mickey and the rest of it will also have to wait until we're out of the woods . . .

"Ah, *bonjour*, Adolphe. *Comment allez-vous?*"

Jemel still held Mickey's letter in his hand.

"*Mais certainement*, Adolphe. If you have a company with a new issue that looks promising, Incombank will be happy to help float it."

. . . newly married sisters and prospective di-

vorcées were burdensome extra mental baggage at the moment.

"*Mon ami,* like you, I always seek the largest profit margin."

He crumpled the letter, dropped it into a wastebasket, took a fountain pen from its holder and jotted figures on a memo pad as he listened.

Shrewd, slippery sons-of-bitches, both of them, Russell Stanton thought.

He had the duplicate annotated sets of his three successive "reports" laid out on the desk in front of him.

Goddamned clever, he admitted. The obfuscations and false trails would have been enough to deceive him indefinitely—if he hadn't known from the start that he was being deliberately misled and wasn't looking for the 10 percent of truth in the 90 percent of camouflage.

Normally, it would have been overkill, for neither Jemel Karami nor Brian Lockhart had any reason to suspect that he was looking.

Now, however, Russ finally had enough raw material for analysis and deciphering. Especially since it was at last plain that Karami and Lockhart each created his own particular varieties of red herrings. Jemel's were like his basic nature: freewheeling, wideswinging, impulsive. Lockhart also conformed to type. His were methodical, meticulous, overly logical.

This simplified the task of separating the horseshit from the stew, Russ told himself. Jemel's blindgrab queries regarding such matters as Hancock Oil's stateside refinery operations could all be discarded as pure, scatter-shot horse manure. That done, Lockhart's annotations were transformed into truth-test mirrors. His reasoned, outwardly reasonable, interest in terrain and geological surveys, seismographic testing, the mechanics of drilling operations, field and lease storage and similar facets of the oil business were reflected as diversionary feints. As more horseshit.

The process of picking the annotations apart, weighing them against one another, matching parallels, identifying inconsistencies and incongruities, checking and rechecking required several hours. In the end, Russ Stanton was satisfied that he'd discerned the major ingredients of the stew. What Karami and Lockhart really wanted to know were:

1. The actual versus the book value of the major oil properties in Saudi Arabia, Kuwait, Muscat and Oman, and the Trucial States.

2. The gross annual production of the existing fields (the true gross as opposed to the published figures).

3. Estimates of the actual (as against the reported) profit margins and profits.

4. Accounting methods employed in financing, depreciation, cost determination, and royalty computation.

To here, almost legitimate, Russ reflected. Almost, They were already probing beyond the limits necessary if they only intended to go after oil-company banking business. What followed were the giveaways.

5. The locations of the most important and the most vulnerable oil company installations and facilities.

6. Which of those installations and facilities, if put out of commission for any reason, would cause the most serious disruptions in operations, yet could be repaired or replaced most readily and at least cost.

7. What were the oil companies' own security measures, and what arrangements did they have with host governments to augment security in the event of emergency.

8. Which companies had experienced the most difficulty with native labor.

The pieces were falling into place, Stanton mused grimly. Not all, by any means, but some. R. D. Whitehead had foreseen an oil grab. That was certainly confirmed. He'd said it would be on a large scale. That was an understatement.

Furthermore, the grab would be violent, involve destruction and bloodshed. No doubt bigger Nuqayr incidents—many in number and coordinated to cause the maximum effect, Russ reasoned.

A thousand and one questions—questions—questions, my ass, enigmas—remained. First of all, what was the underlying strategy? There were several possibilities. The aim could be to scare oilmen and oil companies so badly that they'd sell out to some fake syndicate—or a number of bogus companies—organized anonymously by Incombank. Not very probable, Russ decided. R. D. had mentioned that Jemel was spread out, and such a deal would require tremendous amounts of cash.

He went through a dozen other alternatives. Only one seemed to cover. Incom—and Karami and Lockhart—were working with dissidents. Their intent was to foment a major Middle Eastern upheaval, not only rock the boat but sink it. Then a takeover.

It covered, but it raised more questions than it answered. Years of Middle Eastern experience had taught Russell Stanton that any three Arabs made three factions, each violently opposed to the next. Even supposing—and I have to do some fancy imagining to suppose—that some group had been organized in any given Arab country, what about the others? That those in two or more would work in concert was an impossibility.

Assume the impossible is possible, he ruminated. *Take it for granted. Raiders, terrorists, revolutionaries —give them any label—couldn't carry off an operation of such scope without trained leaders and modern arms, ammunition, explosives. The Saudis and Kuwaitis were on constant alert for shipments of weapons. Only a few rifles here, a machine gun or two there, ever dribbled through to dissident elements. Hell, some of the Bedou were still using ancient single-shot rifles—even muzzleloaders!*

Russ picked up the papers on his desk, read through the notes made by Jemel and Brian yet again. Now, he was struck by the undercurrent of urgency he found in them. The 10 percent was masked, but when the meaningless 90 percent was disregarded, it became clear that they were pushing, pressuring him. What they wanted to know, they wanted to know fast—much faster than it had previously seemed.

He tossed the reports back on the desk.

Karami and Lockhart were in a hell of a hurry. And if time is closing in on them, it's closing in on me, too, he reasoned. *R. D.'s guess was off—and so, probably, was the one I made to Marv Saturday at Baalbek. And that throws everything off—and all preconceived plans out of the window.*

They're working against a tight deadline—and I don't know a thing that would be of any real use. The Whitehead idea that I should play along until I "learn the detailed pattern" has to be junked. Play detective —snoop around? Sneak into Karami's office and rifle the files?

I wouldn't get past the door!

There was only one out.

"Go for broke," Russ said aloud. *Scared?* He asked himself silently—and answered the same way. *Sure I'm scared. Those two killed forty-eight people just to get the forty-ninth, Abdul el Muein. They engineered the shelling of Ramim—how many dead there? Twenty, thirty? How many others—to say nothing of Lloyd Emmerick and Shorty Vosburgh—and how many more to come?*

The bastards wouldn't hesitate a second to have me . . .

"Go for broke," he repeated.

He glanced at his watch. Four-thirty. He'd been mulling and thinking straight through since just after ten. He'd lost all track of time, and he hadn't dictated a word. He wasn't going to dictate anything, either.

He looked around his office. There was no typewriter. Top executives didn't use their own typewriters. That's what secretaries and stenographers were for. Russ buzzed his executive secretary on the intercom.

"Yes, Mr. Stanton?"

"Get a typewriter table and typewriter wheeled in here right away."

"Mr. Stanton . . ."

"Goddamn it, do as I tell you!"

The table and typewriter arrived within moments. "Thanks," Russ said. "Now leave me alone—and close the door behind you."

He pulled the wheeled typewriter stand close to

his Workcomfort chair, rolled a single sheet of paper
into the platen. The executive chair wasn't designed to
permit its occupant to use a typewriter, and he worked
clumsily. Nonetheless, he finished the memorandum to
Jemel Karami in fifteen minutes. He pulled it out of
the machine, read it over, scrawled his name on the
bottom. He folded the paper, placed it inside an envelope, sealed the flap, printed "Mr. Jemel Karami" on
its face with his pen.

He got up and went out into the executive secretary's office.

"Do you have any Scotch tape?"

She did. He tore off several lengths, plastered
them over the flap and back seams of the envelope.

"I want this on Mr. Karami's desk at nine tomorrow morning. Not two minutes before and not two
minutes after. At nine sharp."

"Yes, Mr. Stanton." A pause. "Do you have any
recording tapes for the girls today?"

"No," Russ replied. "Everything Mr. Karami
needs to know is inside that envelope."

Jemel was going out to a dinner party, and Russ
saw him for only a few minutes that evening. He did
not mention his day's work or the message he'd typed.
He'd let Jemel find it on his desk in the morning.

8

Beirut. Tuesday, May 21st.

"There's an envelope on your desk, Mr. Karami,"
Jemel's secretary informed him. "Someone from Mr.
Stanton's office brought it down and said it was per-
sonal—and important."

What the hell, Jemel thought. *Stanton playing
jokes?* The envelope was thick with tape. He ripped
open one end with annoyance, jerked out the sheet of

paper inside, unfolded it, and began to read. His back jolted ramrod-straight; his eyes narrowed to slits.

A hand shot out, depressed an intercom key. "Have Mr. Lockhart come to my office immediately!" he barked before his secretary could speak.

Lockhart appeared moments later.

"Sit down and read this!" Jemel rapped, thrusting a typewritten sheet at him. Lockhart took the paper, sat and began to read.

Memo:
To: Mr. Jemel Karami
Subject: PROPOSAL TO SAVE TIME AND TROUBLE.
From: Russell T. Stanton

Dear Jimmy,

1. While I don't like disagreeing with the boss, I've come to the conclusion the old Dunhill College around-the-table system would beat the one we've got going all hollow. Natch, Brian Lockhart would sit in where Marv used to be when we were starry-eyed freshmen.

2. We could get to the points you want to know a damned sight faster than by having me dictate reels of tripe that doesn't really interest you any more than a dissertation on the formulae and techniques of zymurgy.

3. For example, I've wasted hours describing how to spud a well, fish for a twist-off and operate blow-out valves—and similar nonsense. Sitting across a table, I could tell you in three minutes that the Saudi labor delegate to Whitehead MidEast hates both the company and King Feisal. For a thousand bucks—cash—he'll call every native laborer out on strike. For ten, he'll have them stage the goddamnedest riot you ever imagined. Almost in the same breath, I could throw in a choice piece of inside dope about how Shelby Oil's regional manager at Ghawar punks his houseboys—and will give away his company's all in trade to anyone who threatens to tell the home office about his paraphiliac practices (buggery, to you).

4. In other words, Jimmy I read you loud and clear—but you've been missing my message completely. I wouldn't mind owning my own oil company—or a fair-sized piece of one—a-tall. I'm not sending a copy of this to Brian, but between us, I have a sneaking hunch he's probably picked up one or two of my ultra-high-frequency signals. We ex-majors seem to operate on the same wavelengths.

5. If this tees you off, you can consider it my resignation—and I don't know a thing.

Russ

Lockhart chuckled. "Can't fathom why you're in a flap, Jimmy," he said, waving the memo. "You're the one who touted Stanton as being brilliant at analyzing the complex, reducing it to essentials. He's even better than you believed. Saw through all our smoke screens." He stroked his moustache. "He's even right about what he says in his fourth paragraph. I did sense something—and mentioned it to you, in a round-about fashion."

Jemel's anger had not subsided. "How can we trust him now?"

"He's already proved he can be trusted—provided he gets a share of the profits," Brian shrugged. "You were searching for ideas about how to keep him on—and he's volunteering!"

"We . . ."

"Jimmy, if you have doubts, resolving them is a simple matter. You tell him just so much—and no more, observe his reactions. Then, to provide all the insurance needed, we simply take him with us tomorrow night—to be present when the Damascus and Cairo Export Co.'s specialists prepare our canned goods. If he balks—there can be an accident. If he takes it in stride, we'll be certain he's with us . . ."

"And he'll be in it as deeply as we are," Jemel finished the sentence, suddenly cool, relaxed—even pleased.

"Implicated and equally guilty are the words you want," Lockhart murmured. "I'll go a step further. I'll wager he'll come through as well as either of us. Stanton is tougher and harder than you think. I recognized that the day I first met him."

"Maybe he is," Jemel mused aloud. "I want proof, though." He flicked an intercom switch. "Tell Mr. Stanton that Mr. Lockhart and I would like to see him up here right away." He neutralized the switch. "We'll give him the overall picture, but not many details until after tomorrow night," he said to Lockhart. "If he stands up then, we'll still play safe—keep him in the dark about Saturday and how Pan-Arab will deliver the guns."

9

Beirut. Wednesday, May 22nd.

It was dusk, and the three men sat in Jemel's bar lounge. Russ was aware of the steadily mounting tension in Jemel and Brian Lockhart. They were going somewhere—exactly where and why, they hadn't revealed—and Russ was to go with them. They would leave at nine-thirty. Forty minutes more.

Jemel paced nervously. Lockhart had downed three drinks, was working on his fourth, and he fidgeted. *Not like either of them,* Stanton thought, his apprehension increasing.

I managed to force the issue, and while I'm much further ahead than I was, or would have been if I hadn't taken the big chance, I'm still far behind them.

Karami and Lockhart had given him the broad outlines of their scheme yesterday. Simultaneous "popular uprisings" in the oil-rich Arab countries and sheikhdoms. Overthrow of existing governments. Their replacement by "nationalist" juntas and the seizure of oil-company properties—with an Incombank-organized consortium to operate them under management contracts. A job guaranteed to pay him half-a-million or more a year in salary and in profit sharing—if he played along.

Stanton had agreed. Convincingly. And he'd spent the rest of Tuesday and most of Wednesday answering their now-straightforward questions, giving them every bit of data they desired—adding more, tossing in additional facts that would help strengthen their hand.

I'd got less than I hoped in return, Russ berated himself. *I might have found out more if I'd used different angles of approach, but no matter how I tried, none presented themselves. I still haven't a clue when they plan to pull the plug or any of the key specifics that Whitehead must have before he can take countermeasures.*

To top it all, there was tonight's mysterious trip. Where—and for what purpose? The possibility that it might be a gangster-style one-way ride for Russell T. Stanton had not escaped him.

Jemel ceased his pacing, went to the bar, poured himself a stiff whisky. That was something else. The barman had been sent packing an hour before.

"You, Russ?" Jemel asked.

Stanton looked at the half-filled glass in his fist.

"I advise you to get a couple more under your belt before we leave," Brian Lockhart spoke up. "You'll need them."

Russ emptied his glass, got to his feet and went to the bar. "Okay," he agreed, keeping his voice even. "Only I wish you people would tell me what this is all about. It's like a scene from a fifth-rate movie."

Jemel gave him a cold stare, shoved a bottle towards him.

"Go on—tell him, Jimmy," Lockhart said.

"No!"

"Why not? There're only a few minutes to go before we leave." He pulled open the left side of his jacket. He was carrying a gun in a shoulder holster. "There's nothing he can do."

Jesus Christ! Russ Stanton froze, the bottle in his hand. It was a scene from a fifth-rate movie—but it wasn't a movie. His muscles tensed. If he could throw the bottle at Lockhart . . .

"No intent to do you any harm, Russ," Lockhart said easily. He wasn't drunk, but he wasn't sober either. "Preventive medicine, solely. To discourage you from doing anything foolish—even though I've made a bet with Jimmy that you won't." He looked from Russ to Jemel. "Give him the gin."

Stanton swallowed, poured his drink, replaced the bottle on the bar.

"Since you're so damned eager to talk, you do it, *major*," Jemel said, edgy, sneering. He turned away from them both, stared at the bottles behind the bar.

"We're going to watch some people get killed," Brian said. "In cold blood. It'll be unpleasant—so we're fortifying ourselves. With this." He drained his glass, held it up empty. "I'm sure you had occasion to do the same during the war."

"Often." Russ forced the words through his constricted throat. "Booze before the battle—or whatever." He picked up the bottle, crossed to Lockhart's chair, sloshed more scotch into the glass, returned to the bar, leaned against it.

Good man, Lockhart thought. *Cold.* "A regrettable bit of butchery, but with a purpose."

"You're talking too damned much!" Jemel exclaimed, whirling around.

"No he isn't, Jimmy," Russ declared. "As long as no one's going to take a shot at me, I'd rather not have surprises. I like to have a little warning of what to expect."

Jemel lapsed into a surly silence. Brian began to speak again.

They took the Rolls, Jemel driving, Russ Stanton beside him, Brian Lockhart in back, the threat of his holstered pistol never mentioned aloud, yet implicit. *At that, it was a help*, Russ thought, *a sort of counterbalance for the horror I feel, for the God-awful sense of frustration that comes from knowing I can't do a thing to stop what's going to happen—and that I'll have to stand, watch, hear . . .*

They took the highway leading east to Hammana for ten miles—10.3 according to the odometer, on which Russ kept an eye. They were in the foothills behind Beirut. It was dark, and the car's headlights swept left as Jemel turned off the highway on to an unsurfaced secondary road. Another 1.8 miles—Stanton was memorizing the distances—and a right turn on to what was nothing more than a deep-rutted dirt track. Hillside wasteland. Straggles of trees. Rocks. Dry bushes. For six-tenths of a mile.

"There they are." Jemel's tone flat. His foot on the brake pedal. Two men with Russian-style burp guns stepping from darkness into the headlight beams, hurrying forward to the car, one on each side.

Jemel switched off the engine, pulled up the handbrake, got out. A rapid exchange in Arabic, the words indistinguishable. The men with the guns nodding respectfully.

"We leave the car here." Jemel had stuck his head and shoulders through the open window. He switched off the headlights. Brian was already out of the car, waiting for Russ.

Stanton opened his door, climbed down, acutely aware that Lockhart was staying close to him.

". . . *la, karibi*—it is near," Russ heard one of the burp-gun-carrying men say to Jemel.

They walked less than a hundred yards around a small knob of rocky earth. On the other side, flashlights. Men. Two Dodge panel trucks. Russ could make out the letters painted on the side of the nearest truck: "Damascus & Cairo Export Co. S.A.L."—in English, French and Arabic.

Russ estimated there were fifteen men—including the two who had accompanied them—in the group. All were heavily armed. Lockhart and Jemel left him behind, went forward a few paces and spoke to a black-moustached Arab in a business suit who was apparently the leader. Russ could not hear what they said. The Arab raised his voice, rasped out some guttural orders. Men responded. Two turned on the truck headlights, which lit up a large section of the rock-studded rise in the ground that now appeared to be almost like a wall. An execution wall. Others opened the back doors of one panel truck.

They came forward, into the light, carrying four heavy, limp bundles.

The bundles were men. Or had been, before they were beaten into semi- or complete unconsciousness.

"Our canned goods." It was Lockhart's voice. He'd returned to where Russ Stanton stood. "Notice the uniforms."

Stanton's insides were heaving. A hundred, a thousand, thoughts jetted through his mind. All worthless. A single move and Lockhart or any of a dozen others would gun him down. His death would not save the lives of the four Beirut Jews who had been grabbed, forced to put on Israeli commando uniforms and then battered senseless. They'd be killed anyway.

Russ thrust his hands deep into his trousers pockets to prevent Lockhart from seeing his clenched fists. He clenched them hard, stabbing his fingernails deep into the flesh of his palms, feeling blood.

The four bundles were dumped on the ground. One moved feebly. A pitiful groan came from the mouth of another—a mouth smashed, cut, the lips swollen huge.

"The PLF buggers in Jordan are taking care of the three who're supposed to make the attack on Hussein," Brian Lockhart said. Reflected light showed the glint of half-drunken sadism in his eyes.

"Brian." It was a nothing-chance, but a chance just the same. "Look at those men." Russ fought to control his voice. "They resemble commandos about the way Twiggy resembles a circus fat lady. I recommend you have these PLF guys take 'em back to whatever gutter they were fished from—and some reasonable substitutes found." Any delay. Any delay at all. If the massacre could be prevented tonight, maybe something could be done by tomorrow.

"They are a sad, puny lot, aren't they?" Lockhart laughed. "These PLF heroes picked the weakest and most helpless they could find."

The butchering would start at any moment.

"You're missing the point, Brian!" Russ said urgently. "Anyone seeing the—the bodies afterward will realize it's a put-up job." He grabbed wildly at straws. "Suppose foreign correspondents—or maybe even the U.N.—investigate . . ."

"No fear. Abdul Kamal will control the Lebanese investigation. Won't be a soul who'll look beyond the fact they're Jews and in Israeli uniforms." He edged forward. "Be all over in a minute now."

Some of the Arab guerrillas were propping the four uniformed Jews up into more-or-less standing positions against the side of the little hillock. When they'd done the best they could, they moved away quickly.

"Brian . . ."

Russ Stanton's voice was drowned out by the sudden bark and pound of rifles, pistols and sub-machine guns. Bullets tore into the earth around the four men, struck rocks, whining off in ricochet—and chewed into human flesh and bone.

Lead slugs ripped into one man's chest. He pitched forward. The third in line was gut-shot by the first bullet that struck him, and a long, agonized scream came from his throat—to be cut off by a hammered burp-gun burst. The other two died silently, sliding or slumping down.

Blood gushed and spurted from wounds. The entrails of a man whose belly had been punched open by several bullets were spilling out, and the corpse next to him slid sideways, falling with its face pressed into the ghastly tangle of bullet-shredded intestines.

The shooting had stopped. The PLF terrorists were laughing and jabbering, pounding each other's backs. Brian Lockhart moved closer to the four mangled corpses. Jemel and the Arab in the business suit also came forward to examine them.

It gave Russ an opportunity to edge away for a moment. He walked unsteadily to the nearest panel truck, leaned against it, fought down the urge to vomit, used main force on his willpower to control himself, to prevent himself from making the insane mistake of trying to grab a burp gun from some guerrilla. *I swear —I swear by whatever there is, by everything there is—that I'll get even for you,* he said to the dead.

The black-moustached leader barked more orders. His men quieted down, began to obey. Russ remained where he was as a group of them hurried past him. They dug into the back of the truck, returned with heavy, waterproof canvas tarpaulins and two or three shovels.

The bodies were rolled into individual tarpaulins. The shovels were used to turn the earth, hide the pools of blood. The canvas-covered cadavers were carried back, heaved inside the truck.

"Stanton!" It was Lockhart's voice. "Where are you?"

"Right here." Russ eased himself shakily away from the truck.

"All over. We're ready to go."

Jemel said nothing until they had returned to where they'd left the Rolls. "You drive, Brian," he said. He climbed into the back.

Lockhart got behind the wheel. Russ took the same position he had on the trip from Beirut. "Abdulrahim knows his business," Brian remarked, starting the engine and turning on the headlights. "Y'know, he even thought to put *mezzuzehs* into the pockets of all those Jews."

"Abdulrahim? *Mezzuzehs?*" Russ asked, feigning casualness with immense effort.

"Um. Abdulrahim's the black-moustached chap. Heads Damascus & Cairo Export. *Mezzuzehs*'re like Jewish religious medals." He snickered, spoke louder for Jemel's benefit. "The Jewish equivalents of *sibahs*, like the one Jimmy carries. When they're found on the bodies, they'll drive home the religious issue—*jihad*, for certain."

Jemel spoke curtly. "Get us back to Beirut quickly. You two are through for the night. I still have to meet Kamal."

The Rolls-Royce was parked a thousand yards from the ornate traditional Moorish palace on the southeast outskirts of Beirut.

The dashboard light was a dim bluish glow. Just enough to illuminate the clock. Three minutes before one.

"The truck should be delivering the bodies now," Jemel told the oily, exceedingly nervous man who sat in the front seat beside him. "The shooting will start precisely at one o'clock and last for a minute and thirty seconds. We drive into the grounds about a minute later, Abdul. You rush into your house. I'll drive away immediately. Provided you've given instructions that will be followed, the first police should not arrive before one-oh-five." His eyes were glued to the clock. "Remember to ask about the safety of your servants and if any of your heroic guards were killed or wounded before you say anything else. And—there it is!"

Kamal flinched, seemed to slide lower in the seat, as though to protect himself, as the night was rocked by the pound of automatic weapons and the sharper crackle of rifle fire.

The din rose, fell, rose again.

A minute.

Jemel started the engine, counting himself. One. Two. Three . . .

"How much longer?" a shaky plea.

"Quiet!"

. . . twenty-seven . . .

The firing was already ragged. A second later, it stopped. Then there was one last rifle shot.

The Rolls surged forward, gathering speed. Jemel was doing over sixty when the gateway to Kamal's mansion loomed ahead. He braked hard, swung into the grounds. PLF men dressed in the uniforms and red berets of Beirut's notorious "riot-and-subversion-control" Squad 16 milled around the grounds. They had been told to expect the Rolls-Royce, made no effort to stop it. Jemel drove fast along the graveled driveway. Shit! The fools had dumped one of the bodies squarely in the middle of the driveway. No time to stop. The right-hand wheels bumped twice. He skidded to a stop in front of the entrance. The headlights revealed windows shattered and walls stitched by bullets.

"Go!" he snarled at Kamal, who sat immobile. Jemel leaned across him, opened the door, practically shoved him out of the car. "Inside the house!"

He slammed the car door shut after Kamal was clear, swung the Rolls around in the broad turning circle, stepped on the accelerator. This time it was the left-side wheels that bumped twice.

10

Beirut. Thursday, May 23rd.

The miracle of modern communications, Jemel mused. Full-blown news broadcasts describing any upheaval from all parts of the world poured back into its epicenter almost as soon as the first bulletins were dispatched from it.

He had returned to his house before two, slept three hours and was showered, shaved and listening to the radio before six. Every station broadcasting in every language was already blaring . . .

. . . only alert action by guards saved the life of the Lebanese political leader. The Israeli commandos, in full uniform, penetrated the grounds in which his official residence is located, spraying it with sub-machine-gun fire. Lebanese authorities have revealed that the four Israelis, all of whom were killed, also carried deadly explosive charges which it is presumed they intended to use in . . ."

Try the VOA station beaming from Salonika.

". . . a simultaneous attempt to assassinate Jordan's King Hussein apparently misfired before the Israeli commandos got within a mile of the king's palace in Amman. Early and fragmentary reports from the Jordanian capital indicate that three Israeli soldiers were intercepted and shot down at the intersection of two residential streets located . . ."

Balls. The Jordanian PLF had fouled up—or Hussein had been even jumpier than Kamal. The bodies should have been dumped right outside the palace, and the gun battle staged there. He dialed the BBC Middle East service.

". . . and many observers have expressed dismay that such an attempt be made on the life of the Lebanese statesman"—ah, Kamal was a "statesman" now —"who has long been considered a moderate in his views on Israel. Lebanese officials have suggested that the abortive attack was in reprisal for a terrorist shelling of the Israeli town of Ramim on May third . . ."

Ties together beautifully. Change bands, pick up the States direct.

". . . Lebanon, Jordan and other Arab states' representatives to the United Nations have already declared they would seek a special session to consider what action can be taken . . ."

That's fading. Good. Here's another.

". . . Israeli Defense Minister General Moshe Dayan held a predawn press conference and flatly denied that Israeli troops had been involved in the two assassination attempts . . ."

Not even the Jews would believe him.

". . . However, foreign correspondents who have been permitted to view the bodies of the attackers unanimously report that the dead men wore the uniforms of Israeli commandos. That none carried identification papers is, according to military experts, customary practice with commando-type units in all armies. All such documents are left behind by troops engaged in raiding or surprise-attack operations. In Beirut, authorities displayed what objects they had found on the bodies. These included cigarettes known to be made in Israel, a map of Beirut printed in Hebrew, and several Jewish religious talismans . . ."

Jemel's smile was predatory as he turned off the radio.

Jemel watched Russ Stanton very closely across the breakfast table.

Stanton looked bad. Haggard. Shaky. He usually ate heartily in the mornings. Now he was eating nothing. Not even drinking his coffee. A sign of dangerous weakness? Prod and see.

"A little queasy?" Jemel inquired, moving the silver dish on which the *labeneh* was served closer to himself.

Grip tight, Russ thought. *Tighter.* "Sure. Didn't sleep at all last night. Why should I kid you? I'm scared shitless."

That could be a debit or credit. Depends. "You surprise me."

"I do, huh!" Russ exclaimed, glaring. "Listen, Jimmy!" he said, loudly, angrily. "I'm a very junior partner in this venture—and I've gone up to my neck in it, knowing exactly what I was doing!" God, it was good to vent rage, even if it was only to cover up and maybe pry another splinter of information loose! "The trouble is if something slips up—if one of those characters last night opens his yap, starts to brag around what he and his buddies did, we're cooked! And you're *'surprised'* that I'm scared shitless?"

So far, a credit, Jemel judged. The reaction checked out against the other facets of the new Russell T. Stanton. A man who'd sell out—even for a half million plus a year—would be scared. Of losing what he'd sold out for—and losing his hide. It checked out —and showed there'd be no problems keeping Stanton tame and docile in the future.

"Tranquilize your nerves, Russ. I own Kamal, and Kamal runs Lebanon. He'll keep us all safe." Unsaid, but implied: *Your only danger is that I tell Kamal you're expendable.*

Make an attempt to goad him. "Lebanon!" Russ snorted. "One country out of how many? There's Jordan. You don't own Hussein!"

"I can depend on Abdulrahim and the PLF to keep the lid screwed tight there."

"Abdulrahim and the PLF can't screw many lids in Saudi Arabia or Kuwait or the Trucial States! From what you and Brian told me, they're the . . ."

"Now, that's where you're all wrong," Jemel grinned. It couldn't hurt to throw Russ a scrap of reassurance. It'd bring returns. "Abdulrahim and the PLF furnished the cadres—the 'liaison men' is the neat euphemism Brian and I use to describe them—who've done all the work for us with the dissidents."

Keep going, Russ begged silently. *Keep talking, you son of a bitch.*

"That's why there's organization, coordination—why we can use inside dope like you've been supplying and rely on rebel factions to hit at point 'B' instead of 'A' and blow a feeder line rather than a tank-farm when . . ."

Jemel's majordomo entered the dining room. "*Pardon,* m'sieu Karami. M'sieu Hruska is here. He says it is imperative that he speak to you."

Russ had never met Tom Hruska, although he knew him to be the president of Pan-Arab Airways, but he wished that Hruska had suffered a heart attack —anything—before reaching the house. He'd arrived at the worst moment, breaking into Karami's flow of words, interrupting his train of thought.

Jemel frowned. Whatever Hruska wanted to talk about, he didn't want Russ Stanton to hear it. To stay on the safe side, Stanton had to be kept in ignorance of the Saturday deadline and the mass airlift of munitions.

"Where is he?" Jemel asked.

"Waiting in the foyer, m'sieu."

"Excuse me a minute, Russ." Jemel got up from the table. "I'll see him out there."

Goddamn it—and goddamn Hruska, Russ thought.

The house was quiet. Voices carried, if only faintly.

". . . mobs forming in the city, streets cordoned off!"

A voice—doubtless Tom Hruska's—was raised, excited. Russ paid little attention.

Jimmy's voice now, a murmur, practically inaudible.

"But all that equipment is supposed to come over from the docks today, Jimmy . . . the mobs . . . you never know . . ."

The slaughter last night, Russ was thinking, the

words spoken by the excited, worried voice barely registering.

". . . we have to separate and store according to lot . . . or we'll never be able to load everything Saturday . . ."

More murmurs from Jemel, and the man—Hruska —to whom he was speaking dropped his tone to a level that could no longer be heard.

Russ tried to drink some coffee. He gagged on it, set the cup back on its saucer. The front door closed. Footsteps. Jemel returning.

"Sorry, Russ. Seems there are mobs gathering in Beirut. Hruska was driving from his place towards the airport and saw them. He was afraid they might riot and go after banks—mobs usually do."

That isn't what I heard, Stanton reflected. *Hruska was talking about some equipment coming from the docks. Or maybe he did mention banks, and I didn't hear him. No matter.*

"I've got to run, Russ," Jemel said. He wasn't sitting down at the table. "Have to put the clamp on Kamal, make him control the mobs. We can't afford to have wild riots and pogroms here. I'll see you later at Incom Central."

He obviously doesn't want me to ride with him. That's good, Russ thought. "I'll be along in an hour or so. That okay?" He needed the time to do a couple of things. "I'll take a cab, and if I can't get one, borrow one of the cars, if it's all right with you."

"Sure."

Russ waited until Jemel had been driven away in the Rolls by Ahmed. He telephoned for a taxi. Yes, they were still operating. To Mr. Karami's house? Within minutes!

Stanton made a hasty double-check of his wallet. Eight hundred in cash. American money. Much more than he'd need.

"Yaiziji's on Hamra Street," he told the cab driver.

A Westerner can buy a handgun in Beirut as easily as he can a package of cigarettes. Normally, he must show his passport and have its number and his name and description copied down on "Central Gendarmerie Form 92." However, if he pays a 50 percent premium over the tagged price, the "sporting goods" dealer will write down a passport number, name, and description invented on the spot. In times of crisis, both original prices and premiums double.

Yaiziji's Sporting Goods was open for business, and the base prices had already been doubled. There was crisis in the air, talk of mobs and riots . . .

Russ looked over the stock of handguns rapidly. For himself, he chose a Walther P-38—a leftover from the war, but new—an automatic that had been used by Nazi officers and greatly admired by American troops. It was a deadly accurate weapon, and could be made to fire full automatic, simply by depressing the sear.

"I'll take it—and fifty cartridges," Russ said. He didn't know of any weapon with which Marv Jacobs was familiar except the standard, Army issue Colt .45 automatic. It would have to be an automatic for Marv. He couldn't reload a revolver with only one good hand. Yaiziji's had only two—both used. Russ stripped them both down, chose the best. "This, too—with fifty rounds and two spare magazines."

"Your passport, sir?" the Armenian sales clerk requested.

"Oh!" Russ went through the set routine, tapping his breast pocket. "I must've left it at the hotel." He took out his wallet instead.

"That will be five hundred dollars, sir," the clerk said smoothly.

"Two separate boxes, wrapped neatly in plain paper." Russ counted out the bills. "An extra twenty for you if you make the packages look like they contain anything else and do it in ten minutes flat."

"Yes, sir." He produced two shoeboxes—and crinkly new wrapping paper imprinted with the name of the Tamima Shoe Company, "Specialists in Shoes for Men, Ground Floor, Nasouil Building, 25 Allenby Street." One of the best shoestores in Beirut. There was a question in his eye. "Forty if you use the paper, too," Russ said. Assent replaced question.

The driver of the next taxi Russ took was delighted that his passenger spoke Arabic, relieved to hear he wanted to go to the Saint Georges.

The angry crowds forming throughout Beirut were nowhere near that area, he said. The people were furious at the *yahud*—the Jews—and might well wreak their vengeance on *yahudi* shops and sack the Jewish quarter. But police and troops would keep them away from the better-class sections of the city. Even though there were many foreign Jews in some of the big hotels. Especially the Saint Georges. *Ya di'a'no*—it was a pity—but the foreign *yahudi* would have to be protected!

Russ paid him off at the hotel entrance, entered the lobby. He and Marvin Jacobs had agreed they wouldn't risk being seen together in Beirut unless the situation came to a final head—or there was a serious emergency.

"Emergency there is," Russ told Marv, whom he found in his suite. "And I've forced one issue. Now I'm going to do my damnedest to force the rest within the next few days." He nodded toward the door. "Lock it, huh?"

He told Marv everything he'd learned—and what he'd failed to find out. But he omitted mentioning the previous night's experience with Jemel and Lockhart. He didn't want Jacobs boiling over—yet. He'd tell him later. When they'd both have to be at peak fuck-the-consequences pitch.

Stanton unwrapped the shoebox containing the Colt. Marvin's eyes grew wide when he saw the automatic.

"You think it might wind up like that?"

"Right now, I don't *think* anything. I just want to be ready for it." Russ took out the magazines and began loading them with cartridges. "You should be able to change magazines with the artificial hand."

Jacobs laughed. "You're slipping. You forget I

led an infantry company with one arm in '48 and '49.
I can even punch loose rounds into machine-gun-belt
loops faster with one arm than most guys can with
two."

Russ looked embarrassed. "Yeah. I guess I did
forget." He'd finished loading the last magazine
though, slid it up into the handle of the Colt, put gun,
spare magazines, and leftover cartridges into the box
which he rewrapped with care. "You can leave this
lying around without making any of the chambermaids
curious."

"What now?" Marv asked.

"I'd like to have you get sick. A bad cold or the
drizzles. Nothing serious. Only enough to make you
buy up a load of drugstore medicine and hang around
the hotel for four-five days. I have to be sure I can get
hold of you immediately at any time."

"I'll find an excuse." Marv's thin face was grave
"You have an idea?"

"Like I said, I'm going to try and force things."
How, or whether I can, I haven't a clue. He took the
other shoebox with him when he left.

Downstairs in the Saint Georges lobby, Russ no
ticed a turmoil. It couldn't have reached such pro
portions in the twenty minutes he'd spent with Marv
I was preoccupied when I came in, he reflected. *I too.
it for granted the piled-up luggage and the peopl
surging around the reservation and concierge's desk
were normal, usual hotel morning check-ins-and-outs*

Now he realized people and baggage were all out
going, and the twenty minutes sufficed to make their
numbers and the clamorous atmosphere of apprehen
sion grow. Every flight leaving Beirut was overbooked
Tourists, businessmen—everyone who could—wanted
to get out before the crisis brought on by the assassina
tion attempt erupted into something worse. The shriek
of sirens throughout Beirut—evidence that the police
troops and ambulances were being rushed to troubl
spots—sawed away at the people's nerves. Their fear
mounted.

"Ladies and gentlemen! *Mesdames et messieurs!*

harried hotel executive was trying to announce above
he excited babble. "We cannot make any airline reservations. It is utterly impossible to obtain a seat aboard
any aircraft! We have tried every line . . ."

Russ made his way through the milling, babbling
hotel guests, took a taxi from the rank outside the ho-
el. The driver said they would have to make a wide
detour in order to reach the Incom Central Tower. The
rue Georges Picot and other streets had been cordoned
off. The mobs were multiplying in size and number.

Russ Stanton put his shoebox in a desk drawer,
old his secretary to call Mr. Karami and Mr. Lockhart
and tell them he'd arrived and was ready to see them
whenever they wished.

"Neither of them are available," she reported a
few minutes later. "I understand they're in conference
in Mr. Karami's office with Mr. Hruska and gave instructions they're not to be disturbed under any circumstances."

Hruska? He was supposed to be on his way to the
airport more than an hour ago, Russ thought. With
several thousand people battling to reserve seats and
get out of Lebanon, that's where Hruska should be—at
he Pan-Arab Airways offices. The chaos there must be
fierce. A hell of a way for a man to run an airline,
he mused—and forgot about it.

There were some "Distributions to All Department Heads" memos and notices on his desk. He rifled
hrough them. To distract his brain, give it a brief rest,
rather than any other reason, for none really concerned
him. The Lebanese government was monitoring overseas cables, Telexes and telephone calls; therefore, until
further notice, no client's confidential business would
be mentioned in such communications. Military guards
would be provided to protect Incom Central and all
Lebanese branches of the bank by noon. No papers
or documents pertaining to bank business were to be
taken home by executives while the threat of civil disturbance remained . . .

Crap. He dumped all the slips into a wastebasket,
fed his mind back into the grinder.

Two gaping holes remained. Until they were filled, everything else he knew was worthless.

First, when and how would the rebels be receiving their weapons and, second, when would the "simultaneous popular uprisings" Jemel and Brian described begin? "Soon" was all that they had told him —and "soon" could mean tomorrow or two months from now.

That the dissidents did not yet have their arms and explosives was a foregone conclusion. Not even the tightest PLF-imposed discipline could hold down a dozen or more rebellious factions in several different countries and sheihdoms if the rebels had weapons in their possession. Arabs were emotional—hysterical—and they'd work themselves into a lather, try out their new guns on a neighboring tribe if no one else. Storing munitions in places like Kuwait and Saudi Arabia was almost impossible. Inspections were frequent, bribes and torture equally familiar—and effective—means of learning the locations of arms caches.

The material would have to be shipped to the dissidents at the last possible moment, delivered to the various groups at pretty much the same time. Difficult. The places in which Jimmy and Brian had seemed most interested were mainly well inland. The Suez Canal was still blocked, nothing could get through.

Overland? Railroads were, for all purposes, nonexistent. Truck convoys couldn't move fast enough, and would be subject to innumerable en-route inspections. Air freight was the only remaining answer. Jemel had Pan-Arab Airways, and there was a score or more limping nonsked airlines around Europe, North Africa and the Middle East that existed almost entirely on revenue from illicit air-freighting operations.

I've been over that before, Russ told himself. The nonskeds were out. Their planes didn't have the carrying capacity or the dependability—and no Arab country would give them clearance to overfly or land without having their cargoes inspected by someone at point of take-off.

Pan-Arab? I've mangled that possibility, too. Scheduled airlines operated between regular airports

nd regular airports had customs guards, government
fficials and bureaucrats swarming all over them. A
an-Arab plane crossing into, say, Sáudi Arabian air-
pace would require clearance. Its destination and ETA
/ould be known. When it landed, freight manifests
vould have to be handed over to customs officers—
/ho would check the load, haul it off to a customs
hed, at least spot-check even the most innocent-ap-
)earing shipping containers.

I've been through it with them often. Bring a keg
f nails in by air, and the Arab customs men would not
nly open the keg, but count each nail—and take
nonths doing it.

Still, if he was going to "force" any more issues,
e'd have to start the forcing somewhere. Thin and im-
)robable as the Pan-Arab Airways angle seemed, it
vas a point at which to start. The best, but only be-
ause he could think of no other. And damned near
ny other would be an improvement, Russ confessed
o himself.

Karami, Lockhart and Hruska were in confer-
nce in Jemel's office—or had been half an hour ago.
*4ll right. I'll go up to Jemel's suite and if the conference
sn't over, wait in the outer office until it breaks. I'll
eed a plausible excuse. I know. I'll suddenly "remem-
er" that the telephone-telegraph line connecting Jed-
ah with Medina and Riyadh passes two hundred yards
utside the Whitehead MidEast administrative em-
loyees' housing compound, and that a couple of men
an cut it, put it out of commission for days with a
ew minutes' work. That'll do for openers.*

"Mr. Karami is still in conference, Mr. Stanton,"
emel's administrative assistant told Russ. "I haven't
ny idea when he'll be through."

"I'll wait for him here," Stanton said. "It's rather
rgent I see him."

A long forty minutes passed.

Then the door to Jemel's private office opened.

". . . then you can count on it. Twenty-one-hun-
red Saturday . . ."

The same voice Russ had heard at Jemel's house

earlier. A man who looked like a tank-town college
tackle who'd begun to run to fat emerged, followed
by Brian Lockhart. Lockhart closed the door behind
him.

" 'Morning, Brian," Russ said, standing up.

"Good morning, Russ." Lockhart appeared a shade
nonplussed, made an immediate recovery. "You want
to see Jimmy, I take it."

"Uh, both of you, if you can spare the time."

"Yes. I think I can. Tom is leaving." He remembered Stanton and Hruska hadn't met. He introduced
them to each other.

"You must have a madhouse on your hands,"
Russ said sympathetically to Hruska. "I hear every
foreigner in Beirut's bellowing for reservations on the
very next flight out."

"There's a stampede, all right," Hruska agreed.
"These are the sort of things that make me wish I'd
never shifted to a desk job."

"Pilot?" Russ inquired, aware that Lockhart was
watching them both closely.

"Was. Four-striper. Checked out on everything
from DC-3's to DC-7's and Super-Connies." With
pride. "You fly?"

"A very little. All in the Piper-Cub class." Brian was getting restless. "Let's have lunch or a drink
one of these days, Tom," Russ said, shaking hands.
He and Lockhart went in to see Jemel.

". . . save for radio communication, that'll isolate
Jeddah," Russ concluded, displaying a sketch plan of
the housing compound and the cable route he'd drawn
while he spoke. He saw Jemel flick a glance at Lockhart;
it clearly asked, "Do we have time?" The split-second
look and blink Brian returned said with equal clarity,
"Yes—by a hair." *Not much help,* Russ thought glumly. *Can't judge how they pass on orders. May take
them several days to get them down to the right people
and receive confirmation they'd arrived and would be
followed.* He improvised another ounce of weight on his
forcing lever.

"I can make the job easy," he spoke up. "I'll write nd sign temporary I.D. letters and passes that'll alw whoever's going to cut the cable to enter the housg area and which can explain why they're roaming round the section."

"You're no longer with Whitehead MidEast," emel objected.

"I backdate a few weeks. The company won't ave got around to replacing all such papers with my ame on them yet. They'll be good."

Another exchange of glances between Karami and ockhart.

"Yes," Lockhart mused aloud, reaching for the ketch map. "Having that cable cut before midnight at . . ."

"Let me see that thing!" Jemel said, several shades oo loudly and suddenly. He snatched the sketch from rian's hand.

Did Lockhart almost blurt out something, Russ ondered. *Did he intend to say "before midnight Saturay"? Christ, if he did . . .*

"It's worth a try," Jemel said, casual almost to ne level of indifference. "If you want to make up the apers, fine. After lunch today, tomorrow—there's no eal rush."

He's studying me through a magnifying glass, Russ nought. *Nod, say yes, and clear out. In a hurry. Beore he reads me.*

"Okay. I'll pick a couple of names. I suppose any wo will do."

"Any two will do."

"I'll see you both later."

He departed with a feeling of helpless horror. Alnough it had not yet tripped all the contacts needed o close the circuit completely, the coin was dropping a his brain.

A "Saturday" evidently loomed very big in Jeel's plans. If it marked the beginning and was next aturday—the day after tomorrow—it was already too te for R. D. Whitehead or anyone else to prevent ne onrush. Even if the American or British ambassa-

dors would listen to Russell Stanton, they could onl
dither, promise to contact State Department or For
eign office.

Then what? More procrastination, maybe a bot
tom-level meeting somewhere along the line—an
nothing. Calling on Kuwaiti or Saudi diplomatic rep
resentatives in Lebanon would produce zero result
Arab bureaucracies were the slowest on earth, an
there was always the risk—more a certainty—tha
he'd draw some Arab diplomat who was himse
nose-deep in one kind of plot or another against hi
own government or who'd already been got at b
Karami.

Besides, what proof did he have? None. Only hi
word—and suppositions.

Then, whether it was going to be next Saturda
the Saturday after or any other—*I'm still not sure c
how the arms are going to be delivered,* Russ re
minded himself. True, despite all the arguments tha
could be mustered to the contrary, it *did* appear tha
Pan-Arab Airways was going to be the transporta
tion medium. But then there was Tom Hruska. Jeme
and Brian both held him in open contempt, and h
wasn't smart. That had been obvious from what he'
seen of the man during their short meeting. Hruska-
hell, he couldn't be trusted to run a wheelbarrow dow
the block. He was certainly one of the least likely type
in whom Jemel Karami would place any genuine tru
and confidence when something as big, as immens
and as immensely complex, as this was involved.

Returning to his office, Stanton sat, trying vainl
to massage life back into a brain that felt num
burned out. For want of anything better to do at th
moment, he pulled open the drawer into which he'
put the shoebox. He opened the box, loaded th
Walther P-38 clips, closed the box and rewrapped i
all inside the drawer.

It was painfully restrictive, frustratingly slo
work.

Fitting, he mused, and his big frame sagge
Symbolic. I'm doing with my hands what I'm doin

with my head. Fumbling in a box that's inside a drawer. Hemmed in. Walled in.

I'm in too far to quit. I'll keep trying, keep forcing—even if it does mean that I'll just run up against another wall. He tied the knot of the string on the now-rewrapped shoebox with a vicious jerk. He wished with raging desperation that it was a noose he was tying around Jemel Karami's neck.

11

Beirut. Friday, May 24th.

Russ Stanton gave a last bleak look at himself in the mirror before going downstairs for breakfast.

He'd had another hellish night. Sleep made possible only by Nembutals downed somewhere in the neighborhood of three-thirty. Sleep? Five hours of semicomatose bedclothes mangling, of battles with nightmares, with ghosts and fears.

Jemel had the radio on in the dining room.

". . . so far, Lebanese authorities have managed to maintain relative calm in the country. Sporadic outbreaks of violence, largely directed against the Jewish minority population, have been quelled by police and troops using tear gas . . ."

"Good morning, Russ." Jemel turned off the set. "Lebanon's become the center of attraction . . ."

"Aren't you worried there's too much attention on Lebanon?" *No alternative left but to force at every opportunity.* Russ sat down. *At least, I'll be able to eat this morning. Not much. Enough to keep him from thinking that I'm cracking.*

"The more, the happier I am," came the reply. "Did you get those papers finished yesterday?"

"Yes. Gave them to Brian." Russ pulled at

strings to form a grin. "Mind if I try some of your cheese-on-toast special?"

"Not at all. I warn you, it's habit-forming."

They went to Incom together. Police and military patrols were very much in evidence. Roadblocks had been set up, but Jemel Karami's Rolls-Royce was known, not stopped.

Russ couldn't ease himself away from Incom Central until mid-afternoon. Jemel had Lockhart alternately called down to his office, asking questions. They were filling in the last chinks.

"I'd like to take off the rest of the afternoon," Russ told Jemel around four. "Any objections?"

"No. Go ahead."

Russ went to his office, opened desk drawer and shoebox. The P-38 slid beneath his belt and trousers waistband without showing a bulge. Over on the left, fully covered by his jacket. A spare clip in right pocket, another in left, shoebox and wrapper in wastebasket.

He went downstairs. Lebanese banks stay open until four-thirty. He went to the Arab Bank down the street, cashed $2,000 worth of travelers' checks into American dollars. Next, he rented a new Ford Anglia from a car-agency. The agency wanted a "special extra deposit" of $200 "because of the increased insurance risk at the present unsettled moment." He paid it without argument.

His American passport and credentials identifying him as an executive of Incombank got him through the roadblocks easily—and with smart salutes from the cops and soldiers. The salutes were for his Incombank connection—not for his passport.

Russ drove to Beirut Airport, parked, went to the Pan-Arab Airways administrative offices, asked for Tom Hruska, was informed Mr. Hruska was out in the hangar area.

"I'll go find him."

"Afraid that isn't possible. No one is allowed there without special authorization. The unsettled situation, you understand."

My ass. "I'm Russ Stanton. Work with Mr. Karami. Can you reach Hruska?"

"Oh, sorry Mr. Stanton! I'll get him on the telecom."

Hruska, taking it for granted that Stanton had been sent by Jemel, rushed to the administrative offices, arriving red-faced and out of breath.

"Any place we can have a drink—alone?" Russ inquired.

"My office."

"Nope. Too many ears."

What the hell did Stanton want, Hruska wondered. "Our VIP lounge. Should be empty. Last flight just went out. Won't be another for two hours."

"Sounds better."

The airport terminal itself was jammed. People with tickets and reservations. Those with tickets only, begging or trying to bribe reservations. Some who had neither, were offering insane prices, pleading, making threats, using the "but-I'm-a-friend-of" whoever headed the particular airline in front of whose counter they stood, shoving, waving money, yammering . . .

The Pan-Arab Airways VIP lounge was deserted save for a bartender, a waitress and a forlorn couple evidently taking the long-wait sweat via the nerve-steadying cocktails route.

"I suggest the table in the far corner for us—and I want a gin and tonic for myself." Russ said with an arrogance he did not feel.

"Okay." Hruska cautious, noncommittal. He relayed Russ's order to the waitress, asked for a bourbon-and-water for himself. They went to the table Russ had indicated, sat, waited for the girl to bring the drinks and retreat to the bar. Now for the blindfolded broad jump, Russ thought, then spoke.

"I'm going to level with you, Tom. Maybe you've heard. Jimmy and I are old friends. We went to college together." A shallow sip of gin and tonic. "I like him. Wouldn't double-cross him for anything." Another sip. "Just the same, I sometimes can't agree with his methods."

"What're you driving at, Stanton?"

You'll be calling me "Russ" and falling all over me in a minute. "He asked me to come out here and check up on you." *Drop the bait, even though I don't really know what I'm fishing for.* "To check on your security." A bigger swallow of gin-and-Schweppes, all very confident—and confidential. "I don't buy working behind a top executive's back. Either you trust him or you don't—and I don't give a shit how important the project." The "project" was loose, could cover almost anything. It'd be for Hruska to react, narrow down.

Tom Hruska gulped bourbon, wished there wasn't so much water in it. His brain machinery made a few ponderous revolutions. Yeah. Karami *was* known to triple-check on everybody. This character Russell Stanton had come from some huge stateside corporation, where they did things differently. More straightforward, like. By God, Stanton was a white man. *He can't be trying to twist, because I heard he's on a big salary, more than twice as big as mine. The guy's just being decent. A squareshooter. I've got nothing to lose if he isn't—long as I watch what I say.*

"Thanks for telling me, Russ." That was safe. Something more needed, though. "The security's tight. I can guarantee that."

"I know," Russ grinned and elasticized the truth, but not so far it could snap into his face. "Found out when I started looking for you. Your people wouldn't let me out to the hangar area even when I told them who I was." Finish the drink. "That was enough to convince me." Next improvised hook. "On the q.t., Jimmy's sweat is over Saturday." *I've tossed out "project" and "Saturday." Pray he rises to the bait.*

"Damn it—if he doesn't think I can keep security tight another day . . ."

Then it was *this* Saturday—tomorrow!

". . . he must take me to be the world's biggest jerk!"

Maybe not the biggest, but close. Keep talking, boy.

". . . I got ten men guarding the stuff in the hangars

around the clock. Nobody gets close—and won't until we start loading."

Let him ease off momentarily. Russ pointed to his empty glass, nodded when Hruska asked "Same?" and signaled to the waitress, telling her to bring two more —but make his straight.

"Aw, you have to make allowances for Jimmy," Russ remarked tolerantly. "He's always been an inside man. Great guy, mind you. Only he doesn't think the same as people like us. We're outside men at heart. You'd rather be on a flight deck. I'd prefer being on a drilling rig." Camaraderie. Buddy-buddy. The drinks were served. Russ raised his glass. "We do make more money inside, Tom, remember that. It coats the pill."

"Sure does." Big gulp of bourbon. *Stanton wasn't like that high-hat Limey, Lockhart. He might even put in a good word for me with Karami.* "You—uh— seeing Jimmy this evening?"

"Yes." *Quick-hunch titillator.* "I stay at his house. Didn't you know?"

No, I didn't. Stanton must be an even bigger wheel than I'd figured. Down the rest of the whiskey. "Well, Russ, you can tell him whatever you want. I'm satisfied I've done a fair job so far."

"I am, too—and that's what I'll tell him," Russ shrugged. He offered a mentholated cigarette; when Hruska shook his head, took one himself and lit it. Another feint. " 'Course, he might want me to come out again tomorrow."

To check on the loading. I've got that worked out. How to make it sound good without "leaking" anything in case it's leakage Stanton is really testing for? "Won't be much going on before eighteen hundred. Then you might see some real activity—from a distance." A rib-nudge laugh. "My people still won't let you through."

Hruska was saying "you can count on 2100"— 9:00 P.M.—when he and Brian Lockhart had come out of Jemel's office yesterday. A last thrust in the dark, then drop it. "Eighteen hundred as against twenty-one hundred," he mused aloud, let it dangle there

as though he knew what the hell he was talking about
—and waited.

"Three hours is plenty. I've got five crews with
forklifts. All the loadings are worked out. Numbers
matched . . ."

His voice trailed off, his eyes narrowed. He was
saying too much—or . . .

Russ luckily caught the look, fielded it. "Do me a
favor, Tom. Don't make me listen to all the details
again." *I'd give everything I own—plus—to hear them
for the first time, only I'd bleed to death from the
gash I'd cut in my own throat if I allow you to guess
that.*

Hruska had relaxed. "Another drink?"

"No thanks. Have to go talk with our boss." He
stood up. "I'll probably see you tomorrow, Tom."
Level look, old-pals smile, all-male handshake. *If I
don't get any information out of Jemel tonight, I'll
be seeing you earlier than you imagine. And it'll be
an ugly confrontation.*

New York City. Friday, May 24th.

Television, newspapers, radio—all were giving
maximum coverage on the "new Middle Eastern crisis"
that had caused a global uproar.

> . . . Lebanese authorities permitted camera
> crews inside the ground of the official residence.
> These films show how the entire front of the
> house was sprayed by sub-machine-gun bullets.
> The commandos reached within a few yards of
> the entrance. The four strips of cloth pegged to
> the ground indicate where the men fell after be-
> ing shot down by guards . . .

> SPECIAL UN SESSION
> CERTAIN TO CONDEMN
> ISRAELI TERROR RAIDS

> . . . the United States cannot offer the hand
> of friendship to any nation, large or small, that
> resorts to criminal acts of attempted murder
> against the heads of other countries, he declared

during a press conference held at his Texas ranch . . .

RUSSIAN FLEET BOLSTERED IN MED
FRANCE WILL INCREASE AID TO ARABS

. . . . and strong repercussions are being felt in such oil-producing Arab states as Saudi Arabia and Kuwait. Although providing financial support, these countries played no active military part in the three Arab-Israeli wars that have rocked the Middle East in the past two decades. Public clamor sparked by the assassination attempts is demanding that the rulers send troops and equipment to reinforce Jordanian and Lebanese forces against further attacks from Israel . . .

ESHKOL, DAYAN REPEAT DENIALS
THAT ISRAELI TROOPS RESPONSIBLE

. . . in Beirut, famed Lebanese-American banking tycoon Jemel Karami praised Lebanese measures taken to maintain calm and protect foreign lives and property. "There has been no disruption of the economic life of the country," he stated in an interview today. "Lebanon's banking industry has not felt any adverse reactions as a result of the deplorable incidents." Karami further declared he was confident the failure of the assassination attempts would discourage further incursions and forays. "Thus, in the long run, I think the incidents will serve to ease rather than increase Middle Eastern tensions," he said . . .

"The entire picture's changed now," R. D. Whitehead rasped wearily. "The Israelis made a worse blunder than the Bay of Pigs. They haven't got a friend left in the world. Everybody's sympathies are with the Arabs—and they'll make the most of it. So will Jemel Karami. This gives him a clear field. We can consider ourselves licked, steam-rollered."

Quentin Yeager made no comment. Whitehead's defeatist conclusions were unassailable.

"Quent, let's face up to it," the veteran oilman continued—and he looked and sounded very, very old.

"From here on it's just a question of time before we have to kiss off Whitehead MidEast." He paused toyed sadly with a letter opener that lay on the desk before him. "I'd already decided I was going to retire whenever the Karami thing was over. It's over. I'm re tiring. You'll take over as head of all the Whitehead companies. Russ Stanton will move into your place a president of Whitehead MidEast—to preside over its last throes. With the understanding that he'll be shifted to presidency of one of the other companies when the books are closed on Whitehead MidEast."

Yeager simply nodded. Anything he could have said would have been out of place.

Whitehead tossed the letter opener aside in a gesture of final resignation. "Send a Cousin-David gravely-ill cable to Marvin Jacobs at the Saint Georges."

That was the message they'd agreed would indicate Whitehead had changed his plans and wanted both Marvin and Russ to return to New York.

"They'll have difficulty getting out," Yeager said "According to the papers, every flight out of Lebanon and Jordan is booked solid for day's ahead."

"They might be able to swing something," White head said. "Anyway, a few days more or less won' make any difference. There's no longer any need to hurry."

"R. D., you worked Stanton and Jacobs up into a fury against Karami. Aren't you afraid they might take matters into their own hands? Do something far worse than just foolish?"

"No. They agreed to follow my instructions—and having agreed, they will. In any case, they'll have no reason to think I'm throwing in the sponge. They'll believe I'm calling them back because we've figured a new and better strategy for busting Karami."

Miles Palmer held the telephone to his ear with one hand, adjusted the set of his rimless bifocals with the other and listened.

". . . and he requested me to obtain a consensus," the voice at the other end of the line was saying. "H particularly wanted the views of eight key people, and you're among them, Mr. Palmer."

The Texas twang that set Moon-Face into motion must be at its peevish, angry worst, Miles thought with relish, and said, "I feel, sir, that the most reliable appraisal of the situation was made by Mr. Jemel Karami —who, I might add, is a man I have known for many years. I'm sure you've read the press report of the statements he made during an interview in Beirut." Pause. "Yes, that's the one I mean. When the man who owns the leading bank in the entire Middle East is unruffled and optimistic, we can all breathe easily." Another pause. "Yes, I concur with his views."

When the conversation ended, Palmer hung up his telephone, leaned back and permitted himself a vicarious canary-glutted-cat smile. Jemel Karami's luck was fantastic. The Israeli bungle was a perfect smoke screen behind which Karami would be able to operate with absolute impunity. It couldn't have been better or have occurred at a more opportune time. Not even if Jemel had planned it himself.

12

Beirut. Saturday, May 25th.

The cable, delayed in transmission and briefly caught up in some hotel muddle, wasn't delivered until almost 11:00 A.M.

> COUSIN DAVID GRAVELY ILL. COME HOME IM-
> MEDIATELY SIGNED MELVIN

Marvin Jacobs had almost an hour to ponder what he should do, take a chance and telephone Russ Stanton—or wait until Russ contacted him—before he heard the knock on his door.

It was Russ. Grim-faced, tense. Marvin handed him the cable.

"Forget this," Russ growled, crumpling the cable into a ball, flinging it in the general direction of a wastebasket. "R. D. has fallen for the phony crisis just like everyone else." He made certain the door was locked. "Sit down, Marv, and listen. Don't interrupt me. We don't have much time."

"Hold on. What do you mean, 'phony crisis.' "

"For God's sake, shut up!" Stanton ordered. "The whole fucking thing—the assassination attempts, everything—is phony. Rigged. By Jimmy." He reined in his rage, described the massacre, fully aware what his words were stoking inside Marvin Jacobs. "Official channels are out. Jimmy has the Lebanese government in his pocket. Even if an embassy would listen to my unsupported testimony, it'd take days to get action—and minutes count now." He hurried on. "I've got most of the scheme pieced together. I know how to get the rest. After that, it's up to us. You and me. I made up my mind days ago I was going for broke. How about you?"

Marv's look was the answer.

"Have you any friends from '48 and '49 who can give orders, get them carried out—people who know and trust you?" Stanton asked.

"Yes. All the way up to . . ."

"Never mind. Then we can gamble on the one chance that's left. Gather up your passport, dough, any personal papers—and the Colt and the extra clips. Leave everything else—and shag your butt, Jew-boy!"

Russell Stanton had rented the same model Ford Anglia as before. His Incom credentials again rated salutes as he and Marvin passed through the roadblocks between the Saint Georges and the airport.

"Stay meek and quiet until we're alone with Hruska," Russ said, parking the car. They got out, went to the Pan-Arab administrative offices.

"Please call Mr. Hruska. Tell him it's Russell Stanton."

Thomas Hruska made his appearance minutes

later. He was surprised to see Stanton so early—it wasn't even 1:00 P.M.—even more surprised to find he'd brought a short, scrawny, Jewish-looking character with him.

"Hello, Tom. Can we all go into your private office?"

"Uh—yes." Something peculiar about Stanton today.

He led them into his office. Once inside, Stanton moved toward Hruska's desk. *What in hell,* Hruska thought, looked around. The thin Jewish guy had locked the door, stood with his back against it. He turned again.

Stanton eyed the Pan-Arab Airways president coldly, did a final sizing-up exercise. *Hruska's a good three inches shorter than I am,* he thought, *and much of the muscle's gone to flab.* The man's hometown-football-player face showed its weak, bumbling undertones even more clearly now that he was in a situation he couldn't understand. "Came by to look over tonight's loading schedules and flight plans, Tom," Russ said.

Another Karami test, Hruska decided. "Sorry. Not without Jimmy's okay." He edged towards his desk, reached for the telephone. "I'll call him up . . ."

He stopped, eyes bulging from their sockets. Stanton had yanked a vicious-looking automatic from his belt. He whirled. The other guy had a gun, too. A big U.S. Army-issue Colt .45!

"Where are they?" Stanton demanded.

Goddamn it, Karami didn't have to play melodramatic games! "I said you can't . . ."

Russ grabbed Hruska's shirt front with his left hand, slammed his fist—and the butt of the automatic —against Hruska's jaw. The blow was hard, painful. "After the next one, you'll be spitting teeth, Tom. Now where are those fucking papers?"

Hruska struggled, opened his mouth to shout for help. The gun butt struck his jaw again. Much harder. A tooth splintered. Hruska groaned, sagged. Russ held him up. "Yell—and I'll kill you, Hruska!"

My God, the bastard meant it!

No bonus, no job was worth getting killed for.

"Okay," he muttered. Russ let him go, watched, poised and alert, while Hruska took a handkerchief from his pocket, spat blood and tooth fragments into it.

"In my desk. Manila folder in the bottom drawer."

"Shoot him if he moves, Marv." Russ moved around behind the desk, found the folder, opened it. He went through the papers it contained. Everything was clear now. "They're using sixteen planes, Marv," he said. "They're loaded in rotation starting at eighteen-hundred. Take off in rotation starting three hours later. All timed out so each plane reaches its destination a little before midnight."

"I thought you said you knew," Hruska grunted.

"All shipments classified as 'machinery and equipment,' " Russ continued, ignoring Hruska. "Consigned by Pan-Arab to Pan-Arab. Flight plans filed and cleared as special house charters. Cute."

"Stanton . . ."

"Shut up, Tom. You think there's machinery and equipment in those crates you've got in the hangars, don't you?"

"I don't give a shit what's in them. I take my orders." Hruska had suspected there was something more than what Jemel Karami told him behind the mass airlift. He didn't care. The responsibility was Karami's —and Tom Hruska was only interested in earning his bonus and holding his job.

"Rifles, sub-machine guns, mortars, ammo, demolition charges," Russ muttered. "And that doesn't bother you?"

"No. Why should it?" How did Stanton imagine most nonscheduled airlines managed to survive? Tom Hruska had handled many gun-running shipments while working for such lines. Some loads for Uncle Sam and the CIA—as maybe these were CIA shipments—he argued.

"They're not," Russ said coldly. He had to make the final decision. He and Marv could do nothing—not in broad daylight with ten guards in the storage hangar. In any event, the point could be proven only when the planes were loaded and waiting for takeoff. Settled. He folded the papers, thrust them in his left-hand jacket pocket, picked up the P-38.

"Hruska. Stand near the intercom box, but don't touch it." Flat menace in Stanton's voice made Hruska okey mechanically. "Pay attention. You're taking two old friends up on a sightseeing hop." No flight plans or clearances needed. "Give orders to have a DC-3 ready on the flight line within ten minutes. Screw up—and I shoot. Got it?"

"Yes." *No. Where do they imagine they can go in Lebanon? Or anywhere else without being arrested the moment we land? But you can't argue with a man holding a gun. Not when he has a look like Stanton's in his eyes.* He leaned down, called operations on the intercom. "Hruska talking. Is there a DC-3 available for an hour or so? I'll fly it myself."

"Baker one-one-seven, Mr. Hruska. All fueled, too."

"I'm—uh—taking two friends up. Be right over." He cut off. He was afraid. "Stanton. I've got a wife . . ."

"I did, too. Once." Stanton's voice a solid-ice harpoon. "That's one of the reasons I'm here and we're going to take a flight."

Jesus. That was it. Stanton must be nuts. Insane. Hruska swiveled his head. The other guy hadn't moved. The Colt rock-steady in his hand. *His good hand. By God, the other was artificial. I hadn't noticed that before.*

"We'll walk close to you," Stanton was saying. "The guns will be in our pockets. Neither one of us is afraid to shoot you."

Tom Hruska was in the pilot's seat, Russ in the copilot's position. Both men wore earphones and throat mikes. Marvin Jacobs sat on the jump seat behind them, a chart spread open on his lap.

"Forget procedures," Russ ordered, pressing the snout of the P-38 against Hruska's side. "Try to flub, and I'll kill you. Remember I know a little about airplanes, and I'm monitoring your tower conversation."

Hruska stuck his head from the slid-open cockpit

panel, gave some instructions to the men standing below, pulled his head inside, slid the panel shut. Switches. Energizers. Whine. A splutter. The port engine caught, took hold. Then the starboard.

"Pan-Arab Baker one-one-seven to Beirut Tower. Taxi clearance. Over."

"Pan-Arab Baker one-one-seven clear to runway nineteen. Over."

Russ nudged Hruska's side with the gun muzzle. Hruska worked the controls. The DC-3 began to roll across the apron, down the taxiing strip to where it intersected with the end of runway nineteen.

"Clearance to line up and take-off. Over."

"Pan-Arab one-one-seven. Left turn out. Cleared for takeoff."

Hruska gave Russ Stanton a last pleading look. The pistol dug more deeply into his ribs. Hruska swallowed, glanced up and around at the cloudless sky visible through the plexiglass, nodded, gunned the engines, lined up on the runway. Wheel brakes locked. Throttles forward, Hruska's eyes skimming the instrument panel. The RPMs built up. He popped the brakes.

The moment they were airborne, Russ pulled earphones and throat mike off Hruska. "Marvin will tell you what to do."

"Climb to three thousand, make a 180-degree turn, set your course southeast—105 degrees on the head—and climb to eight thousand."

"You're telling me to head for Syria!" Hruska protested. "They'll . . ."

"Do as you're told." They'd be over the line long before the sloppy Lebanese air force could react—if anyone got the idea it should react—and the answer to the problem of how to handle Syria had been worked out.

Beirut disappeared behind them. Hruska was on course. They were over the foothills, climbing steadily to clear the slopes of the mountains. Now, the Bekaa Plain, a green slash with the brownish-yellow thread of the Litani veining. The town of Rashaya. Over the crest of Mount Hermon with a thousand feet to spare. Syria.

"Dive!" Russ commanded. "Get down on the deck —in the grass." Hruska hesitated. Russ used his free hand to shove the control column forward. The DC-3 nosed down sharply. Hruska, terrified, took over, holding the craft in a steady, steep dive. "Level out at about three hundred!" Russ yelled at him. At that level, any Syrian radar that was working would pick up nothing. As for Syrian ground forces—no Arab soldier would fire at a transport flying that low and clearly marked with the green-and-gold Pan-Arab Airways insignia. It would be assumed the plane was in trouble.

Hruska leveled off at 300 feet or so above the ground level.

Three minutes. Five. Six.

"Straight south!" Marvin barked.

"That's Israel!" Hruska croaked, banking. When he was on a direct-south course, Russ reached out, shoved the throttles full ahead. The airspeed indicator climbed—190,200,210—far past the red line.

"You'll burn out the engines!" Hruska yelled.

"Maybe." It was about twenty miles to the border. If Syrian troops realized what was happening, they'd never manage to hit a plane roaring a few hundred feet over their heads at 210-plus miles per hour.

"We're over!" Marv announced.

Russ grabbed the throttles, hauled them back. The airspeed indicator unwound—down to 200, 190, 170, 150, held at 140.

"Rock the wings!" Russ told Hruska. Two specks, angling up, growing larger, were proof the Israelis had scrambled a pair of interceptors. Tom Hruska obeyed. The old DC-3 pitched and heaved from one side to another. Minutes later, they were flanked by Ouragan jets, the pilots staring at them, shepherding them down to land at an airstrip.

It was Marvin Jacobs's turn to do the talking. He did, in fluent Hebrew, to the Israeli air force officer commanding the units based on the air strip. Russ Stanton and Tom Hruska stood aside, guarded by soldiers. Stanton was calm. Hruska glowered, fidgeted nervously, muttered curses.

Marvin and the officer talked for ten minutes. Then Jacobs came over to Russ. "We're okay so far," he said. "You and I are being flown down to Jerusalem."

"What about me?" Tom Hruska demanded. The officer had joined Marvin. "Listen!" Hruska barked at him. "These two sons-of-bitches kidnapped me and hijacked an airplane! I want them arrested—and I want to see the American consul. I'm an American citizen!"

"May I please see your passport?"

"I'm the president of Pan-Arab Airways!" Indignation, wrath, bluster. "I don't carry my passport around with me when I'm in Beirut. Goddamn you . . ."

"I am sorry," the officer shrugged. "If you have no passport, you entered this country illegally. We must detain you, determine your status."

"But those two are hijackers, criminals. . . !"

Soldiers restrained Hruska. Russell Stanton, Marvin Jacobs, and the officer hurried off towards an STOL Porter Pilutas' parked on the apron.

Five-oh-five P.M.
The loading would start in Beirut in fifty-five minutes, Russ thought.

"Jacobs! Marvin Jacobs!" the one-eyed general exclaimed, entering the whitewashed staff officers' conference room in the Jerusalem military headquarters compound. Stanton and Jacobs had been waiting for his arrival almost two hours. They'd told their story over and over to the staff officers—some of whom also remembered Marvin from the 1948–49 war—but the matter required top-level decision, and the general had been out inspecting troops emplaced along the Jordanian frontier.

More rapid-fire exchanges in Hebrew; then Marvin introduced Russ to the general. The story was gone over; the papers Russ had taken from Hruska's desk were studied yet again. Stanton glanced at his watch when that had been completed. Five forty-seven.

"General," he said. "Time is getting down to nothing. I know you couldn't care less what happens inside Arab countries . . ."

"You are wrong." The general with the black eye-patch spoke excellent English. "We"—he nodded at the staff officers—"have every reason to care very much. The kind of uprising you and Jacobs say is about to take place will destroy what sanity remains in the Arab world. Israel will have a fourth war to fight—one the Saudis and Kuwaits won't sit out. Of no less importance, if we prove the existence of the conspiracy, we prove to the entire world that Israeli commandos did *not* try to assassinate Hussein of Jordan and Kamal in Lebanon."

Stanton nervously lit a cigarette. "It's all true."

"My staff raises questions. The key to them all is this: You and the man named Hruska have vanished from Beirut, taking a Pan-Arab plane. This—Jemel Karami—will have learned of it by now. He has certainly drawn the conclusion that you fled from Lebanon to reveal his plans. Agreed?"

"Yes." Another look at the watch. Five fifty-three. God!

"What makes you think he will still carry on with his scheme?"

"He can't call it off. He, Incombank, several hundred million dollars—all finished if he does. And, he's certain there wasn't enough reaction time left for anyone to stop him." Russ groaned. "He's right. You people were the last hope."

"*Were?*"

"General. The first plane takes off in three hours." Russ crushed out his cigarette, his broad shoulders slumping in dejection. "It would take hours to organize an operation, and you haven't even made a decision yet."

"Oh, but I have, Mr. Stanton. Subject to one reservation. I remember Jacobs well. I trust him—and I trust you. Unfortunately, any decision I make involves a great many people besides me and the troops under my command. Where there is one plot or conspiracy, there could be others. My trust in you and

Jacobs *could* be a tragic—a disastrous—error in judgment." His single eye looked from Russ to Marvin and back. In it was a question any front-line combat soldier would have been able to read.

"Of course I'll go along," Russ said quietly. "I have my own reasons for wanting to go."

Marvin spoke just as quietly in Hebrew. The general appeared satisfied.

"Can you mount a raid in the time that's left?" Russ asked—dubious, but the spark of hope glowing again.

"Our men are trained to move quickly. You can be flown to Haifa within thirty minutes. Our troops do not have to leave Haifa until after eight—and they'll still arrive in Beirut before the first transport takes off."

Five big Alouette helicopters with the Star of David painted on their sides were lined up on the airstrip a few miles northeast of Haifa, their broad rotor blades already chopping lazily at the air. Standing in formation near them were fifty-odd khaki-clad Israeli airborne troopers, each carrying an Uzi sub-machine gun and heavy sacks of demolition charges slung from their shoulders. They stared curiously at the two men in civilian clothes who approached, accompanied by their commanding officer.

One civilian was tall—over six feet in height—blond and wearing a dark gray lightweight suit. The other was much shorter, dark-brown-haired, dressed in open-throated sports shirt, slacks, and contrasting jacket.

The commander stopped in front of the troops, spoke in Hebrew. These two Americans, Mr. Russell Stanton and Mr. Marvin Jacobs, were going in the lead helicopter with the first section. *At their own request.* No officer or noncom had any authority over them. They were not to be given any Israeli weapons. However, they had entered Israel with pistols of their own; they would be allowed to carry those. At the end of the operation, Mr. Stanton and Mr. Jacobs were to be brought back. If possible. Any questions?

There were plenty, but none that the soldiers dared ask aloud.

Very well. A last-minute briefing. Also in Hebrew. Simultaneously translated into English for Russ by Marvin Jacobs.

"Upon arrival at Beirut Airport, Mr. Stanton will point out sixteen aircraft. Any air or ground personnel aboard or near these planes will be ordered—or herded—to safety. The aircraft are loaded with ammunition and explosives. They must be destroyed. Demolition teams will set charges fused to detonate at specified intervals. Once the fuses are primed, *all men will get clear of the aircraft immediately.*"

A pause, heavy with significance.

"You will inflict no—repeat no—human casualties unless absolutely unavoidable. No—repeat no— damage is to be caused to any—repeat any—aircraft other than those specified by Mr. Stanton. Any final questions?"

A sergeant asked if antiaircraft fire could be expected.

"No. We come in from the sea at minimum altitude. Five meters above the water, then just clear rooftops when we get over land."

Soldiers are soldiers the world over. The airborne troopers with whom Russ and Marv were jammed onto the hard, fold-down benches running the length of the Alouette's interior joked with each other as the chopper rose from the landing strip—and for the next ten minutes or so. Then, glancing out through the tiny ports, seeing the waters of the Mediterranean scarcely fifteen feet below, realizing each moment brought them closer to their combat objective, they fell silent, introspective. Each man mummy-wrapped in his own thoughts—and fears.

The engine noise was loud. The thwack of rotors whipping air even louder. The Alouette shuddered from torque, as all large copters do.

Russ and Marv looked at each other, their expressions grim, yet somehow underlaid with satisfaction. They'd taken insane risks and more lay ahead.

Knowing the stakes, both felt it was worth it. Neither regretted any of his decisions. If their luck held, scores would be settled.

A green light flashed on. Fifteen minutes to landing.

Karami and Lockhart, Russ mused. One—or both—must have taken over personal direction of the loading after hearing that Tom Hruska had taken "two friends up for a sightseeing ride in DC-3 Baker one-one-seven" and had not returned.

Marvin's thoughts followed related lines. Jemel will crap his handmade shorts and $500 suit if he finds out I was the third man aboard the plane. And somehow or other, I'll make certain he does find out. He forced himself not to think of his wife and children.

Yellow light. Ten minutes.

The five choppers had followed a course out to sea. Now they swung in, heading towards Lebanon, their flight plan calling for them to sweep in over Khaldeh Beach. Russ and Marv had the same impulse, checked their watches. Eight forty-one. The copters would touch down at 2050, ten minutes before the first plane—the one bound for Al Mubarraz in Saudi Arabia—lined up on a runway for takeoff.

Russ speculated whether or not the orders for cutting the "telephone and telegraph cable" near the Whitehead MidEast housing compound had got through. If they had, there would soon be two parboiled dissidents. It was no telephone and telegraph line. It was high-tension power-transmission cable and anyone cutting through the insulation would frizzle . . .

Red light.

Five minutes.

The soldiers stirred. Equipment and weapons checked. Straps and buckles adjusted. Old reflexes came into play for Stanton and Jacobs. Russ went through the motions with the Walther P-38. Dump magazine. Work operating mechanism. Point muzzle between feet. Snap trigger on empty chamber. Replace magazine, jack round into chamber, click on safety. Marvin followed suit on the Colt with remarkable facility despite the hindrance of having an artificial hand. He dropped the magazine, pulled and released the slide, slid the magazine back into the handle, set the hammer at half-cock safety.

Four minutes. After an eternity, three—and still over water. Now the beach. Copter rising a few feet to clear buildings—by a hair. Two minutes. Then the first runway-limit-marker-lights. Minute and a half. Another eternity. The grating squawk of a klaxon. Chopper touching down. Troops on their feet. Russ and Marvin up, too. Doors flung open. Men piling out at exactly spaced split-second intervals, dropping three feet to the hard surface of the runway.

Perfect, Russ observed, following the soldier ahead of him through the door. The five choppers were all down. In a tight, diamond-shaped formation. At the far end of the airport. Smack in front of the storage and maintenance hangars festooned with great green-and-yellow neon signs reading "Pan-Arab Airways—Airline of the Arab World" and blood-red neon signs blaring: "Incombank—Largest Bank in the Middle East—Welcomes You to Lebanon."

Gaudy bullshit, he thought . . .

More than two-thirds of the Israeli troopers were already fanning out, running with their Uzis held at high port, to form an improvised perimeter and seal off the area.

"Mr. Stanton." It was the Israeli commander with about fifteen men. "We're ready to go."

"Right over there," Russ said, and set off at a run toward the hangars. Their doors yawned open, and they were empty. The loading had been completed. The planes were lined up, nose to tail. Caravelles, Comet IVs, DC-6s and DC-4s. Some flight crews were aboard their aircraft. The first plane—a Comet—was already starting up its engines.

Marvin and the Israeli commander ran alongside Russ. Behind them, the soldiers, moving as though their sub-machine guns, ammo belts, and sacks of demolition charges weighed ounces rather than more than sixty pounds per man.

"The number-one plane's ready to start taxiing!"

Stanton warned—needlessly, for five soldiers had veered off, running toward it.

The first hammering burst of sub-machine-gun fire. Russ jerked out his automatic.

"That's our people shooting. An Uzi," the commander said. They reached the planes. Some were buttoned up. Most still had their loading doors open. These were ships scheduled for later takeoffs, shorter hops. Their flight crews had been lolling around outside them a few moments earlier. Now they were fleeing in terror towards the hangars and beyond.

Soldiers!

Jew soldiers—raiding!

"*Yalla*—you sons of whores!" The triumphant shouts of the Israeli troops. "Run, you women!" More bursts of sub-machine-gun fire, all aimed high, intended to terrify, cause panic. Succeeding beautifully.

Troopers tore open the hatches of the first three aircraft, clambered up and into the planes. Moments later, pilots and copilots leaped out, hit the runway and fled, screaming for help. Here and there, one fell to his knees, begging for mercy, swearing by Allah. A thick-soled army boot in his rump sent him galloping after the others.

The engines of the number-one Comet went dead.

"I'm leaving you here," Russ said to the Israeli commander.

"We both are," Marvin Jacobs added. "I'm going with you, Russ."

The officer gave them both a long, hard look. "We take off in precisely thirty minutes," he declared. His tone changed, softened. "We won't be able to wait for you if . . ."

"I know that," Russ nodded. The Israeli shook hands quickly with Stanton. Then Marvin and turned, ran towards one of the Caravelles.

Russ and Marvin stood for a moment, surveying the scene of howling chaos. Men, some in Pan-Arab flight officers' uniforms, others in mechanics' and ground-crew garb were stampeding from planes and hangars towards the dark, empty 2,000-yard gap that separated the Pan-Arab maintenance and storage area from the main airport terminal.

"It's my bet they're here—and the only ones not running," Russ muttered. He sensed he'd find Karami and Lockhart in the Pan-Arab operations building. To the left, immediately adjacent to the hangars. They'd be where Tom Hruska should have been. Possibly, they'd be stunned, dismayed, cursing and berating Russell Stanton, each other, themselves, everyone. More likely, they were frantically trying to obtain help, stop what they must have by now realized was the final disaster for their scheme—and thus for Incombank. For themselves.

He began moving towards the one-story, white cinderblock operations building.

A dozen—probably more—fear-driven men who had streamed out of the hangars were running past its doors in a loose, blindly rushing column. Stanton and Jacobs waited until they had gone by, otherwise they would have been bowled over, trampled, then went to the door. Inside, a very large room, brightly illuminated by fluorescent lights. Huge maps, equipment-status and maintenance charts and bulletin boards on the walls. A long counter along the length of the room on the left. Behind the counter, desks, now in total disarray, loose papers lying where they had been dropped or knocked by men seized by terror and the impulse to flee. Chairs, two or three upset on the floor. Beyond, at the rear, a door, a trilingual sign proclaiming "Operations Chief."

"That's where they'll be." Russ opened a gate built into the counter. Habit made him allow Jacobs to pass through ahead of him. Marv hurried to the door, tried the handle, flung the door open. By then Russ was directly behind him.

Flash-tableau.

The operations chief's desk squarely facing the door. Jemel sitting behind it. Lockhart standing to his left. Both men holding telephones, raging or pleading into mouthpieces that curled around their faces but failed to hide the desperation contorting their faces.

Lockhart stared at the open doorway, recognized Russell Stanton towering over a slightly built man he had never seen before. He froze for a millisecond, then took the telephone he held with his left hand from his ear and, as though obeying an unspoken command, leaned and twisted slightly to replace it on its cradle.

The movement was enough to divert attention, mask the lightning motion of his right hand.

"Stanton!" He had clawed his gun from its shoulder holster. "You cocksucker!" The gun blasted. Marvin Jacobs was jolted backward, spun, fell, the side of his head suddenly bathed scarlet by fountaining blood.

Action and instinctive reaction. The P-38 bucked in Russ Stanton's hand. Three shots triggered off so fast the explosions were a single, deafening rip, the bullets spiking into Lockhart in plumb-bob-vertical pattern—belly, chest, throat—killing him before he could feel pain, even before Russ could regret that he wouldn't feel pain.

Jemel still sitting behind the desk. His mind having registered everything, he'd hung up his own telephone, placed his hands flat on the desk in front of him. The falcon-featured framework of his face kaleidoscoped expressions with almost subliminal speed. Desperation to fear to fury to squalid cornered-bird-of-prey cowardice—then cerebrally directed composure. Left eyebrow slightly raised. Full lips canted into something only a shade less than a cynical smile. Behind the mask, the mind crackling, gaining velocity.

By any standards, the finish.

The coup a ruin. Israeli troops swarming everywhere, doing God-knows-what to the loaded aircraft. Incombank? By Monday morning—a rubble heap of accounts and balances exposed as phantasms, as created mirages. Lockhart dead. Kamal cowering, refusing to send troops. Stanton alive, knowing all I know, more that I don't, and holding a gun.

By any standards, the finish.

By any standards but mine.

Capitaine Raoul Andrieux had held a gun, too. In

heir own way, the publisher of the Pittsburgh *Herald,*
enator Rodney Whalen and Governor Alvin Miller,
Abdul el Muein and Sheikh Nasib al-Harith—and a
ost of others—each had held even more dangerous
veapons.

*There's always an escape hatch, a defense. Incom
Central has several millions in cash left in its vaults—
ind I have twenty-four-hour access to those vaults.
The Asharat was in the harbor. It couldn't get me very
ar—but far enough—to Cyprus or Izmir—and a bit
arther in the amphib before the hunt started. By then
could get lost, disappear. Do as Beidas did without
naking Beidas's stupid mistakes.*

*At the moment, what I need is an immediate
counterweapon. I'll build it. On the spot. As I have
efore.*

"Russ." Jemel spoke evenly. "Take a look at
Marv. See how badly he's hurt. I won't make a move."
won't, either. That's the first step.

"Stand up, Jimmy. Get over in the corner. Face
nto it."

"Sure." Jemel stood up. Slowly, even gracefully,
lid as he was told.

"Stay there."

"Yes."

Stanton knelt, gun still in hand, one eye on
emel's back, reflexes honed and ready to shoot if
emel made so much as a gesture.

Marv lay sprawled on his face. His blood, spread-
ıg across the floor, soaked through the cloth of Russ's
ousers where his right knee touched the floor. He
ırned Jacobs over gently, examined the head wound.

"Thank God!" he muttered, to himself—but aloud.

"Is he alive?" The question came as from an
cho chamber. Jemel was speaking into the angle of
ıe wall, not turning his head.

"Yeah. Grazing wound. Scalp laid open. Probably
concussion. Bullet didn't penetrate the skull." The rely automatic, precise. *Thank God—and shit! Nothing
led worse than a scalp wound.*

The echo chamber seemed to echo his thoughts.
Scalp injuries bleed badly, Russ. Edge away from

him—let me turn around and come over there. I'll bandage him with something—and you can keep the gun pointed at me."

"Why should you want to do anything for Marvin?" Sneering contempt layered atop openly hostile suspicion.

The answer had to be shaded to zero tolerance. "Why not?" The tone itself a casual shrug. "What more can it cost me?" Now, an instant switch to glacial cynicism, made to sound forced, tinged with a note—faint but discernible—suggesting a hope, an underlying plea, for mercy: "An unselfish act, Russ. The villain redeeming himself before the final curtain."

Stanton weighed the situation rapidly. Marvin was continuing to bleed. *I can't bandage him myself. Not without risking that Karami will jump me.* Lockhart had fallen on top of his pistol. Jemel couldn't get at it. Marv's .45 lay nearby. He picked it up, shoved it into his jacket pocket, rose from his knees and backed away from Marv.

"All right, Jimmy. Turn around. Come on over." He watched warily as Jemel advanced, crossed the room to the doorway, stood beside Marvin.

Russ held his Walther leveled at Jemel's belly. He had two clean handkerchiefs. One in his breast pocket. Easy. He took it out with his left hand, tossed it to Karami. The other was in his right-hand hip pocket. More difficult. He managed, threw that to Jemel also.

"Take out your own breast-pocket handkerchief," he said. "Tie all three together and see what you can do."

Jemel knelt, looked at the wound. "I'll use one as a pad, tie two together around his head to hold it."

"All right." About twenty minutes left before the copters would take off. Five to tie up Marv's head. Ten at most to force Jemel to scrawl out what I'll tell him to write, another thirty seconds—and still time to make it out . . .

Jemel was on one knee. He applied a handkerchief as a compress, sought to tie it into place. "Keeps slipping off," he mumbled. Pretending to adjust the already soaked-through compress, he worked a finger

ato the wound, tore skin and thin layer of flesh a little
urther. A new rush of blood. "It's getting worse."
till a mumble. Only a quick, haphazard glance up at
Russ, then concentration on the makeshift bandage
gain. "Look, Russ. You can lean down, hold that gun
o my head and still use one hand to hold this pad in
lace while I tie a knot."

Russ hesitated, moved. The Walther had about a
wo-pound trigger pull. Hair trigger. The muzzle stuck
lmost into Karami's ear—and a twitch would do it.

"Over there, if you don't mind, Russ. Uh-huh."

Stanton bent down. The P-38 muzzle was almost
ouching Jemel's face. He was standing in blood, Russ
oticed as he stretched out his left hand, pressed the
ne tips of his fingers against the compress.

"That's it. Now I can get it . . ."

Jemel was tying a knot. His hand slipped, stuck
uss's fingers, pushing them off the compress, which
arted to fall. Russ clutched at it.

Jemel's muscles burst free of the tight, perfectly
oordinated grip he'd held on them. He propelled
imself into a flat dive, under the gun muzzle, one hand
nopping up at Russ Stanton's arm, the other seizing
is dangling necktie. Jemel swung himself around as he
ell on Marvin Jacobs, unheeding the twin blasts of the
-38, because he knew Stanton's shots would miss.
astead, he kicked at Russ's feet, his hand still holding
ne necktie, jerking viciously at it.

Russ's shoe soles slithered in fresh blood. His
et went out from under him. He cursed, fell, struggled
 get the gun aimed at Karami.

Jemel chopped the side of a hand against the
ridge of Stanton's nose, seized his wrist, jerked it to
s mouth, sank teeth—fangs—into the flesh.

Pain was exploding through Russ's head. He
ught to remain conscious, to see. More pain in his
rist. His fingers went limp. The gun dropped from
em.

Karami rolled off Marvin Jacob's body, scrab-
ed for the gun. Stanton lashed out with his right leg,
ught Jemel on the side of the face with his shoe, the
le leaving its imprint, red, sticky.

"Fucking hero!" Jemel snarled, rocking back an now flinging himself forward, reaching once mor for the P-38.

Russ was up on all fours. He lunged, collidin with Jemel. They grappled, rolled over. A shar bruising pain in Stanton's left side.

Marvin's Colt!

Jemel was on top of him, one hand gripping h throat, the other chopping at his nose and cheekbone They were both splashed and splattered with bloo Marvin's. Their own. Jemel Karami's fingers dug in Stanton's throat, their hold made viselike by desper tion, by the will to survive, to escape. His face w mad, diabolical.

Russ tried to tear the hand away from his throa A savage chop stunned him, made his eyesight bl yet again—but as it blurred, something snapped in focus in his brain.

"Jimmy—please!" he groaned in agony, gaggin choking—and went limp. He heard the harsh laug felt the spittle strike his face.

Jemel released his throat, eased himself up to h feet, leering.

"You're a dumb bastard, Russ." He stepped lithe to where the P-38 lay, stooped slowly to retrieve it.

Stanton groaned, rolled to one side, then th other, lay in a near-fetal position, his face showin pain—and defeat. Lay on his left side, his arm an hand under him, Jemel saw, and his movements we feeble.

Jemel picked up the gun, balanced it in his han for a moment. He smiled inwardly, his rage for ve geance finding the means to whet its appetite ev further for final outlet. Give Russell Stanton a la thought to take with him.

"You had a great wife, though, Russ." He point the gun at Stanton. "Wild. We used to have some gre parties when you were away. I'd fuck her with . . ."

The muzzle blast of the Colt seared Russ Sta ton's thigh, drove shreds of wadding into his fles He didn't feel it. Not then nor an instant later when h pulled the trigger again. He only saw. Saw the fir slug slam into Jemel's stomach, slam him backward, staggering, the P-38 dropping from his hand, the look of dismay come over his face—and the second bullet hit him in the right side of the chest, spin him, send him crashing to the floor.

"Your own kind of trick, Jimmy," he said, his voice almost normal. He stood up, a little shaky, aching everywhere, otherwise all right. He glanced down at his left-hand jacket pocket. Two holes like overgrown cigarette burns. Smoldering. *A Colt vomits a lot of flame when it goes off,* he mused absently, inanely. *Should never fire one from inside a pocket.* He pinched out the glowing edges of fabric with his fingers.

His brain cleared. He went to where Jemel lay spread-eagled on his back, stared down at him. Not dead yet, but would be in minutes. Russ wiped his jacket sleeve against his face, scrubbing at the place where Karami had spat on it. *No, I won't do the same.*

Stanton's thinking processes picked up momentum. He went to where Marvin Jacobs lay, picked him up, moved him several feet. The bleeding from the scalp wound had almost stopped. Good. He'd be able to carry Marvin out, back to the copters. Very soon now.

He took the .45 from his pocket, dropped it into the pool of Marvin's blood in the doorway. Then he went back to Jemel, grabbed his feet, ignoring his agonized groans, dragged him to where Marvin had lain. He picked up the P-38, pocketed it. There. That would give the Lebanese authorities the easy answer. They'd grab at it. A twist on the customary pattern. Ivar Kreuger, Serge Stavisky and most of the other master world rapers had "committed suicide"—according to the official versions—when their empires collapsed. Jemel Karami and Brian Lockhart had killed each other—and no Lebanese would worry about such loose ends as ballistics tests or the blood tracked all over the Pan-Arab Airways operations office.

He stood beside Jemel Karami another moment, looking at him.

Jemel gazed up, his eyes fading. The fury had

drained from him, had been replaced by something else. He knew he was dying—and even in dying, he'd win.

There was enough acid left in him to make him want to tell Stanton: *You've done me a favor. Now I won't have to run, constantly looking over my shoulder, seeing the pyramid crumble. That would have been worse. It would have hurt more . . .*

His lips wouldn't respond. He stood at the apex of the pyramid—and as his eyes closed, he stepped off into space.

What do I feel? Russ demanded of himself. *Satisfaction? Contempt? Pity?*

I don't know.

He picked Marvin Jacobs up in his arms and walked out of the building. They were inside a copter and a medical corpsman was taking care of Marvin and the five Alouettes were airborne when the first of the sixteen Pan-Arab Airways planes erupted.

Apodosis

1

*Fuck everything. Fuck the world. And I'm
?ocked. And fuck my brain that doesn't want to
?nction.*

Elinor Randolph forcibly restrained herself from
?ancing into the mirror that covered half the wall to
?e right of the Charles Cressent table she used as an
?fice-away-from-the-office in her top-rent, top-floor
?pper East Side high-rise apartment.

*Oh, no. No mirror. I know what I'll see in it.
?m afraid of what I'll see.* She knew her gold-flecked
?een eyes were red-streaked, her face puffed, mottled.
?he coppery hair was lifeless, dry, brittle—tangled
?irelike strands clinging to a scalp that was as numb
? the brain that lay within the skull beneath it.

The numbness went further, deeper, down inside
?d in every direction.

I am exhausted. Gutted, Elinor thought. *But I
?ve to try again. Keep on trying.*

She had been trying.

For three full days and nights. With coffee and
?casionally liquor substituting for food, spansules for
?eep.

She had to do it ALL—the word formed in her
?ind in all upper-case letters six inches high and
?tra boldface—ALL by herself. Whatever was to be
?blished, read by millions—then probably forgotten
? hour later by most—could not be an item dictated
? a secretary or droned into a switch-on, switch-off
?mp of machinery.

If words were to be written, they would have to

509

find their own way out of the honeycombs—the cata
combs, Elinor corrected herself—of her memory
banks. Then they'd have to take on their tones and
shadings from the waiting filters, amplifiers, dampers
distorters—the mental extrusion molders and emotion
al turning lathes—they'd encounter on their trip from
subconscious storage to conscious expression.

Only thus could they be placed on paper. By
Elinor Randolph's own fingers, their muscles activated
by whatever finally emerged to strike the keys of her
SCM 350.

"I have to keep on trying," Elinor muttered
echoing aloud her thought of a few moments before

She stared at the wide table. Electric typewriter
in the center. Directly in front of her chair, foam rub
ber padding protecting the delicately gold-tooled mo
rocco leather tabletop. To the typewriter's right an
left, stacks of clippings, wire-service tissues, type
transcripts of radio and television news broadcasts and
commentaries.

The stacks had been sorted into categories, th
papers piled in inverse chronological order. The old
est—how old is three days?—on the bottom. Thre
days are an age, an eternity. The most recent on top

Elinor shifted her eyes to another pile of papers—
these untidy, disarrayed; evidence that she'd read an
reread them countless times. She knew the headlines c
the clippings and the key sentences in the newspape
stories, wire-service dispatches and transcripts by hear

Gazing at the disordered heap, Elinor visualize
the memorized words and lines unreeling across he
mental scanning screen in jumbled, disjointed se
quence. To be read from left to right as they raced b
from right to left on a searing neon-lighted tape.

". . . INCOMBANK CLOSES . . . FINANCIA
WORLD ROCKED BY FAILURE OF GIAN
LEBANESE BANK . . . in Beirut, official spokesme
hint of enormous cash shortages . . . MOBS O
BANKRUPTED DEPOSITORS RIOT BEFOR
BRANCHES OF DEFUNCT BANK ON FOU
CONTINENTS . . . no information concerning th
whereabouts of the bank's founder and board chai

man, the widely publicized international playboy, Jemel 'Jimmy' Karami has been released . . . Reports of massive frauds and defalcations persist . . . 'A swindle on a scale that has few if any historical precedents,' is how the situation was described today by . . ."

Her eyes remained fixed on the heap of scissored-out newspaper clips, torn-from-teletype sheets and typed transcripts. And the tape continued to unreel.

". . . estimates of cash losses to depositors range upward of half a billion dollars . . . KARAMCORP STOCKS PLUMMET IN WAKE OF INCOMBANK CRASH . . . the United States government and several leading New York banks are reported to be among the heavy losers in the collapse of INCOMBANK, the largest bank in the Middle East. U.S. government losses stem from Commodity Credit Corporation credits extended to the bank . . . DISAPPEARANCE OF JEMEL KARAMI SAID REMINISCENT OF YOUSSEF BEIDAS FLIGHT AFTER INTRA BANK FAILURE . . ."

Elinor pressed her fingers against her closed eyes. She knew what the speeding tape would carry next, and her efforts to blot out or even blur the words would be futile.

". . . INCOMBANK HEAD DEAD . . . after what some observers consider an unusually long delay, Lebanese government spokesmen have finally revealed that Jemel Karami, the Lebanese-born but long-naturalized American head of the recently defunct Incombank, committed suicide . . . RUMORS HOLD KARAMI SUICIDE COVER-UP . . . Beirut police say that the famed international banker shot himself with a heavy-caliber pistol in the master bedroom of his palatial home in Beirut . . ."

"I don't believe it," she said to the tape, and the tape paused to listen, going blank for a moment. "Jimmy wasn't the type to kill himself—no matter what happened." The tape shrugged, lighted up, continued to spool at its former speed.

". . . while the body has been positively identified by several persons, including foreign correspondents, who have been allowed to view it, many have openly expressed doubts about the official suicide theory. The remains were exhibited fully clothed, and Beirut police refused to permit inspection of the allegedly self-inflicted mortal wound. The clothing in which Karami's body was dressed showed no signs of bullet holes. According to police sources, the corpse was clothed in fresh garments after being discovered, 'out of respect for the dead man and because the original (unspecified and not displayed) garments were blood-stained to an extent that would shock the sensibilities . . .' "

God only knows what happened, Jimmy, but you didn't commit suicide.

". . . REVELATION THAT KARAMI AIDE ALSO SUICIDE HEIGHTENS MYSTERY . . . knowing Wall Street traders flatly predicted that the almost 90 percent plunge in the value of the stocks of Karamcorp and its subsidiaries presages inevitable bankruptcy for all the companies. 'They will be brought down by the backwash from the Incombank bust,' one broker stated. In the meantime, it has been learned that Douglas Ford, president of Karamcorp, has been undergoing questioning by members of the New York agencies' District Attorney's staff and agents of other investigatory agencies . . ."

Damn you, Elinor cried out silently. *That doesn't mean a thing to me. I don't care . . .*

For once, the viewing-tape apparatus inside her head—now throbbing rather than just numb—obeyed. It raced ahead in a meaningless blur, slowed to its usual speed.

". . . Lockhart, fifty-two, and a British subject, served as president of the bank. He, too, is said to have shot himself, also in the bedroom of his home. Whispers circulating in Beirut charge that the Lebanese government is hiding the fact that the two men, seeing the inevitable collapse of Incombank, quarreled bitterly and ended by killing each other. A different version, rapidly gaining currency throughout the Middle East, holds that both men were 'liquidated' on the orders of powerful oil-rich sheikhs who had an unknown number of million dollars deposited with Incombank . . ."

The first is preposterous, Elinor told herself. *Jimmy in a gangster-style shooting fray? Impossible!* It had to be the second. The tape, seeming to sense that she wished to ponder, obligingly stopped, went dark.

It could only be that rich men who'd lost money had ordered Jimmy murdered—Elinor didn't know Brian Lockhart, didn't give him an instant's thought. They'd learned the bank was in some sort of difficulty —and sent their killers to get blood when they could not get their money.

But what difference did it make *now?*

Jimmy was—she braced herself before forming the word in her mind—dead. That was the impossible, impossible to believe—and then all the roiling mental and emotional conflicts that had blocked Elinor Randolph from writing her own "good-bye, Jimmy" in her column geysered up once more.

Jimmy. When I first saw him—my first job, with Decker Publications. The Longchamps menu, lunch at the Plaza. Bed. How many, many times in bed—and how very, very wonderful. Then the freeze—and the sudden call. The drinks—actually at Longchamps. In the Chanin Building. Jimmy. How I teased and tormented you that week—and finally went to bed with you again.

Jimmy Karami. The charming, the magnificent lover.

What were some of the things I said about you? That you were one of the world's bigger sons-of-bitches. And the world's greatest lay and you know it and that's what makes you such a son-of-a-bitch. That it's your prick that makes you such a prick.

And I helped to build you, make you into an even bigger prick. How big, how very big, I only realize now. You were a thief and a crook at heart. And more. God, even the wife of your best friend—what was her name and his? Sefton? No. I have it—Stanton. Pat and Russell Stanton.

But whatever you were, you had something— something not one in a million, not in ten million, men have. Good Christ! The night we were aboard your yacht, coming over from England, I lay in your bed,

*with you inside me—and I realized you no longer
wanted me. That you were doing me a courtesy—
though, God knows, never showing it outwardly. I
went out of your cabin, got you that young actress,
told her to go and take my place. And I did it willingly
—because I wanted you to be satisfied, happy. I guess
I must have loved you, you bastard, and if I still knew
how, I'd be crying.*

The run through the wringer calmed her. She
reached for a fresh sheet of paper, rolled it into the
platen, allowing a generous top margin, flicked the lever that made the typewriter purr quietly. She pushed
the automatic tabulator key, started in once more,
stroking the keys, seeing the letters print on the paper.

"Jemel 'Jimmy' Karami has long been front-page
news material. How many of Busybody's readers can
remember when his name first began to appear in this
column? It was a long time ago . . ."

Elinor wandered around the room aimlessly for a
few moments, finally paused in front of the TV set on a
table. She turned it on. A canned-soup commercial
came alive on the screen. She changed to another channel. Beer—the very best beer. Click over another. A
detergent commercial fading out with that hint of fi-
nality that indicates there will—or there might—be
something other than hard-sell pitch following. Elinor
cocked her head, waited a second.

A still house-ad for the station.

TONIGHT ON THIS CHANNEL
at 11:30

That great, Academy-Award Winning Classic
THE BEST YEARS OF OUR LIVES

Elinor wrenched at the switch, turning off the
set, turning away from it, not wanting to see any
more before the image faded completely.

She went to the bar in the corner of the room,
took a glass, reached at random for a decanter of
whisky, tipped four fingers of the whisky into the

glass. She replaced the bottle, stared into the glass for a moment, raised it, then placed it to her lips.

All down—and no more tries.

Whatever she might, could, force herself to write about Jimmy Karami was going to stay right where it was.

Right in the catacombs. Never fully dormant, always gnawing.

"This one was for me, Jimmy," she whispered, waggling the empty glass in one hand, reaching for the bottle again with the other. "This next one's going to be for you." She poured, lifted the glass. "Jimmy." She drank. *Wherever you are, you're probably still one of the biggest—mind you, I didn't say "bigger"—bastards in the place, and still a magnificent lay.*

Elinor replaced glass and bottle on the bar. Turning, she found herself facing the television set. *The damned thing is off.* The screen was dark—black. Nonetheless, Elinor Randolph imagined she still saw the words:

THE BEST YEARS OF OUR LIVES

2

Marvin Jacobs and his vivacious, attractive wife, Russell Stanton and a lovely, slender brunette were seated around a Manhattan restaurant dinner-table.

It was a warm, pleasant evening in mid-June, and they were just starting on the first round of cocktails.

Marvin's head still had a fair-sized bandage on it —but that would come off soon. He smiled quietly to himself as he observed Russ and the girl. The signs were evident, obvious. Russell Stanton had been purged, changed, renewed, brought out of his emotional spin—and then some.

The two men looked at each other across the table. The two women, their feminine intuition telling them of the strength of the bond between Russ and Marv (although knowing practically none of the reasons that comprised its strands), were silent.

"*L'chaim*, Russ," Jacobs said, raising his glass. "It's not often I get to drink to a guy who's got himself an oil-company presidency on a silver platter." He laughed, a short laugh that signalled something far different from the humor that seemed intended. "To think, a good Jewish boy like me drinking to a *goy* who's going to run a whole damned oil company in an Arab country, yet."

Russ got the code, deciphered it. The drink was not just to his promotion by Whitehead MidEast— but yet again an expression of gratitude. Personal and otherwise. For saving Marv's life—and Jacobs insisted that Stanton had done just that—and on behalf of what Marvin would call "the *ganze Yiddische mishpocheh*." And, beneath it all, for years—hell, a quarter of a century now, if you want to look at it that way and cringe—for that long a period of genuine friendship.

But I owe you just as much, Jew-boy, Russ replied silently. *God only knows what sort of wreckage there'd be in a hell of a lot of places if you hadn't been there. At the right place. At the right time—even a little ahead and to the good. As for the friendship— that's two-way, kid.*

"Thanks," he said aloud, lifting his own glass. "In return, I'll drink to the hopes that turban you're wearing comes off fast—and that there either won't be any scars, or that at least your hair will grow and cover them."

Their eyes met, locked, compressed hours of grim, bitter dialogue into seconds.

They both knew that their years of knowing Jimmy Karami—as many years as they'd known each other—what they'd learned about him and how they finally settled the account, had left scars on both of them.

"Care to join us, ladies?" Russ grinned as he and Marv broke their mutual gaze.

The women nodded, reached for their glasses. They could now rejoin Russ and Marv in the here and now.

3

The Fourth of July was hot, oppressive in New York City.

Manhattan was virtually deserted. All who could, had fled to mountains, seashore—anywhere to escape the heat for the holiday.

Inside the Wickpark Towers Apartments penthouse, the temperature was infinitely cooler. Sealed-in windows and air conditioning defeated sun and weather.

But the huge apartment was almost as deserted in feel as the avenues and streets outside. There were only two people in it. The "Count" Federico Bellini and his bride of only some six weeks, the former Felicite Karami.

They were in the library—where Bellini insisted they be, rather than upstairs, in the bedroom, where Felicite had been begging him to go for over an hour. Ever since noon. Ever since he'd gone into the kitchen, nicked a finger while opening a soup can—an incident that had sent him off on a roaring, semihysterical tirade.

"No!" he bellowed. "I refuse to stay in a house without servants! I am not a *cappone* of an American husband!" He switched to Neapolitan gutter *dialetto* and continued to rave.

Felicite tried one more "Rico, stop pacing and shouting so we can think," found herself unheeded and unheard, and gave up. Wearing nightgown and negligee, she started toward the double doors that opened onto the hallway.

That stopped—and momentarily silenced—Federico Bellini.

"Where do you think you are going?" he demanded.

"Back to bed," Felicite replied, pressing hard against her head as she smoothed back her honey-blonde hair, pressing hard to ease her headache at the same time. "And you may not be an *American* husband—but you're not much better than a capon!" she sneered at him. "Not of late."

"You slut! How can a man think of sex when his 'wife' has drowned him in scandal! For weeks, the reporters! Then the police as well. Your brother . . ."

"He's dead," Felicite muttered. "Leave him alone." *Poor Jimmy. He refused to ease up, to move more cautiously—but who am I to criticize him for that? We're very much alike. We* were, she corrected herself. She still could not accustom herself to the realization that he was gone.

"A coward! A suicide! And a failure! A bankrupt!"

"Kiss my ass!" Felicite reached for the door handles.

Headache or no, she was still fairly dreamy-high. And hot, she told herself. Hot as hell for a man. *Rico hasn't raised one in weeks—and his depression fits have ruined every ball I organized with other couples. I'll go up and play with myself until I fall asleep.*

Bellini lunged, clawed his fingers into her arm, whirled her around.

"You stay!" he snarled. "I want to talk to you. About how we are going to live!" His contorted face was close to hers, and Felicite felt the mist of his saliva as he spat out his words. "We must have money—do you understand?"

That money was a need, Felicite was aware. Anything else that had happened—no, she couldn't understand. Not really. The money had always been there, when and where she wanted it.

Now they had told her at the bank that her accounts were closed out—in fact, one was overdrawn. More? No, unfortunately, it was most unlikely that any more would be forthcoming from the normal sources. At least not for a very long time. Not until receivers—or something like that the manager had said —were appointed and somehow—"ah, excuse me, Countess Bellini, until they have brought some order out of the Incombank situation." He'd babbled on— about things that Felicite could not comprehend.

Even the servants had gone. Their salaries had come from one of the New York branches of Incombank. Jimmy's bank. They were closed. Shut tight. On Monday, July 8th, someone was "taking over"—or was "seizing" the word that had been used?—the penthouse itself. She and Federico had been warned to move out by then.

"Money, do you hear me?" Bellini was screaming. "Do you think I married you for that Galleria Mazzini you call your cunt? I had that whenever I wanted it—and so did everybody else!"

Headache, a giddy feeling—and a burning cunt. I've got all three, Felicite thought. She tugged her arm out of Bellini's grasp, frowning. He released her, but watched her with a fixed, malevolent glare.

"I own some property," she said. "In France and in the Bahamas. Maybe someplace else, too. I liked some houses and I left it all up to Jimmy to take care of buying them."

"If he bought them in his own, the bank's or one of his nonexistent companies' names, you have nothing!"

"I bought the house on the Riviera myself. That's in my name. So is the place in the Bahamas. We can sell them, can't we, Rico?"

Bellini scowled. "Yes, but that will take weeks. What do we live on in the meanwhile?" He'd gone through a small fortune of Felicite's money during the first week or two of their marriage, settling up old bills. Since then, he'd contracted many more debts. He'd been certain her millions were safe, intact, available— not pissed into a pool of Incombank money by Jemel

Karami. A pool from which Felicite's money migh
never be recovered.

"We need cash! Immediately. I have less than .
hundred dollars!"

"I have two hundred upstairs in my purse,
think." She smiled. "Come upstairs and sock it to m
for a while, Rico. I want to feel that big dong of your
sliding up into my—what did you call it?"

"Galleria Mazzini!" he rasped contemptuously
"An enormous cavern. A monstrosity!"

"If you can't get it up, maybe you'll eat me a littl
—just so I can come a few times. Please?" Anothe
thought—bumped gently against her. "Rico! I know!
have my jewelry. We can always sell some of *that!*"

Bellini's eyes narrowed, and there was a sly glean
in them.

"Are they in a bank vault?" he asked.

"What?"

He gritted his teeth. "The jewels. Where are they
In a bank vault?"

"Oh, no. Almost everything I have is upstairs i
the bedroom closet. Jimmy"—Jimmy, who's reall
dead now—"had a safe in there. He never kept any
thing in it, so he let me have the combination. He ha
it made easy for me to remember—1941, that's th
year we came to the United States . . ."

Her voice trailed off into a moan. Rico had steppe
closer to her. His hand was rubbing against her pelvis
His left hand. The other was opening his trousers fly
He was erect, and now he rubbed the glans against he
through the fabric of her nightgown.

"Rico!"

"Come upstairs, Felicite. We shall make love.
*For a long while, until you're so tired that you'll fa
asleep. The ship is sinking, my half-mad, sex-craze
wife—and I'm leaving it. Through the courtesy of th
coincidence that 1941 was the year you and you
greasy Levantine family arrived in the United States*

Felicite awoke in Jimmy's vast round bed wel
before sundown. She was a little groggy, but headache
drug effects, and erotic demand had all subsided. Sh

elt hungry and thirsty. She sat up, her mind clearing, triving to remember everything in order.

Oh, yes. The argument with Rico. About money. Then he'd finally managed to get himself worked up. he reached between her thighs, touched herself. She was deliciously sore. Rico—aah, the recollection. He'd ept going for what seemed like hours. Doing everything. Just as he had before. *Why does he always remind me so much of Jimmy when he's like that,* she sked herself. *Funny. Like Jimmy—and in Jimmy's ed.* A small thrill of responding glands releasing megma. She'd momentarily forgotten Jimmy was ead.

Felicite looked to the right. The place Rico usually occupied was empty. He must be in the bathroom.

"Rico!"

No response.

Louder. "Rico—where are you?" Her voice eemed to echo through the house. Once more. "Rico!" Muffled reverberations of her own voice. Otherwise, ilence.

Strange. He almost never left her alone. Felicite ot out of bed, slid her feet into slippers, started towards he bathroom. She stopped. Something white, with vriting on it, propped on a dresser. A card or something. She didn't remember seeing that before. She vent to the dresser, picked it up, turned so the late fternoon light coming through the window struck quarely on the card.

"Ciao, putana . . ."

Felicite, 'Countess' Bellini, snapped into full, rightened consciousness.

"Thank you for a most enjoyable marriage—and or 1941."

It was signed simply "F"—Federico's initial.

Full—now terrified—consciousness.

Phrases came back to her from earlier in the day.

"Think I married you for your . . . we need cash immediately . . ."

Then her own responses. "Property . . . sell . . . ny jewelry . . ."

She stared at the card again ". . . and for 1941."

No! He wouldn't! He couldn't!

She let the card fall, rushed to the closet. The door was partly open. Inside, hangers and clothes had been pushed aside. The safe door was wide open. The safe itself: empty.

She backed out of the closet. She saw her purse on the floor, automatically stooped down, picked it up. It, too, was open. The miniature wallet she carried in it to hold currency was gone.

That, Even that. The $200!

It all struck Felicite at once—and with terrible force.

Jimmy was dead. Really dead. Gone. She wouldn't see him again. Ever.

Rico—he wasn't dead, but her chances of ever seeing him again were small, lessened by the fact that now she had no money, nothing she could readily sell.

She let the purse fall to the floor, went down into the library—she didn't really know why. Then she toured the other rooms like a somnambulist, switching on lights when the sun no longer provided enough light, leaving them switched on behind her. She lingered several minutes in the rooms that had formed her private apartment once—before she became of legal age—a little less time in the completely changed rooms that had served as Mademoiselle Claire Viete's own suite.

Mademoiselle was dead, too. So was Hassan. So —Felicite felt an icy chill of memory—was Nuri.

Jimmy.

Why?

She somehow made her way back to the bedroom. Her mind was clear. Clearer than it had been for a long time, Felicite told herself with a strange, secret smile.

She looked at Jimmy's bed. She looked at it for minutes, the fire building inside her. At last, she moved away from it, went to the bathroom, opened one of the medicine cabinets.

There was the bottle. A large bottle. More than half-full of capsules. She filled a water glass with water from the tap, put the glass on the glass shelf next to

he basin. She reached for the bottle, uncapped it, be-
an a routine. A handful of capsules spilled into her
alm, placed into her mouth, then a swallow of water.
he repeated the process three times. The glass was
mpty. *What I've taken should be more than enough—*
ut I'll make sure. She refilled the glass, took and
wallowed another handful of the bicolored capsules.

Then she hurried from the bathroom to the bed.

Felicite lay down on it quickly. On her back. She
pened her legs, thrust her right hand between her
highs, caressed and kneaded her breasts with the
ther.

She pressed down hard, moved her fingers vio-
ently. She wanted to achieve as many orgasms as she
ould before the capsules took effect and she wouldn't
e able to have more.

At last, the Seconals began to have their effect.
Felicite sensed that she had taken more than
nough.

She smiled.

"Anyway, this is *one* thing I've never tried beore," she murmured drowsily.

Then the fatal overdose really began to take
old . . .

4

Michael Ferrenbaugh was worrying at the topic
hat had cropped up frequently in his conversations
ith his wife Dorothy and daughter Mickey over the
ast few months.

He sat at the head of the family dinner table,
Dorothy on his right, Mickey on his left, waggling his
ead sorrowfully from side to side.

The women made no effort to stop what they
new would be an endless discourse. Talking about
emel Karami and Incombank helped the old politi-

cian get his mind off Mickey's impending divorce an
his break with Frederick Hayworth—who, to Ferren
baugh's consternation, appeared to have gone ahea
on his own without begging forgiveness. Without eve
saying a word of thanks for all the help Mike ha
given him.

". . . have to confess that Hassan and Jimmy alway
treated me fair and square," he was saying. "Sur
they pulled some sharp deals—but then what business
man doesn't? But to think that Jimmy turned out to b
nothing more than a downright criminal . . ."

Dorothy took minuscule portions of her appl
pie.

Mickey Hayworth—still, but not for long, sh
hoped—avoided looking at her father or mother. Sh
stared blankly into her coffee cup.

". . . and that whole tremendous empire built o
nothing but sand. Pshaw! Not even sand. Water. Nc
a cent on the dollar . . ."

Mickey tried not to hear, but it was impossible t
close her ears against Mike's resonant, campaign-plat
form-developed voice. *Jimmy,* she thought.

". . . no telling how many people he wiped ou
left broke. And, if you know that, you start to wonde
how many more he and Hassan before him cheate
and wrung dry over the years!"

Ferrenbaugh paused long enough to take a ver
deep breath and swell his chest pridefully.

"We're lucky, all three of us!" he declared.

Oh, God, but aren't we lucky, Mickey said silent
ly. *All three of us. Especially I, Michele "Mickey" Fer
renbaugh Hayworth—who fell in love with Jeme
Karami when I was five. Who stayed in love wit.
him . . .*

"We're lucky—and I'd be the first to allow tha
we should be kinda grateful, too." He harumphed
took out a cigar, punched a hole in its end with a pie
fork tine.

I'm so grateful that I could scream and shou
Mickey thought. *Jimmy is dead and he was crooke.
and he probably swindled thousands of people. H*

as responsible for people being made penniless, for
people being hurt, even for people being killed. Yet,
ll never be sure . . .

"Grateful in general—to the Good Lord, I s'pose.
nd, by gosh, to Hassan and Jemel personally, too.
either of them ever did a thing—not a solitary thing
-that didn't help all the Ferrenbaughs. Whatever they
ere to other people, they were surely the best friends
is family ever had—or ever will have!"

He did not notice the long, eloquent look that
assed like an electric charge across the table in front
f him, the look exchanged between Dorothy Ferren-
augh and her daughter Mickey.

"Yes, sir!" Mike patted his belly and spumed
noke from his cigar. "I feel sorry for them both. Poor
ouls . . ."

The gaze between Mickey and Dorothy crackled
-but Mike remained blissfully unaware of it. He
ouldn't have been able to interpret what it meant,
ven if he had noticed.

5

R. Daniel Whitehead basked in the sunshine. He
ay on his outdoor chaise in the patio rose garden of
is Oceanside, California, estate.

There were no secretaries. There was no tele-
hone extension near at hand. R. D. Whitehead had
one what he'd sworn to do after the "Karami crisis"
vas over. He had retired, turning top-of-the-Whitehead-
ile control over to Quentin Yeager.

But, there were still loose ends that had to be
ucked into place.

There would be for several more months—then
e'd be completely clear. Free as a bird. An old bird,
e reminded himself—but free just the same.

On this afternoon in late August, Quentin Yeager
sat near Whitehead's chaise, tidying up yet another o
the dangling ends. It was a matter that Yeager had t
see Whitehead about personally, and he'd flown ou
from New York. The whole thing took less than a
hour, and when their conversation was concluded
Yeager made as if to stand up from the garden chai
in which he'd been sitting and make his departure.

"Hold it a second, Quent," Whitehead said wit
his slant-smile. "You get a chance to read the paper
out in New York today?"

"Nope, R. D. I didn't. What's new? Has Johnso
changed his mind—or is he converting to Catholic?"

"Nothing at all like that." Whitehead reache
down, fished under his chaise. His fingers made contac
with a folded newspaper that lay under it. He pulle
out the paper and gave it to Yeager. "Read, Quen
The item that'll interest you is circled."

Quentin Yeager took the newspaper, found th
marked article—and his eyes bugged from his head

INCOMBANK
AGREEMENT
ENDS CRISIS

Beirut, Lebanon. August 27th (OPI).

An agreement to solve Lebanon's economy-
shaking Incombank crisis was reached today between officials of the Lebanese government and
representatives of the New York banking firm,
the Palmer National Trust Company.

The greatest of all Middle Eastern financial
firms, which crashed last May, Incombank will be
reorganized and operated as an international investment firm under the management of the Palmer National Trust Company.

Incom's major depositors and creditors will
receive shares in the company, in proportion to
the sums they lost when the bank failed and its
founder board chairman Jemel Karami, and president Brian Lockhart committed suicide. Para-
doxically, the United States government will be
among the larger share holders in the new com-

pany, spokesmen for both the Lebanese government and the Palmer National Trust Company revealed.

The U.S. agency to receive the stock will be Commodity Credit Corporation, which transferred some $11 million to Incombank for the purpose of financing the purchase of American surplus farm goods by Lebanon.

The new Incomvestco—as it will be named—will also manage the far-flung branches and properties of the defunct Incombank. These, of course, include Pan-Arab Airways, which lost a large portion of its transport fleet last May, when Israeli commandos raided the Beirut airport and destroyed sixteen planes carrying illicit arms and ammunition while waiting for takeoff.

Incom's small depositors—thousands of whom were left destitute when the bank closed—have some hope of recovering a portion of their money out of loans which the Lebanese government is seeking to obtain now from the United States.

"Well, I'll be goddamned!" Yeager exclaimed.

"I was somewhat more blasphemous and obscene when I read it," Whitehead grinned.

"Palmer must have . . ."

"He used the leverage provided by his $50 million loan to Karami—remember there was a stock issue involved—his pull in Washington and what contacts he'd made in Lebanon through Jemel. He moved in free—and he'll cart all the remaining assets and whatever profits there may be forthcoming out through the back door and into his own pocket."

Yeager made a sour-apple-eating face. "The ultimate irony. Miles Palmer lost—but he wins, anyway."

"Oh, hell, Quent. He learned from the Levantine masters. I told you once they've been raping the world for over three thousand years—and pass the art down from father to son, with each son improving on his old man's techniques."

Whitehead laughed. "Jemel Karami didn't have any kids of his own—so he just passed the art down to the first and worst son-of-a-bitch he knew. I'll be intrigued to see how Miles improves on the techniques. It'll keep me busy watching while I rest and relax, now that I'm retired . . ."

Author's Postscript

All fiction is rooted to some extent in actual experience, I wrote in my note at the beginning of this novel. Also related in the note was how I received—and rejected—an offer of $30,000 to "ghost" the "autobiography" of Youssef Beidas, head of Intra Bank, then the largest bank in the Middle East and among the largest in the entire world.

There are, perhaps, some readers who might want to know what finally happened to Youssef Beidas. The following few extracts from among a great many news dispatches sketch out the story.

BEIRUT, Oct. 15th, 1966.—Intra Bank . . . closed its doors today for lack of cash liquidity. . . . Its collapse sent shock waves throughout the financial world and was followed by a halt in the operations of . . . its branches in Europe and North and South America. . . . Youssef Beidas, Intra's founder and board chairman, has vanished from public view. . . .

BEIRUT, Jan. 3rd, 1967.—The Beirut examining magistrate today ordered the arrest of four accounting experts accused of having submitted false balance sheets connected with the failure of Lebanon's giant Intra Bank last October. . . . Police here have issued an arrest warrant for Intra's former board chairman and founder, Youssef Beidas. . . . Police sources said they received word that Beidas was in Brazil.

SAO PAULO, BRAZIL, May 18th, 1967.—Routine inquiries made by newspaper correspondents here indicate that Youssef Beidas, the fallen Lebanese Midas whose Intra Bank failed last October, has apparently again disappeared. . . . Although Lebanon formally demanded his extradition, Beidas was not returned to that country. . . . Lowest estimates of losses to depositors in the crash of Intra place the total at more than $250 million. . . .

LUCERNE, SWITZERLAND, Nov. 27th, 1967. —Youssef Beidas, former head of Intra Bank, was arrested here last Thursday on an Interpol arrest warrant issued in Lebanon, Swiss police announced today.

Beidas was carrying a forged Brazilian passport in the name of Jose Carlos Curi, police stated. The Lucerne police inspector who arrested the fugitive in a Lucerne street said Beidas was driving a "very conspicuous" American automobile with New Jersey license plates.

The inspector declared Beidas's identity was quickly established, though he refused to admit it for twenty-four hours after his arrest. He carried $7,000 in cash, $30,000 in travelers' checks and keys to "scores" of safety deposit boxes in several European countries.

LUCERNE, SWITZERLAND, Nov. 29th, 1968. —Youssef Beidas, former head of Intra Bank, died in a hospital here yesterday, an informed source said. Beidas was arrested here a year ago on an Interpol warrant following the multimillion-dollar crash of the worldwide Intra Bank in 1966.

He was released from prison early this year by Swiss authorities. . . . There has been no official explanation of the cause of his death. . . . However, a source close to Beidas indicated that he had suffered from a "severe internal condition."

The source also said Youssef Beidas had almost completed his memoirs at the time of his death and had intended to publish them. They included details of the rise and fall of Intra Bank, the informant added. . . .

I have but three comments to make on these extracts from published news stories:

ONE: I have lived and worked abroad long enough to be familiar with the many connotations of that handy euphemism, a "severe internal condition." Beans, bullets, knives, knockwurst—an infinite number of things can cause such "severe internal conditions." Odd, indeed, that the official Swiss record does not specify!

TWO: I would like to have seen the manuscript of Youssef Beidas's memoirs. After all—save for its ending—that was the book I was offered $30,000 to ghost-write for Beidas. Unfortunately (if not predictably) the manuscript seems to have vanished (or so any officials contacted would have us believe).

I'd be most particularly interested to read the late Youssef Beidas's version of how Intra Bank acquired a 60 percent interest in MEA (an airline consolidated out of Middle East Airlines and Air Liban). It was in December 1968 that helicopter-borne Israeli troops staged a real—not fictional—raid on Beirut Airport. They destroyed thirteen MEA aircraft on the ground (without causing death or injury to anyone). Of course, by then, Intra Bank was under the management of a U.S. investment firm which also had taken over management of MEA, according to published reports confirmed by officials of both the firm and the Lebanese government.

THREE: As of this writing, the premier of Lebanon is the Most Honorable Rashid Karami. It should be needless to say that a real, living person could hardly be in any way related to or connected with a fictional character—namely, Jemel Karami.

Withal, it seems justifiable to reiterate the statement made at the end of my opening note: People and events in the arcane world of world rapers tend to conform to type and pattern.

ABOUT THE AUTHOR

JONATHAN BLACK knows well and intimately the lives of the power men and the money men. In addition to *The World Rapers*, he is the author of *Oil* and *Ride the Golden Tiger* and is the "writer" of the J. Paul Getty autobiography.

RELAX!
SIT DOWN
and Catch Up On Your Reading!

THE MONEYCHANGERS by Arthur Hailey	(2300—$1.95)
THE GREAT TRAIN ROBBERY by Michael Crichton	(2424—$1.95)
THE EAGLE HAS LANDED by Jack Higgins	(2500—$1.95)
RAGTIME by E. L. Doctorow	(2600—$2.25)
THE BOURLOTAS FORTUNE by Nicholas Gage	(2742—$1.95)
THE PROMETHEUS CRISIS by Scortia & Robinson	(2770—$1.95)
THE ODESSA FILE by Frederick Forsyth	(2964—$1.95)
ONCE IS NOT ENOUGH by Jacqueline Susann	(8000—$1.95)
JAWS by Peter Benchley	(8500—$1.95)
TINKER, TAILOR, SOLDIER, SPY by John Le Carre	(8844—$1.95)
THE DOGS OF WAR by Frederick Forsyth	(8884—$1.95)
THE R DOCUMENT by Irving Wallace	(10090—$2.25)
MAVREEN by Claire Lorrimer	(10208—$1.95)
THE HARRAD EXPERIMENT by Robert Rimmer	(10357—$1.95)
THE DEEP by Peter Benchley	(10422—$2.25)
DOLORES by Jacqueline Susann	(10500—$1.95)
THE LOVE MACHINE by Jacqueline Susann	(10530—$1.95)
BURR by Gore Vidal	(10600—$2.25)
THE DAY OF THE JACKAL by Frederick Forsyth	(10857—$1.95)
BLACK SUNDAY by Thomas Harris	(10940—$2.25)
PROVINCETOWN by Burt Hirschfeld	(11057—$1.95)
THE BEGGARS ARE COMING by Mary Loos	(11330—$1.95)

Bantam Book Catalog

Here's your up-to-the-minute listing of every book currently available from Bantam.

This easy-to-use catalog is divided into categories and contains over 1400 titles by your favorite authors.

So don't delay—take advantage of this special opportunity to increase your reading pleasure.

Just send us your name and address and 25¢ (to help defray postage and handling costs).

BANTAM BOOKS, INC.
Dept. FC, 414 East Golf Road, Des Plaines, Ill. 60016

Mr./Mrs./Miss_____
(please print)

Address_____

City_____State_____Zip_____

Do you know someone who enjoys books? Just give us their names and addresses and we'll send them a catalog too!

Mr./Mrs./Miss_____

Address_____

City_____State_____Zip_____

Mr./Mrs./Miss_____

Address_____

City_____State_____Zip_____

FC—6/77